ABDUCTED BY THE ALPHA

THE ALPHA KING'S BREEDER
BOOK FOURTEEN

BELLA MOONDRAGON

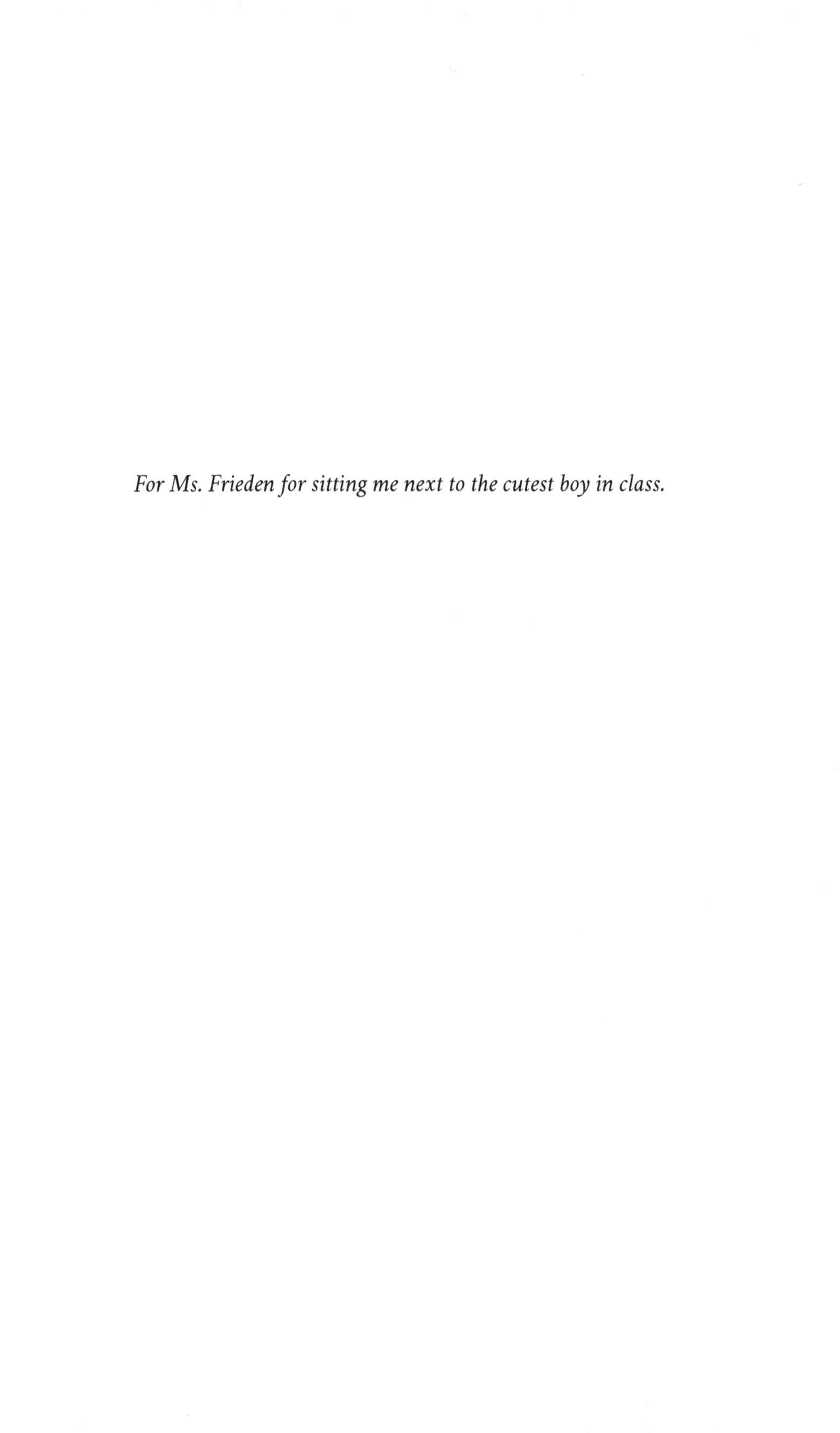

For Ms. Frieden for sitting me next to the cutest boy in class.

CONTENTS

HE'S A NIGHTMARE

Maeve

Kieran, my two-year-old nephew, is a strange creature. I'm not sure if all toddlers are this way, or just him, but I find it hard to believe that any parent would live through this and decide to have another–and another. It must be hard having so much feral energy packed into such a tiny body, which explains a lot, honestly. His dark, curly hair bounces around his pointed ears as he races down another long corridor, screaming at the top of his lungs just to hear the sound of his own voice. I grimace when he trips on the carpet runner and falls face first, not even bothering to use his hands to save himself.

I stand perfectly still several feet behind him, waiting for the wail to begin, but he hops up, teary eyed, and turns to me. "Mama now?"

"Mama's still in her meeting," I tell him with a sigh. He pouts, those big, hazel eyes welling with alligator tears that slide from his impossibly long lashes. He's a cute kid, I'll give him that. Everyone says he's Logan's spitting image, but I beg to differ. He looks like Brie to me. He has her non-existent grace and flair for dramatics, at least. But he's… funny, and soft, and kind, just like his mom.

Just like my big sister.

He's also an ankle-biting little monster who I've been stuck with all afternoon. After the third time he nearly cracked his skull on the same coffee table in my apartment within the castle, I had a group of maids scour the palace for a bike helmet, which seems to be working in our favor now.

"Itchy," he grumbles, scratching the chin strap.

"Keep it on, K." I smile, motioning for him to continue following me through the dizzying hallways. I can tell he's getting tired, but that's the whole point. His next sudden burst of toddler energy is only a few minutes later, where he cuts a corner too sharply and collides with a column, knocking himself backward with a whoosh, but he jumps back up and runs off again, giggling and calling out, "Mabe! Mabe! MABE!!!"

I chase him up the stairs, which he loves. At just over two years old, he's a spritely little demon but also the sweetest, squishiest thing I've ever seen. That cuteness has an off switch, however, and before I know it, he's rubbing his eyes and whimpering, telling me he doesn't want me anymore, that he doesn't like me, that I look funny, and asking for his mom, again.

"You need a nap," I tell him, crouching so we're eye to eye.

"No! No nap!"

"Well, that's your problem. You're tired. That's why you're so fussy."

"NO NAP!"

"Has anyone ever told you that you have the loudest voice in all of the Allied Kingdoms?"

He blinks, tilting his head, and yeah... there it is–Logan's dominant genetics shining through those polished, imperfect emeralds he has for eyes. Kieran doesn't like to be bossed around, and the only person he truly likes is his mom. Just like his dad.

Exhausted, Kieran howls, which turns into a pitched scream that's enough to make my ears ring. I do what any good aunt would do... I scream too, but *louder*.

He cuts off his scream immediately and blinks up at me, his little mouth hanging open in surprise.

When my scream cuts out, he grins, giggling, and his bad mood is all but forgotten. Of course, several maids come sprinting in our direction because it did, in fact, sound like we were being murdered, but I'm the baby of the family. My direct family, at least. I have no idea what to do with him. I never babysat any of Misty's or Sarah's kids–that was always Brie's job, her pleasure, actually. I was often the one who needed babysitting, even in my teens.

Now look at me, trying to keep a two-year-old boy entertained while his mother meets with the Council of Elders–our parliament, essentially. Elders are voted in by the Alphas of the large territories, like the Roguelands, Tarsian, the Deadlands, and even Emberfyll, acting as liaisons for the Alpha Kings and lesser Alphas of those massive kingdoms while my grandmother rules over all of them. Those elders live here in Moonrise now, ensuring our king and queen continue to have their kingdoms' best interests in mind.

I had to meet with those old bastards earlier this morning in regard to the upcoming coronation, of course. That thing no one will shut up about? It's happening in a little over a month, and the past week has been full of festivals and merriment in honor of *me*, the princess who hasn't shown her face to the world for three years now.

Three days ago, I attended my first, and so far only, public event during what will be a month-long festival. It had been a masked ball, which I'd requested. I liked the idea of maybe being able to be anonymous, and that had worked for the most part. People remember me for being tall and spindly. They remember my dark brown hair and sea-green eyes, but I've changed a bit over the years. I finally went through puberty, for one, thank the Goddess. I got a little bit taller but not by much, which means Lexa is still, and forever will be, the tallest woman in our family, which was a tough pill to swallow, but I digress.

I'm not a teenager anymore. I'm a woman–a woman old enough to come into her wolf powers and find her mate, if I were a shifter.

I could have found my mate last year, but I just… can't. I'm not like

Brie, or Lexa, or any of my other cousins. I'm a witch... who terrifies everyone, even while wearing a mask and a beautiful gown.

No one other than my own family looked me in the eyes. No one asked me to dance. No one asked what my interests are, what I like to do in my free time, or my opinions on movies and books.

I don't think my people see me as a person. I'm just a... being. A demigoddess trapped in human form.

When I was younger, I craved that. Especially after Brie and Logan disappeared for a minute and our lives crumpled, forever changed. I wanted people to fear me. I wanted them to stay away from me. I wanted to sit in my office and play the kingdoms like a game of chess.... So I've spent every waking minute over the last two years preparing and perfecting being queen. It was just easier that way.

Now I'm just... alone. Alone—and bored out of my fucking mind.

"Mabe, watch me," Kieran says before raising his tiny hands in the air. He attempts a wobbly summersault, tipping to the side with a giggle that echoes down the corridor.

I clap dramatically as he bows, then opens his mouth wide, and I toss him a jellybean from the pile rolling around in the pocket of my sweatshirt.

This goes on for some time—me chasing my nephew through the castle, him doing little tricks and me feeding him candy. Eventually, we reach the empty ballroom, which is bathed in rich light from the sunset, casting the mosaic marble tiles in a blanket of gold. Kieran loves this room because it's big and wide and his voice sounds even louder here, so I sink to the floor and cross my legs, smiling as he darts around, asking me to watch how fast he can run from one side to the other, and I do.

But my mind wanders back to the masquerade ball, to the man, *the* man, in fact, who I hadn't seen for nearly three years who suddenly appeared again.

At first, I thought he'd been a trick of my mind, a hallucination brought on by too much champagne, but the moment he raised his glass to me in greeting, I knew.

Those lips. That sharp jaw. That wry smirk. They belong to one man, and one man alone.

Tea shop guy.

Otherwise known as *Gloves*. At least, in my journals… not that I've been journaling about him or anything…. Not that much, at least.

"Mabe, look." Kieran runs up to me and squats, clutching something between his hands.

"What do you got?" I extend my palm to him, not knowing any better, and feel every fine, downy hair on my neck stand on end when he drops a live spider into my hand. I swallow my discomfort and give him a wobbly smile, nodding as I choke out, "Wow. That's really cool, Kieran."

He darts away, and I viciously shake my hand free of the creeping, crawling sensation now taking over my body and causing my moonstone necklace to shine.

Smoothing my hand down my thigh, I watch my nephew skip from tile to tile. He's so innocent. So perfect. It's hard to believe that my brother Aris and cousin Blake were that young once. It's impossible to think of Gloves as a toddler, as well. Did he wear masks as a kid, too? Did he sneak around in the dark, disappearing in the rain like a phantom spirit when he was still in diapers?

"Sorry about that," Brie rushes out, her voice bouncing down the long ballroom.

Kieran's light-up sneakers skid across the tiles before he tumbles to a halt. He hops up, breathlessly calling out, "Mama! Mama! Mama!" as he sprints in Brie's direction.

She drops her briefcase and catches him when he launches toward her and smiles, swinging him into a tight squeeze. "Were you a good boy for your auntie?"

"No!" he giggles, wriggling while she kisses his cheeks.

"Yeah, well, I didn't think you would be."

"You just missed seeing our new pet," I say with marked sarcasm as I lean my back against the gilded wall. Everything in this room is wrapped in gold, from the floor to the shimmering wallpaper, to the columns, trim, and delicately welded crystal chandeliers. Just a few days ago, this entire space was swarming with bodies dressed in their finest regalia. The air had been spiced with champagne as soft, classical music wafted through the air over the constant hum of haughty conversation.

I glance toward an archway on the far side of the room... the same archway I'd watched Gloves slip through. I'd followed him, of course. I figured he was just looking for a bathroom, or something, and I hate to admit that I felt like I needed to corner him even if just to confirm he's the same man I'd seen twice in the course of a month and then never again.

But he hadn't been looking for a bathroom. He slipped through a servants' entrance into the narrow hallways that snake throughout the entire castle–a system the maids use to move from one wing to the next. Then, I watched him try to access the doors to the private wing used exclusively by my family–the wing where all the private apartments, suites, and informal offices and sitting rooms are located.

There was no reason for him to be there. None at all.

"Maeve?"

"Yeah?" I turn my attention to Brie, who has her hands resting on her hips. She's wearing those trousers again–the beige, satin ones. A dark belt and casual, button down, white shirt compliments her curvy figure, and her sun-bleached brown hair is pulled back in a delicate, well put together bun at the nape of her neck.

I look down at my raggedy sweatshirt and athletic shorts wondering if the wrong sister is about to ascend the throne, and not for the first time.

"What pet? You better be joking."

"He handed me a spider." I laugh, hugging my knees.

She purses her lips, tilting her head to the side as she watches her son spin in dizzying circles several yards away. "Is that the worst thing that happened? Why is he wearing a helmet?"

"He was fine, really. We had a good time."

She checks her watch, but I feel her gaze scanning my profile. "Did you... did something happen during your meeting with the Elder Council this morning?"

"Why?"

"They were in a horrible mood. Several of them made comments about your... *lack of effort.*"

"Lack of effort in what, exactly? Listening to them bicker over things that have nothing to do with the welfare of the people they were voted in to protect? What kind of lunch they could expect after a morning spent getting absolutely nothing on the agenda accomplished?"

"Maeve–"

"I'm getting rid of all of them when I become queen."

Brie startles, her eyes going wide. "What? Really?"

"The Alphas and Alpha Kings will hold new elections in their kingdoms and territories. I told the council that this morning."

"But they're the *Elder Council*–"

"Of Grandma and Grandpa's Eastonia," I tell her bluntly, finishing the words with a soft smile. "*Not* mine."

Brie sighs, leaning her weight against the wall beside me. "I can't totally disagree with you, I guess. Fresh ideas are needed. Over half of them were against the new railway from Moonrise to Tarsian and now try to act like they had something to do with its success."

I look up at my sister, but her eyes are on Kieran. She's leaving for the Deadlands to visit Ryan and Aviva this evening, taking our parents with her. Logan will be joining her from Emberfyll later this month, and the whole group will make their way back to Moonrise for my coronation.

Grandma and Grandpa have already left for their three week long vacation in Maatua. I understand why they did. The next month is the calm before the storm. There's nothing pressing to do. There are no summits to hold or conferences to attend. It's been a peaceful spring and even more peaceful early summer.

So, for a month, I'm on my own. Getting a feel of things, so to speak. I think it's like a final test from my grandfather, actually. I know he's stressing over it.

"You should consider coming with me and Kieran to the Deadlands, Maeve. You haven't been to Silverhide in ages," Brie says as she slides down the wall to sit beside me.

"I have too much to do here. I'm looking forward to the peace and quiet."

I think about Gloves and the horrible scars on his arm. I think about the silver bracelet and how he was bent over in pain when I padded up to him in my cat form.

"What are you thinking about?" Brie asks, her voice lifted in a laugh. "I've never seen you look so serious before."

"Nothing," I lie, but my powers simmer beneath my skin in a silent warning that the next month might not bring me the peace and quiet I've been looking forward to.

In fact, I have an odd, creeping feeling that something might happen… tonight.

TAKING IT ALL

Soren

I'VE BEEN PREPARING FOR THIS MOMENT. I HAVE ONE SHOT, IN REALITY, to do this and succeed. The palace of Moonrise is a fortress–heavily guarded and an absolute maze within, but I'm an expert in my trade, so to speak.

The brown delivery uniform doesn't fit well, but it has to work. I try to keep my shoulders relaxed so I don't burst through the fabric as I hike the steps to the main entrance of the clinic on the far, backside of the palace while the sun sets over the lake in the distance. Music from the festival continues, never ceasing, not in the week since it began. It's the perfect cover. The chaos in the city square just outside the palace walls has been keeping the guards busy and distracted, which means the clinic is quiet and nearly empty as I skirt inside. A long, circular front desk is manned by only one witch in a starched, white nurse's uniform. She looks up from a tablet, smiling faintly at me as I move toward the counter, reaching up to adjust the brown ball cap that matches the horrendous uniform I stuffed myself into an hour ago before setting out on foot.

"Evenin'," I tell her, leaning my elbow on the counter as she scans my face, my wry, charming smile. "My truck's parked outside. I'm supposed to deliver a few crates to the kitchen."

"Well, this is the clinic," she says with a laugh.

"I understand, but I'm a trainee, and the guy who was supposed to be with me today called in sick, so I'm on my own. I couldn't get around front, you know, with the festival going on."

She sighs knowingly, nodding. I wait for her to ask the questions I'm mostly prepared to answer, like who I work for, if she can see my badge, if I have royal clearance to enter the castle, etc. She slides a piece of paper in my direction and clicks a pen, her light brown eyes meeting mine. She taps her pen on the desk. I give her my best, most dazzling smile, and she folds. *Melts like butter.*

"There's a gate just around the corner. Just punch in these numbers, and it'll open for you. You can back right in. The loading dock for the kitchen is to the left. The princess had her dinner early tonight and let the staff go to attend the festival, so if the loading dock is locked, there's a door to the right of it, and this is the code for that..." She scribbles a series of numbers. "Someone's likely still working because we have patients staying overnight, so most of us are pulling overnight shifts."

"Overnight shifts, huh?" I smile, forcing my cheeks to burn with a blush as I ask, "When do you get off, then?"

Now she's blushing, too. *Perfect.* "Hopefully soon."

"I have two more deliveries after this." I lean against the counter, smiling down at her. "Are you gonna be here? Maybe I can grab you something to eat? Or a coffee?"

She bites her lip, her eyes narrowing in a slightly seductive look that would make a normal, hot-blooded man know he has it in the bag. She reaches for the phone currently ringing off the hook and slides it up to her ear while keeping her eyes on me. I back away, winking at her as I tuck the piece of paper in my chest pocket and turn for the door, that practiced, charming expression fading in a single heartbeat.

It was almost too easy. Takes the fun out of it, if I'm being honest.

I don't have a truck full of deliveries, of course. I don't have a truck at all. I hike back down the steps and follow her directions, punching the code into a gate that's, thankfully, not guarded, keeping my head bowed against the soft, flickering red light of several cameras. I already know the king and queen aren't here. I stood in the curious crowd watching the princess say goodbye to her sister at the train station earlier this evening, confirming Princess Brie—now the Luna Queen of Emberfyll, wherever the hell that is—has also left.

Princess Maeve is alone. I know that for a fact. I know because I've been purposefully going to the bars and restaurants frequented by the highest ranking staff of the castle—those closest to the princess—infiltrating their circles and gathering information.

This wasn't something I cooked up in a week. No, it's been weeks. Months. Maybe even years spent plotting my *final* job.

At least, I keep telling myself that it's my final one.

The nurse was correct about the loading dock being locked for the night, but it doesn't matter for me. One last code gets me into the castle where I immediately duck into a storage room, shed my stolen uniform, and slip on my black gloves. I flex my hands once or twice, and within a blink, dark, shadowy armor covers my entire body. Don't ask me how I got these gloves because the story is long and complicated, but they're the most important piece of gear I own.

I pull my usual black mask out of the pocket of my discarded pants and slip it over my eyes, then move like a shadow through the quiet, lowest level of the castle. It's a maze of servants' hallways, small personal apartments and suites used by the staff, and rooms dedicated to cooking, cleaning, laundry, and whatever else these spoiled royals need.

I take the first staircase I come across and climb two stories, popping out in one of the hallways that runs adjacent to the main, luxurious hallways used by the royals and their guests. I'm on the third floor now, I believe. I hope. Because I need to find one more staircase leading up to the fourth floor to officially enter the private wings of the castle used by the royal family without having to break into the private wing on the first floor, which I'd tried and failed the night of the ball.

A door opens along the hallway, and a pair of maids step out. I take a silent step into the shadows, blending into the darkness. They chat back and forth as they carry baskets of laundry, turning for the same staircase I just exited, but by the grace of the Goddess Herself, they don't see me.

It was too close of a call. I check my watch. I gave myself an hour to get in, and out, and I've already wasted twenty minutes. The guards work in shifts, patrolling not only the main corridors bathed in gold but the servants' hallways, as well. They break for an hour this time of day before a new set of guards moves in. I have forty minutes. That's it. If I'm caught, it's likely a death sentence, and I really don't want to kill anyone tonight—especially myself.

I move, holding my breath while relying on vague details from a story I overheard at a pub in Old Moonrise about some staff member fucking another one in this hallway. He'd mentioned they'd closed themself in "the stairwell to the fourth floor," which caused a ruckus at the table I was spying on because of how close they'd come to getting caught…. But I'd been thinking about how easy it would have been to just climb those stairs and be surrounded by wealth in a matter of seconds.

I check every door, finding more storage rooms, a few closets, nothing of substance until I reach the very end of the hallway, and an open door beckons, the darkened stairwell leading to my freedom coming into view.

"Thank fuck." I hiss, already sweating in the Ghost issued armor. A door down the hall behind me opens with a crack, but I'm already at the top of the stairs when voices drift my way. I slip through the door at the very top of the stairwell and step into an ornately decorated, but shadowed, corridor lined with antique furniture and vases full of fresh flowers.

Ceiling height windows run along the far wall, giving me a startling view of the festival taking place below. Six crystal chandeliers hang from the ceiling but cast no light. No, the only light comes from the flickering, gem-like glow of the festival beyond the gates.

It's not even midnight. I'd expect a twenty-two-year old woman to be up later than this, especially someone like *Maeve*. Someone who creeps through the night, scheming, plotting, misbehaving in general.

But what do I even know about her? More than I'd like, I think.

I know she likes chamomile tea with enough honey to drown out the taste. I know she drinks black coffee from cheap diners and spends a whole hell of a lot of time standing aimlessly in the rain, like an idiot, out in the open with no guards, no one to protect her. I know she uses her magic on strangers. I know she puts herself in harm's way with no regard about how valuable she'd be if she fell into the wrong hands.

I hope she's still as dumb as she was when I first encountered her all those years ago, and so far, my suspicions are correct. I move through the hallways like a phantom, encountering no guards, no maids, no one...

Until I turn a sharp corner and soft footsteps make me halt my progress to her private apartments immediately.

I sidestep into the shadow of an alcove shielded by two heavy, red velvet curtains.

"I think you should go to the festival with him," the princess says to her companion. "He's just *obsessed* with you, Jane."

"He's *not* obsessed." Jane, whoever she is, clears her throat. "He asked me because he feels sorry for me. It was probably a joke. He probably thought I'd say yes, and then he'd have the chance to laugh at me."

"Jane, for fuck's sake, he *likes* you. I can see it in his eyes. Just go with him tonight. There's a concert, and you're missing it!"

"Why aren't *you* going to the concert? Shouldn't you be out enjoying the festivities held in your honor?"

"You know the people of Moonrise use any excuse to throw a festival. I am, actually, looking forward to sitting in the library alone and reading something other than dusty books about history and law, for once. The kitchen maids gave me some rather spicy recommendations for romance novels."

Jane giggles as their shadows pass my alcove. Princess Maeve walks side by side with a dainty little woman in a maid's uniform and *absolutely* towers over her. Dark, thick brown hair is pulled back away from her face as the princess passes within feet of me, but she doesn't pause, or even look over shoulder.

My eyes drift down to the tight, black shorts she's wearing. She's barefoot, too, her arms and stomach covered by a sweatshirt that looks like it's made for someone five times her size.

Such a strange woman. This–this creature of flame, of untamed power–wearing a sweatshirt and shorts, will be our queen in a month's time.

"Are you sure you don't want company tonight?"

"I really don't. I do love your company, though, but I know you're sick of me." She nudges Jane's arm. The maid's head barely reaches Maeve's shoulder. I've never seen a woman so tall, in fact. She has to be close to six feet, if she hasn't surpassed that already.

"I'm never sick of you," Jane says with a little squeak, her voice fading as they turn the corner, "You just stress me out, that's all."

Princess Maeve's laugh is... melodic. I banish the warmth spreading through my chest as I step back into the darkened hallway, my heart hammering, and continue to move toward the private apartment where the princess keeps her valuables.

That's what I'm here for. Not for her. I'm not that kind of man. She's useless to me, but her jewels aren't, and when I reach the wide double doors of her private rooms, I slip a pin out of my pocket and pick the lock with ease, slipping inside unseen.

Again, this is far too easy, but I have mere minutes before the second night shift starts, and new guards begin their patrol.

The princess's rooms are immaculate and smell like magnolia–a sharp, deep, almost heady floral scent that makes my mind spin as I ignore my surroundings and head directly to her bedroom. My contact was correct about the princess leaving her gems out all over her rooms. I pocket bracelets, necklaces, and a few rings within the first thirty seconds I spend picking over her vanity. Two tiara's rest on top of her dresser, which is a mess of little knick knacks and pictures that I ignore. I'm not here to spy on her. I've never needed to spy on her. Those two times we were in the same place at the same time had been odd coincidences, nothing more.

In fact, the second time felt more like *she* was the one spying on *me*, and I didn't like it. I didn't like it at all.

My watch beeps in warning, alerting me that I have ten minutes to finish up and get the hell out of here. I open drawers in her bathroom, pocketing heavy diamond earrings and another ruby necklace. Finished, my pockets full and the black bag I brought along now bursting at the seams, I move through her apartment, but then come to a halt. A shadow moves near to the floor, snaking between the legs of an armchair.

That fucking cat again.

"Well, well," I sigh as the white cat stares at me from across the sitting room. I glance at the door, which I purposefully left ajar, wanting easy access back to the main hallway. "Nice to see you... *again.*"

The cat just stares at me with those big, greenish-blue eyes, but it has a collar on. A huge diamond dangles from it, catching the moonlight drifting from the window directly above it.

I lick my lips, wondering if the cat bites, because I'm taking that collar, too.

Being bitten is a risk I'm willing to take. I walk toward it, expecting it to run away, and I really don't want to have to chase it. It sits completely still as I crouch and reach along its fluffy neck, unclasping the golden chain. I resist the urge to sneeze as I hold up the collar, smiling down at the cat. "I'll be taking this."

It lets out a low growl.

"Pleasure doing business with you." I smirk, giving the feline a wink, and slip the collar into the nearly invisible pocket on my chest.

NOT A FAIR FIGHT

Soren

Storm clouds roll in as I lean on a wooden counter rapping my knuckles against the surface while a pudgy man in grubby clothing inspects the gems. Sapphires, rubies, and emeralds glimmer in the lightbulb swinging over the top of his bald head as he squints through a pair of glasses that make his eyes ten times bigger than they actually are.

I glance over my shoulder at the narrow, dimly lit hallway leading back to the heart of a pub in Old Moonrise. This room is a secret, closed off from the public, and open to only a select few.

There're places like this all over Eastonia. We call them *Fences* here—a place to barter and sell stolen goods without questions being asked. In Crescent Falls, they simply call it the black market. If I had time on my side, I would have traveled there to fetch a better price.

Thunder rattles the building, followed by the roar of sheets of heavy rain hitting the tin roof. I glance at my watch. It's already 3:00 in the morning.

"How long is this going to take?"

The man scowls up at me. "You wanna good trade or not?"

"I'm not here to trade. I'm here for cash."

"Well, this one's worth nothin'," he says, tossing the cat's collar on the counter. "Don't know where you got it. Don't need to know, but that's useless to me."

"What do you mean?" That's a fucking diamond!"

"It's a moonstone, boy. Moonstones grow on fuckin' trees round here, ya know? I don't need it. The chain is worth more to me than the rock."

I growl as I snap the moonstone off the chain and toss it back down to him. "Better?"

"Fuckin' thieves, always wasting my time." He grumbles under his breath as his thick fingers reach for a pen and pad of paper. His mouth twitches into a teasing smile when he asks, his voice laced with sarcasm, "I'm guessin' you ain't got a bank account?"

"Hurry. Up."

He smirks, writing a number down and tearing the paper off the pad. I grind my teeth while looking at the number. It's not what I thought it'd be. Far less, in fact. "You're joking."

"Ain't nothing funny."

"That lot is worth–"

"Ain't worth shit to me if I'm caught with royal jewels in my possession," he snaps. "I subtracted a handling fee for my troubles. Forty percent off the top."

"You fucking dick–"

"Do you want the cash or not?" he asks, raising his brows as he stands. Two large, lumbering men appear nearby–his bodyguards, no doubt.

I'm tall, but they have weight on me for sure.

I run my tongue over the edge of my lower teeth and nod. "Fine."

With a frustrated sigh, the man reaches into a metal box and pulls out three thick stacks of crisp bills and two small bags of coins. I snatch them off the counter before they even touch the gnarled, faded gray surface, slipping the moonstone into the pocket of my leather jacket.

"Better not be seeing you here for a while," he hisses in farewell, but I ignore him. Come morning, I'll be leaving Moonrise and not returning for the foreseeable future.

I stuff my pockets with the cash and walk through the pub, side-stepping through the groups crowding the bar. I shove through people blocking the entrance, having come in recently to take cover from the rain. I can't remember the last time I slept. I've been up for days planning this, researching the castle, figuring out the movements of the staff and guards, and for what?

It might be enough, I think, as I walk down the street, cutting between alleys and crossing intersections until I reach a run-down block of apartment buildings near the outskirts of town. There was once a great crystal castle built in this same area, overlooking the lake and valley where the new city of Moonrise now rests. Now, it's nothing but rubble and the forest has taken it back, new growth trees bending in the wind as the storm funnels over the lake.

I climb the exterior staircase to my third floor apartment. It's nothing but a studio with a small kitchen and bathroom. Holes in the plaster give a view of ancient stone, which leads me to believe this building used to be a manor of some kind before it was crudely reno-vated into small, separate living spaces.

I wouldn't call it home, but it has a bed, and that's really all I need.

I immediately take the cash, coins, and the worthless moonstone out of my jacket and tuck them in a hole in the wall where I keep my valuables. A few other stacks of cash rest inside, painted in shadows. I have to be close to paying off this debt. I might actually have enough to cover it and then some at this point, but I'd need to count it all out to be sure. If that's the case, I could buy a train ticket to Crescent Falls. I could set myself up there, get a bartending job or something in the inner city, and kiss Eastonia goodbye, for good this time.

But I've done this before. Paid off the debt that kept me in a silver shackle, unable to access my wolf powers.

The people I work for… have their ways when it comes to keeping their boots pressed to our necks, and I learned that in the worst way. Maybe it'll be different this time.

I take a shower and rummage through the fridge for leftovers. The sun is just beginning to rise over the lake, poking through the clouds as rain pummels the roof. Water drips into a bucket in the center of the room where a deep, bulging stain continues to creep across my cracked ceiling, but it doesn't matter. My bags are already packed and waiting by the door. In two hours, I'll be on the first train out of Moonrise.

Coffee in hand, I climb out my only window to sit out on the rusted fire escape to watch the sunrise like I do every morning. Rain trickles down the aging metal, but it's warm and humid–the best kind of weather. It's going to be another hot summer.

I scan the street. The only shop open is a corner store that never closes. No one's out and about. But my eyes land on a shadow moving through the alley directly across the street. The shadow stretches under the glow of a street lamp before its owner comes into view.

I'm seeing things. The white cat staring up at me is a figment of my imagination after days without sleep. I'm sure there's other white cats around. I don't see cats often. Shifters don't tend to keep pets, and the witches that do tend to keep them inside, out of harm's way, but....

The cat moves closer before sitting on the curb, and turns its flat face in my direction. Blue-green eyes hold on mine, unblinking.

"What the fuck," I whisper into my coffee as a prickle of unease licks up my spine. I blink to clear my vision, to erase the hallucination perched on the curb two stories below me, but the cat remains.

I slowly, carefully, slide back into my apartment and shut the window. I change into fresh clothes, pulling on a pair of thick socks before slipping into my boots. I return to the window as I'm shrugging my jacket back on and notice the cat is gone. It's likely an omen–a reminder that I need to get moving. There's no point in waiting around here for the train. I'll just go to the station and wait there.

Still, my heartbeat skips several times as I start moving toward the hole in the wall where I just stashed all of the money I have to my name, but the moment my fingers brush over the coin purses, footsteps sound in the hallway outside of my door. The knob jiggles, just once. I glance at the deadbolt, some of the tension leaving my shoulders when I realize I'd remembered to lock it. The floor creaks as the footsteps move away, then to the side.

They stop. I freeze, going perfectly still to try to slow my racing heart. I move my fingers until I feel cold, hard metal, and curl them around the hilt of a knife when the floor outside the door creaks like someone is stepping further away from it.

I pull the knife from the hole at the very moment the door bursts off its hinges, splintering like glass. Dust flies then settles as knee-high black boots appear, followed by a body hurtling in my direction, a crimson cape flying out in *her* wake.

Princess Maeve collides with me, ignoring my knife, and tackles me to the ground with impressive strength. I roll with her in my arms, slamming her against the foot of the bed, her head bouncing against the metal base, but she hooks her leg around mine and flips us over, her nails sinking into my wrist as she fights me for the knife.

I rip her cape off, the clasp biting into her neck before snapping free with enough force to cause it to career through the air and ping off the wall above my bed. I tangle my fingers in her hair and pull—hard, her neck bent back and teeth bared as she grits out a yelp of pain, but then I finally get a look at her face. She tries to yank out of my grip, but I twist my hand, my fingertips pressed against her scalp.

She's panting, her chest heaving with each shallow, pained breath she takes. Her wide, full lips pull back in a sneer, showing off her perfect, pearly white teeth. She has sharp canines like a shifter, but she's not a wolf. She doesn't smell like one. She smells like her room did—like magnolia, with an underlying sweetness that's hard to ignore, but I can't place it. It's familiar in some way, like an old, almost forgotten memory.

Her sharp, manicured nails sink into my wrist as she claws for the knife, drawing blood. She has my wrist pinned to the ground while I have her stuck in place with my hand fixed in her hair, but she's straddling me. She has the advantage right now; not for long.

"Let me go," she grimaces, her blue-green eyes wide with murderous rage.

"So you can stab me? No."

She tries to pull out of my grip, but I yank on her hair. She hisses in pain, her eyes watering, and sinks her nails into fresh wounds on my wrist.

I wait for her to blink, to give into the pain, then bend my knees in a sharp, controlled motion and thrust her to the side, rolling on top of her and bringing the blade down against her dainty neck. She doesn't look like she should be this strong. She's lean but hiding what I assume is a muscled build beneath a black long-sleeved shirt and tight dark jeans. It's taking all of my strength to keep her pinned. She's tall. Abnormally so, but so am I.

"I know who you are." She sneers, arching her neck as if in invitation to slice through her throat. It wouldn't be too hard from this angle.

"I'd hope so. We've met. Twice."

"Three times. You came to the ball."

I arch a brow. She's lost the baby-faced innocence I remember from the tea shop and the diner. Her cheeks have hollowed out. She's shed her youth after all these years. She's beautiful in a fierce way—like a flame—and just as dangerous. I lean down until our noses are almost touching. "You owe me a door."

"I don't owe you shit," she sneers. "You stole from me."

"Did you send your little kitten to follow me, witch?"

Her answering smile is totally unnerving—delirious, like she's possessed by a blood-hungry demon of old. I lick my lips, smirking down at her while she tries to catch her breath with me pressing her into the floor.

"Why don't you use your powers on me? I know you have them."

"It wouldn't be a fair fight."

"Like it's fair now?"

"What? Because you're a man?" She laughs, her eyes narrowing. My mouth begins to pull into a smirk, but she thrusts her knee between my thighs, and any humor I felt vanishes, replaced by blinding pain, then fury.

Maeve grunts with effort, taking advantage of my momentary

weakness, and gets out from underneath me with practiced grace, like she's been sparring all her life. She leaps to her feet, sending her boot into my ribs, but I grab her ankle and twist, forcing her back to the ground. Her other foot locks with my jaw in a crunching blow that has me seeing stars, but I grip her calf, dragging her toward me. She kicks the knife out of my hand and lands another kick to my face, my nose this time. Blood sprays. *"Fuck!"*

"Where is my necklace!" she screams in a blood-curdling rage, sitting up and slamming her fists against the back of my head.

I roll over, roll away, and stand on unsteady legs while the room tilts and spins. Maeve rushes me. I grab her arm and toss her into my dresser, which splits into pieces on impact. She's up on her feet in an instant, but the smell of blood is thick, and I can't tell if it's my own at this point. She's gone absolutely feral.

She throws a punch. I catch her fist, squeezing with all of my strength.

With a grunt of pain, she kicks out, swiping my leg, and I fall through the bed, the metal collapsing under my weight, then hers.

"Where is it?" she shrieks, punching me in the jaw so hard my teeth crunch together. I clutch her waist, shoving her far enough away that I can draw up my knee, then kick, sending her flying into the wall.

Her impact sends a deep vibration through the room. She hits the ground, the sound of plaster cracking and falling all around her mingling with her sharp cry of pain. I slide off the remains of the bed, crawling to her, then grab her by the throat and drag her back to me. She regains her composure enough to fight it, clawing at my skin with her nails, but I squeeze her neck.

"Use your powers on me," I command with a rough laugh. "I know you can. Do it, Princess. This fight isn't as fair as you thought it'd be. There's no shame in admitting it."

She spits at me, so I tighten my grip.

"Do it! Make killing you worth my while!"

"My necklace!" She growls, struggling for breath. Her hands warm my skin, and at first, it doesn't feel like much... but then... heat–blazing, boiling heat–erupts over my wrist, traveling through the dense scar and burrowing under the silver band. A soft clinking sound pings through my ears before the band falls away.

I look down at her, shaking my head. "You shouldn't have fucking done that."

Her smile is bloody. "You shouldn't have stolen from me, you fucking idiot."

The room tilts off its axis and spins out of control before the world goes black, and my eardrums burst.

BROKEN AND BOUND

MAEVE

MY BACK HITS SOFT, CREAM-COLORED CARPET AS THE SITTING ROOM IN my private apartment in the palace materializes. Gloves's hand is still wrapped around my neck, but his grip is loose. His body is a dead weight pressing mine into the carpet. My vision blurs as pain like I've never felt before cascades through me like a waterfall of pure fire. My ribs ache from multiple cracks. My cheeks, jaw, and nose are bruised. My head pounds where his fingers were tangled. I'm sure I'm missing chunks of hair… and I taste, and smell, blood. Lots of blood. Probably mine *and* his.

I suck in a painful breath and shove him off me. My arms tremble against his weight, but I manage to slide him to the side and kick out.

Gloves is completely unconscious lying face down on the carpet when I roll onto my hands and knees, gasping for breath he'd stolen from me. I spit blood and tooth fragments onto the carpet, wiping my mouth on the back of my swollen, bruised fingers.

I, of course, didn't think my actions through. I've sparred enough in my life to know that punching someone in the face, especially along the jaw, is enough to bust open the skin along my knuckles, but I think my fingers on my right hand might actually be broken.

"Oh, gods," I groan, rocking back into a kneeling position and cradling my hand. I glance at the man bleeding onto my favorite rug. He looks like hell—just as bruised, swollen, and bloody as I am.

I don't have healing gifts like some of the people in my family. I didn't even get a drop. If he's dying, I can't save his life. I can't knit my own bones back together or heal the abrasions on my skin.

I sniffle, shaking my head to dry my tears and take a deep, restorative breath just as Jane, carrying my usual breakfast on a tray, enters the foyer. She's humming a song, her footsteps light as she rounds the corner into the sitting room and sees me, then him.

"Don't scream," I croak.

She drops the breakfast tray, coffee spilling in a spray and strawberries bouncing around her feet as fine china shatters. She claps a hand over her mouth, and her eyes widen, but she chokes down that scream, turning it into a muffled, gargled moan.

"Go get one—no—three healing drafts," I tell her shakily, sniffling again as blood drips from my nose. "Some rope, and the biggest bucket of ice water you can carry."

"Are you all right?"

"Jane," I grind out as she starts to tremble, losing what little nerve she has, but she's my favorite maid, her timid, mousy personality aside. She's trustworthy and loyal to a fault, which means I keep her in my corner. If I had real friends, she'd be the best one. "Don't tell anyone. Don't alert the guards. Do you understand?"

"Three healing drafts, rope, and a bucket of ice water."

"Yes," I tell her, watching as she slowly backs away, her shoes crunching shattered porcelain into dust. "*Hurry.*"

She turns and darts for the foyer, and to her credit, doesn't slam the main door behind her like I would have done.

I look back at Gloves, watching his chest rise and fall. Normal people like him can't jump, or spirit, from place to place like I can, especially not on a whim. Maybe I should have done that before, first thing, but…

I feel along my chest where my moonstone necklace should be and find nothing but fury instead.

I force myself to my feet, ignoring the sharp, throbbing ache in my hand as I use the toe of my boot to roll him onto his back. His shirt is shredded and bloodstained, but I finally get a good look at his face without the mask for once. He's younger than I expected him to be. Mid-twenties, maybe. Maybe just a few years older than me. He's clean shaven with clear skin, and his cheeks are a soft pink under the vicious bruising starting to spread across his cheekbones and his straight nose.

His hair is a chestnut brown and highlighted from the sun just like I remember, softly curling around his ears and forehead. He's handsome, even with three deep scratch marks dribbling blood down his left cheek, swollen and angry. I look down at my broken nails. I just got them done, too, damnit.

I roll my tongue across my teeth, spitting out another chipped tooth fragment. Oh well. The healing drafts will fix me up just fine… and I don't plan to share any of it with him.

Using what's left of my strength, I pull him into an armchair. I rip off his leather jacket and dig through his pockets, finding a wallet and a few pocket knives but nothing else. No moonstone.

It wasn't at the Fence. I followed him there. I lingered near the bar, using the hood of my cloak to shield my face from onlookers, while he sold my jewels. I bought the jewels back from the disgusting man who runs the Fence, not wanting to have to cause a scene. Grandpa Ryatt will notice the money missing from the family coffers, but a stern talking to about my spending habits is better than what he'd do if I'd killed every man in that tavern and then burned it to the ground, I suppose.

The man had given up Gloves's address quickly and without hesitation, and from there I just… lost my ever-loving mind.

Jane appears carrying a bucket of ice water, the rope I asked for hanging around her neck, and the healing drafts stuffed in the pocket of her apron. She struggles with the weight of the bucket but manages to carry it across the room while I baby my broken fingers.

"Here," she whispers. "I need to go back and lock the door."

I nod, curling my good fingers around the three vials of medicine as she drops the bucket and hurries away again. I wrench each one open with my teeth, draining them. They're not as powerful as my great-grandmother Isla's tears, but Misty's tears do help. I'll heal over the next couple of hours and be fine by nightfall, I'm sure.

Jane returns. I don't have to tell her what we're doing. She has an uncanny ability to guess my next moves, and begins tying the man to the chair while I crouch, pulling everything out of his wallet.

"Do I want to know what happened?"

"No," I reply, my voice like gravel.

"Did he–did he attack you?"

"Yes."

"Here?"

"No, I went to his place." I pull several identification cards from his wallet and a passport, which surprises me. The passport is old, but the IDs are all different while his picture remains the same on each one.

"Oh," Jane murmurs, obviously struggling to maintain her composure. She's a witch, like me. She went through years of training, years of schooling, like all witches do, but her skills have always been domestic in nature, and apparently knots strong enough to hold a grown ass man are included in that. She steps back to inspect her work while the healing drafts swim through my body, targeting the worst of my injuries. I stretch my broken fingers with effort but notice they're no longer hanging from tendons, which is a good sign.

"Why–what happened?" Jane asks. "Who is he?"

"He stole from me."

"Stole?"

"He broke into the castle last night and rummaged through my room, taking anything shiny he could find, including my–my necklace." I touch my chest, curling my fingers around... nothing. "I followed him home."

"Is he going to die, you think?"

"I don't care," I huff, rising and holding out the cards for her to see. "Look at this. These are fake, but well made."

"He's a criminal, then. He has to be."

"Well, of course he is," I murmur, eyeing him as his slumps forward. I open the passport, looking down at the picture of *Gloves*, and the name beside it. "I think this is his actual ID. This is real, for sure."

"How do you know?"

"Because getting dual citizenship between Eastonia and Crescent Falls is damn near impossible. He would have been given this when he was born if his parents were from both places."

"What's his name, then?" Jane fans through the fake IDs.

I look at the man, then the passport, growling, *"Soren."*

We both look at him as my fury rises, turning deadly again now that my pain is subsiding. I toss the passport on a coffee table and pick up the bucket.

Jane swallows a squeak when I dump the ice water over his head, soaking him to the bone. Water splashes over my boots and sinks into the carpet, but he gasps, jerking against his restraints.

"Good morning," I grin wickedly.

He spits water tinged with blood, panting as he jerks, trying to free himself. I watch him try to clear his vision, blinking rapidly before squinting to scan his new surroundings. His eyes slowly inspect the room that I know he finds familiar because he was just here, in my space, stealing my things, but then his gaze lifts to my face, and I feel... odd.

I've never seen his eyes before. Even during our fight, I hadn't had the chance to really look at him, not like this, not with space between us.

One of his eyes is a startling glacier blue, bordering on white. I've never seen a color like that before, never. It rocks me to my center almost as much as the fact that his eyes don't match. His other eye is a perfect split between a dark, leather brown and pure steel gray.

He pants out a breath, the corners of his busted lips twitching into a smile, his teeth tinged with blood.

"Where is my necklace? I followed you to the Fence. It wasn't there when I took back what you stole."

"What necklace? I took several." He spits blood onto the carpet at his feet.

My lips curl into a sneer. "The moonstone necklace."

"The cat collar?" he laughs. "It was worthless."

"It wasn't worthless to me."

"Maybe if you'd given me a chance to explain instead of attacking me in my own home—"

"You broke into my home first."

"And you beat the shit out of me," he sneers. "We're even."

I laugh hotly, taking a step in his direction while Jane trembles behind me, her arms hugged tight around her chest. "I could have killed you, but I chose to take the high road, which is something you know nothing about."

"You want to talk about the high road with me, Princess? You left those jewels out like they meant nothing—"

"I don't care about the rest of it. I want my necklace back. I need it back, and you're going to tell me where it is!"

"Well, apparently it was worth something," he says wryly, his voice low as his eyes hold on mine. No wonder he wears a mask to somewhat obscure them. I've never seen eyes like his before and it's totally unnerving. I would recognize him anywhere now with just a glance.

He glances at Jane and notices her holding his wallet. He rolls his eyes back to mine, arching a brow. "So, Princess, are you going to kill me? If so, I'd love for you to just get it over with. If not, I have things I had to do today and this... this is wasting my time," he drawls in a patronizing voice that makes my blood boil.

I lean down so we're eye to eye. "I need to make one thing clear," I hiss. "I'm not someone to fuck with, *Soren*. You took something important from me. Something I cannot replace. Where is it?"

"I don't fucking know," he snaps, and the sound of my palm hitting his cheek reverberates around the room.

"If you *ever* use that tone with me again," I growl, nose to nose, "you'll be wearing your spinal cord as a belt. *Have I made myself clear?*"

He smiles. He fucking grins like a cat with cream. "Crystal."

"*Fuck you*," I growl, shoving him back. I can feel that smile sinking into my skin as I turn to Jane, waving a hand in dismissal. "No one enters this room. Do you understand? No guards, no warriors, not until I'm done. Go down and fetch another bucket of water and a few... butcher knives, and something to sop up this blood. There will be more."

She nods and turns but glances wearily at Soren before setting his wallet on the coffee table. I pace, debating my next moves. I suppose I could kill him. The moonstone wasn't at the Fence. I didn't get a good look at his apartment during our battle, and I know for a fact my powers would have reached for it, had it been there. If he sold it somewhere else... I need him alive to retrieve it.

But while Soren spits blood, trying to wriggle out of the tight knots binding him to the chair, I look out the windows bleeding morning light into the room, and see the fading outline of a new moon.

This couldn't have happened at a worse time. My powers are tied to the moon cycle, and they're naturally at their weakest now, but more so than usual, because a month from now, the next full moon will come with an eclipse, and the first Rite in over two decades will take place the same night as my coronation.

Until then, I'm pretty much powerless, especially without the moonstone.

My bloody clothing starts to dry and stick to my skin. I hate it. It's a gross feeling that makes me want to crawl out of my own body. I want a shower. I want to change.

"You're fucked, you know that?" I tell him, growling the words.

"I've been in worse situations," he replies with a shrug.

I lick my lips, looking at his arm where that gnarly scar breaks through his strange tattoos. The silver band is gone, nothing but scar tissue and a red, swollen wound left behind. I need to ask him about that. He's too skilled to just be a random criminal–a street rat, a thief.

"Who do you work for?"

"Who do you think I work for?" he asks, his mouth tugging into another smirk.

I can't think past the sensation of my bloody clothing any longer. He won't be able to free himself from those knots.

Jane might be timid and shy, but she has her qualities.

"I'll kill you for this," I tell him, and turn toward the hallway leading to my bathroom.

"I can't wait to see you try, Princess," he replies under his breath.

ONE-WAY TICKET

Soren

I yank against the knots, ignoring the pain in my body. I have to give credit where credit is due, I suppose, seeing as the two women who tied me up did a fine job of it. I hear a door close and water running, then make my move. Maeve thinks she has the upper hand because she's a princess, because she's a witch, but I know she's more powerful than how she's acted so far, and that makes me nervous.

She could have bound me here using those powers. She could put a ring of fire around me, preventing me from escaping, but she didn't. There's something about the moonstone that's not sitting well with me now, which means I need to go get it before she does.

I yank on the ropes until they loosen just a touch, then slam my weight into the chair several times until it starts to break. I grit my teeth, praying that she's showering and taking her time with it instead of, I don't know, washing my blood from her hands. Another jerk and the chair begins to snap. A second jerk, and it breaks completely, caving in on itself. I fall to the ground but lean forward, shaking the splintered pieces of wood and stuffed fabric out of the ropes. I can't walk through the castle at this point. I have mere seconds to find a way out of this apartment before she comes back into the room.

I limp toward the window. There's a balcony that stretches the entire length of her apartment, but below is a four-story drop right onto a street now teeming with people going to work or setting up for another night of the festival that won't end. I open the door to the balcony and slip outside then race toward the very edge, the corner of this wing of the palace, the top branches of a large, hopefully sturdy tree scraping against the railing.

The wall to the front garden is built around the ancient tree. I could climb down, then walk along the top of the wall, then jump from roof to roof…. Yes, that'll work. It has to work because I have no other options.

I rip the rope free of my wrists and ankles before climbing over the railing. My boots leave bloody footprints on her perfect mosaic tiles. I close my eyes, say a prayer, and jump.

Branches snap against every inch of my body as I fall through the canopy. My back crashes into a large, thick limb, breaking my fall enough to allow me to reach above me, grasping for more branches. My swollen, bruised fingers lock around one and hold, stopping my fall to what could easily have been death, and I hang for the space of a breath before finding my footing and climbing down.

I don't have time to hang around, no pun intended. I watch a trio of guards walk along the wall only ten feet below me and make a move when they dip out of sight. I swing from a branch with all of my strength, using my weight to send me flying over the wall to freedom, landing with a crunch on the roof of what I think is a bookstore. The second my boots hit the ground, I run. I run like my life depends on it—because it does.

The princess isn't what I'm worried about. It's the silver band that's no longer around my wrist and the hunters who would have been alerted by now that I'm free, and probably on the move, which means I have to get the fuck out of Moonrise if I want to survive the day.

A few people shout up at me in alarm as I sprint across the flat roofs of buildings hugging the main square. Old Moonrise comes into view, but I don't jump down to the street until I'm out of the festival district. My body aches. Yet, adrenaline keeps me moving, and in a few long, painful minutes spent sprinting, I cross the stone bridge into Old Moonrise and skid into a turn toward my apartment building… which is gone.

"Fuck my life," I hiss under my breath as I watch smoke funnel into the early morning sky. Half of the building gone, the rest burnt to a crisp, and what was once my shitty studio apartment is now a gaping hole of scorched plaster and old stone.

A crowd lingers nearby, watching royal warriors canvas the space, roping it off.

I run my hand down my face and curse into my palm. *My money.* The money I meant to use to pay the debt.

It's gone.

I cut through an alley, walking briskly to the backside of the building. The sunrise sets the side streets and small shops in shades of gold and light pink as I look up at the only surviving wall of my apartment with a sigh. The fire escape survived, which is now my only way up, so I take it, ignoring the warriors teeming two stories below me and the idea of falling through the scorched floorboards as I climb through what remains of the window, the glass shattered and falling through the grates in the metal fire escape.

The hole where I hoarded my treasures is gone. Burnt dollar bills flap in a soft breeze, scattered across what's left of the floor. I gather any that remain intact, stuffing them in my pocket, and search for what I came back here for.

I kick a piece of debris away and see the pale, opalescent gleam of the moonstone. I must be the Goddess's favorite this morning, because Her light is most definitely shining on me right now as I pluck the moonstone from the ground without even looking at it and tuck it in my pocket.

Maeve has my leather jacket. She has my watch and my wallet, too. I don't have a fancy cellphone. I have a burner phone which is now living up to its name when I crunch its burnt remains beneath my boot on the way out.

I walk at a calm, steady pace through Old Moonrise, my mind blank save for the task at hand–getting out.

I missed the morning train, but there's another at ten, which is only two hours away. It means reaching the Roguelands in the morning instead of this evening, but so be it. I have enough money for a train ticket, at least.

I pass a clothing shop where racks have been set up outside, various items of clothing swaying in the wind. The shop girl is busy entertaining other customers and doesn't notice me pulling new pants and a fresh shirt from one of the racks as I walk by. I cut into an alley, walking into a tight hovel between two buildings, and change out of my bloody clothing. I stop in a bodega next, buying a sandwich and a small coffee just to gain access to the bathroom, where I wash my hands, face, and hair in the sink, blood swirling down the drain.

I hate this. I've always hated living like this, but it's not the first time I've had to scrub myself down in a bathroom with flickering fluorescent lights illuminating my every move. I thought the last time would be exactly that–the *last time*, but no. If I don't leave Moonrise now, the hunters will find me, though I have a feeling the princess will find me first... and if she gets roped into my mess...

I look at my reflection in the mirror, running my fingertips over the scratch marks across my cheek.

She can fight. I'll give her that. But it won't be enough to save herself if she lands in the same mess I've been drowning in since I was a teenager.

The trek to the train station takes over an hour. I steal a ball cap from a shop catering to the tourists currently swarming the city for the festival, tilting the bill low over my face to keep it in shadow when I buy a train ticket, using the last of my money to secure a private room for the overnight leg of the journey to Twin Rivers, the last stop of the line.

I'm not going all the way, though. I sink onto a metal chair and hang my head, exhausted beyond belief. I let myself drift for a moment, mentally mapping my course, trying to conjure memories of the Roguelands. It's been at least three years since I've been there. I have friends there–friends who live off the main roads. Friends who work against their will for the same people I do. Friends who can help, even if it just means helping me lie low for a few days.

I look down at my busted knuckles, my bruised hands. I think of the princess, shaking my head at her memory. She's... infuriating. So confident but lacking the skills to use that trait to her advantage. Maybe giving me such an easy route of escape will be a lesson for her–a hard one to swallow, but a lesson all the same.

I know what the press says about her. She doesn't do interviews or hold public events, not since her older sister was considered dead for a month and miraculously returned, unharmed, with a mate.... Yeah, that situation caused a frenzy, to say the least. The news of Princess Brie's marriage to a relatively unknown man, a captain of her father's army, was quickly overshadowed by the announcement regarding a new kingdom joining the Allied Kings, a kingdom led by her own mate. Emberfyll remains, however, closed off to tourism. I know there's a naval base there, but that's it.

Then, King Ryatt's father died, and the news of that overshadowed Princess–Luna Queen–Brie, or whatever she is now. And for a while, speculation about Princess Maeve died down.

Now, she's all anyone can talk about.

And I had the pleasure of coming face to face with her.

The train pulls into the station right on time, and I board, but it'll be a while before I'm allowed to close myself into the private overnight room. I choose a seat in the farthest car, where I end up being the only passenger for the first two stops before the train departs Moonrise and the surrounding cities completely and dives into the heavily forested border between Moonrise and the Roguelands. I'm just starting to fall asleep when something smashes against the window directly beside my head. I startle, turning my head to watch a little gray bird slide down the glass before falling out of sight.

I ignore it, checking the watch I swiped from an unsuspecting passenger, and decide to see if I can go ahead and close myself into my room for the night.

The sun is setting when I close the door to the snug private cabin, which has nothing more than two benches facing each other and a few thin blankets folded neatly on the table between them, tucked under the window.

I throw myself onto one of the benches, closing my eyes. Sleep washes over me like a tidal wave, dragging me under into pure, blissful, silence.

A sharp series of knocks wakes me up. I haven't been asleep for more than a few minutes judging by the golden light of the sunset still flickering through the window.

"What? This room is occupied," I grumble, rubbing my eyes and blinking to adjust them to the light. The knocks continue, then pound, shaking the entire door. "What?" I snarl, turning the lock and throwing the door open before my brain has a chance to catch up to my body.

Maeve crashes through the door, her cheeks flushed and eyes glazed with… rage? Maybe, I'm not entirely sure. She braces herself on the doorframe then weakly tries to throw a punch, but misses, her entire body slumping and tilting forward.

I'm not sure what force propels me to act in this way. My brain is telling me to knock her ass out cold, to carry her over my shoulder and toss her from the train, letting nature run its course, but my instincts take over, and I grab her as she starts to fall, her eyes rolling back in her head.

"What the fuck is wrong with you?" I hiss, turning in the snug space to kick the door closed, but I knock her head against the wall accidentally, and she yelps in pain. I turn the lock and dump her on a bench, then step back, raising my fists in preparation to defend myself from her again, but she looks… different.

She looks all wrong.

"Are you… okay?"

"Fuck off," she gasps, baring her teeth, but her eyes water. "Where the fuck is my necklace? I need it."

"How did you get on this train?"

She takes a single, shallow breath before her eyes flutter closed, then promptly passes out.

UTTERLY USELESS

MAEVE

I'M VIBRATING. I'M LYING ON MY BACK, BUT I'M MOVING... WHICH IS strange. I open my eyes to darkness and an unfamiliar room with gray plastic paneling and... handles fixed to the low ceiling. An incessant rattle makes my ears ring. I squeeze my eyes shut and open them again, expecting to be back in bed in Moonrise, in my room, but I'm.... Oh, *shit.*

I sit up, whirling toward the man resting on a bench across from me, his arms tucked around his chest and head leaning on the wall by the tiny window overlooking a dark, never-ending forest. He slowly opens his eyes to slits. He's holding a plastic butter knife, twisting it between his fingers as he looks at me through this thick, dark lashes.

Adrenaline cuts through the power fog weighing me down, but not enough to drag me out of the haze, not yet. I need... I need rest. I need sleep. I need something, something he has, or had. I lick my lips, holding his gaze as I debate my next move, my next words.

"I was really looking forward to sleeping tonight," he says dryly. "Alone, I might add."

I feel dizzy as I drag my knees up to my chest. I rest my chin atop them, barely able to hold my head up, let alone say anything, not just yet.

He smooths the dull edge of the butter knife over the pad of his thumb, his eyes locked on mine in silence.

"Were you planning on killing me with that?" I ask.

His tongue swipes across his lower lip before he smiles softly. "That would've been too messy, taken too long. I would have just strangled you. Snapped your neck."

"Oh, well, I'm sure that would have saved you a lot of time."

"I'm still debating it, so don't do anything stupid, Princess."

"I think you win when it comes to stupid behavior, *Gloves*," I grumble, closing my eyes for just a moment.

"What did you call me?"

"Gloves," I reply, looking at him again.

"Why?"

"Because that's what I've been calling you for… three years now. Because you wear Ghost-issued gloves. Those must be stolen too, huh?"

His wry, damn near flirtatious smile works its way into my bones and makes me feel warm in a way I don't appreciate. "You've been… you've been thinking about *me*? For three years?" he teases, his eyes dancing with amusement.

I growl, my upper lip curling over my teeth. "Don't mess with me. You're lucky I haven't killed you yet, you son-of-a-bitch!"

"I'm starting to think you can't."

"Of course, I can–"

"Have you ever killed anyone before? Anyone? Stabbed someone in the heart? The back? Slit their throat? Watched their life drain behind their eyes?" He leans forward, his eyes shining in the dim light coming through the window. "I don't think you have."

"No one has ever dared to cross me before."

"Well, judging by how you reacted when I so *easily* broke into your home and took your things, I supposed if they did cross you, they wouldn't really suffer for it."

My answering snarl pings from wall to wall. We're barely three feet apart. I can smell him, smell his clothing. Two conflicting scents mingled, turning into something that seems off, wrong, not all him.

He smells like a man, like musk and sweat–like rich warmth and the promise of strength and power.

But his clothing smells like floral soap and the breeze coming off the lake in Moonrise. They don't mix.

"Did you steal those clothes, too?"

"Of course. You beat me nearly to death. I was covered in blood. I highly doubt I would've been allowed on the train looking like I did when I escaped you." He purses his lips into a mocking grin. "You need to work on that, by the way. You never leave someone you're planning to interrogate and torture for information unsupervised."

I grind my teeth, struggling for something sharp and witty to say in response, but my moment of hesitation only makes his smile widen.

He leans back, sighing deeply. "If I had been in your position, I would have knocked you out first. Showering right before a torture session is also kind of a waste of time, seeing as they normally involve a lot of blood–"

"Shut up!"

"I don't have to do that. I paid for this room. You barged in and passed the fuck out in my arms. I gave you a place to land out of the graciousness of my heart."

"Just tell me where the moonstone is. That's all I want."

"Why? Why is that rock so important to you?"

"It's none of your business. I could have you arrested, you know. I know your name. I have your fucking wallet back in Moonrise will all of your fake, and highly illegal, IDs. I have your passport, dumbass! I could sick my warriors on you, and you'd never see the light of day again!"

"You could also use your powers to just end my life right now."

"Why are you so concerned with my powers? You were pressing me to use them on you earlier. Do you have some sick, demented curiosity about death, Soren?"

"I'm awfully curious about why you're sitting here with no shields up, knowing I could hurt you," he replies, his voice dropping and softening just a touch. He licks his lips again, a slow motion I can't help but follow.

"I'm not afraid of you."

"I think that's your problem."

I eye him wearily, trying to grasp whether or not this man is, in fact, a serious danger to me right now.

To be completely, brutally honest… I'm… I'm super disappointed. Crushingly so, actually. When I met him for the first time, in those days after all of us thought Brie was dead… those minutes spent in his quiet company had been… well, I'd needed it. Unlike my family, he hadn't offered words of comfort to help me through my grief. He'd just stood there while we watched the news, two strangers in a tea shop.

I felt normal. I don't think I've felt normal since then.

The diner had been when I wondered if…. Never mind. It's silly. It's stupid, really.

I lean back and fix him with a glare. "I need that moonstone, Soren. I'll leave once you tell me where it is. I'll leave you alone, and you can go free. You'll never see me again."

"I don't believe you."

"I need it–"

"Why?" He's so serious right now. That charming smile fades to a look of cold, brutal intensity. It's enough to make me stiffen and seriously consider my next words. No man has ever made me feel like *that* before, that's for damn sure. Soren bleeds violence. That's the only way to describe him. I can just feel it.

And right now, I can't feel much else.

"I used–I used all of my powers to chase down the train," I admit, swallowing past the knot forming in my throat. "I saw you in the window as the train left the station, and shifted into a bird–"

He barks a laugh, then mumbles a half-hearted apology.

"What's so funny?"

"You can turn into a bird?"

"Yes."

"Did you, by chance, fly into a window earlier?" He rolls his lower lip between his teeth, biting back an amused smile.

I lean forward, scoffing. "I'm glad you find this funny, you asshole. It hurt, a lot!"

"Anyway," he says, motioning for me to continue. "You... followed the train?"

"I used up my powers, all of them. The Moonstone–"

The train jolts, sending a rattle down its snake-like body. The power flickers, causing us both to look up at the strip of dim lights above our heads. Soren rises methodically. I can feel tension pouring off him as the train grinds to a sudden stop, and the lights go out like someone blowing out a candle. Silence settles. It's eerie and misplaced, and my skin begins to tingle with a sense that something's terribly wrong.

"Stand up," he says in a near whisper.

"Why–"

"Princess Maeve, *stand up*."

I bristle at his tone. "No. I was just saying that the moonstone–"

He reaches into the pocket of his pants and pulls something out, thrusting his fist in my direction. The moonstone drops into my hand, but my stomach twists, then sinks, when I unfurl my fingers and...

"You *broke* it." I croak, feeling like the floor of the train is caving beneath me. I smooth my thumb across a crack along the face of the smooth stone. "What did you do?"

"What are you talking about?" he hisses, his patience worn thin. "Get up right now!"

"Why?!"

A scream rips through the train. I jump to my feet, whirling in the direction of the sound. More screams and shouts of alarm, then pain, cut through the air, muffled by the door of Soren's cabin room.

"What's happening?" I ask, clutching the moonstone in my palm, trying to warm it, but it remains... cold, and useless.

Soren bites his lip, nodding to himself as his eyes stay fixed on the door. I'm not prepared when he grabs me by my upper arm and yanks the door open. He pulls me into the hallway, his body pressed to mine as people run in our direction, shoving past us.

Soren takes several deep breaths, his eyes locked on the door leading to the next car. I rise on my toes to look over his shoulder and see four large shadows lumbering toward us, just one car over.

"Who are they?"

"Remember how I said you shouldn't have broken that silver band around my wrist?" he growls under his breath, then sighs. "Now's the time to use those powers, Princess."

"I can't."

"What do you mean you can't?" he asks, tugging me along as he backs down the narrow corridor, away from the shadows currently ripping apart the next car.

"My powers are gone. I need time to recharge."

"You're fucking joking–"

"I can't handle all of my powers at once, not yet. The moonstone stored the surplus. I could call on them, siphon my powers from it if I needed more, but you fucking broke it, and now those powers are just… out in the universe, useless to me!" I shout, shoving against him, but he keeps a tight grip on my arm, tight enough to bruise.

"So you have nothing?" he snarls. "Nothing to defend yourself with?"

"No–"

"You can't shift?"

"I'm not a shifter! What's happening? Who are they? What do they want?"

"Me," he says under his breath, letting go of a long, slightly annoyed sigh that ends in a nearly silent curse when four big, ugly, vicious looking men charge into our car, and spot us.

"Soren, Soren, Soren," their leader, I assume, says as he takes a few steps in our direction, chuckling. "The Viper's lookin' all over for ya. Says you broke your tether. Sent us out to find ya."

Soren shoves me behind him, forcing me to match his steps as he backs us toward the opposite end of the car.

"I was already on my way to see her," Soren says lightly. "Your services are unnecessary."

"Viper says you've been ignoring her summons for months now," the biggest, ugliest man I've ever laid eyes on says, clicking his tongue. "You've been a bad dog, so she sent us to find ya and bring ya home to get you back on a leash. A much shorter one this time."

Soren smirks, shrugging. "You're wasting your time and your breath."

"Who's he got behind him?" one of his companions rasps in a slithering voice that makes my skin crawl.

"Looks like we might've interrupted Soren and his most recent lady friend," the leader chuckles. "Why don't you hand her over? Let us have a turn?"

Soren goes completely, utterly still. I'm pressed against the door leading to the very back of the train. There's nothing but tracks behind us, nothing but a steep drop off over a bridge into the woods, no nearby lights, nor lit roads, just foggy, dark nothingness.

My heart races. I've never felt so useless. I stretch and curl my fingers, trying to summon my powers of fire, but nothing happens, not even wisps of smoke.

"I believe I'll be keeping this one to myself," Soren says calmly, which surprises me. I'd think at this point he'd be happy to get rid of me, but then I feel him tap my wrist in a silent command... to what?

"Don't make this hard for yourself, boy. You know how the Viper feels about her pups getting all tangled up with us Hounds. She wants you alive, but if you make any moves... I can't promise you'll make it to her in one piece."

"Then she'd be your problem. I'm one of her best," Soren smirks, which enrages Ugly Man and his minions. I don't know who the Hounds are, but they must be them. "And crossing the Viper is a one way ticket to hell itself. You wouldn't want to be caught in the Spider's crosshairs, would you, now?"

My blood runs cold as ice as Soren's words lace through my brain. The Spider?

Soren works for *Hannibal*?

He taps on my wrist again, taking another step back to press me into the door in a silent command to open it.

"I'm done fucking around," Ugly Man sneers. "Get em. Keep the girl alive. She's got those long legs *I like*."

I scoff, then twist the handle. Soren doesn't waste a single second. He turns, grabs me around the waist, and leaps off the train, past the tracks, sending us into a free fall.

YOU OWE ME

MAEVE

THERE IS NOTHING I CAN DO BUT FALL. I STRETCH MY ARM, TRYING TO summon any power I can siphon from the sliver of moon visible through the clouds. I'm empty and falling at what feels like the speed of light. I'm honestly thankful for the fear and adrenaline buzzing through my veins at the moment because it's the only thing keeping me from being sucked in a full-blown power-depletion coma.

Soren's arm is ripped from my waist when we breach the trees. He shouts in pain, but his voice is drowned out by snapping branches and rustling leaves as I plummet to the forest floor.

I land with a crunch in a thicket of thorn bushes. I'm wearing jeans and a light sweater, but it's not enough to stop the thorns from shredding into my clothes, piercing my skin as I try to roll out of the bush.

"Maeve?" Soren shouts, panting my name somewhere nearby, but I can't see him. It's the middle of the night, and without the moonlight to illuminate the forest, I can't see a damn thing. "MAEVE!"

"I'm right here!" I snarl, whimpering in frustration as I try to untangle myself from the thorns. My hair is stuck in the branches, wound painfully in the same places where Soren yanked entire chunks loose not even a full day ago.

The forest around me rustles as Soren appears, his eyes glowing in the darkness while he assesses my situation and decides to just pull me out of the bush, but my screech of pain makes him question his next move. "You need to relax!"

"Get the fuck away from me!" I scream, swiping at his face with my nails. He rears back, catching me by the wrist, and yanks with all of his strength. My hair pulls branches free and my howl of agony is covered by the sound of the wind rushing through the forest, but Soren wraps an arm around my waist, limping us away from the thorn bush.

Tears I refuse to shed sting my eyes when I shove him away, hard. "Don't fucking touch me," I choke out, shaking as the adrenaline fades, and the pain of the thorns covering my body allows that freezing, bone numbing chill to creep in. I stumble away from him, bracing myself on a tree and lowering to my knees.

"What's wrong with you now?" he asks from several feet away. "We can't stay here."

I realize I no longer have the moonstone. I must have dropped it when we fell. I close my eyes, shaking my head before reaching down to start pulling thorns from my sweater, then my fingers. My hands shake when I reply, "Don't talk to me right now."

He huffs a breath. I glance at him as he stares up at the massive bridge–a true marvel of engineering designed by Blake's father, Sydney, and his grandfather, Isaac. It took over a decade to build just this section of the railroad, the miles-long bridge coasting over the treetops by seventy feet, keeping the ancient forest untouched. Blinking lights flicker along the bridge high above the trees.

I shakily rise and pull my sweater over my head, discarding it at the base of the tree. It's not a cold night by any means, but my skin still tingles in the night air. My tight tank top is going to have to do, for now.

I'm more worried about the thorns stuck between my fingers and the twigs tangled in my hair at the moment, and I have to keep my mind off my depleted powers.

I glance at Soren, who has his back turned to me as he stares up at the bridge.

"There's a town nearby," I say into the dark, sniffling while yanking out a particularly stubborn splinter.

"I know, but that's the first place they'll look," he replies dryly, turning to face me. He scans my bare arms before his eyes slide to my discarded sweater. "There's another village ten miles from here. We have to backtrack. They think I'm headed to Twin Rivers, so they'll go east. We're going to go west."

"I'm not going anywhere with you." I snarl, reaching up to pull twigs from my hair.

"Great," he says with a relieved sigh, promptly turns on his heel, and… walks away.

I stay stationary for a few seconds in complete shock before coming back to my senses. "Where the fuck do you think you're going?"

He stops roughly fifty yards away, turning back in my direction. "Exactly where I said I'd be going. To the east. To a village to the east." His tone is sharply condescending and frustrated, like he's not talking to a royal. Not just any royal, either. *Me.*

He's not…. He's not afraid of me in the slightest.

He's looking me in the eyes without flinching.

That's entirely new for me.

"Shift then," I shout, plucking a thorn from the tender skin on the side of my neck, drawing a few drops of blood. Under my breath, I grumble, "*Dumbass.*"

"I heard that."

"Well, you are one! You're going to walk ten miles in the dark, unarmed?"

"And what are you going to do? Huh? Stand around and wait for someone to save you?"

"My powers will return, and then I'm leaving, and I'm putting a fucking bounty on your head the second I get back to Moonrise!"

"Thank the Goddess!" he shouts, barking a sharp laugh. "Gods, I've been so bored lately, Maeve. Please, sick every warrior in your kingdom on me, I beg you!"

"It's *Princess* Maeve to you, dickhead!"

He raises both hands and boldly flips me off, then turns, and continues walking into the night.

"Soren!"

"WHAT?!" he whirls, his expression etched with exasperation. "What do you want? Do you want my help or not? For fuck's sake–"

"You don't get to yell at me," I growl, limping in his direction. "You started this. You stole from me–"

"And you made the stupid decision to try to follow me–"

"You STOLE from me! You're a thief! You–you came to the ball to scope out the castle that night, didn't you? That's what you were up to in the western wing–"

He cuts me off with a wave of the hand when I close in on him. "How did you know that?"

"Because I was there."

"You weren't. I was alone–" he cuts himself off, his expression shifting from utter annoyance to that bright, charming smirk. "No way."

"What?"

"*You're* the cat?"

I straighten my shoulders. "Yes. What about it?"

"You're a cat shifter–"

"No, those don't exist. I can just… shape-shift–"

"And out of all the things you could choose from, you shift into a cat? A big, fluffy, white cat?" He blinks down at me, then breaks into howling laughter that makes my cheeks burn with a blush so fierce I feel it heat me from within.

"Don't laugh at me," I rush out, my lower lip trembling. "You don't get to–to stand here and make fun of me!" I give him a rough shove, but he barely budges and continues that laughter that sinks into my bones and makes me see red. "You know what, fuck you! You're laughing at me when I should be the one laughing because you're nothing but a thief. You have to steal your way through life–"

"You don't know anything about me–"

"I know you're broke. You don't have a single dollar to your name–"

"I have ten dollars, to be exact. How much cash do you have on you at the moment, huh? Does your bird form come with a little purse–"

I smack the hell out of him. He flexes his jaw, grunting softly. "That hurt."

"Good."

"Are you done? Or are you going to continue to pout in the middle of the woods? Those guys… they're going to come for us. You don't want to be here when they come looking."

"Who were they?"

"Bounty hunters."

I shake my head. His tone makes me believe he's not telling the full truth. "Why are they called Hounds? I've never heard that term before."

"Well, you wouldn't, being a prim, proper, well-bred lady," he says with a smirk, then rolls his eyes to the east. "Seriously, if you're going to come with me, we need to go–"

"You work for Hannibal."

The charming smile is scrubbed from his mouth in an instant.

I take a step toward him. "You work for Hannibal Arachnis. The Spider–"

"I don't work for him."

"That's a lie. You know who he is."

"Yes, I do. But I don't work for him. Not directly."

"So you were lying–"

He grits his teeth, his eyes shining in the faint glow of the flashing red beacons on the bridge looming over our heads. "You need to come with me. I can keep you safe for the night, and you can go back to your castle in the morning, once you get your powers back."

"You work for Hannibal–"

"I don't," he asserts, growling the words.

"But you work for someone he knows—"

"I owe a debt, nothing more."

"For what?"

A distant howl breaks the silence in the forest all around us. Soren looks over the top of my head, his hand absently wrapping around the curve of my bare upper arm. "We need to move."

He gives me a little tug, but I dig in my heels. He glares down at me.

"Maeve—"

"Bring me to him."

"What?"

"Bring me to Hannibal. Take me to him."

He scans my eyes, arching his brows. "Did you hit your head, or are you always this fucking stupid?"

I wind back and send my fist flying toward his face, but he catches it, squeezing until my bones scrape together. Another howl, closer this time, jolts me back to total awareness and sends a chill of warning licking up my spine, but Soren's eyes are locked on mine.

"We're leaving. I'm not going to have your blood staining my hands. Come on." He tugs me roughly once, then twice, until my feet finally start moving.

"You owe me an explanation," I growl, letting him lead me to the east, away from the bridge and deep into the forest.

His hand doesn't leave my arm, his touch warming my skin as he guides us through the dark like he's been here before and knows exactly where we're going.

"For what?"

"Stealing my jewelry."

"I'm a thief. You said it yourself."

"There's more to it. You said you owe a debt—"

"It would have been paid off had you not burned my apartment down with all of my money still inside."

"I didn't—" I cut myself off with a sigh. "You know what, I probably did do that. Nothing I can do about it now, as it stands, seeing as I'm hundreds of miles away from Moonrise." The mountains nearby are still topped with snow—snow that never melts. Miles west of here, along the base of those mountains, a tunnel acts as the border to Crescent Falls.

We're about as deep as we can be in the Roguelands now.

"Why aren't you shifting? I could just ride on your back."

"I can't."

I pause my steps, forcing him to come to a halt. "What? Why?"

"Because I've been wearing a silver band for five years," he says with marked frustration. "Is that enough? Have I answered all of your questions?"

"What was it for?"

Soren exhales deeply, nostrils flaring with annoyance. "What do you think it was for, Princess?"

There's a glimmer in his eyes I don't think I like. Grief, I think. Deep seated, something that's been festering for a long, long time.

"Is the Viper your boss?"

He doesn't say anything, but his expression gives me my answer. He starts walking again, tucking his hands in the pockets of his stolen pants. I struggle to keep up with his swift, long stride, but we walk like this in silence for several achingly long miles. The howls fade in the opposite direction as the stars tilt overhead, barely visible through the treetops.

When the silence becomes too much, I ask, "How old are you?"

"Twenty-six."

"So you've been wearing silver since you could shift? Or longer than that?"

"I was twenty-one when she—when I joined."

"Joined what—"

"Enough. I can't take it anymore," he says under his breath. "Please, I haven't slept in days."

"You owe me—"

"I don't owe you shit, Maeve." He points through the trees where a small town erupts into view, only a few lights flickering in the dead of night, but there is a small hotel tucked on the outskirts along a narrow, dirt road just to the left of us through the trees. "We're here."

"You owe me an apology," I cut in, and his eyes meet mine. "For breaking my necklace."

He's quiet for several seconds. I watch him take a breath as he holds my gaze, looking into my eyes like he's totally, completely unfazed by the promise of what I am, what I can do, what kind of pain I could inflict if I had my powers.

He sees right through me.

"I'm not sorry in the slightest." He turns from me, stalking into the village, giving me a view of the tension gripping his broad shoulders and the way his hands curl into fists in his pockets.

SAYONARA

MAEVE

I LIKE TO TRY TO LEARN SOMETHING NEW EVERY DAY. TODAY, IN THE dead hours of the night, I learn that ten dollars does, in fact, cover the cost of a hotel room in the shittiest little hotel in all of Eastonia... which includes a twin bed with what I believe might be a rather large blood stain, a blanket that has seen better days, and a single pillow that should probably be thrown into a fire.

Soren chews his lip as he leans on the door to close it, sighing deeply as he scans our new surroundings. I refuse to look at him when his eyes graze my profile, however, and keep my focus on the disgusting, yellow-stained pillow and bed likely crawling with little bugs.

"I can go ask if they have extra satin sheets," he says sarcastically, which earns him an absolutely scalding glare.

"I'm not sleeping on that bed."

"Yeah, you're not. I bought the room, so the bed is mine anyway." He strides past me, opening the only other door in the room, which leads to a bathroom I'm not sure he can even fit inside. He shuts the door, tucking his hands in his pockets. "I'm going to go find us both new clothes while you sleep. The floor looks cleanest over there." He points to the far corner of the room, winks, and brushes past me toward the main door.

I'm fuming but bite my tongue to stop from mouthing off. I decide in the moment that I have nothing else I could possibly say to the man, the monster, aside from what I've already said.

But his absence in the room weighs on me in a way I hadn't expected.

I sit on the edge of the bed and busy myself by picking rogue thorns and splinters from my jeans. An hour passes, and when he doesn't return, I take a cold shower because there's no hot water to be had, but at least there was a small bar of soap to help wash the remaining twigs from my hair.

Wrapped in a towel that barely fits my body, I lay on the mattress, cringing as I cover myself with the measly blanket, and fall into the deepest sleep of my life.

I've gone through a total power depletion before, but only once. It had been after I summoned my powers and said the spell to open a portal, taking Logan and Brie to Emberfyll. The pain of it... Goddess, it's hard to describe. It's like being frozen solid and thawing slowly, like I have shards of razor-sharp ice beneath my skin.

This time feels different, however. I just feel... numb and empty.

I've been storing my powers in that moonstone amulet since I was six years old. It was a solution to the dangerous powers a child my age had no way of ever being able to handle. Up until that point, I'd been catching things on fire, spiriting away from home on accident, and being an overwhelming liability to my powerful family members. I couldn't be around my cousins unsupervised. My maids and tutors were terrified of me.

I thrived in Moonrise, however. Something about that place just calls to me, calls me home.

When Arthur, the historian in Veiled Valley, presented the necklace to my grandma and my mother as a possible solution to my overwhelming gifts, it worked.

All I needed to do was wear it. It held my powers warm against my skin, safe and secure. I've worn it every day, every moment, since then.

Until Soren took it, and broke it, releasing those powers back into the world... and now it could take... days, maybe even weeks, to build those powers back up again. I've never just... let my powers materialize to their full strength before without a buffer.

What if I can't handle it?

I wake hours later to warm morning sunlight creeping through a single, circular window and fanning over the bed. I roll into the sun, letting the light heat my skin, but my legs brush against something stacked near my toes.

I sit up as a shadow passes over me carrying the scent of soap. Shielding my eyes from the spray of the sun, I watch Soren walk wearing nothing but a towel tied around his waist, his heavily muscled back and arms on full display as he runs his fingers through his wet hair. He grabs what looks like a pair of worn-in jeans and shirt from the clothing pile at my feet and watches me draw up my legs, his eyes drifting over the blanket clutched to what I realize with a start is my naked chest.

I fell asleep in nothing but a towel. I can feel it gathered around my waist now.

"Morning," he says, narrowing his eyes as he scans my face for threats, I think, like I have my powers back and can now blast him into fiery oblivion if I wished for it.

"Did you steal those clothes, too?"

He frowns, unamused, and turns from me, dropping his towel.

I blink, startled by the very naked view of his back and... rather sculpted ass, then look away, my cheeks burning crimson.

"You'll be surprised to know that I don't just steal my way through life like you assume," he mutters, slipping into the jeans and pulling them up to his waist. I don't dare look at him, but out of the corner of my eye, I see him turning back in my direction before shrugging into a simple, gray T-shirt, smoothing the fabric over his chest.

"How did you get them, then?"

"I noticed a guy with a crooked chimney and offered to fix it for him. He paid me well for it, and I bought some clothes. For you, as well. You owe me forty bucks."

He sits on the edge of the bed only inches away from my legs to put on a pair of socks, then his boots.

"Did you... did you sleep?"

He glances at me, shaking his head. "There wasn't room for the two of us, and I couldn't wake you up. I felt bad about dumping you, naked, on the ground and taking the bed."

"Well, thanks–"

"There's some clothes for you and a couple dollars to buy breakfast downstairs if you need it." He rises with a grimace like his back is sore, then reaches for a ball cap and fits it on his head. "We're about twenty miles from the nearest train depot, but I'd avoid it if I were you. You should do your little disappearing and reappearing in a new place trick instead." He scoops a thin piece of navy blue fabric off the corner of the bed and ties it around the top of his face, shielding his eyes from view.

"Jumping."

"What?" he asks, smoothing the fabric.

"We call it jumping, or spiriting."

"Kay'." He gives me an odd, disinterested look before tossing some money on the bed near the stack of clothing he mentioned. "Take care of yourself, Princess."

He moves toward the door, and my chest convulses with sudden panic. I can feel a flicker of power in my chest, but that's it. Just a flicker. It could be enough to get me by... but what if it's not enough? Hell, I can't even mind-link as it stands.

He hesitates for a split second, his fingers curled around the doorknob, before he pulls it open and slips away, shutting the door with a soft click behind him.

Leaving.

Just like that.

※

Soren

I PACE AT THE END OF THE DIRT ROAD, GRUMBLING AND SNARLING under my breath while every fiber of my being begs me to turn around, to go back to the hotel where I just left the royal princess of Eastonia–the queen in a little over a month–alone, unarmed, and naked in a filthy bed.

In my defense, I didn't touch her. I just sat on the ground with my back to the wall and watched the door all night, acutely aware of every creaking floorboard and wondering footstep, a knife I swiped from a man at a nearby bar resting in my lap.

And, I had, in fact, fixed a man's chimney. He'd overpaid me, but he'd also been so drunk I couldn't understand a damn word he said. I'm not that bad of a guy, just an enterprising one.

So, I bought the princess a little sundress with blue flowers on it and a cardigan at the only store in the whole Goddess-forsaken village and planned to go on my merry way until this moment, when walking away from her feels like something I'm going to regret for the rest of my miserable life.

I rub the scar on my forearm where a tingling sensation began to erupt last night. I'm not sure if I'll ever get my shifting powers back after years bound in silver, but this feeling is new, and maybe that's why I'm on edge, not because I feel... guilty or anything.

I should have chosen a different royal. I should have chosen a different royal apartment. Had I known what door I was opening by stealing from Maeve, I would have... still done it, honestly, just to bear witness to her fury because that was....

She's....

"Fuck, man," I hiss at myself, rolling my shoulders and groaning as I turn toward the narrow, dirt road leading out of town and start walking.

Morning turns to midday, and midday bleeds into the afternoon as the sun beats down on my back. I don't stop walking for what feels like dozens of miles, but eventually, I come to a fork in the road, still trapped in the dense forest. I sit on a rock to rest, rolling out my aching muscles. I'm still heavily bruised from when I let the princess rough me up. Keyword–let. But the sharp pain of fresh wounds has turned into a dull, ever present ache.

Engine noise rattles toward me. I turn my head to an old, beat up truck bumping in my direction, its bed full of small bales of hay. The man driving the truck slows down, looking out his window at me, then waves me over.

"Need a ride, kid? It's hotter than hell out here and you're miles from the nearest village."

"Yeah, actually," I tell him, flashing him a smile. "My car broke down a few miles back. I'm trying to get to–" I cut myself off, shrugging to make it look I'm just uncomfortable and hot in my sweaty shirt instead of trying to come up with a rapid plan. "I was headed to my cousin's place near Emerald Creek."

"Yeah, I know where Emerald Creek is. I can take you as far as Lonesome Gorge, though. I'm headed south to the Deadlands myself."

I nod, clapping the hood of his truck in thanks, then walk to the bed of the truck and pull myself up. He starts driving again, and the miles speed by, but the forest only grows thicker.

I try not to think of Maeve, but it's impossible. All I could think about last night was taking her by the shoulders and knocking some sense into her. She has... she has all of this power–Goddess-like power–and kept it locked away in a fucking necklace? Why?

The truck turns off the main road onto a smaller, terribly maintained road that travels directly through the forest, which is odd. I stand as the truck slows to a crawl, the road cast in the shadow of the trees, and comes to an abrupt, jerking stop.

"Hey, you good?" I shout toward the driver, but he's silent.

Confusion washes through me as I leap out of the bed of the truck and walk up to his window. I'm just about to knock when I notice him staring forward, his mouth slightly ajar, his eyes unblinking... and hazy.

I slowly follow his gaze to the masked man dressed in black Ghost armor blocking the road several yards away, standing calmly, patiently, his masked face turned to mine.

My chest tightens as I walk toward the man, flexing my hands. I glance back at the driver before closing in on him, growling under my breath, "You told me we were done with this. That was two years ago, man."

He says nothing but slips me an envelope–a thick one.

I look into his mask, trying to catch a glimpse of a face I should know well by now, but I've never seen it.

With a heavy sigh, I look inside the envelope, arching a brow. "This is more than you've ever paid me."

I pull out the handwritten note stuck between several tens-of-thousands of dollars' worth of bills, and realize why. It's a single name written in the neatest handwriting I've ever seen.

"This one dies," the stranger says, then disappears in a burst of star flaked mist.

OUT OF JUICE

Maeve

I'm not one to wear sun dresses and cardigans. I've never considered myself softly girly, by any means. I like clothing I can move in–athletic shorts, sneakers, a sweatshirt if it's chilly... or the sweeping, ethereal fashions I grew up with in Veiled Valley–gowns and cloaks of satin and silk.

I look in the rust-eaten mirror in the tiny bathroom, running my fingers through my frizzy dark hair. It's the best I can do as it stands. I don't have a comb. I don't have pins or a scrunchy to keep my mane pulled back away from my face. I'm just... me in my rawest form, I suppose.

I stare at my reflection. My eyes are bloodshot and glazed, and my fingertips prickle with adrenaline as I swipe toothpaste onto a shiny new plastic toothbrush Soren left on the counter for me. I spent most of the morning in bed, finding it hard to move. My body feels numb and stiff, and every breath is a struggle, but I manage to brush my teeth and limp back into the main room where a pair of brand new, rolled up socks are sticking out of one of my sneakers.

I'm not sure what he did last night. He said he mended a chimney to get the money he needed to buy these things for us, but… given the circumstances, I find that hard to believe.

What I can't deny is that he plucked every single thorn and splinter from my sneakers. It must have taken him hours. He did the same for my jeans, which he then folded neatly and sat on the corner of the bed with my tank top resting on top of them.

He had no reason to do it. He's a criminal, a thief. He broke into my royal apartment and stole my jewelry, and he's… not ashamed of it.

People have their reasons to be bad, to do bad things. He said he had a debt he needed to pay, and I'm well aware of the gnarled scars on his forearm. He'd been… shackled, robbed of his shifter powers for years.

I almost feel sorry enough for him to forgive him, but the phantom weight around my neck where my moonstone should be–now useless and lost in the forest forever–stops that feeling from fully materializing.

It takes some effort to get into my socks and sneakers, but I manage it, then leave the room, abandoning my old clothes. The hotel is… mostly empty. No one mans the counter, and the small deli sharing space with the bottom floor is silent, save for a flickering TV in the corner playing some soap opera from Crescent Falls.

I stayed in the room too long to get breakfast, but I'm not hungry. I know I should eat, but this wobbly, tingling feeling in my body makes me wonder if just a few hours of sleep is enough to spirit back to Moonrise.

It's a simple jump–a short one, even if the capital of Eastonia is at least a hundred miles southeast of here–but I don't even really know where I am. The Roguelands are full of rural villages and communities. The territory has dozens of Alphas that guard a handful of villages and towns at a time, and this tiny, one road town isn't familiar to me.

I walk down the street, not bothering to shield my identity to try to conserve my powers, and reach a gas station that marks the end of the village. Beyond it, a dirt road winds through the thick woodlands where the trees are so dense the sunlight doesn't even touch the road. I tug my cardigan close, smoothing my hands over the thin, gray fabric, then step into the gas station.

The attendant doesn't even look in my direction as I pluck a pamphlet sized map from a magazine rack, then a pair of sunglasses, a roll of elastics for my hair, and the best looking gas-station sandwich.

"Anything else?" the old man behind the counter asks, ringing my bounty up without looking away from his newspaper.

"Do you have coffee?"

"Just around that aisle, in the corner." He tilts his head in that general direction.

I place the money Soren left for me on the counter, telling him he can keep the change, which is only a few pennies. Plastic bag of things to get me through the morning in hand, I pour myself a cup of coffee, black, and slide the sunglasses up the bridge of my news before perching on the curb, in the shade, eating my sandwich.

I've never really been… out like this. I don't get a lot of opportunities to explore. I'm constantly bouncing between Veiled Valley, Moonrise, and Crescent Falls, of course, but I've never been a nobody–never been just a girl sitting on a curb somewhere, enjoying the soft, early summer breeze whispering through her hair and the way the sun dances through the treetops.

I think of Jane, however, with a long, dramatic sigh. She knows I've gone after Soren. She tried to talk me out of it when I stepped out of a very short shower and found an armchair in shambles and a trail of blood on my balcony. I told her not to tell anyone where I'd gone, and if anyone asked, I was in Silverhide, with Brie, visiting family.

While being nearly powerless is extremely inconvenient at the moment, the timing of this… adventure couldn't have been better. I have nothing pressing on my agenda back in Moonrise. The family is busy, out of the loop of my shenanigans.

I stuff the last bite of sandwich into my mouth, chewing slowly as I let my mind reel. I do, in fact, have a few weeks of quiet before the family descends on Moonrise again… and for the first time in years, I have a lead on Hannibal.

Even the thought of his name makes me see red. What his people–people like Soren–did to my sister makes me want to scream, but that was years ago, and he's been quiet since.

Yet, I think I believe Soren when he said he doesn't work for Hannibal, not directly. He's probably a fringe member of some other criminal underlord with ties to Hannibal, who seems to have his fingers in the underground crime network constantly plaguing the Allied Kingdoms.

Soren left, though. I have no idea where he is. He left me here, and it's over. Whatever the past two days were.

I rise and tie back my hair then move, walking at a slow pace down the road. Wolf trails cut through the forest for a while, but eventually, the forest swallows everything whole, and the road narrows, becoming more hilly and less traveled by vehicles. I have no direction in mind because it doesn't matter. I'm just waiting for my powers to return enough to jump, and then I can sulk in Moonrise, wondering if I missed my shot at taking Hannibal down for good.

Once, that was my only objective when I became queen.

Now, I'm not sure how to feel.

I cut into the woods, into a clearing with pockets of sunshine that dance across soft grass and fresh flowers. I close my eyes, imagining my powers drifting through me, warming my skin, but it's likely just the sun beating down on the clearing.

Rogue locks of hair begin to lift around my face, however. My skin tingles, and I smile, whispering, "That's it. Just a little more–a little more–"

A snapping sensation erupts all over my body before the world tilts on its axis and dissolves. A vacuum of sound and darkness swallows me whole before spitting me out again in a matter of seconds but…

I gasp, filling my aching lungs with desperately needed air. It's dark. I can see the outline of the trees overhead cast in the shadow of full night. Thunder booms nearby, and I'm soaking wet. Soaked to the bone. I flail my arms to the side and grip moss and snapped twigs, not the carpet in my apartment.

Pain reverberates through my body in throbbing waves as I take another breath, then another, and grunt with the effort of sitting upright.

I'm in a forest. I'm not in the clearing where I tried to jump. I turn my head, scanning the shadows, seeing nothing but miles upon miles of trees.

Rain patters against the top of my head as I stumble forward. My cardigan and sunglasses are gone. So are the elastics and plastic bag from the gas station.

I look up, trying to find the moon. Did I jump? I had to have jumped because this isn't where I started, but it's night now, which means I did jump, and I've been lying prone all day, passed out.

A chill wraps up my spine as voices drift toward me through the rain, carried by the scent of smoke. Hushed voices—calm voices laced with laughter.

Without a second thought, my body twists into my bird form, but it's painful. I can't hold it for very long, not with my powers so weak.

I flutter toward the voices, landing in a tree overlooking a cabin resting along a burbling creek. Three men are sitting out by a fire, ignoring the sprinkle of rain as they pass a bottle of what looks like whiskey.

"You still have that safe house near Twin Rivers, right?" one of them says, and through the darkness, against the glow of the fire, I can see his face. He's young and handsome, with dark curly hair and what must be light colored eyes because they reflect a bright amber hue when he turns to one of his companions, and my heart skips a beat.

Soren, sitting on the ground with his back against a tree stump, stretches out his legs and crosses his ankles, tapping his fingers on the bottle of whiskey. "Yeah, I do. She doesn't know about that place yet, and I'm hoping to keep it that way, but I need to go to town. I need to face her myself and get this sorted out."

My powers flicker as I gaze down at the men, at his companions who he seems to be perfectly comfortable with. Both men have silver bands on their forearms.

My stomach curls as the rain drips down my wings, and my powers thrum in warning that my time in this form is limited.

The dark haired man clicks his tongue, aggravation lacing his words as he says, "This isn't even your debt to pay."

"Neither was the last," Soren says under his breath before taking a pull from the bottle.

"I say you go to the safe house and lie low for a few weeks," his companion argues. "She can't find you without the band. It's quiet now, anyway. Neither Duke nor I have been called in for jobs in months."

I glance at the man who hasn't spoken yet. He has short-cropped blond hair, but his back is to me, so I can't get a look at his face.

"That's going to change with the coronation coming up, and you know it," Soren replies dryly. He sighs, closing his eyes for a moment, continuing, "The Viper needs me and can't kill me because of that. I can take a beating from her guys. What I want to avoid is the Hounds."

"You must have really pissed her off for her to call those guys in."

"I've been ignoring her summons the past few months."

"Why?"

"Because I haven't needed the money," Soren replies with a shrug, but his mouth ticks into a smile. "I have no interest in going deeper in her debt just to stay alive, and she knows it."

"You're still doing outside work? That contact of yours?"

"He's still around," he mumbles, and if I had brows to furrow in this form, they'd be pinched together in confusion.

A squawk high above my head steals my attention. A hawk spots me, circling in interest. I look back down at the men and freeze when Soren meets my eyes through the darkness, his gaze narrowed as he peers up at me.

Shit, twice over.

The hawk dives. I flutter from the tree, diving through the branches and gliding out of sight of the cabin. The hawk chases, but I roll out of the bird form and into my human body, which startles the hawk so much it screeches before flapping aggressively away.

Panting, I brace my hands on my knees, gulping down fresh, rainy night air. That freezing ache spreads through my joints like a fever, but I have to ignore it. I can't keep doing this. I need to rest. I need to find a train depot or hitch a ride somewhere. Hell, I could hitchhike to the border of the Deadlands and call on Ryan–

Soren's body collides with mine. He cages me in against a tree, his hand wrapped around my throat.

SHE'S NOT SUPPOSED TO BE HERE

Soren

"WHAT ARE YOU DOING HERE? HOW DID YOU FIND THIS PLACE?" I sneer.

Maeve blinks up at me, her expression relaxing into what I can only describe as relief. She gives me a rough shove, but I tighten my grip, arching a brow in challenge. "Don't fuck with me right now, Maeve."

"I'm sure you'd love that," she replies hoarsely, the corner of her wide mouth pulling into a smug smile bordering on... seductive. I'm seeing things, obviously. There's nothing about her I even remotely desire. Especially her company.

"Why are you spying on me?"

"I'm not."

"Then why–"

"My powers," she grits out, shoving me again, but her hands hold on my chest. "They're not coming back."

"You said all you needed was food and rest–"

"It doesn't work that way."

I ease my grip on her throat but keep my arm pinned over her breasts. She's soaking wet, water droplets gliding down her collarbones and seeping into the bodice of the dress. I look into her eyes, scanning them for any threat, anything that would make me decide against letting her go, and see nothing but... exhaustion, maybe a shred of disappointment and fear.

I lower my arm and step away from her, shrugging out of the jacket Patton loaned me when I arrived at his cabin. "Here. Put this on. You're trembling."

She nods, lowering her gaze and allowing me to help her into the thin, but waterproof coat. Her skin is like ice, again, and I'm starting to feel that guilt and regret burrow through my chest once more–the same way I felt leaving her in that shitty little village by herself.

With a hand on her arm, I guide her beneath the cover of a tree, glancing over my shoulder to ensure I wasn't followed. "Explain it to me, then. Everything."

Maeve grimaces, shrugging my hand off her arm, and scowls up at me. "Like you care–"

"I left you behind because I thought you could get yourself home. Obviously, that didn't happen. So, you either need help or you purposefully followed me here, which I find hard to believe because we're over fifty miles away from that village now."

Her cheeks flush as she looks down at her mud-stained sneakers. I lick my lips, struggling with not only words but action. I have no desire to coo at her, to stroke the top of her head and tell her everything's going to be okay. That's what a normal person would do, right? Empathize, sympathize, rest my knuckles under her chin and tell her to buck up, buttercup, then offer to personally escort her home?

Maeve isn't a damsel in distress. She's a fucking demon in a sundress. A whimpering, miserable looking demon, but a creature from my wildest nightmares nonetheless.

"I tried to jump home," she admits, sniffling before closing her eyes and turning her sorry-ass expression back to cold, hard steel. "I thought I made it, but I woke up in the woods nearby, soaking wet, freezing cold and… I think I'd been lying there for hours. For the entire day, actually. I was just… I can't do it yet, Soren. I didn't follow you. I wouldn't waste my time on you like that."

There she is.

"How long until you can?"

She purses her lips, the column of her throat bobbing as she swallows hard. "A few days–"

"A few days?" I hiss. "Why didn't you tell me–"

"What would you have done? Nothing, Soren. I didn't want your help, anyway. You got me into this mess–"

"You got yourself–"

"Don't. I don't have the energy to fight with you right now. You are so far below me, Soren. I don't think you realize that. You're nothing. I'll be queen in a month. I would never have even turned my head in your direction had you not stolen from me."

"That's a lie," I say, my voice a hushed whisper over the rain.

Her eyes–those strange, polished sea-glass eyes–lift to meet mine.

I step into her, arching a brow as I wait for her to react to the way I'm closing her in against the damp bark of the tree, but she doesn't swing on me like I expected her to. "You were there both times I broke into the castle. You saw me in the hallway while in your cat form. You had to know then that I wasn't supposed to be there, that I was snooping around. The second time, I was actively stealing from you, yet, you did nothing. You let me take that collar off. You didn't even react."

She swallows again. I follow the motion against my will, feeling a twisting, unsettling kind of heat flame to life deep in my body, and it's her powers. The rain sparkles on her skin. I reach for her, swiping my thumb across her collarbone to collect the shimmering droplets on impulse, and I swear on the Goddess, she leans into my touch.

Something… sharp echoes through my chest, and I pull away from her, wondering if she does, in fact, have enough power left to create this heat, that sharp pang echoing through my heart, but she just stares at me, silently.

"Why didn't you stop me?"

"Why were you at the tea shop that night?"

Thunder booms in the distance as I conjure the memory. "I lived nearby. Moonrise was too quiet that day. I couldn't take the silence any longer." It strikes me then that she would have been reeling from what she believed to be the loss of her sister during that first encounter.

She doesn't have to say she felt the same way, felt the same pull to the sanctuary of yellow walls, hot tea, and barely functioning TVs as I did, but there we were. Together.

"Why were you at the diner?" I ask to break the sudden silence.

"I lived nearby," she echoes, the softest, saddest smile touching her lips. "And… and that night, my sister got married, and I gave away the only person who ever saw me for what I am, the only person who ever understood me and loved me anyway." Her eyes meet mine, but shed that softness I'd just witnessed a moment ago. I realize how rare that look must be, and maybe she hadn't meant for me to see it–that vulnerability. "Why were you there? In Veiled Valley?"

"I was visiting friends who live there," I say, and it's a half-truth.

We seem to be at an impasse. This is the calmest, and longest, we've actually spoken without beating the shit out of each other. I suck in a breath and glance around the darkened forest, needing to come up with some solution. Being the princess's personal bodyguard wasn't something I ever anticipated, but here I am, and here she is, totally and completely at my mercy.

"Are you going to be able to trust me?"

"No," she replies without skipping a beat.

I ignore her, asking, "If I get you to the nearest depot, will you go home without a fight?"

"I want to make a deal–"

"I'm not making deals. There's nothing you can offer me–"

"Your friends have silver bands, like you did. I know they hurt, and I know none of you can shift. If I… if I rest for a little while, get warm, and what-not… I could remove them, with my powers–"

"No."

"Why not?"

"Because you'd be putting them in the same kind of danger you put me in."

She bites her lip. I glance down, noticing the raindrops shimmering on her lower lip, biting down on my own to stop... some feeling I find hard to describe from taking over. I can readily admit she's beautiful–stunning–an absolute work of art, carved by the Goddess Herself, but I have other options if I'm really feeling that desperate.

And I'm not a desperate man. I never have been. Love and companionship has never been on my radar.

So why the fuck is she getting under my skin and making me feel like... like...

"Are you going to be sick? You're pale," she asks, stepping away from me.

I suck my teeth, glaring down at her and running a hand through my wet hair. "I've been drinking."

"I saw."

The glare deepens. "I'm thinking about what to do with you tonight. Can you shift back into a cat, maybe?"

She shakes her head. Her lips are tinged blue, which makes me nervous. She's cold, even under the cover of my jacket.

I have one option as it stands, and I don't like it.

I tilt my head, beckoning her to follow, and guide her back to the cabin.

It takes all of thirty seconds for Patton, my friend from childhood, to recognize her.

"Where's Duke?" I ask, keeping my fingers curled around Maeve's upper arm.

Patton's blue eyes widen as he braces himself in the doorway, glancing from me to Maeve, who smiles kindly up at him.

"Uh, what the fuck is going on?" he says nervously, his eyes meeting mine again. "Soren?"

"This is Maeve," I say, shrugging the tension from my shoulders. Under my breath, I rasp, "She's a little lost."

"Fuckin' Princess Maeve?"

"Yes," Maeve grins.

Patton's lips part before he slowly straightens, his eyes on mine, unblinking. "Soren, can I talk to you for a moment?"

"No." I sigh, yanking Maeve into the cabin, forcing him to step out of my way. Maeve's head swivels as she takes in her new surroundings. It's not much, but Patton made himself a home here out in the middle of nowhere, smack dab on the border between two Alphas who either don't know they have a rogue in their midst or don't care. Patton isn't a threat, never has been. He was just in the wrong place at the wrong time a decade ago. Just like me.

I let go of Maeve's arm and turn to my friend, who bows deeply to her, his cheeks flushed pink. But his eyes narrow on mine, his mouth pulled into a tight line as he tilts his head toward his bedroom on the first floor in a silent command to speak in private.

I ignore him, turning to Maeve. "There's a bedroom upstairs in the loft. There's some dry clothes in the closet, something to sleep in at least. Pat, you got hot water, right?"

Patton nods stiffly, his eyes shooting daggers in my direction.

I turn back to Maeve. "Take a bath or something. Warm up. We had dinner already, but there's leftovers. I'll heat them up."

Maeve glances between me and Patton before nodding, giving Patton another kind smile that betrays who she is, at least to me, and goes upstairs, her footsteps light on the floorboards as she disappears from sight.

Before Patton can get a single word out, I snatch his arm and drag him into his bedroom, kicking the door closed behind us.

"What the fuck, man?" he says in a whispered hiss, his eyes going wide. "Why is the princess of Eastonia in my fucking cabin?!"

"It's a long story–"

"Well, you better start talking!"

"Where is Duke?" I ask sternly. "Is he here?"

"No. He said he had to meet up with someone. He's on a job and was just stopping through."

I let out the breath I'd been holding. I've known Duke for a long time, but he's a hot head, and I don't fully trust him, not like I trust Patton.

"Look, I fucked up in Moonrise. That final job I was talking about a few weeks ago didn't go as planned–"

Patton gapes, glancing at the ceiling. "You better not be saying your final job was kidnapping the princess–"

"Why the fuck would I need to kidnap her?" I ask in all seriousness. "I was robbing her, dumbass. And at first, I was successful, but she's... she's not letting me go. If anything, I'm the one being kidnapped right now!"

"So she followed you here?"

"It's more complicated than that," I try to explain, but I'm tired. I had a long ass day just trekking here. "Look, she just needs a roof over her head for a few days, and then I'm taking her to Twin Rivers. I need to go there anyway, and she'll be able to take the train back to Moonrise from there if she's not better by then."

"What's wrong with her?" he asks, genuinely confused.

Where do I even begin?

"Just–just be cool about this, all right?" I turn for his bedroom door, my entire body screaming at me to go check on her for some reason. "And if Duke comes back, wake me up. I want to talk to him about this directly."

DEN OF THIEVES

MAEVE

I BUTTON UP THE MEN'S SHIRT I FOUND IN THE CLOSET. IT BRUSHES MY thighs as I turn to inspect my reflection in the foggy mirror, sighing heavily but immensely relieved to be totally clean.

Soren's friend keeps his upstairs bathroom, which isn't fancy by any means, fully stocked with not only soap but shampoo and conditioner.

I found a comb in one of the drawers and ran it through my hair, which is now starting to dry in soft, hydrated waves... not the frizz I'd experienced yesterday or the day before. I'm not sure how much time has passed, honestly, and the memory of waking up in the woods only a few hours ago is weighing heavily on me.

I'm better than this. I'm more powerful than this. I understand I completely depleted my powers. I get it. But the last time this happened... I'd opened a portal, whisking me and two other people to an unknown land, using my powers to not only guide us into oblivion while keeping us alive, but through an impenetrable veil... whereas this time, chasing down a train in my bird form had done me in.

I found a pair of sweatpants that might fit. I slide my legs into them, tightening the drawstring, then pad barefoot down the hallway past the open loft overlooking the lower level of the cabin, and into the upstairs bedroom.

Soren is rummaging in the closet, but his eyes catch mine, his nose wrinkling as I step past him to look out the window. "What's that face for?" I ask, glancing at him over my shoulder.

"You smell like a man."

I frown at him as he turns back to the closet, shoving several flannel shirts out of his way.

"Well your friend must not have women here often because my only options were soap and shampoo scented like cedar and suede."

He chuckles, keeping his back to me. I fold my arms under my chest and turn back to the window overlooking the front... yard of the cabin, if I can call it that. The fire is burned down to flickering embers in the rain, but a shadow passes next to them then nears the house.

"Who's that?"

"Who?"

Soren steps around the bed to stand at my side. He eyes the shadow, then curses under his breath, saying, "Stay here."

He leaves the room, shutting the door with a snap behind him, but I've never once obeyed a man, and I'm not going to start now.

I follow him out to the railing, but he's already halfway down the stairs. Patton comes into view below wearing a pair of oven mitts as the third man, I assume Duke, steps into the cabin, shaking out of his raincoat. His silver band catches the light coming from a scone directly above his head.

"I didn't think you were coming back," Patton says, but the smell of roast chicken distracts me from the sharp look Soren's giving me from the bottom of the stairs. I take a single step off the loft, and Duke lifts his face, his eyes scanning mine, then narrowing.

He's shorter than both Soren and Patton by several inches, and maybe a few inches shorter than me, but that doesn't matter. He's built like a brick manor–his shoulders and heavily muscled arms bulging beneath his fitted navy blue Henley. Those shoulders straighten as he looks me up and down then turns to his friends in a silent command, a silent question.

Patton looks between them before turning on his heel and disappearing into the kitchen directly below the loft and out of my line of sight.

"This is Maeve," Soren says, but his tone... it's harder and darker than it was when he briefly introduced me to Patton, and dripping with possession. "She's staying the night. With me."

Duke and Soren stare at each other. I can taste the tension between them. It's thick—so thick I'd struggle to cut it with a knife. I slowly move in Soren's direction, feeling like the best place I can be is directly at his side. He hasn't moved from the last step, and his hands are flat at his sides, his thumb resting on the clip of a knife hanging from his belt. My fingers graze his lower back as I come to stop on the step above him, my eyes not leaving Duke's, who watched every move I made down the stairs like a predator stalking his prey.

"Nice to meet you," Duke says low in his throat after a very long, tense few seconds, then his eyes meet Soren's. I have a feeling these two don't like each other. There's history there, for sure. Duke's dark green eyes shine like polished gems as he takes a breath and turns from us, saying to Patton, "The creek is swollen and the rain's not stopping. I'm staying here for the night."

Patton's pulling a baking dish of leftovers from the oven, his blue eyes wide as he nods, but his gaze slides to Soren's, then mine. He grimaces, mouthing, "Sorry," before setting the dish on the stovetop.

I shiver involuntarily as the tension continues to rise. Duke makes a move for the half-empty bottle of whiskey on the mantle only a few feet away from where me and Soren are standing, but Soren steps off the stairs, his tone like ice as he says, "I need to speak to you. Outside."

Duke looks him up and down, smirking. "I'm not after your leftovers, Soren, if that's what you think."

"*Outside,*" Soren growls.

I look at Patton, who's standing perfectly still near a dining table with two plates in his hands, his eyes locked on the tense exchange.

Duke's smirk turns to a flat line when he looks at me again, but Soren steps into him, his dark brow raised. "Don't fucking look at her."

"If you're going to fight, do it outside," Patton says sternly from the table, setting the plates down.

"We won't be fighting," Soren says, "Right?"

The threat in his voice is clear. My heart skips a beat, a warmth spreading through my chest at his promise of violence… over me. For me. It shocks me to my core, and before I can blink, Duke whirls and heads for the door with Soren hot on his heels.

I flinch when the door slams shut, rattling the picture frames I hadn't noticed before. Patton exhales deeply, his eyes on the door, before he meets my eyes. "Soren said you'd be hungry."

"I am," I reply weakly, not liking the knot of unease forming in my stomach.

Patton turns toward the cabinets and starts rummaging in a panic. "I have cloth napkins somewhere–"

"Oh, don't worry about it–"

"I–I'm sure this isn't what you're used to," he rushes out, clasping a trio of chipped, slightly dusty wine glasses before thinking better of it. "I don't have wine."

"It's okay, really," I say, trying to sound soothing, but Patton looks horrified when I sit down on a rickety stool before he has a chance to pull it out for me. His cheeks flush crimson as he bows deeply. "You don't need to do that. You don't need to bow to me."

"Oh–uh, yes, Your Highness–"

"Or that," I say, smiling up at him. "Just call me Maeve."

Patton blinks at me for a moment, then nods, sinking into a stool across from me. He doesn't eat, but I do. I pile my plate with chicken, roasted vegetables, and fresh baked bread with creamy, salted butter. But just as I lift my fork, I pause, the tension still hanging heavy in the house as I look up at Patton, who's staring at the window overlooking the table.

It's pitch black beyond the glass. It has to be the middle of the night at this point, maybe the earliest hours of morning.

I set my fork down, clearing my throat. "What's their problem?"

Patton sighs heavily, knitting his fingers together on the table's surface. "It changes from day to day," he says, like the answer is actually that simple.

My eyes lock on the silver manacle on his forearm. He has the same lifted, web-like scar from here the silver cut into his skin repeatedly over the years. I wonder if he even feels its burn at this point. I wonder if he's worn it as long as Soren has.

"Soren–he told me he works for someone named the Viper."

Patton seems to be having a hard time meeting my eyes. He chews the inside of his cheek, nodding gravely.

"Do you work for the Viper, too?"

"From time to time." He briefly looks in my direction but quickly looks away, rising to fetch the bottle of whiskey off the mantle. Instead of coming back to the table, he leans against the dormant fireplace, fiddling with the cork.

"Does Duke work for the Viper?"

"We all do." He lifts the whiskey to his lips and drinks deeply before resetting the cork. "Soren less often these days, but yeah. We've been working together for over a decade now."

An angry shout echoes from beyond the walls. Patton looks down his hands, flexing them, and I see the soft, silver outlines of scars cross-crossed over his knuckles.

I want to ask what he does for a living, what they all do, but decide to finally take a bite of the food while Soren and Duke shout obscenities at each other only a few yards from the front porch, their shouts lifting over the rain.

"This is really good," I tell Patton, smiling around a bite.

His cheeks warm, and his eyes sparkle. When he smiles, he even shows a bit of teeth. But when I raise the fork to my mouth again, the door opens and shuts with a slam so loud it makes my ears ring.

Soren stalks inside, looking at Patton, then me, then back to Patton. "Duke decided to cross the creek and continue on his way." He tucks his bloodied hands into his pockets, but I catch the smears of crimson, wondering if the blood belongs to him or Duke.

Patton nods, his brows raised as he looks down at his hands while Soren stalks across the room to the stairs, climbs them, and disappears into the bathroom.

Silence hugs the cabin until I hear the shower running, and then I turn to Patton, arching a brow.

Patton pops the cork and drinks deeply, gulping once, then twice, before shaking himself off and rasping, "Duke and Soren got into some shit a few years ago that made things pretty hard for Soren."

"What happened?"

He clears his throat, moving back toward the table. "I–I don't know much about how you and Soren got into your... situation–"

"He broke into the palace and stole most of my jewelry."

"Yeah... well, he's not a *bad* guy."

"He's an absolute angel," I murmur sarcastically, and Patton's soft smile is touched by a sadness I hadn't expected.

"He got dealt a bad hand. I don't know all the details about what happened between him and Duke, but they've never been friends. We just run in the same circles, end up in the same places sometimes."

"Is Duke dangerous?"

"Yeah. We all are," he says, and I stiffen, but Patton doesn't notice.

He moves past the table, putting the unused dishes away, and for a while, it's quiet. I have more questions than answers from these men. I can tell, however, that Soren and Patton are friends–good friends. Based on Soren's behavior when Duke was here, looking at me... Soren wouldn't have let me be alone with Patton if he hadn't trusted him with my life.

Not that it matters to Soren. He's probably counting down the minutes until I leave, just like... I should be. I can, however, readily admit this is the most exciting thing that's happened to me in years. I'm eating delicious, perfectly roasted chicken in a den of thieves... thieves who can cook, apparently. Thieves who have dried flowers hanging in frames along the walls... but maybe that's Patton.

He takes my empty plate in silence. I thank him for the meal and start moving toward the stairs, but Soren appears in the loft, towel drying his hair and walking toward the bedroom in nothing but a pair of shorts.

My chest tightens when he meets my eyes, tilting his head toward the bedroom door in a silent command to follow.. Below, Patton does the dishes, humming to himself in a way that reminds me of Jane, totally oblivious to the fight about to begin the second we close ourselves into the bedroom.

At least, I expected a fight.

Soren pulls the curtains closed, his back muscles tense as he grips the fabric for a moment before turning to me.

"Are you okay?" I ask, scanning his face for new injuries, new bruises and scratches that weren't from our battle in his apartment. Scratches and bruises not left by me.

I shouldn't feel territorial about that.... This weird, suffocating feeling is because–because I'm stuck here, with him, and he just growled and snarled at a man who dared look in my direction. He jumped from a train, off a bridge, with me in his arms rather than leave me behind despite several threats to end his life.

"I'm sorry for what he said," Soren says, reaching for a T-shirt he left on the corner of the bed.

"What do you mean?"

"The leftovers thing." He slips into the shirt.

I watch his muscles flex with the motion. "Patton is a great cook. I don't blame him for being territorial about the chicken–"

"That's–" Soren says, then laughs lightly, the corners of his mouth ticking in the first real smile I think I've seen. "That's not what he meant."

The sudden intensity of his eyes on mine nearly steals my breath.

Something feels... I'm not sure what this feeling is. Lunacy, perhaps.

"Go to bed, Maeve," he says, and brushes past me, but pauses in the doorway. "We'll talk in the morning."

"About what?"

"A truce between us. Sound good?"

I nod my head, and he smiles.

WE'RE NOT FRIENDS

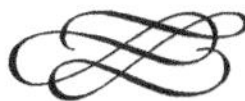

Soren

PATTON IS ALREADY AT THE KITCHEN TABLE DRINKING COFFEE WHEN I sit up from the couch, blinking into hazy midmorning sunlight. My body rejects the idea of moving, my joints popping and head swimming for several seconds before I fully rise and stumble to my feet.

He hums a laugh, but his eyes are on a newspaper spread out across the table, which he keeps so clean and polished I can see my reflection in its surface when I sit down. "What time is it?"

"Almost eleven," he says with a small yawn, flipping a page. "Didn't feel like waking you."

"Is she up yet?" I blearily reach toward the window to pull the curtains closed against the intense sunlight pouring directly into my eyes, but Patton beats me to it, then rises to fetch a coffee mug from his tidy cabinets.

"Not yet–"

I rise, turning for the stairs.

"I already checked on her," Patton amends, clicking his tongue at me. "She's fine. She's still asleep."

I grip the top of the chair, scanning his face for inconsistencies in his story. Patton has never given me a reason not to trust him, but bringing Maeve into the picture has me on edge more than usual. The idea of anyone hurting her, touching her, or even looking in her direction other than me makes me want to... to do violent things. Patton arches a brow as he sets the mug on the table and slides cream and a bowl of sugar in my direction.

"Did Duke come back?"

"Nope. Haven't seen him this morning." He sinks back into his chair while I make my coffee the way I like it, mostly black. I rarely have fresh cream on hand, though, so I add a heavy dose just for the hell of it. "What exactly was that about?" he asks.

"Me and Duke?"

He nods, leaning back in his chair. "You haven't seen the guy in months."

"I haven't seen you in months, either."

"I thought the two of you mended things."

"He's the reason I owe another debt to the Viper," I tell him flatly before taking the first, blissful sip of pure caffeine. "He knows it, I know it…. Last night was a long time coming."

"Coulda fooled me."

"What do you mean?"

He flips another page in the newspaper. The printed date in the top right corner is from two months ago, which was probably the last time he ventured into the nearest town, I'm guessing. "You looked like you were ready to snap his neck the second he saw Maeve–"

"Princess Maeve," I cut in, but Patton smirks, rolling his eyes to meet mine.

"She told me to call her just Maeve."

"Well, seeing as the two of you are best friends now, you can be the one to escort her to the nearest train station."

"Isn't she magic? Doesn't she have those–those powers that make her fly or whatever?" He wiggles his fingers before flipping another page.

"Are you even reading that thing?"

He snaps the pages shut and shifts his position to face me, bracing his elbows on the table. "What are you doing with her, Soren?"

"I told you everything. There's nothing left to say."

"The future queen of Eastonia is in my house right this minute, sleeping. Sleeping without guards to watch over her."

"I'm watching over her."

"Why?"

"Because she's fucking helpless," I reply, losing my patience. "She can't access her powers for some reason, and now she's stuck."

"So she can fly–"

"It's not flying, Pat, for fuck's sake–"

"I'm just trying to make sense of this–"

I run my hand down my face and groan into my palm before just... telling him everything–from the beginning. From the very beginning.

Pat listens intently, occasionally nodding, laughing, or smirking depending on the context, but when I tell him about seeing her last night, spying on us, his expression falls flat, then turns skeptical.

"Why would she come here?"

"I don't think she meant to," I admit. "I'm not sure what happened, and neither is she, but it's obvious I'm stuck with her, and I just can't–I tried to wipe my hands clean of this. Robbing the castle was a huge risk. I spent months preparing. She is the one thing I didn't prepare for."

"Did the Hounds recognize her?"

"No," I breathe. "No, I don't believe so."

"She's been out of the public eye for years," Patton says, rising to pour himself another cup of coffee. "That's on your side, I suppose."

"You recognized her immediately."

"You know I like my gossip magazines," he says with a soft smile. "It's the eyes, Soren. She needs to keep them covered, just like you do."

"Duke recognized her," I add with a huff, leaning my elbows on the table.

"So? What is he going to do? Run to the Viper and tell her where you are and who you're with? He's in heavier shit with her than you, you know. He wouldn't risk it if he knows what's good for him."

"What do you mean?"

"I don't know the details, but he fell out of her good graces. He's broke. She's keeping him shackled but blue balling him on jobs. He's been coming here off and on for a few weeks. I think he's got a den where he's been gambling a few towns over. He's asked me for money a time or two."

"And you say no."

"I say no," he confirms.

"I don't want him around Maeve."

"I can tell," he deadpans, but his eyes search mine before he leans forward, whispering, "You're sure you're not, like, kind of *into* her?"

I grind my teeth. "You wanna go there?"

"Just asking."

"She's a princess."

"And?"

"She's the most annoying, aggravating person I've ever met in my life."

"Well, it seems the two of you have that in common."

I narrow my eyes to slits, but Patton shoots me a playful smile. "Just saying I feel the tension pouring off you, Soren."

"I'm tense because this isn't how this was supposed to go."

"You thought she'd just let this slide?"

"She's a royal. She has an endless supply of money–"

"You know who her grandfather is, right? King Ryatt? King of the Rogues? Shadow King of the Roguelands? He's the reason we're not under the yoke of the old kings anymore. He was a slave, like us. You think he lets the women in his family forget where they came from and how easily their life of luxury could be taken away? I don't think you're giving the princess enough credit."

I lean back in my chair, crossing my arms over my chest. Patton is a total royal family freak. He knows every name, every familial connection. It's like a hobby of his. I know for a fact he has a picture of Alpha King Ryatt and Queen Ella hanging in his bedroom, like he prays to them every night.

Having Maeve in his cabin is likely the highlight of his life so far.

"Would you like me to ask Maeve to autograph your fancy linen napkins?"

His eyes go momentarily wide. "Would she?"

"What's wrong with you, Pat? Seriously?"

"What's wrong with *you*? You had the gall to steal from her? You know what the press says about her. She's–she's the most powerful being in our world. She's a full-blooded Firestone witch. The first in– what? Three thousand years–"

"You really believe all that?"

"You don't?"

"I believe," I growl, losing my patience, "that she's a whole lot more powerful than she's ever led herself to believe and terrified to show it." I lean forward, my entire body reacting to the sudden onrush of fury as the memory of fighting with her in the apartment comes rushing to the forefront of my mind, exploding in full color. "She's terrified of herself because everyone around her is scared of her. She thinks she's tough, cruel, and cold as ice, but it's a front."

"And you're not scared of her."

"Not at all."

A creak on the stairs makes us both turn to the shadow looming over the living room. Maeve appears looking lost, rubbing her eyes. Her thick mane of brown hair is mussed from a deep, dark kind of sleep, and her eyes are slightly puffy when she brings her hands down and blinks at us.

Patton nearly falls out of his chair in his haste to stand, bursting into chipper, lifting questions, asking if she's hungry, if she likes eggs, telling her he can brew fresh coffee and baked two loaves of bread this morning because he wasn't sure if she likes whole grain or sour- dough, so he made both, and also baked blueberry muffins, none of which did he offer me in the last half hour he's been grilling me on my fucking intentions with the princess.

And Maeve just... beams at him. Her beautiful mouth pulls into the most genuine smile I've ever seen, her eyes creasing and bright as she nods.

I feel a sudden, choking rush of jealousy.

I want that smile. I want it for myself.

I want to wring Patton's neck when he asks if she wants to meet his flock of chickens, and she excitedly claps her hands.

Because she looks at me and that smile instantly fades, replaced by something more tight-lipped, something that makes me want to either curl my fingers around her dainty neck and command her to smile at me like that or get on my knees and beg for it.

What the actual fuck is wrong with me?

So, I sulk on the porch, sipping my coffee and frowning while Patton and his princess feed his chickens. Maeve's barefoot in the grass, her hair spilling down her back as she gathers eggs and admires their color and shape while Patton grins with pride. He'll never forget this. I was right–this moment will go down in history as the best day of his life.

I'm more happy for him than I'm annoyed, though. He's a good guy. He's not the kind of man who should be wearing that silver shackle. He's not the kind of guy the Viper needs, nor wants. No.

He's in that silver band because of me. He's my tether to the Viper. He's the reason I need to pay off this debt. If I step out of line, Patton is the one who's going to pay for it. I can't have that weight on my shoulders any longer. I don't want that for him. He should be able to feel his wolf. He should have found his mate by now and settled, had a few kids. That's the kind of life he's always deserved.

It's why I bought him this property in the middle of nowhere. He's happy here. He's safe here.

Maeve hurries up the steps with a dozen eggs resting in her shirt, cradling the fabric like a basket. She looks so… so peaceful right now.

So, I ruin that peace by reminding her why we're here. "How are you feeling? Powers back yet?"

She frowns at me, shaking her head. "Not quite."

"Not quite, what? Can you go home yet?"

She straightens her spine while Patton absently frolics around the chicken coop, totally oblivious to the flame beginning to burn to life on his porch.

"You act like you're desperate to get rid of me," she drawls sarcastically. "I thought we were having fun. And," she says, cocking her hip, "you mentioned a truce last night."

"Are you prepared to forgive me for breaking your necklace?"

"No."

"Then no truce yet." I bring my coffee to my lips. Her eyes follow the motion for a split second before she turns into the house, her cheeks going a rosy pink.

"You know," Patton says a few minutes later as he climbs up the porch steps, "she might actually want to forgive you, and maybe even be your friend, if you were a little fucking nicer to her."

"I'm not in the business of making friends."

CUT THROAT

I SPENT THE DAY MOSTLY IN PATTON'S COMPANY. HE'S A WONDERFUL man. He reminds me of... well, honestly no man I've ever met before. He's a domestic Goddess who keeps me fed throughout the day but also gives me a fair amount of space, and by the time the sun sets, I feel... better.

I sit on the edge of the bed upstairs, watching smoke curl between my fingers. That's more than I've been able to summon in the days since following Soren's train.

I close my eyes and sigh in relief, curling my fingers into a fist at the same moment Soren, who's made himself scarce all day, walks into the room and spots me, spots the smoke.

He slowly closes the door behind him, those strange, multi-colored eyes locking on mine.

I wait for him to say something, anything, but he just stands there.

So, I say, "My powers are starting to come back, I think."

"I can see that." He crosses the room, rummaging in the closet... again. He finds what he's searching for and slips what looks like money into his pocket. I want to ask where he got it, but... I don't think I want to know.

"I think," I begin, glancing toward the window with a frown, "I think in a few more days I'll be able to go back to Moonrise."

He stiffens, his back to me, but then relaxes and nods. "You can stay here until then. I think that's the safest option as it stands." He turns to me, but his gaze barely grazes my face.

"Are you upset with me for being friendly with Patton?"

Now he's looking at me unwaveringly, his chestnut curls falling in loose ringlets over his forehead.

"No, but he's going to be heartbroken when you leave."

"I'm thinking about taking him with me, actually," I quip, knowing it's going to grind his gears. I can't help myself, honestly, as his eyes narrow on mine. I cross my legs, stretching out my fingers and testing my powers again. "I'll destroy his silver band, and he can come work at the castle. He's an amazing baker." I inspect the smoke curling around my nails.

"He's also a highly skilled killer."

A chill runs up my spine as I slowly meet his gaze again.

"And what are you highly skilled at, Soren?"

He smirks—that stupid, flirtatious smirk that immediately causes my whole body to warm.

"Don't do that. Save your powers."

"But you're free of your band—"

"And I'm being hunted down as we speak." He turns back to the closet and fishes out a coat as the last light of sun fades, casting a cool violet glow through the room. He slips something in his pocket—an envelope, I think—before turning in my direction.

"Where are you going?" I ask, rising.

"North," he says on a breath, purposefully keeping his eyes on the window. "This is where we part, for real this time. You're going to stay here with Patton. I've already discussed it with him. In a few days, when you're well enough to—" he waves his hand, struggling with the words, "—to jump, or whatever you call it, just do it. You'll be safe here with Patton until then. He won't let anything happen to you." He reaches into his pocket, thumbing through the contents of the envelope, and pulls out several large bills, extending them in my direction. "This is for the moonstone–"

I turn away from him so he can't see the absolutely livid expression on my face. "I don't want, nor need, your money."

"I wasn't asking."

I close my eyes as he places the money on the bed beside me.

He leaves, again, and I feel the same way I did when he left the first time–like this is wrong. Like something is gravely wrong.

"Soren, wait–" I leap off the bed and follow him, but his stride is impossible to keep up with. Patton watches us with interest from his favorite chair at the kitchen table, his hand resting on a gossip magazine, but I don't even glance in his direction as I follow Soren outside onto the porch.

"Soren!"

"Maeve," he breathes, whirling around the second I step off the porch. "This is it, okay? I have to go, and you need to get well and go home."

"But I–"

"This isn't some grand adventure," he says hoarsely, his voice just below a shout. "This is over. It ends here. I'm not going to risk you getting into trouble–"

"What if I can help you? I could help pay off your debt to the Viper!"

"I don't want your help. I don't need it. I'm not going to let you get yourself wrapped up in my mess–"

"What happened to you?" I shout, losing my patience. "You're so–you don't make any fucking sense."

He stares at me, his face twisting in an expression I can't decipher. His jaw tenses, clicking, like he's debating his next words.

"I'm a criminal, Maeve. I'm a bad guy. I'm the worst kind of guy. Stay away from me. Don't come looking for me. Go home."

A shadow rips out of the darkness spreading through the forest, hurtling toward Soren. I have two seconds to come to terms with what, and who, I'm seeing before a flash of metal pierces the hazy violet light and… pierces Soren through the chest.

"SO–"

He falls to the ground with a grunt, his hand outstretched for me, but misses.

Duke, wild eyed, lunges at me with a long blade covered in dark red blood. Soren's blood.

I duck, his blade narrowly missing the top of my head. I kick out, using my returning strength and height to knock him off balance, sending him toppling toward the ground, but he slashes his knife across my thigh.

My scream of pain and fury echoes through the air, waking the chickens in the nearby coop. Patton shouts from the porch, cursing as he thunders in our direction.

I'm wearing the dress Soren bought me a few days ago in the little village. Dark blood rushes down my thigh as I debate my next move. My heart pounds, my vision going momentarily hazy as my limited powers simmer. Overhead, the moon rises, but it's not enough.

"MAEVE!" Soren bellows, just as Duke swings the blade toward my face. My powers roar in answer.

I catch his wrist, screaming as I send what little reserves I've built up cascading into his skin, burning him. He drops the knife, howling in pain and fury, and punches me directly in the jaw with his free hand, sending me careening backward.

My vision blurs. I struggle to catch my breath, to move, as a scuffle between Patton and Duke ensues nearby. I vaguely make out Soren's outline in the darkness as he struggles to stand, falling over again, then crawling to me.

But Patton hits the ground with a crunch that reverberates through the grassy front yard, and Duke is on me again in an instant, his meaty hands curling around my neck.

"GET OFF HER!" Soren screams, grunting through the pain, but I can't see him anymore. Duke takes up my vision, his eyes wild and dancing in the darkness as he practically foams at the mouth, squeezing my neck to the point I feel–I feel–

"MAEVE GET UP!" Soren's voice is tinged with panic and… something else. Something deeper, something edging on despair as he shouts my name again, his tone laced with agony. "GET UP!"

My powers burn into Duke's chest, sizzling through his shirt, but— but I can't move past the numbness, the cold now starting to spread as I push what little powers I had to their breaking point.

I don't have enough, and I'm going to die.

Soren's voice cracks as he claws his way to me, begging me to fight it. Patton groans nearby. Yet, all I see is Duke.

I've done too much, trained too hard, to go out this way.

I go completely still, closing my eyes. Duke laughs, rising up, loosening his grip on my neck. He thinks he did it. He thinks he just killed the future Queen of Eastonia.

But I recently fought with a man much stronger, swifter, and deadlier than him. I fought my equal, and momentarily came out on top.

I strike when Duke least expects it, slashing my nails across his cheek. He gasps in pain, rearing back in surprise, which gives me a chance to kick out from beneath him, sending my knee directly into his groin with a devastating crack. His bellow of agony vibrates around me, but I ignore it, my vision going red when I catch of glimpse of Patton on his hands and knees, trying to catch his breath while blood pours down his face and into the grass, and Soren–Soren unable to stand only feet away, clutching the growing red stain on his shirt, directly over his heart.

Soren's eyes are wide as the scene plays out in slow motion. I tip Duke to the side, rolling with him, on top of him, plucking his blade from the grass and sending it… sending it directly into his neck.

"Have you ever seen the light fade from someone's eyes?"

Soren asked me that once, on the train.

That's exactly what this is. I look down at Duke, a man I don't know, and watch as he dies by my hand, his blood pooling beneath him in a crimson tidal wave, gushing into the cool, bright green grass.

How many times have I threatened death to others? Dreamt of it?

Wished for it? Wished to do this very thing to anyone who ever crossed or hurt those I love?

I thought I knew what it'd feel like. I thought–

A strangled sob works its way up my throat.

I drop the knife.

"Maeve," Soren rasps, breathless, his hand coming down on my shoulders. He pulls me off Duke, falling with me in the grass, kneeling over me as I come undone.

Pain whispers over my body as what's left of my already weak powers fade. Soren covers the slash on my thigh with his hand, ignoring his own wound as he shouts at Patton, who struggles to his feet and sways before rushing back into the house.

All I can hear is the gurgling, bloody sound of Duke dying mere feet away.

"Hey, look at me. It's okay," Soren says gently in a tone I've never heard him use before, smoothing his hand over my forehead, brushing my hair out of my face. "You're fine. You're okay."

I look up at him, my lips parting in a choked cry. I can't form words. All I see, and hear, is the knife puncturing Duke's throat.

Patton returns, his body blocking the soft light pouring from the house. He kneels, speaking in a low, rapid tone as he wraps a thick bandage around my thigh. "You both need to get out of here, now. The Hounds will be here within an hour if he found them and alerted them to your whereabouts, I'm willing to bet my life on it. Your chest–"

"I'm fine," Soren cuts in hoarsely, his hand still resting on my cheek. "Get her some warm clothes, whatever you have on hand. A coat, a blanket, a hat. Gloves."

Patton leaves again, and the night erupts around us. Birdsong titters through the air, mingling with rustling leaves as a cool summer breeze skitters through the treetops swaying overhead.

"You're okay," Soren repeats, but his voice is pained. "Maeve, you're okay." He smooths his hand over my cheek again before leaning down, resting his forehead against mine.

I close my eyes, choking on sobs. I can't stop. "I didn't mean to…" I choke out. "I didn't know–"

"It's okay," he says, over and over, so close our noses brush. He grits his teeth, his lips only centimeters from mine, and within moments I'm being lifted, a coat draped over my trembling body, and a hat stuffed on my head.

"Go, now," Patton growls. "Go north for three miles. There's a house in a grove of cottonwood trees. You can't miss it. There's a healer there. *Go.* I'll find you."

Soren lifts me into his arms. I feel nothing but ice as he carries me through the forest, his blood scenting the night air like iron.

TIME TO GET OUT

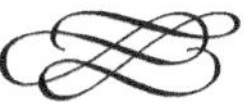

Soren

I'VE NEVER BEEN A FAN OF WITCHES. I DON'T TRUST THEM, AND THEY smell strange. They don't smell like shifters do. They smell like... their potions and herbs, with the underlying metallic scent of magic permeating the air around them.

I tend to steer clear of them even though it's nearly impossible living in a place like Moonrise, their mecca.

Now, it's completely impossible. The ancient stone cottage built in a grove of cottonwood trees tilts to the side, one corner sinking slowly into the soil over the decades. Four witches rush around the main room of the house, speaking in low tones as they grind herbs and toss them into a cauldron, all while I guard the doorway leading into the room where Maeve is prostate on a cot, covered in thick quilts stuffed with goose down, a fire blazing in the hearth only a few feet away from her.

The oldest witch, an elder, skirts in my direction holding a shallow bowl. It's perfectly smooth on the outside, but the inside is ingrained in a series of symbols I don't recognize, all of them inlaid with lines and swirls connecting the symbols to each other.

One of her younger assistants follows closely behind, the two of them brushing past me in a hurry.

"What are you doing?" I snarl when the elder witch hands the bowl to her assistant and kneels at Maeve's beside.

The assistant glances at me wearily but says nothing as her mistress untucks Maeve's arm from the pile of blankets. Her skin is tinted blue.

I brace myself in the doorway, unsure what to do, what to say, and how to feel when the elder witch slices across Maeve's fingertips with a knife and tilts her fingers over the bowl, collecting a few drops of blood from each.

My stomach curls in rage. The doorframe groans and cracks from the pressure where my hands curl around the frame, squeezing, taking the brunt of my fury so I don't go blind with madness and kill both witches for touching her.

The elder witch rises with the bowl, her milky eyes downcast on the symbols as she turns and brushes past me again, ducking under my elbow. I don't look away from Maeve's hand, however. Her skin is just... white. A sickly, whitish-blue that makes my chest convulse as the young witch weaves a bandage over her fingers and tuck her arm back under the covers.

I've been ignoring my own injury–a stab wound to the chest. That fucking bastard. I knew Duke would return. I knew I had to hunt him down and intercept him before he came back, and I should have done it a day ago but... I stayed. I stayed with Maeve. I stayed with her, knowing she was perfectly safe with Patton, and wasted time because I just didn't want to leave her yet.

I didn't want to be anywhere else.

"We need to dress your wound before it gets infected," another witch says somewhere behind me. "Excuse me? Sir? Your wound–"

"I'm fine," I rush out without looking in her direction. When the young assistant witch rises from Maeve's beside, I step toward the foot of the bed, but fingers curl around my wrist.

"Leave her," the elder witch says in a huff. "You're bleeding all over the place. You need stitches. You cannot help her until you help yourself."

I slowly look over my shoulder at the short, older woman. She's in her fifties by my estimation, and beautiful, but dark circles line her eyes as she turns her face to the window. Gray, stormy morning sunlight drifts through faded yellow curtains. Rain hammers the glass, and beyond, the forest is lost in a wall of thick fog.

It took two hours to get here with Maeve slung over my shoulder for most of it. She woke when the rain started again, and from there, we hiked uphill, her arm slung over my shoulder as she trembled from bitter cold despite the heat and humidity driving the storm.

We reached the cottage as night bled into the earliest hours of morning. I pounded on the door, shouting for help, and help came in the form of a household of witches.

Maeve was quickly carried away, but she looked back at me, her eyes wide with fear and… raw emotion I didn't think she was capable of. Fear, grief, and confusion made her eyes burn like fire-lit gems, and it gutted me.

She's never killed anyone before. That was her first time.

I don't understand any of this. I look at her profile, the dark circles beneath her eyes and the puff of cold mist every time she takes a breath. What's wrong with her? Why aren't her powers returning? It's been days of this—this back and forth.

The old witch gives my wrist a tender squeeze, her dark eyes meeting mine. "Please, let me tend to you so you can tend to her."

I hold her gaze for several seconds. "Here. I'm not leaving this room."

"She is safe where she is. I need better light to see your wound. Come."

I allow the witch to guide me back into the main room. Her assistant now sits at a wooden work table in the center of the space, scribbling madly in a little notepad while keeping her eyes on the strange bowl now coated in Maeve's blood. The other witches station themselves at the fire over several large iron cauldrons, neither of them even looking in my direction as the old witch guides me into a chair and picks up a giant pair of steel scissors.

I close my eyes as she cuts through my shirt.

"It's not as deep as I thought," she whispers under her breath.

I breathe deeply, grimacing as her fingers prod the wound. "He got—ugh, fuck that hurts!" I growl, my upper lip pulled over my teeth while she pinches my skin together.

"Another half inch and your heart would've been pierced," she says softly, turning and grabbing a stool before sitting back down and reaching into her apron. "Whatever blade was used hit your ribs. You were blessed by the Goddess at that moment."

"The Goddess has nothing to do with it," I grumble, wincing as my skin burns while she cleans the wound.

"She wants you alive for a higher purpose," she corrects, those sharp, dark eyes meeting mine. "Regardless of whether you believe it or not."

I stare at the woman, taking in her features. I'll forget her. Her face will fade into oblivion like the healers who've tended to my body before, but her hands are soft, her motions kind, and when she finishes stitching my chest closed, I watch her move with a witch's grace to the bowl.

I slowly rise from the stool, shrugging out of the remains of my shirt. The witch turns to me when she notices my movements, narrowing her eyes at the network of scars of my forearm. Her eyes go wide with shock. "Sit back down. I want to look at that."

"There's nothing you can do about it," I tell her. "Other than maybe finding me a new shirt."

The other witches are now looking in our direction. The elder witch moves toward me, clutching my forearm and turning the scar to the light.

"This is a silver burn," she says, almost to herself.

"Yeah," I confirm, not liking the look on her face.

"How long were you bound by silver?" Her eyes search mine, and I have an unsettling sensation that she's looking right through me.

I wonder what she knows about men like me—like me and Patton.

He's practically her neighbor. She must have seen men in silver bands before, especially with an operation like hers. Every shelf is full of healing potions. Every drawer is full of medical equipment to stitch bodies back together. She hasn't even asked my name, and I doubt she'll give me hers.

It's very hush-hush… but I know she's aware that it's the Princess of Eastonia lying on that cot just beyond the door. This situation is suspicious as fuck. I get it.

I'm also not in the mood to explain. I try to yank out of her grasp, but her grip tightens, showcasing an incredible amount of strength for someone her size.

"Years," I answer, my voice low and emotionless. "Five years."

"And she took it off for you, didn't she? You wore a band." She slowly lets go of my wrist, but her fingertips trail over the scars to the newest, still healing wounds. "You cannot feel your wolf powers at all, can you? What does it feel like now?"

"It tingles from time to time, but otherwise it just hurts."

"It's healing. Once that fresh wound on your forearm has scared over, you'll start to feel the call of the wolf again. You'll be able to shift again, one day. Probably soon, given the circumstances." She turns back to the worktable, leaving me standing shirtless, jaw slack, gazing after her like a dumbass.

"What circumstances?"

A sharp, desperate knock on the door startles me, but the witches seem used to it. The young assistant moves from the table and peeks through the peephole before opening the door wide.

Patton steps inside, absolutely drenched, carrying a covered basket under one arm. His eyes meet mine in the fire-lit haze, and he exhales deeply, relieved to see me upright.

Then, he turns to the women, all of whom beam at him, fluttering their eyelashes as he presents the basket full of eggs and the mead he brews himself.

All but the old witch, who is currently still bent over the bowl, her face twisted in concentration. Patton glances at me over the witches encircling him, giving me a sharp nod, then tilts his head toward the door in a silent question. We've never been able to mind-link. Not while wearing silver.

I grab my jacket off a hook near the door, stepping out into the shadow of the covered front porch. Rain pelts the metal roof, which is obviously a new addition. Beyond the porch, the forest is thick and dark, with fog curling around the base of the trees like silver snakes.

Patton steps outside after a moment, shutting the door snuggly behind him. Before he can get a word out, I ask, "Were we followed?"

"No," he says, shaking his head. "There's no sign of the Hounds, nor any of the Viper's guys."

I take a breath, filling my lungs for what feels like the first time in hours. "What the fuck was that about, Pat?"

"I don't know." Patton braces his hands on the railing, leaning over to stretch his shoulders. "I don't fuckin' know, but while you guys were here, getting tended to, I went to Jameston Ridge, about ten miles from my place. It's the biggest settlement this far north. That's where Duke has been hanging out lately, drinking and gambling, trying to make some money. I talked to a few folks I know around town. I was told the Beta there holds the card games, and Duke owed quite a bit of money."

"He went after Maeve," I cut in, shaking my head. "What the fuck does she have to do with any of this?"

Patton rolls his eyes, shaking his head. "Look, Soren, you give me shit for keeping up with the royals, but I know for a fact Maeve's ascension to the throne isn't as popular as it seems, especially with you coming from a place like Moonrise. Here in the Roguelands… they barely tolerate Alpha King Ryatt. These Alphas weren't old enough to remember what it was like before Ryatt and Ella took the throne and united Eastonia. They see someone like Maeve as a threat. She's not like us. She's not like anyone. She's the only one of her kind."

"So?"

Patton stares at me. "She's… she's dangerous, Soren. People are scared of her. *Alphas* are scared of her. You think there's not people out there trying to figure out how to get rid of her? Of doing the impossible and killing her?"

My body feels tight and uncomfortable. My hands curl into fists at my sides around a sensation bordering on rage. I've never cared about the royal family. Never. I don't involve myself in politics. I've always been on the fringes, doing what I had to do to survive, to be free.

Now I want to... I want to cut through anyone who remotely looks like they have anything bad to say about the woman lying on the cot inside, fighting for her fucking life.

Because that's what's happening, isn't it? She's losing her powers. Her body can't handle the constant charging and expelling of those gifts.

I can feel Patton watching me, inspecting my face, trying to see past the expression of neutrality I've spent a lifetime trying to master.

"I don't think," Patton says after several long, tense moments of silence, "Duke was trying to kill her. I think he planned to... I don't know, take her back to town and sell her to one of the guys he's in debt to, maybe, so they could use her to get a ransom from the royal family."

"The royal family doesn't pay ransoms," I reply under my breath. "Alpha King Ryatt and Queen Ella would've burned that town to the ground to find her."

"Duke didn't know that, or he didn't care. Either way, I buried him a few miles from my house. He's gone." Patton straightens, turning back for the door. "You can't stay here long."

"You can't go back to your house for a while in the event he did, in fact, find the Hounds and told them where I was."

"I'm aware. Don't worry about me. Helena owns this place and will get you both out of here and into the Highlands. That's the safest place to be, especially with this storm system rolling in. It'll be like this for a few days, at least. The roads north will be bogged down, and Maeve will have some time to rest." Patton runs his fingers through his hair, then checks his watch. "I'm going to board the house up and leave."

"Go to my safe house in Twin Rivers," I tell him, and he nods.

"I was planning on it." He starts to step off the porch but stops, his hand clutching the railing. "Can I tell you something without you getting fucking pissed off?"

"What?"

"You screamed for her, when Duke was on top of her. I've never heard you–" He licks his lips, his eyes meeting mine in the stormy darkness. "Do you feel anything, Soren, now that your band is gone?"

"What are you asking?"

"You looked like a man who was watching his mate get killed. It–it tore me shreds."

"She's not a shifter, Patton. She can't be my mate." Why does the thought of that–the thought of her being... mine... make me want to set fire to the world that's constantly hurting her, criticizing her, and forcing her into a little box?

This woman–this force of nature–kept her powers in a necklace so she wouldn't hurt anyone.

I get it.

I also fucking hate it.

FULL-BLOODED

Soren

I STAND ON THE PORCH FOR SEVERAL MINUTES AFTER PATTON LEAVES, disappearing into the storm to go board up his house. He can't stay there now. Not with the threat of the Hounds. His theory about Duke's behavior made sense, but I'm not entirely convinced he wouldn't have gone to the Hounds, or worse, alerted the Viper herself that Princess Maeve was with me, in the Roguelands, unguarded. Her boss... well, he'd love a royal in his clutches, especially Maeve, given her skillset.

The thought makes my stomach turn, or maybe that's biting hunger, I'm not sure, but I go back inside, and the witches are disappointed to find out that Patton left.

He must come here sometimes. He left the basket, and it's one of his fancy ones. He'll return for it when it's safe, I'm sure, and I do my best to explain that to the witches while watching the old witch continue her inspection of the bowl in the center of the room.

I start to move in the direction of the room where Maeve's resting, but the elder witch stops me, clicking her tongue. "I need to speak to you," she says, sitting on her stool and motioning for me to sit beside her.

"About what?"

"The princess," she says with a sigh, then looks at her assistants, motioning for them to leave. They funnel through a door leading to the recesses of the house, and silence falls all around us, broken only by the crackling of the fire and bubbling of the cauldrons.

I don't sit. I cross my arms over my chest, looking down at the bowl, its pale, pewter surface now stained crimson. "What is that thing?"

"It reads power in blood," she explains in the simplest terms. "Witches use them often in healing to determine the best routes for our potions and medicines, but they're also used when witches are young to determine what their best practice might be when they go through schooling."

I edge closer to the table, glancing at the notepad beside the bowl, but I can't make out the handwriting.

"You cut Maeve's fingers."

"To determine how best to help her, but she's beyond my scope of power. I'm a healer, wolf. But I'm also just a witch. She is far more than that. Far, far more."

"Is she dying?"

"No. She's experiencing something we call a depletion event. Most witches have experienced one, but they learn early on not to stretch their powers so thin. We see it more in children–those too young to truly understand the scope of their powers. It makes them ill, a little sick to their stomachs, but they always recover with rest. The princess, however… her family is different."

I sink onto a stool, giving up on looking hard and serious. While I hang my head in my hands, she continues, "Powers like the princess possesses are world ending, or world building, gifts. The kind that can topple mountains, create weather, breathe life into the dead. Her entire family is like that. I knew her mother. She was younger than me by several years, but we went through school together in Moonrise, in their healing program." She tilts the bowl, gazing down at the shimmering blood. "Alpha Kenna was a force–a hybrid of two rival powers. From her mother, Firestone gifts, which had only ever sprung up randomly in our modern times, and from her father, the gifts of the Shadowsyngers, which was her dominant power group, for sure. Shadowsyngers are a special kind of wolf, however, not witches, so her blood was… complicated. She wanted to be a healer so badly. She had the hands for it, but not necessarily the powers. She did it anyway."

"And what is Maeve, according to your bowl?"

"Firestone, completely. The first full-blooded of her kind since their downfall three thousand years ago. It's a miracle. It's the return of a demigoddess in our midst, but she… her power depletion spells are always going to be extreme. Her body can't handle it, being stretched this thin, but this happened at a horrible time, I'm afraid. The next full moon isn't for another three weeks, and when it comes, it'll be eclipsed."

I sigh, trying to take in all of the information, but I'm unsure what to do with it.

Thankfully, she doesn't pause before continuing, "Her powers are naturally at their weakest this close to the sacred Rite. It's a time of… renewal. Once the Rite has passed, her powers will return in full, but until then, she'll be weak–weaker than she's ever been, and in her case, using her powers at all for the next few weeks could spell danger. But, of course, marking her could help her along."

"What?" I rasp, unsure I heard her correctly, but the witch rises and walks to the far side of the room, opening cabinets and pulling out lengths of fabric.

"The mate's mark, of course. It's simple, really. Her mate can carry some of the burden of her depletion, giving her a boost, so to speak. It'll speed up the recovery process."

"She can't have a mate. She's a witch."

"Witches have mates. They just have a hard time finding them, that's all. We can't feel the bond like you wolves can, but it's there, destined, finely woven into the heavens." She walks in my direction, placing a pile of fabric in my hands which turns out to be clothing for me and Maeve. "You must leave this place, however, once she wakes. She'll be weak, and if anything comes knocking, I can't guarantee we'll be able to protect you both. My apprentice, Glorabell, her parents own a hotel in the Highlands. Her mother is a witch, a healer, and her father is the Alpha of her pack. She's sent word ahead of your arrival. You'll be safe there. The Alpha is an ally, but his pack is far removed. There's a ghost town two miles north of here at the base of the mountains. There's a tram that's been out of service for a long time, but it does still work. Take the tram into the mountains, and from there, you'll be met by scouts from the pack Juniper Grove. They will take you to the hotel."

"Is it possible for her to get word to her family while she's there?"

"If that's her choice, yes."

She gives me an odd look that makes my chest tighten. I can't decipher it, but it's almost like she's silently asking me if that's what I really want.

"And you," she says on a breath, reaching into her apron. "Take this tonic tonight, preferably on an empty stomach. It'll help heal your wounds, both to your chest, and your arm."

With that, she turns for the door and disappears into the back of the cottage. Silence hugs the room, but after a few moments of rolling the vial of healing potion around in my fingers, I move into the bedroom where Maeve is now sitting up in bed, her eyes glued to the window.

"Maeve," I whisper into the darkness, shutting the door behind me and locking it with a soft click.

She slowly turns her face to me, her eyes watering and her mouth just... just trembling, her lips parted as she sucks in a breath.

I'm out of my mind when I move toward her, kneeling in front of her. She says nothing, but her fingers move to trace the fresh sutures on my chest.

"I'm fine. It's just a scratch."

"There's ten stitches here."

"I've been in worse shape before. You've done worse to me."

One corner of her mouth twitches but doesn't quite form into a smile. Whatever thoughts are behind her eyes weigh her down. She blinks and looks away from me, turning her face to the far wall. "I can't go home yet. I'm sorry. My powers–"

"We're going to the Highlands. It's already arranged. You'll be able to rest there for a few days until you can–" I cut myself off, remember the witch's words from earlier. "Until I can get you to a train station. There's one on the border. You can ride the line all the way back to Moonrise once this storm passes and the coast is clear for us."

She continues staring absently at the stone wall. I can feel what she's thinking. I can see it, the memory of sinking that knife into Duke's throat. Telling her he deserved it isn't going to help. She's not someone who wants, or needs, to be babied through this. She knows what she did. It wasn't an accident. She'd do it again if she needed to, but there's nothing like the first time.

"I was sixteen when I had my first kill," I tell her. "I remember what it was like. You feel everything. It's normal."

She closes her eyes, biting her lower lip. "It wasn't my first."

I shouldn't be shocked, but based on the look on her face... something isn't adding up.

Still on my knees in front of her, I rest my hands on her thighs, planning to ease up if she so much as flinches, but I feel her muscles relax, my warmth permeating into her chilled skin. She's wearing nothing but a white shift, probably given to her by the witches. Her breasts are high, her nipples peak beneath fabric, and she looks... undone. Unraveled and raw.

"I was a baby," she explains, her lips barely moving around the words. "I remember it. I remember my powers, at least, and fear but... a witch tried to take me. So, I took her, spiriting us away, from what I've been told, and when she tried to hurt me, I burned her–and kept burning her until she was nothing but bone."

Her words lace up my spine, spreading a chill in their wake.

"I wanted to kill the Alphas who rejected my sister," she continues quietly. "I planned it out down to the finest detail. It would've been slow. I figured I'd like it that way, watching them suffer. I would have done it, too, if she hadn't come back."

Another chill that I ignore shimmers over my skin.

She turns to look at me, that rawness growing to something unhinged and terribly sad. "I wanted to kill you because you weren't what I thought you'd be."

"Who did you think I was?"

"The man from the teashop," she says with so much heartbreak I feel it snapping through my chest. "The only person other than my family who has ever looked me in the eyes."

My heart skips a beat, starting to thunder. "Do you still feel that way about me?"

She swallows hard, struggling a bit. I watch the column of her throat bob. "Why aren't you scared of me? I could hurt you, Soren. I could burn you. I could light you on fire. I could turn you to ash."

"You don't have powers right now."

"But if I did–"

"So be it. I don't mind. What a way to go out, honestly."

"It's not funny. I could–"

"You could hurt me in a thousand ways. I don't care."

"But you hate me."

"I don't."

"You–you're the only person who has ever–who has ever raised their voice at me."

"That explains so much," I laugh, and she frowns.

"What are you saying?"

"I'm not afraid of you and I'll never be afraid of you. You can scorch me with your powers. You can wrap your little hands around my neck and squeeze until I take my dying breath, and I wouldn't be afraid. I'd let you do it just to see the look on your face."

"Why?"

"Because you know exactly who you are, and you've never seen a reason to change that. You never needed that moonstone necklace." I rise, leaning over her, "You are the most powerful being in Eastonia, and you reduced yourself to a simple witch. You're more than that. That's who I met in that tea shop. A girl with fire in her eyes. If you hurt me, I want that to be the last thing I see. That *fucking* fire."

Her lower lip trembles. She looks away before I catch the tears sliding free from her lashes.

"I'm going to get you home. I'm not going to leave you again, not until you're on that train to Moonrise," I say, and it's a promise. I take her hand, knitting my fingers between hers and squeezing. "You're going to be queen, and you'll have your powers back."

"You're just trying to get on my good side so I don't have you arrested and executed," she sniffles, but the ghost of a smile tugs on her cheeks.

"You know I have my ways, Maeve, to weasel my way out of that."

She turns to me, her eyes shining in the stormy, midmorning light. I'm still leaning so we're eye to eye, now bracing my hands on the bed on either side of her hips, and I feel the sudden, overwhelming urge to just... just see what would happen if I brushed my mouth against hers, just for a moment. A second. The space of a heartbeat.

Maeve beats me to it.

She straightens her back and kisses me so hard our teeth clash painfully but then pulls away with a soft yelp of pain, her face burning crimson as she looks at the wall over my shoulder.

"Well," I say, reaching up to feel along my lower lip for any splits, trying to play off my absolutely thundering heartbeat. "That's not how that's done, but–"

"Go away," she whispers, that blush burning even deeper than before.

I scan her face, running my tongue along my lower lip, then kneel, resting my hands on her thighs once again. She shifts her weight, shimmying away from my touch, but I grip her muscled legs, tugging her closer to the edge of the cot.

"Look at me, Maeve."

"No."

I take her by the chin and lean in, my lips brushing hers in a featherlight touch. She inhales, her eyelids fluttering closed before her mouth chases mine, and then I... I pull away, just a touch, and look at her.

She's a work of art. Undone and raw, she looks like... looks like something the Goddess crafted with a master's touch. Something ethereal, whimsical, and too much for our world.

Too much for me.

She whispers my name. The scar on my arm tingles, sending shooting pains through every butchered, healing nerve ending.

"Get some rest," I whisper against her mouth, and let her go. "We leave in a few hours."

It takes all of my strength to walk away.

CAN'T FIGHT THIS FEELING ANYMORE

I'M AN IDIOT. I CAN'T EVEN LOOK AT MY REFLECTION IN THE MIRROR without blushing so deeply I feel actual heat shimmering across my cheeks. I listen to Soren's deep, monotone voice as he speaks to Helena, the old witch who owns this house, this clinic deep in the woods, in the other room while I dress. It's nightfall, but the passage of time today has been nothing but hazy. A storm of epic proportions raged, flooding the forest, swelling every creek and washing out the narrow roadways that connect the smallest, most rural villages to the large towns and cities in the Roguelands.

Soren says that's in our favor, but I'm still not sure why he's being hunted or how. I destroyed his silver band. The Viper, whoever she is, can't possibly have a way to track him down now, right?

I try to swipe the Viper from my mind, but she works for Hannibal. Soren is a direct link to the most wanted man in the Allied Kingdoms, and I'm… I'm here, with him. I'm… I'm having a hard time not looking at him while my chest aches, and my body does this weird thing where I get all hot and unsteady. And… I kissed him a few hours ago–terribly. Horribly. My lower lip is slightly bruised from it, and the thought makes my stomach twist with sudden embarrassment.

What was I thinking? What drove me to act so stupidly?

But then he'd… kissed me back. Just a touch of his lips against mine. He'd been so warm, his mouth so inviting, and I'd just sat there, my eyes closing against a sensation that wove through my body like ribbons of pure, unfiltered heat.

He's fucking with me, obviously. Soren might be warming up to me, but he doesn't want me in that way. Obviously. Right? I mean, why would he? He doesn't seem like a relationship kind of guy… because he's constantly on the run and being an all-around degenerate, but still.

And I'm… I'm going to be Queen of Eastonia in a few short weeks. It's not imperative I marry. Whoever that is, if it ever happens, will be titleless, a background figure in the royal narrative.

A breeder, essentially.

Because according to what Misty and Aviva know about the Firestone witches, that's what their men were. Means to an end. A way to make children, daughters in particular.

I'm sure there were great love stories during the golden age of the Firestone reign, but I'm the first in a very long time. I can't be thinking like that, yearning for a life of warmth, companionship, and family. A life where I roll over in the mornings and feel Soren's huge, warm, scarred and tattooed hand caress me while he nuzzles my neck, waking me up slowly… taking his sweet time to do delicious, scandalous things to my body–

"Hello?"

"What?" I snap, rising from the edge of the bed so swiftly I lose my balance and trip over the pair of boots I'd been in the process of putting on. Soren stands near the door, his brow pinched and mouth twitching in amusement while I stumble out of the boot and try to tug it back over my toes..

"You good?"

"I'm fine. Why?" Panting, I slide into the other boot and crouch to tie the thick, leather laces.

"You were just sitting there, wide eyed, and didn't respond when I asked if you were ready to go." I can feel Soren's gaze boring holes in the side of my face as I pull up the thick stockings Helena provided me and lower the skirt of the equally thick, corduroy dress. A sweater hangs over my upper body, several sizes too big, but warm. A wool coat hangs on a hook by the door while a hat and mittens rest neatly on a stool right next to where Soren stands, folding his arms over his chest, the material of his thin windbreaker crinkling.

Compared to him, I look like I'm going to an arctic exhibition. He's in jeans, a T-shirt, and the windbreaker to keep him dry. He dusts a ball cap off on his thigh before putting it on backward, and he looks... he looks good. Very good indeed.

I struggle to swallow past a tight knot in my throat when he smirks at me, raising his brows while I rush past him to stuff my hands in the mittens.

"Think you'll be warm enough? It's only, like, seventy degrees tonight."

"Shut up," I warn, pulling on the hat, then shrugging into the coat. "I don't need or desire your commentary tonight, thank you very much."

"Great," he quips, turning on his heel. I step into the main room of the cottage where Helena waits, alone, a canvas bag full of medicine and other things I'm not yet privy to hanging from her fingers, which she hands to Soren with instructions to give it to a friend of hers, another witch, the healer of whatever village we're hiding out in tonight, and for the next several nights, it sounds like.

Helena isn't one for long goodbyes and simply shuts the door behind us, leaving us out on the porch in the rain.

Soren turns to me, inspects me, and roughly pulls the hood of my wool winter jacket over the top of my head, squishing the hat over my eyes accidentally–or on purpose–I honestly don't know.

"Hey!"

He waves me off, reaching into his pocket to fish out a long strip of black mesh, which he tears in half using his teeth. "I'm going to set some ground rules before we go," he grunts, then grabs me by the front of my jacket, yanking me close. "You're going to keep your mouth shut."

He roughly ties the fabric over my eyes. It's already dark as hell outside and pouring rain, but now it's really hard to see. I swat his hand away but he catches my fingers, shoving them to the side as he adjusts the makeshift mask. "You're going to keep your mouth shut," he repeats, "and you're going to keep this mask on until I tell you it's safe to take it off. Understood?"

"What's the point? Helena said the Alpha and Luna of Juniper Grove already know I'm coming."

"They've been told *travelers* are headed their way," he corrects, tying the second piece of fabric around his eyes. "Not the Princess of Eastonia. I want to keep it that way."

"So I have to wear this stupid mask–"

"You have options, Maeve, that we need to discuss." He steps off the porch, beckoning me to follow. "When we reach Juniper Grove, you can show everyone who you are and ask for help getting home, call your family–"

"That's out of the fucking question," I growl behind him as I stomp through ankle-deep water, struggling to see him in the dark.

"Why?"

"Because–because the people of the Highlands are solitary. My grandfather gives them their space to govern as they choose. They're not technically part of the Roguelands and don't fall under his, or my grandma's, jurisdiction."

"I'm talking about using a phone to call and have someone come rescue you."

"I'd rather not."

"Why?"

"Because the only person who knows I left to chase you down is Jane, and knowing her, she's got everything in Moonrise under control."

"Your mousy little maid is running things? Playing princess–"

"I'm not going to bring my family into this and cause a bigger problem, Soren. Do you think before you speak? What happens if my grandfather comes here and finds you, likely a wanted criminal with a bounty on your head, instead? He'll save himself the time I've wasted and just kill you on the spot."

"He sounds like a guy I'd like. I can't wait to meet him," Soren chuckles. "I'm sure we'd have a lot in common."

"Like what? Being all dark, brooding, and absolutely fucking insane?"

"Putting up with your bullshit whining, for one."

I scoff, then kick water at him. He jumps out of the way, shaking his head.

"So we're back to this, then?" he asks over his shoulder as we tromp through the woods.

"You started it."

"And I'll finish it–" He whirls on me, catching me by the shoulders before I run right into him. In a split second, he has me pressed to a tree, his mouth hovering just centimeters from mine. "You need to obey me, Maeve. You need to stay quiet and out of sight. If you're not going to call for help, I'm your only option. I promised you I'd get you to a train station, and I will keep that promise." His breath is warm on my cheek as he leans in, his lips hovering over my skin. "But you can't make this harder for me than it already is."

"What's so hard about guiding a helpless woman through the woods?" I argue, gripping his jacket.

He shakes his head, chuckling low and dark, and for a moment, I wonder if this is where I kiss him again. It wouldn't be so bad, would it? I want to kiss him. I'm not sure why. I find him infuriating, but also... I love this. This arguing, this heated banter. No has ever gone to bat against me as much, or as long, as he has.

His hands move down my arms as he lingers, rain falling down around us like a scene out of a movie.

But this isn't a movie.

"Don't make this hard for me," he says against my cheek, then yanks me off the tree, whirling us in whatever unknown direction he's leading me in.

My heart is absolutely thundering and not from the long, wet, dark walk through the forest. I can't catch my breath after a mile, then another, especially when Soren clutches my hand to help me over increasingly uneven ground while we start to hike up out of the trees. My wet clothes weigh me down, but I'm warm, which was the ultimate goal. With my powers at their lowest, I'm running the risk of another depletion, and I can barely keep my body temperature up, even in the warm, wet, humidity.

Soren's starting to grumble, however. He takes off his jacket, sighing into the rain while tying it off around his waist. Through the mesh, I can make out a sharp incline and the rainy shadow of the rocks ahead of us, and something else, something big and boxy that makes me reach up and shove the mask up to get a better look.

An old tram station rests in the rain just yards away. Red lights no longer blink on its wires, and the building itself is boarded up, but Soren walks to the door, yanking on the handle before it opens with a pop.

"Come on," he grumbles, swiping rain away from his face, then pulls his mask down to his neck. I do the same as I follow him into the darkness. It's a small control room that overlooks a wide, open air platform where two trams rest, long out of use.

I remember my older family members talking about these things, but I've never been on one, and I've spent very little time in the Highlands.

Soren fumbles with what looks like a radio, glancing at scribbled ink written on the palm of his hand.

"Are we really going on one of those?"

He nods then picks up a receiver, speaking directly into it, "This is Soren. Helena said you'd be waiting for me and a female passenger." He waits, his eyes on the closest tram, scanning the platform like something is going to jump out and attack us, right here, right now.

An unfamiliar male voice replies through the static, confirming they heard him, then walking him through how to start it up.

In a matter of seconds, the platform explodes with flickering light and the grinding of gears, and then Soren is stuffing me into the tram, shutting the door, and flipping control switches like his life depends on it.

He's rigid with tension. I know I'm not making his life easy. He's being hunted and unwilling to talk about why. Even Patton, who seemed to trust me, wouldn't elaborate about their lives, their jobs, or their boss.

But he's desperately trying to protect me right now. I can feel it, sense it, damn near taste it with every move he makes. He grunts with effort, struggling to pull a lever, whispering under his breath, *"Come on, you fucking bitch..."*

I come to his side, curling my hands around his, and pull down.

The lever snaps into position with a jolt that has us bumping into each other. He ropes an arm around my waist to steady me as the tram starts to move, whining and grinding as it climbs up wires hanging precariously over steep ridges and shadowed drop offs.

But my eyes are on his face. I reach up, absently swiping water from his cheekbones. He leans into the touch, closing his eyes and I... I...

"I told you not to make this hard for me," he whispers over the rain pounding the roof of the tram.

"What am I doing wrong?"

"Maeve," he says into the palm of my hand, and the kiss he presses there... his eyes locked on mine...

I'm having a difficult time justifying these irrational feelings any longer.

"Soren?" I ask a bit unsteadily. I draw my hand away, swaying on a sudden precipice.

I want him. My body is begging for him. Whatever drops of wolfish blood swimming through my veins are desperate for him.

I clutch his damp shirt. His hand splays over my lower back, his pupils blown wide...

And then light floods the tram as we pull into the station at the very top of the mountain... to safety.

HOW THE TABLES TURN

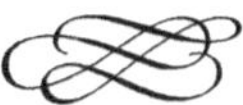

Soren

I HIKE A NARROW STAIRWELL TO THE FOURTH FLOOR OF THE NICEST hotel I've ever stayed in, especially for a town as small as this in the Highlands. The rolling mountain view beyond the diamond shaped windows is bleak, totally dark, and socked in by storm clouds still raging through the valleys below this mountain top village.

I've never been to Juniper Grove, but I've been to the Highlands for *work*. Maeve was right when she mentioned the Highlands weren't technically considered part of the Kingdom of Eastonia, although I know for a fact several of the more powerful Alphas here throw their support behind the royal family…. Both royal families, that is.

The mountains serve as the official border between Eastonia and Crescent Falls. The border itself is only three dozen miles away or so, over a few gnarly mountain peaks and a wide, steep valley where a highway, and most recently, a rail line, connects the two kingdoms.

Both King Ryatt and King Sydney keep their borders under lock and key, however, especially in years past. I'm part of the problem, I guess. The time I've spent in the Highlands has been brief, but it's always been to run contraband and stolen goods over the border and back.

I turn out of the stairwell and stalk down a narrow, but amply, lit hallway with soft blue walls and white trim. Sconces dance with flickering faux-candlelight–electric, perhaps. Thunder booms overhead, and the sconces flicker with more fervor, warning of a blackout, which I hope isn't the case. Not tonight, at least. Not with the hotel full of travelers, which I hadn't anticipated.

No one seemed to notice Maeve when I checked into the hotel, and she'd lingered behind me. Scouts did come for us at the tram, but they were under the impression I was a traveler belonging to a pack deeper in the Highlands who got stuck in the Roguelands visiting his wife's family–and Maeve is that wife. The sick wife, who desperately needed a healer after the roads were washed out, and we became stranded, or whatever the hell Helena and her witches told their contacts here.

Whatever. We're here, we're dry, and Maeve is taking a bath.

I unlock the door to our room and step inside, loudly clearing my throat to warn her of my presence, but she's already out of the bath and sitting in an armchair next to a dormant fireplace, brushing through her wet hair with a comb.

She's wearing that white shift again and… not much else. But her coloring looks better. I'd almost forgotten how she seems to glow a soft gold from within. Her gaze follows me as I walk across the room, stepping past the single, king sized four-poster bed. Of course, it's only one bed, seeing as everyone here thinks we're married, but so be it. I'll sleep on the fucking floor, again.

"I got more towels," I tell her as I cross into the steamy bathroom now scented with whatever soap she used in her bubble bath, something bright and floral. I set them on the counter, checking my reflection and running my fingers through my hair.

"Well, you're absolutely filthy right now. You should take a shower and use them," she quips, tilting her chin in a show of dominance.

I glare in her direction. "You sound like you're feeling better."

"I am."

"Good. Now, go to bed. We're leaving here in three days for the border. You'll catch a train from there, but it does mean dipping back into the Roguelands, and you need to be in better shape before we do that."

She says nothing but continues brushing her hair. *It's so long.* That's one of the first things I noticed about her all those years ago, when I'd gone to waste time and stopped in for something hot to drink. Her hair had spilled all the way down her back in thick, loose waves.

"What are you looking at, Soren?" she asks from across the room.

I hadn't realized I'd just been staring absently at her this whole time, but I shrug it off, turning back into the bathroom to rifle through the cabinets and drawers in search of a razor. "I'm going to shower, and when I'm done, I'll go find us something to eat."

"I thought I heard music coming from downstairs–"

"There's other people here tonight," I cut in sternly, leaning around the doorframe to catch her eye. "Which means you need to stay up here–with the door locked."

"Whatever you say," she sighs, rolling her eyes to the ceiling.

I close the door, and take an approximately ten minute long shower, which is apparently enough time for Maeve to do something incredibly stupid.

I storm down the stairwell, my heart in my throat, my hair still wet from the shower. I pulled on whatever clothing I could find and my ball cap before tearing out of the empty room in search of my demonic princess who'd disappeared mere minutes after I left her alone for the first time in… days. The irony is not lost on me.

Music thrums through the hotel coming from a back room–the bar. The smell of fried food wafts through the air as I walk past groups of travelers mingling in the foyer of the hotel and into what I can only describe as a riotous party.

A live band takes up a corner of the room. People rest at wooden tables drinking beer or something stronger, while more linger near the bar, their faces turned to the group of young women currently tearing the dance floor to shreds.

Maeve, toward the center of the group, has her hands in the air as she twirls to the soft rock music, and spots me glowering.

But that light in her eyes… I haven't seen it since the day her maid tied me up to that armchair.

I reach up to adjust my mask and realize I forgot to put it on.

Maeve is just… in her shift, with knee-high brown boots and a loose gray cardigan covering her shoulders… with no mask.

Great. Just great.

She eyes me for a few more seconds trying to gauge whether or not I'm about to come drag her out of the crowd, but I just… shrug. If the princess wants to play games, we can play games.

Maybe I'll let her fend for herself when whatever dangers headed our way come out of the dark tonight and see how she likes it, because right now, the only thing on my mind is a fucking drink.

The music blares—modern music. Rock and roll, as they call it in Crescent Falls. I like it and find myself relaxing with each passing beat. A man in my line of work doesn't go to bars just for fun. No, it's always for a job. I've never gone to a concert for the hell of it. I've never bellied up to a bar and ordered a drink for myself without needing to be there to scope out a target.

Watching Maeve over my shoulder as I wait for my drink, I find myself… somewhat thankful she snuck away because she looks so… fucking happy right now.

I shouldn't feel relieved about that, should I? Sure, I'm thankful she's starting to recover, but this feeling… this ache in my chest is new and totally unfamiliar. It gnaws at me as she whirls through the increasingly crowded and rowdy group dancing in front of the band, her hair whipping into a frenzy as she closes her eyes and tilts her face to the ceiling, drinking in the sound.

My arm tingles while I drum my knuckles against the bar in time with the music, trying not to look in her direction again, but it's impossible.

Five minutes later, I'm leaning against the bar sipping from a glass of scotch while the music continues, thrumming through the room and up to the rafters. The sound of a guitar wailing cuts through the thunder booming all around the hotel, and...

We're fine.

No one comes out of the shadows. No one snatches Maeve from the dance floor. No one slashes a blade toward my neck.

"That's the princess of Eastonia. Can you believe it?" an older woman says to her companion nearby, her eyes washed in awe and excitement while they watch Maeve bouncing up and down, her eyes pinched shut as she waves her arms to the music. "She's so beautiful, isn't she? I can't believe I got to see her in person!"

I take another sip while scanning the room. Yep, she's getting recognized. One by one, people turn in her direction, whispering as the dancers scream and shout to music I doubt they know the words to.

"Where were you headed?" a middle aged man with kind, blue eyes asks me, leaning against the crowded bar only a few inches from the area I claimed for myself.

"Me?"

He nods, then shrugs, motioning for the increasingly over-whelmed bartender to pour us both another glass of scotch. "I live nearby and usually bring my mate here on the weekend for dinner and drinks. I've never seen the place so crowded. Were you trapped up here trying to leave the festival, too?"

"Nah, we were just passing through."

He hums to himself, sliding a few dollar bills onto the counter in exchange for the drinks. My senses are honed on his every move, trying to decipher whether his kindness is sincere or if I should be weary. I've been around enough ill-willed men to know the differ-ence, and when he turns to the crowd, pointing to a pleasant looking older woman dressed in a fluffy blue sweater and says, "That's my mate. She was bloody surprised when the princess walked in, I'll tell you what. She screamed, actually. I think she's a little embarrassed," I come to the conclusion he's fine. Safe. Just a chatty old man.

"Why is the hotel so full?" I ask, glancing in Maeve's direction as the music grows rowdier, louder. "You mentioned a festival?"

"Aye, a few towns over, down in one of the valleys. Heatherland Falls, I believe, is where it was held. Juniper Grove is one of the last settlements with a hotel before you have to drop down in the valleys again to reach the Roguelands and the border. The storm, I'm telling you, it's worse out there than I've ever seen it. Everyone passing through has no choice but to bunker down for the night, including this hellish band."

I smile around the rim of my glass. He's not wrong. The music is exactly what I like and has an effect on the crowd I'd expect at a concert venue deep in the city center of the neighboring capital. Maeve, in fact, has totally lost her damn mind and is now climbing on a table at the behest of the friends she's made, and the room explodes in excited shouts as she dances across the surface, spilling drinks.

The crowd starts to clap to the music. My hands move against my will, and then I'm... smiling. Smiling at her. Smiling *for* her.

Her cheeks are a deep rose in the dim light of the bar as she twirls on the toes of her boots. She's not graceful at all, but she's an enthusiastic dancer, her body moving with the music and hair whipping through the air as she completes another, then another, turn.

I lean into the stranger, saying under my breath, "You mentioned Heatherland Falls. How far away is it?"

"Not more than fifteen miles north of here," he says, then smiles and waves to the woman in the blue sweater, who's pointing at Maeve with a huge, bright smile. "Usually a cozy little place. I've heard the Alpha's a real fucking prick, though."

I chew the inside of my cheek as the memory of *The Architect*–that strange phantom of man who'd stopped me in the woods–flickers through my mind.

"This one dies."

I know better than to question him or his motives.

"I got family there," I lie with ease, easing onto a stool. "My grandfather. It's his birthday next week, that's where I'm headed. Do you know of any knife shops nearby or someone with... skills in that trade?"

"Your grandfather's a collector of blades, then? I might know a guy."

My arm tingles sharply, the sensation creeping up toward my shoulder.

I look at Maeve as the song ends in a crashing, thunderous finale, and the dance floor erupts in applause… but the lead vocalist turns to Maeve as she's helped down from the table, her face glowing a soft pink. Her lips part as she takes several shallow breaths, laughing and saying something to the women around her, her voice overshadowed by the excited crowd.

"Our *Queen Maeve*, everyone," the vocalist beams, extending his hand in her direction.

The crowd explodes in applause and whistles.

Maeve blinks, her smile wavering.

Maeve scans the crowd as the sound of her adoration reaches a peak. Her eyes shine like shimmering sea glass–so bright I can almost see the gears turning in that confusing mind of hers. She beams, laughing hysterically, then shouts, "Next round of drinks is on me!"

I purse my lips, exhaling deeply through my nose as I fish in my pocket for my wallet, murmuring under my breath, *"She doesn't have any fucking money,"* before tossing a huge wad of cash toward the bartender. She knows it, too. Gods, she loves taking advantage of me, doesn't she?

At this point, I can't say I mind. Not even remotely.

I'm utterly fucked.

But one look at the princess shatters that fleeting moment of frustration. She's easing through the crowd, drinking in the excitement, and her feelings, well, they're clear as day on her beautiful face.

She… she didn't expect this. Being loved. Adored. Having people standing close, some even touching her, meeting her eyes.

She looks directly at me as I bring what remains of my drink to my lips.

I raise my glass to her, smirking as I bend at the waist in a rather dramatic bow, and when I rise… there she is. There's that fire.

There's that flame, and she's currently making her way to me through the crowd.

FIRE AND ICE

MAEVE

I... I KNEW BETTER THAN THIS.

I knew the second I slipped out of our hotel room, chasing that vibration creeping through every surface in the building, that Soren was going to be absolutely ticked off, but I couldn't help it.

There's something about my power that's drawn to sound, as strange as it seems. Like a beacon, the music I heard when I'd been taking a bath wrapped its talons around the traces of magic still left in my system and tugged, hard, begging me to follow, to let go.

I remember the night of Brie's elopement as I side-step through the crowd in Soren's direction, ignoring the curious hands reaching to graze my sweater before pulling back, like they can't believe I'm here, their princess, their soon to be queen, and I'd just been dancing like mad on a table for all of them to see.

That night after the ceremony, Blake told me something that stuck in my brain like a piece of gum, forever ingrained in my memory. *Find something that shuts you off.*

Music gets me going. The lively, riotous kind that squeals and bangs, making walls shake and the ground vibrate with each haunting melody. It makes my powers dance in my veins, even now, when I'm so empty I can still feel the ice beneath my skin.

But the moment I reach Soren's side, and slide my hand up his thigh, I lean in to whisper into his ear, "Are you mad?"

And he says, "What do you think?" giving me that cocky, displeased smirk.... Yeah. My powers sizzle, calming as his mouth inadvertently brushes over the top of my ear to continue, "You owe me a thousand dollars for those drinks you promised these people, Maeve. They're all drinking top-shelf."

My cheeks burn as his soft, low laugh tickles my skin.

"You're not mad at me, are you?" I ask, lifting my eyes to meet his. In the dark gloom of the bar attached to the backside of the hotel, his face is shadowed, and that backward ball cap makes him look... younger, less rough around the edges.

Just a normal man flirting with me at a bar.

He's sitting on a stool, his legs splayed with me now standing between them. It's crowded and loud here, and I feel an intense pull toward going back upstairs to the quiet confinement of our room, but... would it break this spell?

It's possible I'm the only one of us feeling this way. This... this heat that burrows through my body, making it impossible to think past it. This heat that makes me want to claw out of my own skin and into his. Isn't that weird?

"What are you thinking about?" he whispers in my ear, his hand coming to rest on the curve of my hip. The touch is electric, creating an itch I desperately want scratched.

"I'm wondering what the hell is wrong with me," I reply and take his drink, downing what's left. It's scotch, which isn't my favorite but it's better than nothing.

Soren's brows raise as I hand him the empty glass. He chuckles, leaning back to set the glass on the bar. "I didn't take you for a whiskey girl, but I guess I can't see you drinking anything with a girly little umbrella in it, either." He leans forward again, gripping my hip to guide me out from between his legs. "Do you want to stay? Dance a little?"

"No," I reply without a moment's hesitation. "I want to go back upstairs." I hold his gaze, wondering if he can see past the cold look I'm giving him.

He only nods, rising and taking my hand to lead me through the crowd. I can still hear the music, but it's muffled when we reach our room. It mingles with the blood rushing through my ears and the thunder still crackling and groaning overhead. I feel like it takes him an eternity to unlock the door. Every breath, every second that passes, is full of so much tension I could drown it in.

He has to know that something changed between us—that something's actively shifting. I can't be the only one who feels it.

I desperately want him to feel the same.

"Come on," he says quietly, pushing the door open. It's dark in the room. The only light pours from a small lamp on the far bedside table, illuminating clean sheets and what I hope is a comfortable mattress.

I'm still staring at the bed when he shuts the door and locks it tight. I'm still staring at the shadows in the crinkles on the bedspread when his heavy tread echoes across the floorboards behind me, and he stops just shy of my body. I close my eyes when his fingers dance through my hair before letting it fall again, and my heart... it lurches when he says, "I've always loved your hair."

I know now that Soren means every word that leaves his lips. Every single one. He's not a man that dances around the truth.

"What a weird thing to say," I grind out, struggling to swallow as my heartbeat grows faster. I'm about to do something so very stupid again, I can feel it, so I refuse to turn around to look at him.

He rounds me instead, the floorboards creaking under his feet.

"What's wrong?"

"Nothing is wrong. I'm—I'm a little worn out."

"You were dancing on a table. That might have something to do with it."

"I don't like you," I lie, opening my eyes to find him directly in front of me, stepping into my personal space, but I don't back away.

"I think you do. I think you like me, Maeve, and hate it, because it means you're capable of feeling something other than disgust for someone else."

I square my shoulders, scanning his face for answers to the questions bouncing through my skull with no place to land.

"I'm going to get ready for bed," he says, his eyes on mine–intense and bright. "And I'm going to sleep in the bed. It's been a long time since I slept somewhere other than a couch, or the floor. Can you handle that?"

I can't. The idea of him beside me, of only inches of space between us....

He brushes past me into the bathroom. I close my eyes before shrugging out of my cardigan and slipping off my boots. The shift will work as a nightgown, I suppose. It's clean, at least. Soren leaves the bathroom smelling like toothpaste and a hint of whatever body wash he used in the shower earlier but walks past me toward the bag of vials and other medical supplies he brought with him. He sets his wallet on a side table as he cleans out the pockets of his jeans, while I move toward the bathroom to brush my teeth and braid my hair.

He's still not in bed when I return and slide between the sheets, my heart hammering against my ribs. I roll over to face the wall and listen to Soren checking the locks on the door and window, and then the bed sinks under his weight, and here I am–in bed–with him.

"Are you going to turn that lamp off or are you afraid of the dark?"

I reach over and pull the little tassel. The room fades into darkness, but Soren is shifting his weight repeatedly, trying to get comfortable. His leg brushes mine as he rolls over onto his side in my direction, then beats his pillow a bit, making the bed vibrate with each move he makes.

I squeeze my thighs together against a rush of that flaming, delirious heat now radiating through my body.

He wraps his hand around my shoulder, and I startle, my eyes flying open.

"You're freezing," he says under his breath. "I'll go downstairs and see if they have more blankets."

"You don't need to do that."

"You're like ice right now, Maeve."

"I barely feel it," I whisper, keeping my eyes trained on the wall.

His sigh of frustration whispers over my skin, my hair, as he moves closer until his body is flush with mine.

He wraps his arm around my waist, and his warmth is... fevered. Hot enough to make my skin prickle and cheeks warm.

His other arm snakes beneath my shoulder until my cheek is resting against his arm, and then he's folding me against him, curling his body around mine... and I let him do it.

My voice shakes as I say, "You don't have to–"

"Stop talking. You're cold. I'm... not. You can have my warmth until I get tired of this position."

"How do you normally sleep?"

"I don't know. I've never thought about it. My back, I guess."

"You probably snore then," I quip, and his chuckle dusts over the rim of my ear, igniting that flame once again.

"Why is your heart beating so fast, Princess?" he whispers, his hand splaying over my lower belly, his fingers suddenly aching close to the apex of my thighs.

"I've never been in bed with a man before."

"I'm not touching you because I want or expect anything from you," he says under his breath, but his hand doesn't move from my stomach, and for that, I'm grateful.

I feel safe with him. It's crazy, but it's true. He may hate me, be sick of me, but he'll defend me if he has to, and I know it. Deep down, somewhere I've locked away and kept guarded... I trust him.

"I've never even–even kissed anyone before." I swallow against the flaring blush starting to creep down my neck, thawing out more of the ice. His touch and proximity is doing wonders for my power depletion, honestly. I'm not sure it's his full-blooded shifter heat or what, but I'm warming up, and that chill is being replaced by something deeper, something that aches, something that makes my muscles coil with tension.

His mouth brushes over my shoulder, my bare skin rippling with a heated chill. "I figured based on how you tried to kiss me the other night."

I scoff, but his breath fans against the back of my neck as he inhales deeply into my hair, not even bothering to hide it...

I might have been wrong.

He might want this as much as I do.

"Will you show me how to do it?" I ask without thinking.

"Do what?"

"Kiss."

His hand on my belly presses in just a touch, his arm going tight. "Why would you want me to kiss you?"

"I just need–I need a distraction."

His body relaxes, his mouth touching my shoulder again as he inhales slowly. "Maeve–"

"I'm just–I trust you, Soren. Fuck, I–" I swallow past the nerves, my hand coming up to rest over his. "I'm going to be queen in a few weeks," I begin. "My days will be spent doing my duty to my people. Then I'll spend my nights alone."

"You wouldn't be alone. You'll marry some prince–"

"It doesn't matter. You're the only person who isn't afraid of me," I force out, the words wobbling off my tongue. "I just–I'm tired, and I'm freezing–"

He kisses my shoulder, and it's enough to make that flame roar to life, an everlasting heat that burns through me with an intensity to make my toes curl. His teeth gently graze my skin, and it steals my breath away.

That ache between my legs is something I can't deny. I imagine him at the bar, imagine that smile that tugged across his lips when I'd been dancing, dancing for him, wondering if he–if he knew, could feel it, somehow.

His hand moves down my stomach, over my hip. "I've been thinking about doing more than kissing you," he admits as his fingers find the hem of my shift and trace a line over my thigh, toward my center. He exhales sharply, dragging the hem up until his fingertips graze the waistband of my panties. "I've been thinking," he repeats, his mouth still resting against my shoulder, "about what it'd be like to have you at my mercy, Princess."

WORSHIP ME

Soren

MAEVE SMELLS INCREDIBLE. LIKE HER SKIN, A TOUCH OF PERSPIRATION, and that heady magnolia scent that curls through my body with each inhale, rewiring my brain. There's more to it. Things I hadn't picked up before–like her scent is suddenly intensified. Traces of amber and vanilla. A soft, evening breeze over the lake in Moonrise. A cool, late autumn rain.

She's delicious. Her skin is soft as silk, and I can't keep my mouth off her shoulder. I graze my teeth over her skin again, clutching her to me, curling the arm she's lying on and bending her neck back to give me better access to the soft, tender spot where her pulse is going haywire.

My fingers glide over the waistband of her panties before slipping beneath the elastic. It takes all of my strength not to shutter when her soft skin whispers against my fingers and my palm.

This is the only place where she's warm–like she has an internal source of heat and power suddenly radiating from her, mingling with mine.

Shifters call this being in heat, literally. It's when the females are at their most fertile, but from what Patton forced me to learn to ensure I wasn't accidentally fathering several bastards during my younger, more prolific years as a bachelor... this is much more common between *mates*.

I scrub that thought from my mind as my scarred arm tingles to the point of pain.

"Is this what you want," I rasp against her shoulder while my fingers dip lower, parting her folds. My eyes close against the sensation of her shuddering in my arms, and her breathy moan is confirmation enough for me.

She wanted a distraction. I can give her that. I can give myself that, even if every fiber of my being is screaming to mark her, to claim her as mine, mate bond be damned.

"Please," she begs, sucking in her breath as I draw lazy circles over her swollen clit. She shimmies, her ass grinding into my groin.

"Relax," I whisper, pressing another kiss to her shoulder. "Keep breathing for me."

I'm not sure if she's even aware that I'm talking to her, whispering praise against her skin as I slide my fingers through her wet slit. She's... enthusiastic, which makes my own desire, my own want, harder to ignore. I want her *loud*. I want her *unhinged*. I want her legs splayed wide and my cock buried inside of her, but not like *this*.

I cover her mouth with my free hand to muffle her cries of pleasure. She whimpers against my skin as I inhale sharply through my mouth and close my eyes, losing myself to the feeling of my fingers sliding inside of her.

She's never done this before, and the thought of me being the first man to touch her? *Fuck.* It's my undoing.

"I want you to fuck me," she whimpers, her words muffled by my hand.

I chuckle against her shoulder, driving my fingers deeper, curling them as I pull them out. Her knees bend upward, and she turns into the touch, trembling.

"Not here. Not like this."

"Why?" she whines, but her eyelids flutter as I return to the soft, rhythmic strokes over her clit, the exploratory swipes through her folds. Memorizing her. Taking into account the way she writhes, if her muscles tighten and flex when I touch her a certain way. I want this to be good for her. I desperately want that.

"Because," I reply breathlessly, "when I fuck you, Maeve, I want you to be able to scream my name without an entire hotel full of people overhearing us."

She moans, grinding and shaking. She likes this—this stimulation. She likes when I trail my fingers in a featherlight touch between her thighs, teasing her. She can handle a single finger inside of her so far, so I give her two, enjoying the way her back arches against the intrusion and what might be a shimmer of new, fresh pain.

Her inner walls are like silk—soft, hot, and gripping my fingers with an intensity that makes my balls tighten.

"I want to be inside of you," I say against the outer rim of her ear, my hand still clamped to her mouth as she starts to unravel. I'm not done with her yet, so I slow my pace, drawing my fingers back to tease her clit again. "I want you tied up with your hands behind your back while you kneel. I'll fuck your mouth first. That wicked, sharp tongue of yours deserves it."

She moans, squeezing her thighs together to try to keep my fingers inside of her. That's where she wants me. That's where she desperately needs me, and I notice.

"And then," I groan, rocking my hips against her ass, greedily chasing any friction I can find for myself, "I'll bend you over the mattress, and you'll take all of me, Maeve. It won't be easy. It'll hurt you, but I think you want that." I slowly, carefully, lower my hand from her mouth, my fingers trailing over her lips and down her neck. I grip her throat, not enough to hurt her, but enough to get her attention as I continue, my voice warm and rough against her ear, "I'll make you feel things you've never felt before. I'll fuck you until you can't think straight. I'll ravage you until you're spent. *That's a fucking promise.*"

She gasps as I roughly jerk three fingers into her pussy, my thumb pressed against her clit. She's on her way. Her cheeks go a deep rose while her lower lip trembles, her eyes squeezed shut.

"You might be my queen," I tell her, panting against her skin as her inner muscles tighten, "but when I'm between your legs, I'll be the one you *worship*. The one you *obey*. You'll be on your knees for *me*, Maeve."

Her legs quiver, her toes curling as her pussy spasms with my fingers buried inside of her. Her skin warms like waves of heat are washing through her, her chest rising and sharply falling with each ragged inhale she takes between pitched moans of pleasure that settle in my core before licking up my spine.

I'm hard. Uncomfortably so. The urge to sink my teeth into her skin jolts me back to reality at the moment she begins to relax.

I press a rough kiss to her shoulder before releasing her, dragging the hem of her shift back down her thigh. Her panties are soaked and part of me regrets that it's not my seed dripping out of her. That'll come later.

I gather her back to my chest, curling around her while she pants in my arms, and I stare at the wall as stormy darkness cloaks the room in shadow. Minutes pass in silence. She whispers my name at one point, but it's a sound drowning in fatigue, and I lose her to sleep before my heart rate returns to normal.

I promised her I wouldn't leave again, but there's something I have to do tonight before I lose my nerve.

MAEVE

I WAKE TO EARLY MORNING SUNLIGHT DRIFTING THROUGH THE curtains. It's still raining, but daylight, and ribbons of sun dance through swiftly moving clouds. For a moment I forget where I am. I guess I could be anywhere at this point. Moonrise. Veiled Valley. Crescent Falls.

Patton's house. A train. Another shitty inn. The fucking forest floor.

It takes me a moment to remember the details of the room—the light blue walls, the soft finishes and light wood furniture. I'm not entirely sure what woke me up, but when I inhale, arching my back into a deep, luxurious, cat-like stretch... the smell of blood fills my nostrils, and I jerk upright as Soren's heavy footsteps stalk across the room.

He closes himself into the bathroom before I can get a good look at him. I reach for his side of the bed, noticing the chill on the sheets. It can't be later than seven in the morning, but he's been up. He's been up, and apparently bleeding.

The window is open just a touch, but the breeze cuts into the room, lifting a piece of paper off the table beneath the window and sending it spiraling to the ground.

I hear the shower running when I slip my feet out of bed and pad across the room, bending to pick up the paper. My thumb brushes over what I believe is a printed list of coordinates and a set of initials I don't recognize, but the imprints of a pen make me pause. The handwriting is... impeccable. Straight and clear, like it was typed and printed out.

I set the paper down on the table, thinking it's probably just directions here, to the hotel, given to Soren by the old witch at the clinic, but I notice Soren's bloody jacket hanging lazily on a chair near the door, and his filthy, mud-soaked boots beside them.

My stomach begins to turn as I scan the room for more evidence that he's hurt, but the blood doesn't smell like his. That flicker of wolfish power in my blood gives me heightened scent, of course, but that's it, and this blood doesn't belong to him. I know that for a fact because I think I've made him bleed more than anyone.

The shower turns off. I watch his shadow beneath the door as he dries off then appears in the doorway wearing a towel around his waist, his eyes lifting to mine like he's surprised to see me out of bed.

I wait for his questions, his attitude, but he just stares at me, his pupils blown wide, his eyes nearly black in the hazy morning light.

A tingle shoots up my spine as his eyes graze my throat, then dip lower to my breasts. My nipples harden, peeking beneath the thin fabric of the shift.

"What's wrong?" I ask, my voice quaking. "Are you hurt?"

He just... stares at me, reaching up to grip the top of the door-frame. He lowers his head, stretching the muscles in his back and shoulders.

"Soren?"

"I'm not hurt—"

"The blood—"

"It wasn't mine."

"Whose?"

He lifts his head just a touch, and all he says is, "I patrolled for a while last night. I couldn't sleep. I ran into a bit of trouble, but it's nothing. I'm fine."

His tone is... different, however. It's darker, edged with something unfamiliar, and I've seen and heard this man rage at *me* before. This feels off, and the tension filling the space between us confirms it.

I move toward him, carefully picking my way across the squeaky floorboards. He doesn't fully look at me until I close the distance between us and reach for him, trying to lay my hand over his chest.

But he catches my wrist. I whisper his name, confused and uneasy.

Now, we're chest to chest, his arm snaking around my back and tugging me closer—closer than last night, if that's even possible.

His lips drag over mine before he sweeps me off my feet with a kiss that knocks the air from my lungs.

My first *real* kiss.

"Open your mouth," he commands against my lips, and I answer him with a gasp as his hand slides down my back and grips my ass—hard. His tongue slides over mine, and he groans, his body trembling like a shiver's running up his spine. The kiss becomes erratic, desperate. Our teeth clash. He bites down on my lower lip, grunting as I splay my hands over his chest, smoothing them down the hard, broad muscles of his abdomen, and lower, to where he's hidden by the towel.

Memories of last night stir through my head, igniting that heat once again, but this time I want more. I want everything.

"I want you to be my first," I whisper, my tone pleading, edging on begging.

It sends him over the edge, and before I can even blink, he lifts me and carries me to the bed. We fall onto the mattress, my legs wrapped around his waist, and his hands… they're everywhere, clawing at the shift, ripping it from my body.

His mouth presses against mine in a rough kiss before he buries his face in my neck and inhales sharply, and I feel… I feel his teeth– his canines lengthening, pressing into my neck.

"Soren! Wait!" I screech, sinking my nails into his back to try to get his attention. Something's wrong. Something's off about him, and this is–this isn't him. "SOREN!"

He goes perfectly still, then pulls away and stumbles backward until his back hits the door to our room. His towel is hanging precariously around his waist as he places a hand over his chest, squeezing his eyes shut and bending forward a bit, like he's struggling to breathe.

I sit up, gathering my mangled shift to my chest and slide off the bed. "Are you okay? What's going on? You almost marked me!" I shout, my words slipping from concern to sudden fury. "What is wrong with you?"

I start in his direction, but he holds out a hand. "Get out of here. Go take a shower and wash that–that scent off."

"What are you talking about?"

"Get out of here, Maeve," he snarls, his eyes finally meeting mine. His pupils slowly shrink to normal.

"You did get hurt, didn't you? Where–"

"Take a fucking shower!" he shouts, his tone laced with ice.

"Don't you dare use that tone with me. I'm trying to help you!"

"We're leaving in half an hour," he growls, pointing at the bathroom door. "Go. *Now.*"

GHOSTS FROM THE PAST

MAEVE

HAZY MORNING SUNLIGHT BLEEDS THROUGH DARK STORM CLOUDS, sending ribbons of light through the fog gathering at my ankles. We've been walking for two miles, at least, in what direction... I don't know, and I honestly don't care. Soren is several yards ahead of me and hasn't so much as looked in my direction as he leads me down a narrow, paved road in the middle of Goddess-damned nowhere. There're no trees here. Just rolling, grassy hills and a single, lonely, fog-soaked road.

Rain begins to patter against the top of my head. It's gentle, thank goodness, but enough to make me pull the hood of my cloak over my hair.

I keep thinking about what happened in the hotel only two or so hours ago. I rub my neck, still feeling the pressure of his teeth there, and then relive his moment of shock.

Now, I'm watching him favor his arm, the one where he used to wear the silver band. It's bothering him—itching, I believe. He won't leave it alone.

"Soren," I shout, coming to a stop. My boots squeak on the damp pavement, the sound echoing to him, but he doesn't so much as look over his shoulder.

"Yes, Maeve?"

"Did I do something wrong?"

He rolls his shoulders, his hands curling into fists at his sides. "No."

"Then what the fuck is your problem right now?"

I start walking in his direction, and the bastard starts moving again, keeping what I assume is a calculated distance between us.

The rain begins to beat the fog into submission as the path trails down, and the valley opens up, the tree line visible only a mile or so away. The Roguelands bleed back into view, and through the hazy strips of sunlight battling the rain clouds in the distance, I see it. The border.

It's too far away to see the start of the highway that connects Crescent Falls and Eastonia, but we're close. Ten or fifteen miles away.

A pang of guilt and regret whispers through my chest as I stare at Soren's back, noticing the tight muscles, the tension, and his straightened, rigid shoulders.

He's going to take me to the border, isn't he? I can catch a train there and ride it all the way to Moonrise with minimal stops. It'll take over a day by train, but I'll be home, safe, and back to my... my life.

I stop walking again. My legs just... stop working.

Soren lets out a rough sigh and finally turns around, his eyes gleaming in the filtered sunlight cutting through the drizzle.

"Did you kill someone last night?" I ask, the words wobbling off my tongue.

"Yeah, I did."

"Why?"

"It needed to be done."

"Is that all you're going to say? You came into the room covered in blood and then–then we almost–"

He tucks his hands in his pockets and hangs his head. I step closer to him–two steps, exactly–to which he takes two steps away.

"What's going on, Soren? Please–"

"I need you to stay away from me. Keep your distance, please–"

"Please, what? What the fuck–"

"I'm not feeling well," he says with effort, his jaw clenched. "Okay? We're about to drop into the woods. I wanted to be able to keep you in the Highlands for a few more days, but I learned the Hounds have been spotted nearby, and we couldn't stay. They're trailing me somehow, and I need to get you to the border as soon as possible–"

"I'm not ready to go home–"

"We can't do this, Maeve. You have to go home. This isn't a little vacation, or adventure, or whatever the hell–"

"I–" I suck in a breath as my chest goes rigid with the words I so desperately want to say but can't. I just… can't say them. I want to ask if he feels anything for me. If I'm going crazy, and these aching feelings of want are just me, and only me.

But the way he's looking at me right now… I've never seen him so raw, so utterly broken. His face is cast in a shadow of his own making–shadows of regret, maybe even turmoil, as he scans my eyes and then looks down at his boots.

We've known each other for a little over a week at this point. That's… nothing. Nothing at all.

But the idea of never seeing him again shatters me like glass.

I start walking, brushing past him. He walks on the opposite side of the path, keeping pace with me but also keeping his distance, for the next mile, then the next, until the road forks.

The road into the Roguelands is nothing more than a strip of gravel that bleeds into dirt, then a nearly impassable network of roping vines and rocks big enough to stop most vehicles. The remains of small villages peak through thick, dark trees, but we're alone. Birdsong is the only sound as we follow the remains of a very old road, something I'm sure was used to connect these ghost villages during my grandfather's time here.

Soren eventually cuts off the road, following an overgrown wolf trail, murmuring something about staying out of sight, and I dutifully follow until my feet start to ache and the rain returns in earnest.

The sun slips out of sight and the already dark forest descends into shadows when we reach another dead village.

Soren hikes a bag filled with our meager belongings and supplies for this last stretch of our journey over his shoulder with a sigh as he scans the village. Several buildings still stand, forming a perfect circle.

He looks up, squinting against the rain, and purses his lips.

I stand in the weather wrapped in my cloak for several minutes while he internally debates our options. Thunder booms in the distance, drifting closer. The forest bends and groans with the storm creeping overhead, the clouds dark and angry as they funnel and roll.

"I thought it was going to be a nice summer," Soren grumbles, swiping rain from his face, then he turns to a small stone cottage only a few feet away from us, taking one step toward it.

Just one.

The birdsong goes silent. A tingle of unease drifts up my spine, my weak power reserves simmering.

"Don't turn around," Soren whispers over the rain.

A chill snakes down my spine as several twigs crack nearby, behind us, around us.

"Don't be afraid," he says, reaching along his belt for a knife I didn't know he had on him until now. "We're not far from the border. If you can jump that distance, do it now."

"I can't–"

He turns to look at me over his shoulder, and he's… changed. Changing. His pupils expand, turning a glassy, furious black. His canine's sharpen, and I feel it, smell it, sense it deep in my bones.

"Your wolf is back," I breathe as my body reacts to the knowledge.

"*Run,*" he says with great effort, and I do.

I whirl, sprinting between two dilapidated buildings as six wolves sprint into the village, howling and snarling. I turn back to Soren, my feet refusing to move another inch, just in time to see him burst through his clothes with a vicious scream of rage and… shift.

His eyes glow like stars in the stormy darkness, his coat a deep chestnut brown that's thick and glossy–perfect. He's huge. Larger than at least half of the wolves barreling in his direction.

But he's totally, inexplicably outnumbered.

The first two wolves collide with him in a burst of fur, teeth, claws and a spray of blood. My heart quickens. I slide into the shadow of the nearest building, my lungs contracting as my meager powers sizzle to sudden life.

I could use them. I have enough–just enough to send a wave of flame through the village, but not enough to control it, wield it like a weapon. I'd hurt Soren in the process. I wouldn't have enough power left to rein it back in.

I could jump, but how far? The ice beneath my skin is nearly gone, but the moon is not even close to being full, and my powers are taking for-fucking-ever to return.

Tears of frustration spring along my lashes as I watch Soren battle without being able to help him, but he... doesn't seem to need my help.

I find his moves familiar. Shockingly so. He battles with practiced grace compared to the scrappy, more instinctual tactics used by his foes.

He fights like a warrior.

A trained warrior.

Like a Ghost.

My blood rushes through my veins as I straighten out of the shadow, watching Soren use skilled techniques to pin and annihilate two of the wolves at once, ripping out their spines.... Fuck.

Only someone who... trained under my father's command...

I'm suddenly standing in the small strip of grass between the two buildings, within sight of the other wolves. I walked there without realizing it, stepping out of the cover of the shadows.

A large wolf turns his head to me, and I know those eyes. The ugly man from the train–the leader of this pack of hunters, these Hounds...

The guy who'd said he likes my long legs.

He lowers his head and gives me a wolfish smirk that makes my skin tingle with sudden fear.

I hold out my hand, begging my powers to flare. Smoke curls between my fingers, letting off a few pathetic sparks.

"Please," I grind out, "Please, just work. For fuck's sake, please!"

The wolf lunges, jaw wide and teeth splayed. I scream as my powers erupt in a blast of pure heat, pure fire, pure death.

But it's not enough.

Ice rips through my body, and my powers shutter out. I fall backward as the wolf and I collide. He latches onto my cloak, leaping from me and dragging me by the garment back between the buildings while Soren continues his battle just out of sight. I kick out then dig my heels in, desperately trying to wriggle out of the cloak, but the clasp is strangling me, biting into my throat. The wolf tosses me, and I roll through the wet grass, landing on my stomach, and he's on me again, shifting to his human form against a backdrop of thunder, lightning illuminating his old, portly body. His naked body.

"You little witch," he grins, straddling me. His meaty hand curls around my throat and squeezes until I see stars. "I know who you are now. What a fucking treat this is going to be, having you then killing you."

He leans down, his hot, rancid breath dusting over my cheek. "How do you like it, Princess? I can make this good for you, but I do like a little fear–"

His hand suddenly releases from my throat, and he's just... gone. Nothing left but blank, empty space. Something heavy collides with a nearby tree, and a gurgling of bloody, wet pain mingles with another boom of thunder that shakes the ground all around me.

A wet crunch follows, and then silence creeps back into the clearing. Rain washes over me in sheets while I lay prone, too scared to move, too terrified to look to the side.

"Soren?" I gasp, realizing I'd been holding my breath.

I sit up, rolling onto my knees, and turn to the shadow hovering in the trees.

Soren, naked, his muscles tight, and covered in blood, rises with the ugly man's head in his hand. He tosses it into the woods, panting, and slowly turns to me.

Rain washes the blood from his body while I scan him for injuries. He's spotless. Flawless.

Totally unharmed.

My eyes widen as he turns in my direction, wearing absolutely nothing.

"Soren–"

He's on me in a second, scooping me up, carrying me back to the village. He presses my face against his chest, shielding my eyes from the bodies he steps over–every body. Every wolf who dared attack him. Every wolf he killed.

He kicks in a door and walks inside what remains of someone's home. It's dark but spared from the rain. Dust covers nearly every surface, surfaces untouched for decades.

"Are you okay?" I begin as he lowers me to the ground. I turn from him to grab what I believe is a blanket draped over a wooden chair, but he catches my arm, forcing me to turn back to him.

I have a single moment to breathe, to catch my breath. A single moment to look him in the eyes and feel what he's feeling, to know.

To know that everything I feel, he feels, too.

I drop the blanket to the ground at my feet and rise on my toes, kissing him.

Kissing him like he's mine.

MY PET

MAEVE

FOR A MOMENT, I EXPECT SOREN TO PULL AWAY FROM THE KISS. MY body tightens in anticipation for him to shove me away, for his snarl and whatever snide comments await me.

But he backs me against a wall, his tongue darting over mine, and kisses me back in a feral, all-consuming way that makes heat sizzle to life all over my body, igniting my powers.

"Soren," I whisper, pulling back to take a much needed breath. "Are you hurt? Please–"

He shushes me sternly, stepping into me, his body taking up my entire view. I look up into his eyes when his mouth meets mine again, slowly this time, drawing out a wet, hot kiss that makes my knees tremble when his eyes meet mine.

His pupils are fully dilated like he's still riding out his wolf powers, but every touch, every breath, is for me, not battle.

"Fuck me," I command, and he... obliges.

Soren pins me to the wall, his fingers wrapped around my throat, and kisses me again, growling under his breath as I nibble his lower lip, refusing to let go. His other hand travels down the length of my body, over my muddy clothes, pulling my shirt out of the belt loop holding my skirt in place. I gasp when his warm hands touch my bare, chilled skin. His hand drifts up my belly to my breast where he presses, cupping then kneading my sensitive flesh while my nipple stiffens against his palm. He presses his body against mine, and I'm reminded that he's already totally, completely naked.

His cock rubs against my belly–rigid. Hard as steel and huge. My eyes fluttered closed. I don't care if it hurts me. I don't care if I can't walk, or if I cry, or even bleed…. No. I have to have him. My entire body is thrumming with the anticipation he started at the hotel, when he used his fingers to make me feel… wanted. Worshipped.

I want him. I want him more than anything. I need him, and I'm willing to beg. What did he say he'd do to me? Fuck my mouth? Make me pay for every sharp, mean thing I've ever said to him?

Goddess, I want that. I want to know what he tastes like, how he'd feel sliding down my throat.

His teeth graze my jaw as his hands continue to explore my breasts, tugging my shirt out of the way before growing frustrated enough to rip it clean from my body. Cool, rainy air brushes over my naked skin. He presses kisses to my neck, my collarbone, then reaches down and grips my thighs, hoisting me into his arms where he presses me back against the wall with my legs now wrapped around his waist. I cry out his name when he takes one of my nipples into his mouth, his tongue darting then drawing circles before he bites down. I gasp, clawing his shoulders, but he sucks the pain away, leaving me breathless, any rational thought fizzling away from my normally overcrowded, overwhelmed mind.

Thunder booms, but all I can hear are my cries of pleasure as he kisses between my breasts, groaning against my skin as his grip on my thighs tightens. I rock my hips against his stomach as a dull ache spreads through my center, throbbing, pulling my attention away from his ministrations.

"Please," I beg, scraping my nails down his back. I gasp, writhing as his tongue drags another line between my breasts. "Gods, Soren, please!"

I try to wriggle out of his arms, giving him another sharp scratch to get his attention, but he chuckles darkly against my skin, lifting his face to mine. "You're asking for trouble, Princess. Are you sure you want to do this? There's no going back."

"I want this," I pant.

He smiles wickedly against my cheek, still keeping me pinned to the wall. He lets go of one of my thighs to smooth his hand down my side then over my hip, his hand warm on my skin as he brushes the fabric back. "You can't take this back once it's done. I'll be the first man between your legs, and I'll be sure to leave my mark. You'll never forget it. No one will ever come close."

His hand slips over my leg to my ass, his thigh dragging over where my slit is covered by my panties–already soaking wet.

I twitch when his thumb brushes over my clit and holds there.

"Please," I whimper, rocking against his touch, wishing there wasn't a thin layer of cotton between us. "Soren, I'm begging you."

"I just shifted for the first time in five years, Maeve," he explains, closing his eyes and pressing his forehead to mine while his muscles strain against the weight of holding me up. His fingers deftly slide my underwear to the side, his touch featherlight through my folds, but I moan, arching my neck. "I could–no, I will lose control. I'll fuck you like a wolf would, and I don't know if you can handle that."

"Please," I whisper again, the word turning to molten desperation as he slides three fingers inside of me, stretching me in an impossible way. I grind against his fingers, gripping his shoulders for support, and he lets me, watching me chase the same feeling he gave me the other night. He circles his thumb over my clit, sharpening the sensation as I ride his fingers, losing myself, losing control and any shyness I might have had.

"Good," he rasps, his cock hovering just below my entrance, practically wedged between us while he continues to hold me off the ground, my back biting into the stone. "Keep doing that."

"I want *you*," I snarl, losing my patience. Tears of frustration prick the corners of my eyes when he gives me that cocky, wry smile.

"I can tell. You're wet as fuck for me, Princess."

"Do something about it then," I grit out.

"I will, don't worry. I just like hearing you beg."

My heart quakes as that smile wraps around my mind, turning everything to flame. My powers respond, my body warming like this–whatever this is between us–is recharging my powers in a way they hadn't been able to before.

I writhe on his fingers. He taps my clit with his thumb, smiling when I whimper another short, frustrated moan. He's enjoying this–teasing me, drawing out my suffering.

I can't take it anymore. I can't. I lean forward, taking his earlobe between my teeth. He jerks, growling low in his throat until I release him, whispering across his ear, "You can put it in my mouth."

"*Fuck*, Maeve," he breathes, pressing me further into the wall and rocking his hips into mine. His cock is sandwiched between us–hot to the touch.

"I want that," I whisper, squeezing my eyes shut as he jerks his fingers inside of me hard. "I want to taste you. I want you dripping down my throat."

"Where did a high-bred lady like you learn to talk like that?" he whispers into my hair, starting to lose himself the same way I am.

"Fuck me, Soren. Hurt me. *Choke me.*"

"*Fuck*," he snarls, losing his grip on reality entirely. "You have no idea what you're asking," he says through gritted teeth.

My answer is another sharp bite to his ear. His growl reverberates through my body.

"You little witch," he pants. "Bite me again, and see what happens."

So, of course, I do. I bite his cheek, and he snarls, teeth bared, and releases his hold on me. My feet hit the ground, but he doesn't lean a shred of space between us. He bends his arm over my head, resting his forearm against the wall, his face lowered to mine. "Take off your clothes."

I cup my breasts, my eyes glued to his.

"Now," he asserts, breathless, as he watches me pinch my nipples between my fingers. He rolls his lower lip between his teeth, his eyes still trapped in the pseudo-transformation, like he's fighting his wolf for control. "Do it now, or I'll do it myself."

I slowly drag my hands down my bare stomach. My blood rushes in tune with my hammering heartbeat. His gaze follows my hands as I smooth my skirt down over my hips, then my thighs, until it falls in a heap of fabric at my ankles.

"Everything," he says, his eyes lifting to mine, glassy with a feral, animalistic kind of heat.

I keep my eyes on his while shimmying out of my panties, stepping away from them, totally and completely exposed. My hair falls over my shoulders in messy waves, tickling my breasts as I heave a breath. Soren's sweep of my naked body is so heated my skin could blister.

"Now turn and face the wall," he commands, his voice steady, unwavering, and utterly serious.

But I can't help myself when I reach for him, my fingertips traveling down the length of his thick shaft. He flexes his jaw, his eyes still locked on mine, darkening to the point I can't make out their kaleidoscope of colors anymore.

I continue the light, teasing touch, loving the way his jaw tightens, and his hand grips my waist. Wetness drips between my thighs. I squeeze them together, trembling as a jolt of pleasure ripples through me.

His nostrils flare, and that heated gaze turns deadly. He leans in to brush his next words over the rim of my ear, "What did I say?"

I grip his cock, hard, and he chokes out a breath before growling, losing the last shred of control he has.

He grips my waist and whirls me to face the wall. I suck in a breath as he presses his hand flat against my lower belly, forcing me to bend just a touch. His other hand travels down my back, over a globe of my ass, and then he steps into me, kicking my ankles apart, his cock pressed between my cheeks. He slides his dick down, guiding it between my folds. I shiver as pressure like I've never felt before turns to pure pleasure, adrenaline soaring through my veins, thawing my powers.

He steps into me again, my breasts flush with the wall, my face turned to the side and cheek pinned against the cool stone, and thrusts.

I rise on my toes, a scream climbing up my throat that he stifles with a hand around my neck, but he doesn't move. He buries himself inside of me, stretching me out, forcing me to submit in one smooth stroke.

"*Holy fuck*," he growls, his fingers gripping my hip.

"You don't fit," I whimper, gasping for breath, but that low, sensual chuckle works its way through my tight body, my coiled muscles.

"Oh, I just made sure that I do," he replies smoothly, then pulls out just a touch before pressing back in. He doesn't stifle his own grunt of pleasure. The sound works through me, massaging out the knots of pain and uncertainty. "You feel... gods, you're so fucking tight, Maeve."

The hand on my hip slips between my thighs. His fingers graze my clit, sending little jolts of pleasure through my legs, my lower belly, enough to loosen the spasming tightness keeping his dick locked inside of me.

"Relax," he breathes against my temple. "Let me have you."

His fingers find that dull ache and turn it to unyielding fire. My legs tremble but begin to relax, and he rasps a breath, pulling out to the tip and slowly sliding back in.

I whimper a moan, gripping the wall he's keeping me pinned to, but it turns to a sharp exhale of pleasure as he pushes past the soreness and fills me again.

"Good girl," he says in praise.

"Soren," I moan, my breath catching in my throat. "Fuck, I–"

He leans down, kissing my shoulder, his teeth graze my skin as he pumps into me from behind, starting with slow, almost delicate and exploratory movements to something piercing, angled, and primitive.

My muscles tighten as that ache blurs with pleasure. The room fades, and then it's just us, just his hands on my body, his mouth sucking kisses on my skin, his cock filling me to the brim, and my inner walls clutching him tight on his way out.

I start to tremble, meeting him thrust for thrust as he picks up his pace, driving me toward the edge of oblivion, but he notices how close I am and suddenly pulls out, snatching me from the wall, and swiftly lowers me to the ground on top of a blanket.

I barely have a moment to breathe before he's inside of me again, my legs splayed, and his cock buried to the hilt between them. I arch my back while he fills me, crying out his name.

His mouth hovers over mine as he fucks me into the floor. He's not gentle. I don't think that word is in Soren's vocabulary. He fucks me like I'm not a princess. Like I'm not the future queen. He fucks me like I belong to him–his to use as he sees fit–so he does.

"I'm going to come," I warn him, my voice quivering as I bite out the words, clasping his shoulders and bending my neck back as a wave of insane pressure builds and breaks, leaving me breathless.

Soren curses, grunting my name as he pumps into me, once, then twice, burying his cock so deep my toes curl, and then he spills himself inside of me.

Warmth spreads through me like a shimmering wave of fire, settling in my powers.

He presses us into the blanket, panting, his lips finding mine in the rainy darkness.

I look up at him, tracing my fingertips over his cheekbone. "You're mine now," I tell him. "I think I'm going to keep you."

He arches a brow. "I'm not a pet, Maeve."

I steal his words with a kiss, and he leans into it, and I feel him growing hard again already.

"Do it again," I whisper against his mouth.

WHO YOU REALLY ARE

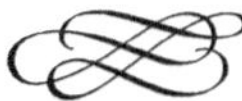

MAEVE

I'M NOT SURE WHAT TIME IT IS NOW, BUT IT'S FULL DARK, AND THE RAIN is relentless. I smooth my hand over Soren's chest while he lays on his back beside me, his eyes open but hazy while he stares at the ceiling.

I'm not sure I'll be able to walk after this. I'm not sure I even want to try. I feel... an overwhelming sense of possession at the moment, especially after the last... three hours or so.

We hadn't stopped after the first time. He took me again, rolling me over onto my belly and ravaging me from behind until I was screaming his name. And again, but with me kneeling, his cock sliding down my throat while he tangled his fingers in my hair. Then... again, just now, but softer, slower, our bodies spent but unable to stay away from each other. He licked between my legs until I shimmered with light–actual light–my powers finally thawing, and I'd spread my legs again and let him bury himself between them, both of us coming undone at the same time, locked together, tangled in an old, dusty blanket on the floor of an ancient cabin, in a clearing, surrounded by the wolves he killed.

The thought has reality spiraling back to me. My breath catches in my throat, and Soren's fingers catch mine before I can pull away. "We're safe here for the moment," he says as if reading my thoughts. I relax for a split second before he continues, "But we'll need to move on by morning. We're not far from a depot where you can catch a train."

"Well, you can come with me," I tell him, perching my chin on his chest. "Back to Moonrise."

He chuckles, but his eyes are still dark, still focused on the ceiling. "That's funny, Maeve."

"I'm serious. Come back to Moonrise with me–"

"I can't do that."

"Why not?"

He glances at me, and his expression… wrecks the bubble of delusion. Pops it. Shatters it.

I sit up slowly, looking down at him. "I–Soren, I want you to come with me. I can keep you safe from the Hounds–"

"You can't."

I frown, searching his eyes for answers. "I'm going to be queen in a few weeks–"

"I'm aware." His voice is suddenly cold. I feel a sweeping sensation cutting through the haze of pleasure still gripping my body, and it's enough to get me to my feet, clawing at the ground for any clothing I can find.

"Maeve–"

"It's fine," I spit out, pulling what might be a man's shirt over my head. It brushes my thighs while I dig through the blanket for my underwear, hoping to find it in one piece.

"What's wrong?"

"Nothing."

Soren rises to his knees, sliding his backpack toward himself. "We can talk about this–"

"So you can tell me we can't do this?"

He rises, stepping into a pair of boxes. He licks his lips, his eyes downcast on his task. "We can't do this–"

"What is this, actually?" I hate the way I sound–like a broken, jealous girlfriend. Like I'm attached. That's new for me, a new tone I don't like. A new feeling I hate–rejection.

Soren pulls a shirt over his head and looks at me, shaking his head. "Whatever you're thinking–"

"Was it not good for you?"

"Of course it was," he says sharply, taking a few steps in my direction. "But that doesn't change the fact that I'm a criminal, Maeve. You can't bring me back to your home."

"If I say–"

"You are going to be queen soon. What am I to you?" he asks, eyes wide and dark. "Nothing. I am so far below your rank–"

"That doesn't matter to me–"

"It matters to me," he admits, shaking his head. "And it will matter to your family. I can't go back with you for that reason, for more than one reason."

"Because of the Viper? I can fix that. When I have my powers back–"

"No, Maeve–"

"Do you know who I am? Who I am when I have my powers at their full strength?" I say, my voice edging on a shout. "This is ridiculous, Soren."

"What do you want, Maeve?" he asks, his voice serious and steady.

"You! You fucking idiot!" I shout, losing my patience, my nerve. My cheeks go a deep red as a blush burns through me. I close my eyes, not wanting to see the look on his face.

"Maeve."

"I didn't mean–you know what, I did mean that. I don't–I don't want to go home. I can't go home knowing you're in trouble–"

"You don't owe me anything."

I open my eyes, turning to him, struggling with what to say. I could tell him how I feel, how he's the only person who's ever looked me in the eyes and seen more than my powers. He's seen me–seen me at my lowest, my most vulnerable.

I draw in a breath, shaking my head, and keep my mouth shut

while ripping the backpack from the floor in search of pants. "I'm sorry. It was just sex–"

"It wasn't just sex–"

"It's okay; it really is. You're right."

"Maeve," he growls, edging toward me. I start pulling things from the backpack, the only thing that survived when he burst through his clothes and shifted. I toss a thick envelope on the ground that immediately spills its contents, followed by a familiar piece of paper... and more cash than even I, a very wealthy princess, have ever seen.

The money falls to the floor around my feet.

I look up at him, confused. "What is this?"

Soren's eyes meet mine, but they're... sad. Guilty, almost.

"Where did you get this?"

"It doesn't matter."

"It matters to me."

He grinds his teeth but then sighs, fixing me with his signature cold look. "I killed someone the other night, after you fell asleep. I got paid for it."

I laugh, thinking he's fucking with me, but Soren isn't laughing. "Wait, you did? Why–"

"Maeve–"

I shake my head, my hands trembling as I kneel to pick up the money. "This isn't right. This isn't right–"

"Maeve!"

"You're being hunted," I whisper, my brain whirling. "Soren, I can help you. We can go to Moonrise, and you don't have to live like this anymore. I can help. We–we can–"

"We can be together?" he asks, but his voice is... hollow. I look up at him, and his expression is enough for tears to begin to well in my eyes. "We both know we can't do that, Maeve."

"Why?"

"You're smarter than that," he accuses me, his eyes remaining... despondent, like he feels the same ache I do when I look up at him. "This wasn't just sex to me, but it can't go any further. We both know it. You know it."

"Then what now?"

"You go home–"

"No–"

"--where it's safe–"

"I said no!"

"Maeve–" Soren holds out a hand, shaking his head while his eyes plead for me to stop, to just shut up.

But I can't. This is insane. "I can help you get out of this, Soren, whatever it is, I can help. Just come back with me if you won't let me go with you–"

"This ends here," he snaps, his voice cutting through my desperation like a knife. "It's done, Maeve. You need to go home. You *have* to go *home*."

"N-no!" I bite out, my powers sizzling to life as sudden, untamable fury rips through my veins, coiling beneath my skin. "What is wrong with you, Soren? Do you enjoy this? Constantly being on the run, having to steal and lie your way through life–"

"You don't know a fucking thing about me–"

"Then explain," I gut out over the thundering rain. Small holes in the crumbling metal roof above our heads begin to drip water. *Drip, drop, drip.* The sound pinging off a nearby chair is the only soft sound to be heard over our raised voices.

Soren just stares at me, his jaw tight, his hands curled into fists.

"What are you so afraid of?" I press, losing my grip, my voice shattering into a pitiful whimper. "Is it me? You're–you're afraid of me, aren't you?"

"I've never been afraid of you," he asserts, but his voice is heavy.

"Soren, you need to understand–"

"I am not going to lead you to Hannibal, Maeve. I won't do it. I can't."

"But you can–"

"I don't work for him directly. I've made that very clear from the start–"

"But you work for someone close to him, someone who could lead me to him, to his assassin–"

"I'm the fucking assassin, Maeve!"

Time slows to a crawl. I hear every lazy raindrop sliding through the holes in the roof. I watch Soren take a breath, then another, watching the muscles under his shirt contract and expand with each inhale. When I look up at him, he's looking down at me, his eyes heavy and dark with raw emotion that makes my stomach clench.

"No."

"I am."

"But you–you can't be?"

"Why not?"

"Because you're–you're just not."

He takes a step in my direction. My body instinctively moves back a step, and it's like a nail being driven through a coffin, sealing our fate.

I think about his recent battle, how he took out six wolves in less than five minutes. The skill needed in order to do that goes beyond the biological, beyond his advantages as a large, strong, obviously well-bred wolf.

I picture his black Ghost issued gloves, long lost, but still clear as day in my mind. I think about our fight in his old apartment, how easily he'd thrown me to the ground over and over, nearly putting me through a wall.

The average man couldn't do that, even when I'm as powerless as I am now.

I grope for a chair, a stool, anything to sink onto before my legs give out.

"We're only seven miles from a train depot. It's small, but I can buy you a ticket there," he says like he didn't just drop a bomb on me and absolutely ruin my life. "You'll be in Moonrise by tomorrow night, maybe the morning after–"

"Are you working with my family?" I ask, my throat going impossibly tight. "Did someone in my family put you up to this?"

"No," he rushes out.

"But you're a Ghost, aren't you? You–you're some kind of spy working on the inside–"

"No, Maeve, that's not what this is."

I stumble across the room, needing to put distance between us. Everything I thought I knew, everything I thought I felt, comes crashing down around me like a crushing blow straight to the heart. My chest just… stops functioning. I can't breathe. I can barely lift my face to look at him as pain like I've never felt before echoes through me, drilling into my bones, pounding the marrow like someone is taking a hammer to my body.

Soren moves in my direction, his face drenched in sudden concern, but I hold out my hand, my powers flaring, flames I know better than to conjure in my state licking between my fingers.

The column of his throat bobs as he watches my powers form then fade. His eyes lift to mine again and hold. I press my back to the wall and slowly sink to the ground, curling my knees against my chest.

Soren, silently and slowly, kneels a few feet from where I'm sitting, and for what feels like several long, aching minutes, neither of us speak. Rain washes over the building in angry sheets that pop across the roof, drowning out the sound of my thundering heartbeat.

His eyes never once leave mine–not once–not until he looks down at his scarred, tattooed hands and says, so quietly I almost miss it, "I'm not going to hurt you."

"You already have."

His eyes briefly meet mine before looking down again. "That was never my intention."

"But it was," I snarl. "It was your intention to hurt me. You stole from me. You tossed me around like a rag doll–"

"I defended myself when a feral witch attacked me," he cuts in harshly, arching a brow in challenge. "We're not going back there, Maeve. We've already hashed that out. It has nothing to do with the present."

"You've been lying to me this entire time."

"I kept you in the dark to keep you safe and out of the mess I am trapped in, Maeve."

"You just refused my help to get out–"

"There's no getting out," he interrupts. "That's what you're not getting."

"Then explain." My voice cuts out, splintering into something weak and barely audible. *"Please."*

He sighs heavily, rolling his neck as he scans the room, looking anywhere but my face. "Then what?"

My heart trembles. I hate this feeling–this fragile, sucking, empty feeling that makes me want to scream and sob, to beg him to just… change.

Soren isn't the kind of man capable of changing. I know that for a fact. He is what he is down to the marrow of his bones and will never apologize for it.

I know–because I'm the same.

"You're the second most wanted man in all of the Allied Kingdoms," I whisper. "What do you think is going to happen, Soren?"

His eyes flicker to mine, unblinking. "If you're going to kill me," he says slowly, his tone deadly, utterly serious, "I want you to do it here. Where I *fucked* you."

My chest quakes, the familiar warmth flooding through me, breaking me.

"Promise me," he continues. "I'll tell you what you want to know, but you'll kill me right here, in this fucking cabin. I want it to be by your hand, Maeve."

I can't do more than nod. My mouth goes painfully dry as I curl my fingers over my knees, my nails biting into my skin. "I want to know everything. From the beginning."

"It's a very long story."

"I have time."

FROM THE BEGINNING

Soren rises and walks to the pile of blankets scattered on the damp ground. Blankets that still smell like him, like us. He pulls a knife from the backpack, sliding the blade's ridge over his palm–not hard enough to break the skin, but enough to feel it, likely imagining his own death by my hand.

The note remains where I dropped it, the ink now bleeding across the water-logged graph paper.

"My father," he begins, "was an abusive, alcoholic gambler with a pension for driving his fists into my mother's face. She wasn't much better." He walks toward me, twirling the knife and extending its hilt in my direction. "When he got tired of beating her, he liked to take it out on me. But I liked to hit back."

I swallow hard as I curl my fingers around the hilt of the knife, and he lets go, but my chest is tight, and the blade is a dead weight as my hand falls to my lap. He holds my gaze for a few seconds before sitting on the ground a few feet away, his back against one of the decaying wooden crates. He allows the rain to rush over the cabin for a few moments before continuing. "He left one night to spend what little money we had for food and didn't come back. I was ten."

"Where was this?"

"A little village outside of Moorn," he replies with a sigh, summoning fading memories of a landscape of rolling, golden hills and a long stretch of highway that flash behind his eyes. I know Moorn. I've been there, seen the empty stretches of road and not much else. "We were rogues. My dad wasn't wanted by any Alphas. He had nothing to offer."

"You're from Crescent Falls?"

He nods, meeting my eyes. "I was born there."

I try not to be shocked. I try not to feel anything right now, especially not the dull ache of heartbreak coursing through my bones. I try to just… listen because I desperately want to know why this brave, proud man became what he is so I can… believe it. So I can rise and drive this knife into his heart knowing he's evil, that he can never change, and that he deserves death despite my overwhelming feelings that are begging me to turn the other cheek.

"My mom was from here, from the Roguelands. When that asshole didn't come back, she left, taking me with her, saying we had family here, but by that she meant… she meant my older brother, her first son. Thomas. We had different fathers. Tom was six years older than me and already out on his own. He had a place in Twin Rivers, and she dropped me off on his doorstep—cold, hungry, and sick—and just walked away. I never saw her again, and Tom… well, he had *money*. I suddenly had food on the table and shoes without holes in them. I gained weight, grew a few inches. He got me into a local school while he… worked. I didn't ask where the money came from. I didn't care. All I cared about was not being hungry anymore. But I was… fucked up, Maeve."

I'm not even breathing. There isn't a single thought in my head when he continues. "I got into a fight at school when I was twelve. A really bad fight. I nearly killed another kid. He deserved it, in my defense. He'd been picking on some of the girls, and I got to the point where I couldn't fucking take it anymore. The teachers wouldn't do anything. My classmates just stood there. So I beat the absolute shit out of him. I was still picking his teeth out of my knuckles when a warrior came to get me. I was in trouble. Big trouble. The local Beta and school master called in the troops because the kid I beat up was the Alpha's grandson, and I was taken to some holding facility for people like me—older kids, troubled kids. Kids without family to keep tabs on them. Tom didn't even try to get me out. He sent a single letter telling me not to say shit about where we were living or where he got all of his mysterious money, so I kept my mouth shut. And then... I kept getting into fights, more and more, until the people running the place couldn't keep me there anymore. I was smaller than the rest of the kids, but they picked on me because they knew I'd fight back. It was entertainment for them. For the facility, I was a liability, but there was someone who didn't see me that way."

"Who?" My voice cracks over the word.

"Your dad."

"Wh-what?"

He nods, his expression distant and grave as he smooths his hands down his thighs.

"One of the guards at the place sent me to Moonrise under the guise of having me detained there, deeming me unwell, an actual danger to society. In reality, I'd been secretly recruited, I suppose, and thrust into wolf training at the age of twelve, the youngest in my class by several years. I had a natural gift. Elevated senses, they called it. The witches who run the academy for wolf arts had my blood tested to see if I was some kind of hybrid, but I was just an *angry* kid. An abused kid. A kid who knew hunger and was willing to do what he needed to do to *never* feel that way again."

"My brother—he went to that training center, but not until he was fourteen. Blake, too."

"Then you know what it's like."

"It's brutal. It's brutal for even the men who attend." I whisper, tears in my eyes. "You were just a *kid*."

He looks away, not wanting to lose his nerve, I suppose. I wanted everything from the beginning, and that's what I'm getting, whether we both regret it or not.

"A captain in your father's army at the academy escalated my training. I was given tutors to help me catch up in school, but most of my time was spent training in the arena. I wasn't anywhere near being able to shift yet, but it didn't matter. I spent two years learning the wolf arts, hand to hand combat, and learning to fight with a variety of weapons on top of that, and by the time I was fourteen, I was on the fast track to training with the Ghosts. Not everyone is accepted into that field of training. The Ghosts are elite, the best of the best. It was all I wanted. I used to watch the Ghost trainees. I'd sit on a ledge overlooking the training grounds while they ran drills, praying for the moment I'd get my chance, and I did. I was going to be the youngest trainee accepted into the Ghosts. I met your father personally. He shook my hand."

My fingers curl into a fist at my side as if I can feel my father's grip there, warm and solid against my skin.

Soren clears his throat, backtracking a bit, "I met Patton there, at the training center. We were roommates. He was… just another lost boy, no parents, just happy to have a roof over his head. He was never going to get into the Ghosts, but we were best friends. We went everywhere together. He was on the academic track. He wanted to be a teacher, I guess. Compared to me, Patton was soft and kind, and that occasionally made him a target. I protected him. No one messed with him as long as I was around, and in turn, he helped me get the grades I needed to graduate early in anticipation of joining the Ghosts."

Soren closes his eyes for a moment. The air between us is thick, the tension so heavy I'm not sure the knife in my lap would be able to slice through it. A shift in the tension in his jaw gives me a single glimpse of what's going on in his head. He's picking through those blurry, fractured memories of a time in his life before he wore silver.

"When I was fifteen… Tom showed up in Moonrise to visit me for the first time in three years. I'd written to him a few times, but he'd never written back. Then, all of the sudden, he was there, acting like nothing had changed, like we even knew each other to begin with, and I was… so fucking stupid, Maeve, for letting him talk me into going back to the Roguelands, just for a visit, using that weakness I felt for him, my only family, to instill the idea in my head that being a Ghost was like licking the boots of the royals who didn't care about people like us. I visited him in Twin Rivers during the Solstice break against my better judgement. Patton came with me. We drank and partied for two weeks, spent loads of money–more money than we'd ever seen before, all supplied by Tom. I met Duke there. He was Tom's friend, just a bit older than us. But things… stopped feeling right. The people Tom surrounded himself with were not… well. The parties often turned violent. Tom would suddenly come into obscene amounts of cash, and I'd watch him blow it in a single evening. It reminded me of my childhood. The things Tom told me to try to turn me away from a future in your father's army started to sound wrong. So I returned to Moonrise with Patton. I finished out the next semester, and that spring, got the official notice that I was now a Ghost trainee and spent the next three months training with them."

Soren rises, exhaling deeply before beginning to pace. Beyond the stone walls of our sanctuary, the storm carries on, funneling overhead. Thunder booms, sending a steady vibration through the cracking plaster, making the crates squeak together, but… my entire body is screaming to move, to touch him, to help him. His face is just… broken. His eyes are dark and heavy as he turns to me, saying, "I met the Viper when I was sixteen. I'd just been put on leave from Ghost training and was able to travel down to Twin Rivers for a month to visit Tom. I hadn't heard from him all summer. I was worried, I guess. His last letter had been… frantic. I'm not sure how else to explain it, but he asked for money. I was making a little bit on the side, acting as a trainer for some of the younger boys going through the wolf arts program, but nothing substantial. I arrived in Twin Rivers by train, unable to shift yet for the journey, and he wasn't home."

Dread begins to prickle across my skin.

"I looked all over for him, and it turns out he'd gotten in trouble with his boss, the Viper. I didn't know much about what he did at that point, but to be honest, I blocked it out. I knew enough to know he was doing illegal activities, likely running contraband across the border, or something, but I didn't know the extent of it until someone came to his house shortly after I arrived, like they knew I'd be there, and brought me to the den."

My blood runs cold as his tone drops, his gaze turning icy.

"The Viper, she…" he clicks his tongue, chuckling darkly, "she's… my brother and Duke were partners in a business sense, I guess. They'd run errands for her, or she called it. Doing her dirty work. In return, she allowed them to live a lavish lifestyle, but you have to buy in to be protected by the Viper. I wasn't in Tom's life when he gave himself to her, fell into her debt, so to speak. There was a gig gone wrong shortly before I arrived, and it sounded like she was already tiring of Tom. He was on a short leash by then, old enough to shift but tethered by silver. He'd been getting too confident, taking too many risks, and when he and Duke inadvertently caused the death of four of her best men when they were caught trying to rob a train full of precious minerals heading to Crescent Falls, she made me watch when she gave Tom the option to save himself or to save Duke."

My stomach hollows out.

"Tom begged and pleaded for his life like a coward, telling her to kill Duke, that he'd be good and do better. She killed him instead, and to be honest, I was happy for it at the time. I watched my own flesh and blood snivel like a little bitch, telling her to kill his friend."

I close my eyes, not sure I can take anymore because I have a feeling it's going to get far, far worse from here.

"I thought it was over then. But they wouldn't let me leave the den. I was grabbed, thrown down, and pinned. Her cronies beat me senseless, despite the fact that I was training to be a Ghost. I still couldn't get out. She told me that I was special to her, that when she found out Tom had a younger brother, a highly skilled warrior, that she knew she needed me, that she *wanted* me. That *he* wanted me."

"Hannibal?"

"Yes. The Spider."

THE BLADE

MAEVE

I CHEW MY LOWER LIP AS SOREN'S EYES SCAN MINE. HE TURNS AWAY,
pacing to the far side of the room, and leans against the wall.

"I told her to get fucked, but a few days later, while I rotted in a
holding cell deep beneath her lair, she'd sent her people to fetch
Patton from Moonrise. She used him against me, threatening to kill
him if I didn't do her bidding. She put my brother's debt on my shoulders—a sum no one should have ever been able to pay off. I knew
she'd kill Patton without hesitation so I... I gave in. I'd been trapped
for several weeks at that point. Patton told me my trainers and
comrades in the Ghosts thought I'd just walked out, changed my
mind, and they moved on like I'd never existed. I started to think Tom
was right. There wasn't a place in the world for people like us, so I
leaned in. I started as a thief, a pickpocket. I was good at it, kept
getting better at it, all while she held Patton over my head. When I
started doing bigger gigs on my own, outside of her command, to pay
down my brother's debt, she used Patton to keep me glued to her,
telling me the debt had doubled because of Patton's needs, his

housing in her den, food, clothes. It didn't matter. I was falling fast, drinking up the same darkness that took my brother's life. I did bigger, and bigger, jobs. I worked fast and clean. I got the attention of Hannibal, a man I'd never met but apparently called all the shots, and just when I'd managed to pay off my brother's debt, I turned twenty-one. All of the sudden I was… a liability again." His eyes hold mine in the growing darkness as the storm rages. "During those years as a thief, she put Patton to work. His skillset was different from mine. She used his charm, grace, and good looks, turning him into a whore, a piece of meat she could dangle in front of people she wanted something from, or that Hannibal wanted something from, and Patton was dutiful because he knew if he ever said no, or refused, the Viper would punish me and vice versa."

A strangled sob rises up my throat, but I choke it down.

"I rebelled when I found out what the Viper was using Patton for. He'd been…" Soren presses his fist against the stone, closing his eyes against what I can only describe as a wave of rage and agony. "One of his regular clients nearly killed him, beat him so badly he ended up unable to walk for weeks. In response, the Viper said Patton was even further in debt for all the medical visits and medicine she had to smuggle for him from Moonrise, and I lost my fucking mind. I killed several of her best guys–slaughtered them." He swallows hard. "That was when she knew she couldn't ever risk losing me. She put me in a silver band, put one on Patton, too, when he came into his shifting abilities. The jobs she lined up for me at that point were all violent going forward. Murders, punishments to our own people, and the like. She also started–started threatening to use Patton for her own pleasure. She'd been making passes at me for years, and I… I did what I had to do so she'd leave Patton alone. I did side gigs as much as I could. I bought that property in the middle of nowhere, put him there to keep him safe and out of her sight, and then kept her busy." His eyes slide to mine. "If you know what I mean."

I want to put the knife through my own heart.

Soren grits his teeth as he looks down at his shoes. "Four years ago, I was tasked with… with killing an Alpha in Tarsian. Normally my marks were smaller guys, random nobodies who owed debts that hadn't been paid and tried to go on the lam, but this was new. The Viper insisted I do it. She said I didn't have a choice, that the order was directly from Hannibal. I was... clawing my way out by then, stealing and robbing to continue paying down my debt and Patton's debt and was making progress, even though I knew I'd never get out, but maybe Patton could. I killed the Alpha, and she left me alone for months, which was new. That taste of freedom was enough to do it again when asked, but that second mark..."

I watch as he traces his fingers over the scar on his forearm. "That second mark was wrong. Something was off. It was an Alpha in Crescent Falls–a smaller one, someone without much rank within the kingdom. I watched him for days, watched his family, wondering why the Spider and the Viper needed him dead. News of the death of the Alpha in Tarsian was making waves at that point. Your Allied Kingdoms had been hunting for Hannibal for years already and tied him to the murder. But I... I had to do it. I killed an innocent man with a family and left him where they'd find him. I made it quick, painless. I let him see my face." Soren turns from me so I can't see the look passing behind his eyes. "And shortly after that, I met *him*."

"Hannibal?"

"No, the Architect."

He turns back to me, walking toward me with sudden purpose shining behind his eyes, but stops short of my legs before crouching down.

"He's the one who wrote the note you found. I've never seen his face. I've only heard his voice once or twice. He's–he's not just a shifter, I know that much. He's something else, something dark and twisted, and when I was given my third mark, one of the Patriarchs in the Deadlands, he found me there and offered me a deal I couldn't refuse."

"I don't understand. You're–you're working with someone?"

He nods. "You have to go to the grave with this information, Maeve. Do you understand? There are dozens of lives at stake."

I nod, but my mind reels.

He kneels, his knees resting against my boots. "He knew where to find me–somehow. He knew what I was going to do and stopped me. He was trying to undermine the Spider and had a way to do it. The money he offered to go along with the plan was immense, and I couldn't say no. He gave me an out, and I took it. The Viper would give me a mark, and with the Architect's guidance, I'd put them and their families into hiding, in a place no one would be able to find them, playing it off as an assassination. A year passed. We moved six Alphas into hiding. I only killed three that year, but they weren't marks from Hannibal."

"But from the Architect," I whisper.

He nods in confirmation. "Alphas who were known to be working with the underground, the crime lords, like the Viper. Alphas who ran illegal breeder auctions and the like–those were the ones that died, that made the news the most, and none of it was directed by Hannibal. He grew suspicious but was drinking in the notoriety. The Viper couldn't do anything about it. They couldn't pin it on me because I was still carrying out their marks, but they had no idea I wasn't killing those Alphas, all while their allies were being slain. And then... then Hannibal got desperate, moved on to tormenting the royal family, your family, directly. He had his men try to kill the princess, your sister. I was supposed to be on that boat that day, by the Viper's command."

My eyes widen. "You were?"

He nods. "The Architect intercepted me in Veiled Valley and sent me to Tarsian instead, where I killed one of their rogue Alphas."

I remember that. I remember seeing it on the news when I'd stood in the tea shop with Soren. Soren, who'd smiled when the news anchor referred to him as the Blade, and I'd called it a fucking stupid nickname.

"What's going on?" I ask, my voice trembling. "Why all the deaths? Why–"

"I don't know. All I know is the Viper has mentioned some grand plan. But I've never met Hannibal. Not once. And things went quiet after your sister disappeared then returned. No more marks, no more gigs, not with the royal family up in arms. We were all told to lay low, to fend for ourselves, and I did. I spent the last two years doing gigs again, stealing, like I stole from you, using this downtime as an opportunity to finally save the money I needed to pay off Patton's debt—and mine. And I have enough now. The money you found is enough to get him out."

The distance between us feels like too much, but the knife is still heavy in my hand.

"You stole from me because it would pay off Patton's debt," I say, already knowing the answer.

But his reply isn't what I'm expecting.

"I stole from you because—because I spent two years... over two years wondering what the hell you were up to, why I hadn't seen you again. I broke into the castle because I knew, admittedly, that I could take what I needed to secure my own freedom, but there was something about you, something about those two times we met, that kept your memory lodged in my head, and I couldn't shake it," he admits quietly.

My breath leaves my lungs in a whoosh, my body reacting to his proximity, to the memory of being beneath him, my hands gliding over his naked back.

He reaches toward my lap, his fingers grazing mine as he lifts my hand and presses the knife I'm gripping against his throat.

"You know everything now," he says.

"I can't kill you."

"I need you to, Maeve. I'm actually asking it of you. I need you to do it."

"I won't. None of this was your fault."

His eyes darken, every conflicting shade suddenly heightened. "I am not a good person."

"You are—"

"I," he cuts in darkly, "killed without remorse, without feeling. I don't regret it. I don't regret stealing. I don't feel guilty about taking and ruining lives. I would do it all again—"

"You were protecting your friend," I grit out through tears. "You were forced to be like this, Soren."

"I was born like this," he says. "I will never change. I can't erase what I've done, what I've become. My death would be a blessing on Eastonia, and we both know it."

"No–"

He leans in, gripping my hand hard so I can't let go of the knife still pressed against his throat. "I hurt *you*. That is the only regret I have."

My lower lip trembles as I search for something to say, anything that'll change his irrational mind. How do I even begin to fix something, someone, so broken? Someone who never knew love, warmth, or protection? Soren was always on his own. Always.

I've never felt that way. I've never known what it feels like to have nothing to eat, nothing to wear. I was never enslaved and held against my will. I was never forced into someone's bed–

The dam breaks. Tears slide down my cheeks in a torrential downpour I can't stop. His grip on my hand loosens, the knife falling and clattering to the ground between my knees. Soren lunges, crushing me against his chest, his arms wrapping around me and clutching me close.

I bury my face in his neck, murmuring incoherent curses, promises, and pleas.

He's immovable, this force of a man. Like a mountain–strong, tall, and forever proud. I can't kill him even if I swore that one day, when I became queen, I'd hunt him down and end his life myself. I can't. *I can't.* Even before I knew the truth, I wouldn't have been able to raise a single finger against him.

Because *I love him.*

The words burn through my head, igniting my powers, making them simmer beneath my skin. My magic calls to him, like it's looking for a way inside his mind, to find the broken pieces and weld them back together again, making him whole.

But I already know it's fruitless. I know the cold, hard, truth of it without him having to repeat it out loud.

This, whatever this was, ends here.

I'm a Firestone witch. I'm… I'm the queen.

Soren is tangled in a mess I can't fix, and we both know it.

And even if I could… he won't let me. He won't drag another person into this.

But I still beg. My voice shatters as I turn to look up at him, my lips resting on his as I bite through sobs of agony. *I can fix this. I can save you. Let me help you. Let me try.*

He smooths my hair away from my face, resting his forehead against mine. "I'm close to ending the Viper's reign, Maeve. Trust me. I can't bring you into this."

"But I'm *me*," I cry out, and he kisses the words away, his cheeks wet with my tears.

"This is not your fight. You have to go home. I have to take you *home*."

THE QUEEN AND THE ASSASSIN

Soren

I'VE NEVER TOLD ANYONE THE WHOLE GODDESS-DAMNED TRUTH before. Not even Patton. He doesn't know everything I've done, everything I've been forced to do or did willingly... but as we spend the rest of the night in that shitty little hovel in the middle of nowhere, I tell Maeve everything.

I tucked us in a corner as rain pounded against the roof. I covered her chilled body in blankets and gave her my warmth while I poured my story into her mind, telling her everything, every insignificant detail, every damning moment, and she took it and carefully folded it, tucking it away.

I don't know what my life is going to look like after this, after her. Once she's safely on that train, I'll go to Twin Rivers, maybe after lying low for a few weeks, but I'll pay off our debts. Patton can return to his home, and I'll... find somewhere to go, something to do.

And she'll be queen, like she was meant to be.

But without me in her life, and that's the best route for her, even if I'm having a fucking hard time accepting it.

My warmth begins to heat her body as night bleeds into the earliest hours of morning. I fall asleep at one point and wake to her stirring, her hand pressed against my lower stomach, her cheek resting against my chest. Her hair falls over her shoulder when she rises to look down at me, her eyes slightly puffy and red from tears that stung and wouldn't stop.

And I shouldn't do it, but when she lowers her mouth to mine and kisses me, I kiss her back, because we both know it's the last time.

I don't believe in fate. I don't believe in second chances. I'm not sure I even believe in the Goddess, but this woman is real. Her mouth on mine, her tongue drawing an exploratory line across my lower lip–that's real. My fingers ghosting over each vertebrae of her spine as my hand smooths up her back–also real.

The kiss takes on a mind of its own when we both give in, let go, and lean into whatever sensation we're seeking from each other in the moment. I pull her onto my lap where she straddles me, giving me the access I crave to run my hands up her thighs, under her skirt, to that beacon of silken heat I can't get out of my head and likely never will.

She's sore from yesterday. I was too rough with her, too hard on her innocent, untouched body. She drags out a breathy moan when I slide my fingers through her folds, the sound turning to a hungry, strangled whimper when my thumb dances over her clit in slow circles. And I just… look at her. I drink her in, memorizing the planes of her face, the sparkles in her eyes. I want to remember everything, even if it's my fault things are ending this way.

At least I'll have this memory of her, and the memory of yesterday, to look back on.

Because there is no one else for me. No one who could even come close to what she makes me feel.

She reaches between us to unclasp my belt, her eyes locked on mine and cheeks flushed. Neither of us speak. We don't need to. We'll let our bodies do the talking this time. There's nothing we could possibly say to make this easier, to make it better, to make it hurt less, because I'm instantly reminded, the moment her fingers grip my cock and guide it to her entrance, that this is it.

It's over.

"Maeve," I grunt, my neck arched backward as she slides onto my cock, her inner muscles flexing and gripping me with so much strength I might actually just come right now.

She gasps, smoothing her hands up my stomach, wriggling to find the best way to do this, chasing friction, moving her hips in a motion that makes me twitch and grit my teeth against a wave of ball-tightening pleasure that's nearly enough to end this before it begins.

She's so fucking tight. It's impossible, really. My breath comes in a rasp as I pull her shirt over her head, groaning as I watch her breasts bounce free. She's exquisite. Perfect. A fucking work of art.

And for a day, she was mine.

I clasp the back of her neck and drag her down to me, kissing her firmly while bending my knees, giving her more support while she writhes, riding my cock. She moans against my mouth–a pleading, whimpering sound that makes my stomach tighten in anticipation.

I flatten her against my chest, my mouth pressed against the upper rim of her ear, and start thrusting, hard, pushing past her soreness, giving her what she wants the way she likes it, with me in control. Me guiding her movements. Me calling the shots.

"Soren!" she pleads, gasping and trembling, her mouth on my shoulder where she bites down, moaning as her walls tighten.

I can't take it anymore. I want her prone, sprawled out like a feast, undone and raw. I roll with her until she's on her back, still buried inside of her, kissing her to distract her as my hands cup her breasts, her hips, her ass, memorizing every sweet inch of her soft skin. I calculate every thrust, every jerk of my hips to meet her needs, grinding my hips into her while she comes apart beneath me, her cheeks wet with fresh tears.

I kiss them away, closing my eyes and eating up the feeling of her pussy tightening, then spasming, her pleasure washing through her body, and mine, like a light. Like the brightest sun. Like a flame.

I grip her throat when she arches her neck, her lips parted as she comes again, and I bury myself deep, letting go of any restraint, and pour myself into her, imaging my seed dripping between her legs while she rides that train back to Moonrise, a small reminder of where she's been, and who claimed her first.

"Did I hurt you?" I whisper against her neck, pressing a kiss there, something gentle, sweet.

"No," she breathes, but her voice is like gravel, choked with the same grief currently ripping me to shreds.

She can't feel it like I can. Maybe it's a blessing. She'll move on, find someone worthy to play whatever part comes with being romantically involved with the Queen of Eastonia. Someone who doesn't have blood staining every inch of his body. Someone that doesn't yet exist in her life, but that I hate, and want to kill, just thinking about him.

We wordlessly dress. Silence hugs the small cottage while we gather whatever supplies survived the attack. We walk out into the drizzle, into sunlight we've been ignoring, rainy, gray sunlight that illuminates the bodies all around the clearing that we forced ourselves to forget about.

I walk Maeve another five miles to another small, insignificant town. The train depot is tiny, but covered. I buy her a ticket. I sit in a metal chair beside her, my hand resting on her thigh while her fingers absently stroke mine, and we wait.

There's nothing I can say. Nothing that would make me believe we have a shot, a fucking future, because that would be insane.

It would almost be better to believe that everything we went through meant nothing, that it was a coincidence, that it was a fray in the fabric that holds our world together.

The train comes on time. Only a handful of people depart. Maeve turns to me as she rises, but I'm frozen, exhausted, and utterly, inexplicably… empty.

I close my eyes when her lips press against my cheek, and then she's gone.

❀

Maeve

I sink onto a plastic bench covered in blue, shaggy fabric at the very back of the train. There's another car behind me, but it's empty, full of sleeper cabins I might use if I find the nerve to shut my eyes. My body feels... broken, numb, and cold, so I knit my fingers together, trying to will myself to take a breath.

This feels wrong.

No one can really feel this deeply, can they? For someone who isn't their family?

My chest caves in when the train starts to move, lurching forward, gears grinding, and I... I look out the window at the platform beginning to inch by.

Soren is standing, stepping to the side to allow a couple to move past him with their suitcases. He's pale, his eyes catching the sunlight as another lurch has the train picking up speed, but then his eyes meet mine and...

I whirl toward the last car and yank open the door, carefully walking over the divider into the next car, where I sprint to the edge, to a door so similar to the one I opened, the one he pulled me out of and jumped to what could have been our deaths, but was the beginning of the greatest adventure of my life. He's running along the platform now. I throw open the door to the back of the train at the last possible moment, and he jumps, crashing into me, pinning me against the door.

The kiss is... damning. Passionate and desperate, it takes my breath away. He pants against my lips, closing his eyes while his hand curls around my nape and drags me closer, throwing everything he is into the kiss like it's a silent promise, a silent confirmation that I wasn't the only one feeling like my heart was being torn from my chest.

"Please come with me," I whisper, looking up into eyes I'll never forget.

"We can't," he says, then backs away. "We know we can't. We both know it."

But he… smirks. That wry, charming, utterly irritating smile that used to make me see red.

"You're an asshole," I laugh past tears.

He licks his lips, and bends into a deep bow at the waist. "Queen Maeve."

I straighten my spine on instinct, and Soren rises slowly, his eyes uncharacteristically wet, and he backs off the train, disappearing in a burst of fabric shredded to ribbons.

I watch his wolf dart into the woods as the train speeds along the track, leaving the Roguelands behind.

That's it. It's over. The end.

I'll never see him again, will I?

It takes over a day to reach Moonrise. Dozens of stops later, I walk onto the busy platform at the grand station, alone, my body worn, my clothes dirty and hair untidy. No one even looks in my direction. No one recognizes their princess in this state, but the castle is another animal entirely.

The guards look confused when I pass through the front gate. Several follow me, asking questions, none of them knowing I've been gone for over a week, which means Jane did her job and did it well.

I ignore the maids casting looks in my direction as I weave through the castle, my heart lodged in my throat. That warmth in my chest? That warmth Soren gave me? It's gone, leaving nothing but a gaping void of nothingness in its wake.

I walk into my apartment and close the door. I shed my clothes on the way to the bathroom, where I shower, scrubbing my skin raw. Familiar scents erupt around me, blurring the memory of the ancient forest, of Patton's house, of the hotels, inns, the bar, and the clinic, turning them into something so distant it could have only been a dream.

But I can still taste him on my tongue when I emerge from my room dressed in comfortable, silken pajamas that smell like *me* and my home–not him.

I can still feel his mouth to mine, bruising and demanding, forcing me, the Firestone princess, the Firestone *queen*, into submission.

Blake told me to find that thing that turns my mind off, that thing that keeps my power in check, and I did.

For a beautifully heartbreaking moment, I had it.

But I was never meant to have something like my parents have, or my sister, was I? That's not the Firestone way. I am still, inexplicably, alone, and I have to accept it.

No matter how badly it hurts.

Jane rushes in the second I drop onto my favorite couch in the sitting room, my eyes locked on the sunset bleeding over the lake.

"Princess Maeve, are you all right? You've been gone for so long! Goddess, I did everything I could to keep it a secret. No one knows so far."

"Good," I say with a click of my tongue, sniffling indignity and wiping my tears away.

I have to move on. It's over. It ended. I will likely never see Soren again, and I have to accept that. Maybe in time, it'll feel like nothing. This ache will fade to something dull, something I can easily ignore. But right now, all I feel is pain. Pain lodged deep in my chest, writhing, clawing, trying to force me to recognize it. But I'm not a little girl anymore. I have to be rational. Soren was right when he told me there was no future for us, no future where we could live together, waking up in the morning together, kissing each other good night.

I am a queen before everything.

He's... the assassin I swore I'd kill and now must forget.

I turn to Jane, giving her my best smile, and it takes all of my strength to ask, "So, what did I miss?"

SOMETHING FOR ME

Soren

Sometimes I feel like I'm still standing on the train, gripping the railing while I just... look at her, memorizing every painful, beautiful, devastating detail. The way the wind whipped her hair into a frenzy as the train caught speed. The way her sea-glass eyes shone with tears. The way her fingers clutched my shirt, wrinkling the fabric. The salt on her lips–tears–that I swiped away with my tongue.

Her scent. Her warmth. Her voice, for fuck's sake.

Then I wake up, reminded how far away she is, and the incredible distance between us that has nothing to do with miles.

Pale early morning sunlight drifts through the window directly behind me, casting rays of dusty sunbeams skittering across the freshly swept floor. Beyond the rusting metal window frame, a patch of sparse trees bow in the wind, and beyond that, the Deadlands stretch for miles of rolling nothingness.

This place, my safe house, is situated right on the border between the Roguelands and the Deadlands, tucked just beyond the shadow of the ever dark, endless enchanted forest where I just spent the last week trapped with… with her.

I close my eyes against Maeve's memory but only for a moment. It's been two weeks. Two quiet weeks. Two weeks where I've watched the news every minute of every single fucking day for a single sight of her to make sure she made it, and she's okay.

I followed the train. I ran through the woods, spying on every stop, taking stock of who got on and who got off, to ensure she was safe. But I lost her once the train whirred toward the bridge hovering over the long stretch of forest. It didn't matter at that point. She wouldn't have another stop until she was safely back in Moonrise territory, but if I could have, I would have ran all the way there and watched her every move until she breached the threshold of the castle walls and disappeared from my sight.

She's still hiding in the palace, but her family is starting to slowly arrive for the coronation–everyone. All of the people Patton knows by name, the younger kids included. If she didn't make it home, I would have heard about it by now.

I scrub my hand over my face, groaning, and slouch into the cushions. A warm breeze whispers through the open windows, carrying dust Patton is going to annihilate within the next hour, I'm sure.

The Viper knows about my safe house in Twin Rivers. I'm certain her goons do, as well. It's nothing but an empty apartment in a shitty part of town. When I told Patton to go there, it had been code for *this* place. This decaying hovel far enough over the border of the Deadlands that the Viper won't risk sending her guys here. No one messes with Alpha King Ryan, not even her.

I reach for the remote on the coffee table and flip on the TV, grumbling to myself as static fills my vision, followed by a hazy mix of reality TV, sports, and then the news.

Somewhere outside Patton is feeding his precious chickens–chickens he carried here all the way from the Roguelands. We're safe here. No one knows I have this place. The house itself is some old shanty left behind from the days of the war of the Old Kings, when this whole area was a city of refugees.

I wouldn't call it home.

I don't have one of those.

But it has a bed. That's enough.

I take my first sip of coffee just as Patton strides through the door, chipper and smiling, squinting against the sunlight. "What're you doing up so early? You're never up this early…" His voice fades as he steps into the hallway leading to the kitchen.

I ignore him, watching the news instead, watching the fanfare reaching a peak hundreds of miles away in Moonrise.

"The capital of Eastonia is *alive* today, I'll say that much," a pretty, but heavily made-up, female news anchor says with a pearly white smile. "It's estimated that over five hundred-thousand tourists have visited Moonrise so far in the past month to partake in the festivities, with another hundred thousand expected over the weekend for the coronation."

"Which means," her partner, an older gentleman in a perfectly tailored suit, says with an equally white grin, "if you were planning on traveling to the city, think again. You'll be hard pressed to find a hotel at this point."

His companion laughs.

I frown, my lower lip pressed to my mug, as live footage of Moonrise plays across the screen. People are already gathering in the main square in anticipation for this weekend's events–the main events of the festival. I listen as one of the anchors, obviously from Crescent Falls, goes on and on in an attempt to explain the Sacred Rite. Neither of them know the significance. Hell, up until three weeks ago I didn't understand.

Now, all I can think about is whether Maeve is getting her powers back, and wondering how she's going to feel when the eclipse ends, and they return in full.

"Soren?"

"What?"

Patton appears with the duster in one hand and a broom in the other, his dark hair swept back away from his face and blue eyes even sharper after several days spent in the sun, building garden boxes or whatever the hell he's been up to since I arrived four days ago. His lips part to ask some question I assume pertains to what we should do for dinner, if we can risk going to the nearest villages for groceries, when he turns to the TV and gasps excitedly. "Wow, do you know who that is?" he asks, pointing to the TV.

I glance at it then turn fully as a beautiful young woman with light brown hair chases something across the sweeping balcony being decorated for the coronation in real time. She crouches out of sight, then reappears looking flustered, holding a wriggling, unhappy little boy in her arms.

"That's Brie," Patton says dreamily, leaning his weight against the broom. "Luna Queen Brie, I mean. And her son, Kieran. He's the Prince of Emberfyll."

My heart hammers as I watch the live feed, watch as Brie, slightly red in the face, waves down at the crowd gathered around the walls of the castle, everyone clambering for a view. A few maids scurry to her aid to get her and the boy off the balcony and out of sight, and I find myself smiling softly when the little boy tries to roll out of his mother's arms.

But then my blood runs cold. A tall, broad shouldered, but lean, older man steps onto the balcony. The little boy reaches for him, wrapping his tiny arms around his neck while the man talks to Brie, his hand resting on her upper back as he guides her back into the palace.

Alpha King Ryatt glances at the crowd, giving the thousands of people below a diplomatic smile, but I see past it.

"The crowd is overwhelming them," I say into my coffee, sipping. "He's nervous."

"I imagine so. I've never seen so many people in one place before."

A prickle of unease scurries up my spine, pinging up and down without a place to land while I rack my brain. I haven't heard anything through the grapevine of contacts I have with other men stuck in the Viper's clutches about any targeted attacks in Moonrise. None of us have had jobs as it stands, not for months. The Viper wouldn't risk any kind of business in Moonrise most of the time, anyway, and especially not with the royal family gathering together like this, all powerful and in one place, at one time. It's why I was able to stay there for months without being bothered.

But still, the idea of Maeve in danger coils through my chest and squeezes so tight I have to stand, resting my hands on my knees.

The footage continues to play on the ancient TV I bought at a pawn shop a few years back, when I found this place and made it mine.

Patton watches dutifully, his eyes scanning the screen as the footage of the balcony zooms out to show the crowd gathered beyond the gates and the extra guards stationed all along the wall. I feel somewhat better until the footage pans to the city center where the festival rages, every street swarmed with people and wolves.

"Goddess above," Patton says under his breath, straightening his back.

I chew my lower lip, my coffee forgotten, as the footage cuts out, switching to similar festivities being held in Crescent Falls in Maeve's honor. King Sydney is her… cousin, I believe. The family is tight knit, that much I know is true.

At least, I've been told as much. Maeve barely spoke about her family. Patton and I watch footage of the royal family of Crescent Falls flash across the screen while an anchor rattles on about how the royals are heading to Eastonia for the coronation, but something catches my eye.

"Which one is that?" I ask, pointing to the screen as a young man with striking violet eyes briefly comes into view before lifting a briefcase to shield his face from the glare of flashing cameras as he leaves a massive skyscraper in the center of the inner city.

"Blake. He's his father's heir. King Sydney's oldest son." He brings his coffee to his lips.

I swear I've seen him before. Something in the way he moves scratches something in my brain, but I blink, and the footage moves on to the weather in the Roguelands.

Patton sighs heavily, leaning against the broom as he downs his coffee. I can feel his eyes boring holes in my profile, but refuse to look at him.

Four days ago, I walked up the front steps and acted like nothing had happened. Like I hadn't followed Maeve's train until it completed its last stops, ensuring I saw the face of every person who got on and off before the train reached the suspension bridge and entered the outskirts of Moonrise territory. Like I hadn't spent three days digging a pit and burying the bodies of the Hounds, leaving their leader naked, prone, and decaying in the woods with his head and hands removed from his body and nailed to a tree for what he did to her.

Like I hadn't set fire to the cottage where I spent a single night with her in my arms, reckoning with every sin I've committed, before I burned it to the ground to scorch our mingled scents from existence. Like I hadn't spent the next week and a half lying low in the Highlands, waiting for news to spread about the Alpha I killed there.

I'd just... walked in, walked upstairs, took a shower, and tried to forget her, but it's... she's burned into my chest like a brand. It's impossible.

"Have you... spoken to her?"

"What do you think?" I ask hotly, bringing my mug to my lips.

"Hey, man, you don't gotta be a dick about it–"

"I'm not sure what you want me to say–"

"What happened between you two? Seriously. You've been on edge since you got here–"

"Patton, please–"

"Look, Soren, I liked her, too. She's great. She's–she's a good person, funny, and kind of a mess, but she was our mess, and we were her mess, for a week, but–" He cuts himself off, humming under his breath. "I worry about her, too. I know you're worrying over her every second you've been back."

"She got roped into my bullshit–"

"With the Viper?" Patton snarls, dropping his good-boy persona in a split second. This is... very rare for him. "You really think the Viper would stand a chance against her? A Firestone? *The* Firestone? That's what you're so worried about?"

"The Viper and Hannibal aren't like us, and you know that. They're not like *her*, either. I'm not taking any chances–"

"So you sent her away, didn't you? That's what happened–"

"What the fuck else was I supposed to do?"

"Something for yourself, for once in your fucking life." Patton whirls, stalking behind the couch on his way out the room but slaps me over the head with the feather duster so hard I see stars for a moment.

I grimace, growling as he hikes up the stairs and out of sight.

"I'm leaving tomorrow," I shout, but his bedroom door slams shut, sending a low vibration through the house. I turn back to the TV where live footage of Moonrise greets me, more views of the dizzying, overwhelming crowd. "There's somewhere I have to be."

REMAINING MAEVE

"It's stunning. Just stunning," Mom says as she walks a wide circle around me, her eyes glued to the gown taking up what feels like half the room. Muted pink wallpaper with gold trim takes up my vision while I stand with my back to a row of floor length mirrors, looking over the heads of Mom, Misty, Sarah, Maddy, and Aviva, all of whom are working in tandem to stretch the train the length of the room—the largest sitting room in the private royal suite on the sixth floor of the castle.

"We're running out of room back here," Aviva says a great distance away, her voice lifted in a soft laugh. "How is she supposed to walk in this?"

"It won't be that far of a walk," Mom replies, matching Aviva's smile, but her eyes give away the crippling anxiety she's feeling as she gazes down the train that easily weighs a hundred pounds and stretches over a hundred yards—at least. "Plus, she'll have attendants to carry the train for her into the temple, and from there, the procession is only a few dozen yards, I believe... I should measure." She whirls away, murmuring under her breath, but I watch my family members continue to look at the train, scratching their heads.

I don't feel the weight of the train biting into my hips hard enough to leave bruises—the deep, angry kind that'll take days to fade. I barely feel the pinch of the impossibly tight corset or the way the boning pushes my breasts to unbelievable heights. I know I look stunning. This gown has been in production for months now, every stitch perfected, every bead of ruby, crystal, and moonstone carved, polished, and stitched in place with impeccable skill. The fabric is a deep, burnt crimson—dark, and heavy—and brings out the golden sheen to my skin. I slowly, carefully, turn just a touch to face the mirrors, running my fingertips over the neckline, which is wide, showing off my shoulders, before long sleeves of the same heavily beaded material cinch at my wrists.

"And once the ceremony is over, I think Sarah and Aviva should be the ones to take her aside and remove the train. You two are the strongest," Maddy says over the soft chords of conversation bouncing through the room. Sarah smirks at Aviva, her violet eyes dancing with both mischief and pride.

Misty scoffs at her mother, but Maddy waves her off, mentioning something about Misty needing to be ready to help stuff me into the car that will race me back to the castle where I'll step out onto the wide balcony overlooking the city and show my face to my public, my people, as their queen—for the first time.

The coronation is a private event—a sacred one. I'm not sure who all will be in attendance other than my family, but I do know my grandma Ella has been fielding press for days now, everyone clamoring to get their cameras into the temple to broadcast the ceremony.

"Maeve?"

I jerk, startled out of my mind as I turn to Maddy who appears at my side with Sarah. "Yeah? Sorry, I was just—just thinking..." My voice breaks as I turn away from my reflection. The dress is beautiful. The most beautiful thing I've ever worn. I picked the color out myself, spent ages going back and forth about the design, the details, the way it should fit.

But my reflection in the mirror was different then. While my powers are steadily, but slowly, returning as the moon cycle drifts closer to the full moon, the light in my eyes is gone, my cheeks hollow, my skin pale.

It's been easy enough to get away with it—with the eternal frown that now pinches my brows together like I have a constant, blinding headache. My family started arriving at the castle a few days ago in droves, everyone settling into their private, dedicated suites and preparing for the coronation and Sacred Rite to follow. The castle is busier than I've ever seen, and the noise is the distraction I needed from the agony tearing my heart to shreds.

I try to ignore it. I've been trying to ignore it since I came home two weeks ago. I'm used to wearing a mask of indifference, burying my feelings, pretending I'm a goddess, the fearless, all powerful witch, instead of just a heartbroken girl who just realized my life was broken into two parts.

Before him and after him.

"Let's get you out of the dress, honey," Maddy says gently. "It weighs a ton." Her silver hair is pulled back in a ponytail that shimmers against her shoulder. She and Misty start removing the train, with me gripping their shoulders to hold myself steady.

I watch Mom, Aviva, and Sarah on the far side of the room, a shouting distance away, while they stretch a tape measure across the width of the fabric, Aviva crawling on her hands and knees across it with the tape measurer clamped between her teeth while Sarah points at places without bead work, and I smile at the sight.

No one knows I was gone. No one knows I killed one man and fell in love with another.

It's killing me.

It takes them thirty minutes to get the gown off. Maddy helps me into a robe, wincing at the deep, red marks the boning left on my hips, breasts, and thighs before cinching the robe in place. "You look tired, Maeve. Are you feeling okay?"

"I haven't slept much," I admit, which is true. I smooth my fingers over my stomach, over the ache where the train rested on my hips. It was a bit tighter than before, but there's nothing I can do about it now other than make Jane force me to stop lying in bed, stuffing my face with chocolates and those croissants filled with vanilla cream I haven't been able to stop thinking about, which is the only time I'm not thinking about Soren.

"Go get some rest. Your grandma is handling the business end of things, so you have the night to yourself. We'll get you up bright and early to begin getting ready, however. Do you still want your hair up?"

I nod, bleary eyed, my gaze sliding to the windows where the golden light of sunset is starting to paint the sky.

This time tomorrow, I'll be kneeling in front of the High Priestess of Eastonia, the head of the church, while she crowns me queen.

My heart skips a beat as I hurry out of the room, nodding and giving tight smiles to the maids scurrying in every direction. I take the main stairs to the fifth floor, and in the wide, open stairwell that drops a dizzying all those stories from ceiling to the grand foyer, I can hear the ever persistent hum of the growing crowd beyond the castle gates.

I cut into a servants' hallway to make my journey to my private rooms a little shorter. At least, this is where I'm staying tonight before I officially move to my grandparents' old quarters, now that my renovations to the place are nearly done,

I slide through the door to my royal apartment and close it behind me with a sigh, drinking in the silence, but it's painful.

Beneath my feet, the carpet—the white, fluffy carpet Jane somehow managed to clean of Soren's blood, leaving not a single trace that he was here once, catches my attention, and I feel the tears I've been fighting every damn day since I came home burning along my lashes. I temporarily give in.

A single tear floats down my cheek. I wipe it away at the perfect moment because Brie huffs a breath as she comes into view, carrying a small suitcase of mine that she must have just fetched from my room.

"Oh, good. I wasn't sure they'd let you go yet." She smiles, looking radiant as usual.

"Where's K?" I ask, my voice like gravel, but I straighten and turn toward the sitting room where the view of the city, and the enormous crowd below, is now blocked by heavy curtains to shield us from view of the public.

"He's somewhere with Logan. I think all the guys have gathered upstairs for the day. Everyone's a little nervous," she adds under her breath, glancing at the windows as she sets the suitcase down. "I was just packing you something to wear to have handy after you go out on the balcony tomorrow. I figured you didn't want to have to walk through the castle in that heavy gown a second time just to change. I know the Mystics will have you in white when you bless the couple performing the Rite tomorrow night, anyway, so this is just a new shift, some slippers, socks, you know." She lifts one shoulder in a shrug, but her eyes are on the floor between us, on the carpet.

I haven't told Brie what happened. I want to. I curl my hands into fists at my sides as the agony of my heartbreak becomes too much to bear, but I just… can't.

I swallow it, burying it, adding another brick to the impenetrable wall of emotion now spiraling through my increasingly empty heart.

"Jane just dropped off a whole platter of pastries–"

I speed past her, nearly knocking her over in my haste to get to the little tea room where I normally take my meals, alone, because I'm constantly going to be alone here going forward, which is something I… I expected. Something I planned for without emotion, without feeling, because I'm already so alone in this world, even surrounded by family.

I grab one of the pastries, stuffing it into my mouth, not even tasting it.

"Are you okay?"

I wave Brie away. "Just hungry."

She gives me a look. "Are you sure? You've been… kind of off since we got here–"

"I'm fine, Brie. Goddess. Why is everyone asking me that? I'm being crowned in less than a day, and people want to know if I'm fine?" The words come out sharp and tangled.

My sister stares at me, wide eyed.

I huff a breath, closing my eyes and counting to ten to try to relax. "I'm just–I'm just due for my courses any day now, of course, and about to be stuffed into that monster of a gown and paraded in front of everyone. I'm tired. I'm hungry. I'm–I'm not feeling like myself."

"It's a lot of pressure, I totally understand," Brie begins, but I snap at her, again.

"You can't possibly know how it feels to be me."

She swallows back whatever reply she was about to say and sighs, plucking a pastry from the dish. "Maybe you should go to bed early tonight. It seems you could use it."

"There's no time. I have too much to do." I bite into another pastry before turning away from her. "Is Blake here yet? I need to talk to him."

"I haven't seen him, but I know he'll be here tomorrow for the coronation."

"Do you talk to him much?" I ask, perching on the armrest of the couch along the wall. "I've been trying to get face to face with him for months, but he's ignoring me. I haven't seen him since the family gathered for Solstice last year."

"That's the last time I saw him," she replies, eyeing me wearily. "Maeve, you're kind of worrying me. Your coloring isn't good. You're a little gray."

My stomach pitches, but I ignore it. "Like I just said, I'm due for my moon cycle. Of course, it's the worst timing possible. I'm a few days late, actually, so I'm just–" I look down at my hands. *Tell her. Just fucking tell her everything. She's your sister.*

"Do you need anything? Tea? Something for the pain?"

"I'm fine. I'm sorry I snapped at you."

"I know this is a lot, Maeve. I know having the entire family here is also… overwhelming. Trust me. I feel it, too." She lays a supportive hand on my shoulder. "But you've been waiting for this for years. You're ready. You know exactly what to do. Being queen isn't the hard part."

"Then what's the hard part?" I laugh, but tears fill my eyes against my will.

"Remaining you," she answers, a sad smile touching the corners of her mouth. "Being Maeve, not just Queen Maeve."

She has no clue. No idea that I spent a week free, untethered by my status, our family, the crushing responsibilities now saddled on my shoulders.

She has no idea I met someone who changed my life, and I have to take the secret of *him* to my grave.

He also… knew that there was no future with us together. He's a murderer, a criminal, and I'm… *this*.

"I love you," Brie says softly, pressing a kiss to the top of my head. "You're going to be fine, whatever comes."

The next morning, the city descends into organized chaos with me at its center.

PUT ON A SHOW

Moonrise roars as I wait in the shadowed foyer of the temple. Just feet away, a heavy set of doors will soon open to the sanctuary of the sacred place where hundreds of people are gathered to bear witness to my ascension to the throne, while a few steps in the other direction, behind yet another set of doors, the city is buzzing with nervous excitement.

I'm alone for the first time since I opened my eyes this morning. My reflection in a mirror on the far wall of the foyer isn't... me. The tall, lean young woman in an immaculate crimson gown stares blankly back at me, her eyelids dusted with gold and her wide, full lips painted a deep, dark red.

Her eyes are hard and hollow–dead–but still that familiar sea-green.

I reach up to run my fingers over the simple updo a trio of maids spent over an hour creating. My hair is pulled tight against my scalp and twisted into a neat bun on the top of my head, not a hair out of place. A band of brilliant rubies and flawless black diamonds rests over the center of my forehead, set in gold, with a veil attached that's made of the same impeccable gems that trails all the way to the floor like I'm being showered in gemstones.

It's heavy, but I don't feel the weight. My mind is blank, honed on the buzz of noise all around me, as I stare at my reflection.

I reach along my neckline where the moonstone necklace should be.

"Are you ready? It's nearly time," Grandpa Ryatt asks from the shadows before he appears, dressed in all black. His ebony hair is peppered with gray. He steps into the faint light pouring through tall stained glass windows. He trimmed his beard and is looking more put together than I've seen him in the days since he and my grandma arrived back at the castle for this very moment.

"I am ready," I reply, but there's no emotion in my voice. I turn away from my reflection, gazing at the doors instead.

"I was told to give you a five minute warning," he says, stepping closer before coming to a stop a foot away and checking his watch.

"Are you going to walk me down the aisle?" I ask after a beat of silence, but there isn't a teasing glint to my voice like I planned. Dead. Dead words, dead heart. I woke up this morning feeling... changed. Changed back, I suppose, to what I was before. Back to the woman I trained to be, the woman I promised myself I'd be because I didn't think I had another option.

Grandpa smirks, shaking his head. "If it were your wedding, yes, but I'm sure your father would like the honor."

"It might as well be," I say under my breath, smoothing my jeweled fingers over my midriff, breathing past the tight ache in my stomach.

"What do you mean?" he chuckles, but music begins to play within the temple, and the shuffle of feet as people rise, just out of sight, make my spine straighten.

I turn to my grandfather, the man who's been ruling beside my grandmother for the past... fifty years, almost, and meet his eyes when I say, "I doubt I'll get married, so this is it. This is my wedding. My marriage is to Eastonia."

Grandpa's smile fades, turning to a tight line as he scans my face. "Is that really how you feel?"

"It's what I know," I breathe, turning to face the door again. I slam a wall against the memory of Soren's mouth against the shell of my ear, his breath hot on my cheek while he whispers, *"You know exactly who you are,"* against my skin.

It was a compliment. It was something he... he saw and liked. Something he reminded me about constantly. He knew what I was capable of and yet never once flinched away from my touch.

In fact, he saw through me, saw the girl beneath the wall of fiery armor I'd built around myself from the moment I was old enough to realize I was something people feared.

And I know without a shadow of a doubt no one will ever see me like Soren did again because... *I don't want them to.*

I suck in a breath as a dozen maids funnel out of a side door, ignoring the skeptical look Grandpa Ryatt's throwing in my direction. His shoulders tighten as I tilt my chin, closing my eyes and forcing myself to tuck every other feeling away.

I am Queen of Eastonia. This is my birthright. This moment is the dawn of a new era.

As the maids unravel my tremendously long train, I turn to my grandpa, giving him a sharp, diplomatic nod. "Thank you for all you've done as king."

"Maeve, we should talk."

"Another time," I reply tightly, but he shakes his head.

"I didn't overthrow a corrupt regime for you to spend the rest of your young life alone," he says, but the doors open wide, revealing the sanctuary bathed in the light of the sunset and the hundreds of people–guests of honor–here to witness... *me.*

I feel his fingers dust my arm in an attempt to make me wait, but I step out of the foyer, ignoring the pull against my hips as the train snaps tight, a crimson river of fabric that cascades behind me as I begin to climb the steps to the rise where the high priestess is waiting for me.

Hundreds of eyes lock on my face, my body, the gathered

onlookers hushed into unnerving silence as they watch their queen, their beast, their demi-goddess, rise to her power.

I think of climbing on that table in the bar as I step up. I pass eager reporters, the blessed few whom my grandma allowed access to the coronation, knowing their cameras are live-streaming my every move to the crowd outside of the temple and around the Allied Kingdoms.

A roar echoes beyond the walls of the temple as the crowded streets erupt in excitement. I pass where my family is gathered. My parents, my cousins–all of them–everyone watches in silence as I pass, but my parents give me small, encouraging smiles.

I wonder what they're thinking, if they're happy, or worried, or maybe a bit of both.

Blake and Brie stand side by side, with Logan on Brie's other side holding a wriggly Kieran, who immediately lights up when he sees me. Blake, dressed in black with his dark red-brown hair swept away from his face, remains stoic and void of emotion, but his violet eyes scan my face before he turns to whisper to Brie.

My sister is just… lit up from within, and it gives me the boost I need to climb the last steps and stand before the priestess.

I already know what she's going to say. I know the ceremony by heart because I've practiced the steps, the words, the vows. Silence hugs the temple, but my heartbeat is loud, booming through my ears, when I'm made to kneel before her, tilting my head down.

Grandma Ella appears before me, Grandpa Ryatt beside her, and I feel the weight of a crown placed on my head. A crown of precious stones–gems from every corner of Eastonia. Emeralds, sapphires, and polished obsidian from Veiled Valley. Diamonds, turquoise, and aquamarine from Tarsian. Rubies and emeralds from the Roguelands.

And moonstones from Moonrise that glow a bright crimson as my powers ignite the moment the crown is placed on my head.

"Rise, Queen Maeve," Grandma whispers, a soft smile in her tone as I slowly look up at the woman who did the impossible, the woman who pulled this ancient city from the lake, who freed a nation with her mate by her side.

They couldn't have known it would all be for me.

I can't let them down.

Grandma and Grandpa take each of my hands, helping me straighten, and then I turn to the crowd.

The applause inside is muted, but outside… Moonrise explodes in noise.

I barely register the moment. Everything is sound and color as I leave the temple, Aviva and Sarah quickly removing the heavy, beaded train while Misty guides me into a waiting car to rush me back to the castle. Brie slips in beside me, trembling with nerves and excitement as we're driven down roads purposefully closed off for this, but it's impossible not to see the groups of people situated on rooftops, clambering for a view of the balcony where I'll make my first appearance to the public, my people, as their queen.

"Did that really happen?" she asks breathlessly, gripping my hand as the blacked out car skids around a sharp corner, the back gates of the castle opening wide to allow my family's procession of vehicles entrance. "You're Queen of Eastonia?"

"I am," I breathe, the first words I've said since the ceremony, when I vowed to protect and serve the Goddess above all others. My heart barely beats as Brie hurries me out of the car, and we rejoin the family, everyone whispering excitedly, uncontrollably, while following me into the castle's depths. Brie stays close, but to my surprise, I feel Blake come up behind me, steadying me with a hand gripping my elbow as we walk the steps to the fourth floor where the wide balcony opens to a view of the city.

Grandma and Grandpa go first, stepping out onto the balcony side by side to the roar of the crowd. The sunset has faded into streaks of violet against the clouds where the full moon begins to rise, the countdown the eclipse, and the Sacred Rite, beginning.

"You look great," Brie says in a hushed whisper as she adjusts the impossibly heavy crown on my head, taking a few pins from her hair to secure it in place. Blake waits beside us, his eyes on the balcony while Grandma and Grandpa give a wave down to their people for the last time as king and queen.

My heart pounds while Brie and my mom fiddle with my gown,

my hair, and my jewelry, but my eyes are on Blake for some reason. I haven't seen him in months.

"We need to talk," I say to him, and he glances at me, his face as emotionless as ever. "Tomorrow morning. I mean it, Blake."

His answer is the slightest of smirks.

I grind my teeth but Grandma and Grandpa start backing up, turning toward the doors. "This is it," Brie breathes. "What are you going to say?"

"Nothing," I answer, which elicits a confused look from both my sister and my mom.

"You're not going to say anything to your people?" Mom asks, genuinely confused.

"No," I say with a shrug, then glance at Blake, who is just... staring at me. Staring at my chest, where the moonstone necklace is missing. "Not yet. Not now. They don't care about that," I continue, looking away from Blake and stepping past my mom and Brie. "They just want to see what I can do."

I turn to look at the rest of my family, everyone dressed in their finery, everyone looking both nervous and excited as my grandparents step back inside, and the crowd beyond the castle walls turns from roars to muted whispers of anticipation.

There's... nothing I can say. We all knew this was coming. I was born for this. I was made for this.

But... that girl–that excited, over-confident idiot who thought she had everything she needed, and wanted, in the palm of her hand?

She's gone. I left her on that train platform when I bent to kiss Soren's cheek, biting back the truth I desperately wanted to share with him.

That I regret it–leaving him. I didn't want to. I wouldn't have. Had he felt the same, I would have thrown all of this away and disappeared, going somewhere we could be... us. Together.

I squeeze my eyes shut against a wave of grief and nausea that washes through my stomach, stifled by the boning of the gown, and step onto the balcony.

The crowd goes silent. All across the city, the massive group of celebrators gazes up at me as I walk to the edge of the balcony. I scan the crowd, my face etched from stone, void and stern.

I will not be known for my kindness, my grace. I will be known for ruling with a fist of iron, with a voice that carries and demands justice. I know Blake refers to me as Bloody Maeve. Some people think he's joking, but maybe he's seen this in my timeline–this heartbreak that serves as the catalyst that turns me to iron, once and for all.

I let the crowd see it. I know my face is blown up, zoomed in for everyone across the Allied Kingdoms to witness. I let them see that fire in my eyes as my powers simmer, scratching and clawing to the surface as I summon them for the first time since I left Soren and returned to startling reality.

The full moon beckons, and even with the eclipse on the horizon, just an hour or so away, I feel… more powerful than I've ever been.

And I don't have a necklace to absorb the excess. I could bring this city to its knees in one swift motion of my wrist.

I could burn any trace of my world from existence in the blink of an eye.

But I look at the faces of my people, taking them in, seeing the excitement and promise of a future in their eyes, a future I vowed to protect.

I know its… impossible, but I look–I search until I feel my knees going weak–for one set of eyes in particular before I raise my hands and let my powers ignite, showing Moonrise–showing Eastonia–who their queen has become after years out of their view.

And I wonder if Soren can see it, and if he's… smiling.

Because I'd give anything to see it one last time.

FROM A DISTANCE

Soren

Moonrise has officially descended into hell.

I can readily admit I'm not one for crowds. I like being alone. I enjoy peace and quiet. I dislike being pushed and shoved, and I sure as hell hate seeing every street swarmed with people, most of them sloppy drunk after a day of festivities, all of them clamoring for a view of the woman who just appeared on the wide, regal balcony of white marble overlooking the city center.

Giant screens project close up shots of Maeve as she walks into view, her face set in an expression so sharp it pierces right through my chest, which warms with pride.

Patton's unable to stand still beside me and begins pacing the rooftop we've been lounging on for what feels like hours. My skin prickles from the insane heat of the day, even now that the sun has set, but I don't pay the sunburn on my cheeks any mind.

No, I just look at her. Watch her. Watch the way her shoulders tighten and that impeccable posture lengthens as she strides to the edge of the balcony, those eyes bright as a flame.

"Do it," I murmur to myself, low and soft enough that Patton can't hear the words over the shuffling of his sneakers. "Do it, Maeve. Come on. Show them who you are."

The gems falling from the band on her forehead look like liquid, bloody rain. The crown atop her head sparkles as it catches the moonlight and soft glow of the scones all along the balcony. I didn't get to see her like this. I saw her at her rawest, dressed in just her skin. Before that, in borrowed clothes that didn't fit, dancing on a table in a bar with the widest, brightest, most sincere smile on that devastatingly stunning face.

But this... this is her, down to the marrow of her bones. The queen. The witch. A goddess reincarnated. The promise of death by fire.

I lean forward, folding my arms over a rooftop AC unit, and drink her in.

"What do you think she's going to say?" Patton asks excitedly, coming to a stop beside me. We both smell like cheap beer and the narrow cigars we've been smoking since this afternoon, taking in the reverie, forcing myself to ignore the plucking, burning sensation in my chest anytime a glimpse of her would appear on the screens hung from the tallest buildings in the city, her image projected for everyone to see.

I'd watched the coronation, of course, like the rest of the city although none of us common folk were allowed within the sanctuary of the temple. I was glued to the scene as she ascended those steps, took her vows, and knelt. She hadn't smiled. Not once. No, her face had been set in that trained expression of conviction, just like I expected, and honestly, I was thankful for it.

That smile is *mine*. There's no way around it, no way to erase the feeling of possessiveness even though it's over before it ever truly began.

"She's not going to say anything," I reply after a beat, watching as she continues to scan the crowd. I catch a single flicker of emotion barely visible to the naked eye. It's something I've seen before, something now branded in my mind.

Disappointment.

I roll my lower lip between my teeth and straighten, crossing my arms over my chest. "Do it, Maeve. Just do it."

"What did you say?" Patton asks, his voice lifted in nervous excitement.

"Nothing," I murmur, but my eyes remain locked on Maeve, blocks away, as she raises her hands.

I can feel the light of the full moon whispering over my skin, calling to my wolf, just like it's calling to those powers I pray she let recover over the past weeks. I drum my fingers against my arms, waiting impatiently, for her to just… unburden herself, to dig past the barriers she's built to keep her magic in check because she's terrified of it and what people will think when they witness it, witness her.

Her eyes glow, turning from that bright sea-green to a sharp, unfiltered amber. A hush whispers through the crowd gathered on the street below, huddled around one of the screens.

I catch the faint golden glow rippling through her skin before she lifts her hands. A tremor washes through Moonrise, the three-story building we're perched atop rattling as that golden glow ignites.

"More," I hiss under my breath, unable to stand still. I brace my hands on the AC unit, bowing my head for a second before watching her again, this time peering past the screen, between buildings, to the balcony several blocks away. "Come on, girl. Give it more."

The lights in the city shudder out, flickering as the hum of electricity dies. Even the power her grandfather still supplies using his magic whispers away, and a wave of darkness washes through Moonrise before Maeve stretches her hands above her head, her brow pinched in concentration.

Shouts of awe spiced with sudden fear echo through the crowd below.

"Maeve," I growl, my eyes back on the screen, on the trembling close-up shot still lighting up the street below. A flicker of hesitation passes behind her eyes, and I… gods, I nearly lose my nerve. I could run to her, parting the crowd, screaming her name and telling her to just do it, to show them, *show them who you are.*

A crackle of energy explodes, followed by a shockwave that tears through the city. A dizzying, damn near unsettling light expands overhead as Maeve splits the sky in half, sending her light over Moonrise in a cascade of fireworks in hues of bright red, deep crimson, and the brightest, star filled purple. Screams of fear quickly turn to shouts of awe, and then the rolling, thunderous applause and shouts of excitement begin, drowning out the blood racing through my ears.

Most people are looking up.

I'm looking at her.

"Good girl," I whisper, my entire body on edge as my chest convulses, making it damn near impossible to fill my lungs. "More."

"How is she doing this?" Patton shouts nearby, his eyes wide and mouth gaping in astonishment.

I ignore him, watching as she strains against her magic to paint the sky with her powers again like she's taking a brush to the stars, creating a masterpiece I can't even begin to put into words. I can taste her magic. It's everywhere, touching everything, coating the city in stardust as it begins to settle on every rooftop and crowded street.

The lights return, flickering back into existence as her fireworks settle, and the roar of the crowd expands, drowning out my thundering heart and Patton's excited laughter.

I'm not laughing.

I watch as Maeve lowers her hands and opens her eyes, her expression tight, and her skin going a ghostly pale beneath the layer of makeup that makes her look like a completely different person— older and harder.

She takes a single stumbling step away from the railing. My body jerks, but I rein myself back in when her sister appears in the background, reaching for her, her hand gripping Maeve's forearm as she slowly moves out of sight.

And that's it.

It's over.

Maeve is now the Queen of Eastonia like she was always meant to be.

The city below breaks into song and dance as minutes rush by. A candle-lit procession weaves through the streets as a dozen Mystics in their silver-white robes guide the couple chosen for the Sacred Rite through the crowd. I stay on the roof with Patton for another twenty minutes before we make our way down to the street, cutting through the crowds toward the lake where a huge party is taking place all along the shore with bonfires and music.

Patton has some friends in Moonrise, people he met during his days as a prostitute, I suppose. A client of his, in fact, is the reason we're here today with a roof over our heads tonight. I don't like it, but I'm keeping my mouth shut about it because I know this means the world to Patton and I just... after seeing the crowds and the look on King Ryatt's face, the beat of unease... I had to come.

While Patton makes the rounds at the beach, I sit on the rocky shore, enjoying the cool night air as I watch the stars reflect on the glassy surface. Across the lake, against the mountain, the ancient temple's gates are open, and the candlelit procession comes to a stop.

I leave forward over my knees, watching as a cloaked figure stands before the couple, her hand moving in a motion like she's blessing them.

The corner of my mouth tugs into a half smile as I watch Maeve turn, returning to the six or so guards who followed her every move to the temple gates to bless the couple, to bless the Rite that marks the beginning of what I know will be a long, prosperous rule.

She has no idea I'm here, and that's probably a good thing. I couldn't handle it otherwise. I thought it would be easier than this. We had a week together, most of that spent fighting, bickering, mouthing off, but...

I scrub my hand down my face, turning away from the lake as I rise but pause when a man dressed in black starts walking in my direction away from the bonfires.

My spine straightens vertebrae by vertebrae as the familiar posture, the broad shoulders, and black gloves, come into the view. The dark mask covers his entire face, like usual. He's not wearing his black beanie, though, and his hair is dark, neatly slicked back as he gains ground, every step he takes dripping with determination.

"For fuck's sake," I growl, giving the Architect an exasperated scoff. "Here? Really, man? There's thousands of people gathered on the beach alone. I thought we were done with this."

He grabs my arm and yanks me closer to the shore, into the shadows of a crop of trees. I rip my arm from his grasp and give him a sharp shove. "Don't ever touch me again. That isn't how this works."

He stares at me for a moment before reaching into the inside pocket of what I realize is a finely tailored tuxedo jacket. I narrow my eyes, watching every move he makes as he pulls a stack of envelopes from the pocket and hands them to me.

I fan through the envelopes, reading the vague notes for each one, everything written neatly in that strange handwriting on graph paper.

"Everyone needs to be moved into hiding," he says in a deep, clear voice. "Their families, too."

I'm not wearing a jacket since it's eighty degrees, even during a full eclipse, but I slide the envelopes into the waistband of my jeans, tucking them behind the cover of my shirt. "Why?"

"You don't ask questions."

"I feel like I'm entitled to know at this point. You're telling me to move three Betas, a commander of the King of Crescent Fall's army, and an Alpha's son into hiding with their families? That could easily be over fifty people–"

"And you've just been paid accordingly–"

"Who do you work for?" I ask sharply, cutting him off.

He stares at me, really *looks* at me from behind that thick mask. I catch the faintest tilt of his head, like he's considering something, before he says, "I work for my own best interests."

"And to whom do those interests align?" I grit out, arching a brow.

"What are you asking?"

I step into him, and he doesn't back away. "Where," I rasp into his ear, "does your loyalty lie?"

Now he backs up, his shoulders rigid as he stares at me, his hands balling into fists.

We're the same height–both tall and equally built. I've never once felt intimidated by him, but there's something strange about the man that I can't put my finger on.

He's dangerous. He knows it. I know it.

The thing is, I'm not afraid of him, and I think he knows that, too.

"It doesn't matter," he replies dryly.

"It matters to me."

A low chuckle echoes from behind the mask. "Don't tell me you're starting to fall into Hannibal's web–"

"I am loyal to my *queen*," I snarl. "Does this benefit her? That's all I want to know."

The Architect flinches like the admission startled him. He starts to turn away then stops, slowly looking over his shoulder to scan me from head to toe and back again. "You need to be more careful," he says, his tone tight and serious. "Move them by next month. I'll find you once it's done." He disappears in a shimmer of black mist that sparkles like purple-hued starlight.

I stand on the shore for a few more minutes, just staring–staring at the place where the man turned to stardust. He's like Maeve in a way that makes me uneasy. Somewhere on the shore, in the distance, I hear Patton's laugh over the chaos of music and excitement, and feel... the urge to get somewhere quiet, even if just for a moment.

My feet carry me back into town with no set direction or end point. Within minutes, I find myself on a quiet street with flickering lights, just outside of the festival's reach. Yellow walls suck me in, and the smell of herbs settles my senses, slowly bringing me back to reality as a young, dark haired woman blinks up at me expectantly over the glare of two wide, but very old, TVs playing chopped up footage of Maeve's light show.

I pick up the pen she uses to scribble orders, clicking it as I slide a large hot-to-go cup from a sleeve on the counter. "Do you deliver to the castle?" I ask.

She shrugs one shoulder. "I suppose."

I pause, the pen tip pressed against the cup. "This is for someone named Jane. She'll know what to do with it," I say under my breath and write the only thing that comes to mind, handing the cup to the young woman. "Double chamomile with enough honey to drown out the taste."

DELEGATION OF POWER

MAEVE

IT'S THE MIDDLE OF THE NIGHT WHEN I FINALLY SLIDE INTO MY PRIVATE apartment. Boxes of my things are stacked precariously around the foyer, all labeled to be delivered to specific rooms in the massive royal suite that takes up an entire floor two stories above me. My head pounds from wearing the crown and all the jewels that dangled from my forehead for hours even though I undressed immediately after coming off the balcony. That was hours ago.

Now, I'm wearing the white ceremonial gown from when I blessed the couple performing the Rite and a dark navy blue cloak. It smells like the smoke that drifted off the lake where dozens of bonfires were burning.

After the Rite, I was escorted back to the castle where a party for my grandparents was being held. It had a very select guest list, but party goers still filled the formal ballroom, and even now, in the dead of night, I can still hear the music drifting through the castle.

I assume everyone else is asleep by now. It's been the longest day of my life, and the reality of what happened today hasn't quite settled in yet, I suppose.

I am Queen of Eastonia.

Now what?

I'm pulling on pajama pants and buttoning the silken, matching shirt when Jane announces her presence. She floats into my bedroom, her figure cast in shadow as she peeks her head around the door, knocking softly.

"I thought you'd be asleep by now, Jane," I say into the shadows, reaching up to rub my tired eyes.

"I have… I have something for you, I think."

I arch a brow, turning from my vanity to face her as she glides into the room holding a large to-go cup. I recognize where it's from immediately and frown, my brows pinched in confusion. "Did you go out and get that?"

"No, it was delivered at the back gate. Niall's on guard tonight," she begins, mentioning the tall, dark haired warrior. I've been impressed by his dedication to his job as a castle guard, taking notes and making plans to promote him when the time is right. "And he said this was for me, but… I don't think it is."

I search her eyes, running my tongue over my lower lip. She knows I was with Soren for a week but not the full extent of it. I told her what I had–that I hunted him down, but was… unsuccessful in bringing him to justice.

It couldn't be further from the truth of what actually happened.

She sets the to-go cup on the edge of the vanity and steps away, giving me a gentle bow before whispering, "Goodnight, Your Majesty."

I swallow hard, nodding, and she slips from the room. I don't move until her footsteps fade, and I hear the echoing, tell-tale click of the main door snapping shut.

I smell chamomile and honey. I let the scent drift around me, settling in my bones, cutting through the waves of nausea that have been plaguing all day. I've barely eaten today. I haven't had time, and the promise of honey makes my mouth water, but I find it impossible to move.

There's a heat sleeve on the cup. I see the edge of a pen mark in thick black ink over the rolled, soft cardboard. I reach for it, sliding it down and gazing at what I realize is unfamiliar handwriting because I've never seen Soren's handwriting before.

"You never needed that necklace."

I sniffle, shaking my head, and bring the tea to my lips while squeezing my eyes shut against the knowledge that Soren was here, in Moonrise. That he could still be here, right now, somewhere in the city, and I... I can't go to him.

But he *was* here. He watched my coronation. He watched me use my powers to paint the sky.

I take a deep breath, fighting the smile tugging at my lips, and take a sip.

The tea is perfect, exactly how I like it.

Three Days Later

"Nothing will change between Eastonia and Crescent Falls," I say from my desk, my words directed at Sydney, who's standing in the crowd of family members stationed around my official office, leaning on furniture or the walls. "As it stands, our trade negotiations need no adjustments. I'm happy with how they are."

Sydney nods, stifling a smile. "I am, as well."

"Then we can table any discussion about our future as allies until later this winter when I come to Crescent Falls for the summit with Lunaria and Celestoria."

Sydney takes this as the dismissal he's likely been waiting for since the family gathered here after breakfast, which I didn't attend. He turns to Sarah, who's beaming at me, trying to hide her excitement at seeing me behind this desk, in this office, that used to belong to my grandmother but now belongs to me.

The family starts to funnel out of the room, but I say, "Lexa and Aris, please stay."

Lexa turns to Aviva and Ryan, tilting a brow as she smirks, and turns back to me as her parents leave.

"You too, Blake," I grumble, but Blake hasn't made any moves to leave the window where he's leaning, watching the sleepy city below. People are literally asleep in the streets. The celebration didn't cease until the sun rose, and even now, days later, music still drifts over the quiet hum of activity within the castle.

When everyone else has left the room, save for my grandpa and my dad, I motion toward Aris, looking down at my agenda while saying, "Aris, I'm going to be moving you to Moonrise for a few months. You'll be in the barracks at the training center and will keep an office there. I'm making you a captain in my royal forces, and you'll oversee the training facility there as an administrator," I tell him, meeting his eyes. I turn to Lexa for my next order of business, "Lexa, I want you in Moonrise as well starting after the Harvest Festival. I need you training with the Ghosts, as well as my royal forces. I want someone like you in command, as well. It would mean spending most of your time in Moonrise this fall, winter, and spring, and returning to your duties in Silverhide next summer."

She crosses her arms under her chest, standing tall and stoic, nearly as tall as Aris, who is currently slumping. Her dark, impressively curly brown hair trembles as her dark blue eyes narrow.

I continue. "I'm making you a captain in my forces, directly below your mother's command. You'll stay here this winter, train not only the Ghosts who run their training camps in the city but my warriors as well. You'll be given a townhouse in the city just beyond the castle gates and will be free to visit the Deadlands any time you like. Is this something you'd be interested in?"

"Of course," she smiles. "I'll plan on it."

"Good." I click my pen, crossing another item off the list.

Aris grumbles his way out of my office, Lexa hot on his heels as she chuckles under her breath about how she gets a townhouse, and Aris has to stay in the barracks, but I pay them no mind.

I glance up from my agenda at my father and grandfather. "Grandpa Ryatt," I say, straightening my spine, "you'll be in retirement, but I may call on you from time to time. For now, you're dismissed." There isn't an ounce of emotion in my voice, and he arches a brow, giving my father a look before leaving the room.

To Dad, I say in dismissal, "I'll be visiting your offices in Veiled Valley next week to discuss my plans for the Ghosts and where I need them stationed. For now, I'm fine as is."

Dad moves toward the desk. I look back down at my agenda when he puts a hand on my shoulder, squeezing, then leaves, shutting the door behind him—shutting me in with Blake.

His soft, deep chuckle reverberates through the room as I flip through the pages of my agenda.

"What's so funny?" I ask, shooting him a glare.

"Nothing," he says, but I see the ghost of a smile touching his lips as he turns from the window. "You just dismissed the most feared man in the Allied Kingdom without so much as blinking."

"He's *my* grandfather," I reply tightly. "Anyway, he's done. He's retired."

"He's still King of the Roguelands seeing as no one has been chosen for that title–"

"It is no longer a title. I am Queen of Eastonia, which includes the Roguelands." I click my pen and scribble a few notes about my meetings this afternoon, ignoring the pang of discomfort in my stomach that woke me up this morning and hasn't stopped since. "This is what they wanted, Blake. Otherwise I'd still be preparing to be queen, and they'd be ruling."

He stares at me, but I ignore the way his eyes are boring into my skull. "You seem off."

"Like you actually care." I chuckle, rolling my eyes. "I'm busy, that's all."

"Did you need me for something? I'd like to return to my parents and prepare to go home. We're traveling together."

"You will not be returning to Crescent Falls with them today." I meet his eyes in a silent challenge.

"This again." He sighs, turning to the window while checking his watch. "You already know my answer."

"I'm not asking."

He glares but my spine turns to steel as I let my powers shimmer behind my eyes.

"What exactly do you need me for, Maeve? Paperwork? Doing your heavy lifting? Being the bad guy?"

"You already know what I'm going to say, Blake. You are not meant for Crescent Falls, and that's becoming more apparent the older you get and the more powerful you become."

"You don't get to decide that for me."

"I don't have to. You know what your future holds. You've seen it. You've seen mine, as well–"

"I have not," he cuts in. "Our powers aren't compatible. I can't see your timeline. I don't know what your future holds, and even if I had the ability to look inside your head, I wouldn't dare."

"But you've seen yours."

"No," he replies in a hushed whisper. "I haven't. Would you want to know the day you die? Or who you'll love and lose?"

I look down my hands, curling them into fists in my lap. I've already done that last part, haven't I? "I need you here in Moonrise to continue the hunt for the Spider. More importantly, I need you to find someone for me who goes by the name the Viper. I believe she's a woman."

He pauses, slowly looking at me like the name is familiar. "What's your business with the Viper?"

"Then you're aware of her existence–"

"She's a powerful underlord with ties to the Spider, yes. I am aware and so is your father. His Ghosts have been hunting her for years."

"Well, I may know where she keeps her den. It'll be in Twin Rivers, if not in what used to be Rifthold. I want you to choose a few loyal warriors, whoever has skills to go undercover and sniff her out. Watch her, at least."

"What do you plan to do?"

"Nothing for now," I admit, leaning back in my chair and swallowing against the sudden urge to throw up. My words tremble as I bite out, "She'll lead us to Hannibal, and that's enough."

"You look unwell," he says, ignoring my statement.

"I'm tired, Blake."

But he's staring at me again with that strange, all seeing gaze. Maybe the gray hue in my cheeks and my bloodshot eyes are making him feel a shred of empathy for me because he sighs, rolling his eyes to the ceiling. "I've been giving your... offer some thought."

"Oh?"

"I will keep an office here, in the castle, one of my choosing. I prefer the east wing."

"I don't care."

He ignores my interjection, pacing to the opposite side of the room and back. "I'll split my time between here and my duties to *my* kingdom, but I'm not giving up my title as Royal Prince yet. Liam isn't ready."

"Liam is already the Alpha of Shadowcrest," I interrupt.

"He's not ready," he reasserts. "He's not ready to rule with you as an ally, I mean. You scare him to death."

"And he's not scared of you?" I chuckle.

"He's used to me."

"So what exactly are you saying, Blake?"

"I'm saying I will act as your second but not full time, not yet. I have business to attend to in Crescent Falls, responsibilities I have to see through. Until then, you can have me a week out of every month or so. And, again, I get to choose my office and keep a private suite in the castle."

"Whatever you want." I shrug. "But I want you here two weeks out of every month."

He glares but I hold his gaze in challenge.

"It's a paid position," I sigh, wincing as another wave of nausea rolls through me. I cover my mouth with my hand, and I can feel Blake eyeing me with marked concern. "That's all I need. You may go–"

"Are you ill?"

"I've never been ill a day in my life–"

"You look sick–"

"I used an incredible amount of power this week during a time when my powers were already at their lowest." I rise, knowing I'm now biding time. My stomach curls as I move swiftly toward the door.

"Maeve," Blake calls out, but I'm already hurrying out of my office and cutting into the servants corridor, racing toward the stairs, which I take to the fourth floor. I'm barely in my suite when the nausea overcomes me.

I'M NOT SICK

MAEVE

MY FAMILY HAS GATHERED FOR A FINAL SUPPER BEFORE EVERYONE GOES back to their usual lives. I sit at the head of the table, picking at my food, my stomach still in knots. I feel hot and cold at the same time, which is unnerving. I don't get sick. Not unless I exhaust my powers, but the last few days have been… a real test of my limits, I suppose.

This isn't a formal dinner by any means. Everyone is dressed comfortably and moving around, mingling in small groups. Kieran is asleep in Logan's arms while he and Brie talk in quiet tones to my parents, while Sydney, my grandpa, and my father talk to Ryan on the far side of the room, glasses of whiskey in their hands as they stand near one of the windows overlooking the city below.

I had the meal setup in one of the upstairs rooms–the pink room, we call it. It's wide and deep, with enough room to fit the entire family comfortably. It used to be a playroom. I remember being here as a kid with Maddy watching over all of us while the other adults held meetings or took a moment to themselves whenever the family gathered.

This place used to feel so warm and inviting. I split my time between here and the castle in Veiled Valley growing up. I have memories of racing up and down the hallways here and scaling the bookshelves in the library. I remember every room being full of people and lively chatter.

But a few hours from now, the castle will be ghostly silent again, with just me in attendance to fill the void of sound.

Aviva moves down the long table to sit beside me, smoothing her wild, untamable red curls away from her face. I've always liked her. She was my age when she married Ryan and joined the family. I was only a year old or so, I guess, but I have memories of seeking her out as a young child. I find her feral nature strangely calming.

"Lexa told me you offered her a position here in Moonrise," she says by way of greeting, glancing down the table at her two daughters, Lexa and Nora.

Both look like Ryan with their height, but Nora, the youngest, inherited her mother's red hair and amber eyes. She's shy and quiet, however, compared to Lexa, who is loud and brave like her parents.

"Is that a problem for you and Ryan?"

"Not at all. Lexa's ready for a bit of separation, I think."

"She'll return next spring, of course. I don't mean to make this a permanent move. I just need my forces better trained. I'd ask you to move, too, but your duties as Luna of the Deadlands make that a tricky process to navigate as it stands." I reach for my untouched glass of wine but think better of it, returning it to the table. "I'll be on my tour of the kingdom for the next four or five months, anyway. She'll be taken care of here, though."

I can feel Aviva watching me closely, scanning my profile, when she says, "I'm sure Lexa's tenure here will be good for her. She's been leading her own group of warriors in the Deadlands for a few months now under my command." She sighs, turning from me to look at her daughters instead. "She'll make a fine Alpha one day. She's just like her father."

"She will," I agree but notice Aviva looking at Nora with a sad kind of expression. "And Nora will... break out of her shell eventually."

"I want to ask you something. Something I hope you'll consider."

"Okay," I reply slowly, not liking her somewhat uneasy tone.

"Would you consider allowing Nora to come with Lexa to Moonrise for the winter? Nora is an amazing painter, like your grandmother Ella. There's a few masters here she could train with, and Ella and I have discussed sending Nora to Veiled Valley for a few weeks to train under her, as well. It's what Nora loves, and I sometimes wonder if she feels like she's stuck in Lexa's shadow."

I glance at the young women at the far end of the table. "That would be fine. Lexa's been offered her own townhouse. It's perfectly safe and in a secured neighborhood."

Aviva nods, smiling to herself. "She'll be so excited."

I shimmy in my chair, scanning the room for Ryan, who's still with a group of the men by the window. "Won't it be odd to have your house to yourself again?" I ask before I can stop myself. "Just you and Ryan?"

Aviva chuckles, taking a sip of her wine before replying, "Relationships happen fast in this family, Maeve. Ryan and I only had a little under a year together before Lexa came into our lives. In a way... I feel like I'll be getting him back after a while apart."

Something shifts in my chest. I feel that sucking, drowning sensation spreading in the pit of my stomach, flaring up my spine and into my chest.

"Are you okay, Maeve? You look sad," Aviva asks, nudging me with her shoulder.

"I'm totally fine," I lie, grinning through tears now beginning to well along my lower lash line. Lie, lie, lie. That's all I've done for the past weeks, especially with my family here. No one has a clue what happened to me, and I'll keep it that way forever, tucking Soren into the furthest recesses of my mind until I forget about him.

It's not like we had much time together in the first place. A single night, honestly, where we both acted on our real feelings. It wasn't meant to be. It was... fun. A moment of distraction. An adventure.

But my heart cracks every time I think of him, or catch his scent lingering on the old leather jacket hanging in the very back of my closet, its pockets full of his old IDs. I never had a chance to give it back after Jane and I stripped him down that day before everything changed.

"Maeve, honey, you look exhausted," Mom says in a rush as she appears at my other side. "You need to go to bed, I think."

"I'll stay to tell everyone goodbye," I argue, but she shakes her head.

"Don't worry about it. Go upstairs and sleep. I know Jane had some of the guards finish moving your things into your new suite and finished setting up the furniture. I put a basket with herbs and salts for your bath in the main bathroom, so that's what you should do tonight. Take a bath, relax, everything else can wait until tomorrow." She squeezes my shoulder.

"I'll miss saying goodbye to Brie," I cut in, shaking my head.

"They're going to the train station with us in an hour," Aviva says. "Your mom's right. You've had an insanely busy few days with little sleep, I think."

I glance between the women with a resigned sigh, wondering why I'm so adamant about staying put when they're giving me the perfect out. I rise, quietly hugging both of them and saying goodbye, and their promises to say my goodbyes to the rest of the family in the room are the last words I hear until I'm tucked in my new, formal ensuite bathroom in the massive royal suite on the sixth floor.

I kneel in front of the toilet, wiping my mouth with a trembling hand. White marble fills my vision as I slowly rise and sway to the sink, washing up, rinsing my mouth for what seems like the thousandth time today.

My eyes are bloodshot in my reflection, and my hair is a mess, sweat prickling along my hairline. My body roils, begging me for rest, for food, even though my stomach protests both at every turn. Whatever's wrong with me is getting worse, I fear.

I turn to the huge bathroom–a small swimming pool, if I'm being perfectly honest. It takes up an entire corner of the gilded room and overlooks a beautiful view of the forest lining the outskirts of Moonrise. It's full dark now, and the stars glow overhead, casting beams of gold and purple through the glass.

Mom did, in fact, leave a basket of herbs and salt for the bath. The herbs… stink. My stomach twists again, and I have two seconds to fall to my knees in time to retch, but there's nothing left. Not after four days of this feeling.

"Mistress? Maeve?" Jane shouts into the recesses of my royal suite–all eight rooms and two huge living areas included. Her voice bounces off the boxes stacked in the oversized master suite just beyond the bathroom door as I rock onto my ass and slouch against the wall, wiping sweat from my brow.

"I'm in here," I croak, and she knocks lightly on the door.

"Are you all right? Danny in the kitchen was making you a tea tray. I told him I could bring it up myself."

Another wave of nausea rocks me to the core. I groan, choking back a sob.

"Maeve?" Jane says hurriedly, knocking again before opening the door. The scent of chamomile tea wafts into the room, the only thing beside Soren's jacket that smells good right now, and it's enough to bring me to tears. "Good Goddess, what's wrong?"

"I don't feel well," I whisper, and I see the look on her face… the sympathy, the worry…. A sob tangles in my throat before bursting free. I gasp for breath, unable to speak as Jane sets the tray on the counter and rushes for me, kneeling at my side. She brushes my hair away from my face before laying her hand over my forehead. "I'm not… not sick. I don't know what's wrong with me–"

"You're late by a week," she says under her breath.

Time stops. The bathroom goes completely still. I blink, rapidly doing internal math and realize, with a start, that she's right. "That's why. I'm just… I'm just about to get my period. No wonder–"

"This never happens to you when you get your courses," she says pointedly.

"There's a first time for everything–"

"You're pregnant, Maeve."

I laugh because it's all I can do. Delirium sets in, and I laugh harder, practically howling at the notion, but that laughter peters out, turning to choking, gasping sobs as the truth tears through my body. She wraps an arm around my shoulder, leaning her head against mine. "It was him, wasn't it? He forced you–"

"No," I whimper. "Oh, Jane, you have no idea–" I cover my face with my hands as the dam breaks, and I let myself feel for the first time since getting back on that train.

I tell her everything. Everything. Painting her a masterpiece of details. She sits in silence beside me while I talk, and talk, unable to stop until I'm totally out of breath.

"I can't–I can't do this. It shouldn't hurt this much," I cry out. "I– we barely knew each other. He doesn't feel the same. I know that. And now my period is late and I–"

"Do you know how to find him? He should know about this," she asks, but I shake my head.

"No. I don't know where he actually lives. I have no idea how to contact him."

"He was the one who sent you the tea, wasn't he?"

I nod, blinking past tears.

"Maeve," she says, swiveling to face me, "is he a good man or a bad one?"

"A little bit of both," I laugh.

She nods, unsure what to think, and I don't blame her. But knowing Jane… she'll handle this. She'll know what to do. "The family left. Everyone's gone. What do you want to do? I can call for your mother–"

"Don't," I rush out, shaking my head. "Not yet."

"We need to confirm you are, in fact, pregnant," she says.

"I don't want anyone to know if I am."

"I understand. There's a healer at the clinic downstairs who I know is discreet. She's a midwife. I'll speak to her in the morning and bring her here to confirm it."

"And then what?" I ask as fatigue washes through my body.

She chews her lower lip, shaking her head. "I don't know, Maeve.

We'll keep it a secret, if that's what you want. But you'll start to show, and from there, your family should know."

"How much time until then?" I ask.

"A few months, I guess. I don't know, I've never been pregnant before."

"Well, that makes two of us." I try to joke, but another tremble of heartbreak ghosts through my chest.

Soren doesn't know, and I have no way to tell him. I close my eyes, listening as Jane concocts a plan of action, and give in to the pain and fatigue, my hand pressed against my lower belly.

"Everything's going to be okay," Jane says. "I promise."

THE ARCHITECT

Soren

Five months have passed since the coronation. Time has been a blur, to say the least. I've been all over the place lately, working my fingers to the bone to move over fifty people into hiding, and now, I'm nearly done.

The man standing in the corner of the foyer of a large, well-built stone house in the plains outside of Moorn stares at the file in his hands, his face gray and washed in confusion, then startles in understanding as I watch the column of his throat bob when he swallows, his eyes flicking to mine.

"Are they in danger?"

"Yes," I reply steadily, but I don't look in the direction of his mate, a woman of maybe thirty currently sitting in the other room with their three young children.

This man, a commander in King Sydney's royal forces, was the one I knew I'd have the most trouble with. Moving the Betas was easy. The Alpha, not so much, but he eventually folded.

I don't know what's in those files the Architect supplied, but it's enough to change their minds, that's for sure.

"How long would we be gone?"

"A year, maybe longer."

"This is…. How? Who's doing this?"

"You're familiar with the man named The Spider, I assume?"

The commander's pales but he nods. He glances at my black ghost issued gloves, my black ghost armor, which is the only reason these people allow me to get close. They have no idea I don't work for the Allied Kingdoms, and it needs to stay that way. He looks back at the file while I turn to face the windows overlooking a stretch of moonlit plains. Snow covers everything, and it's been a cold, bitter autumn so far, but Crescent Falls is always so much colder than Eastonia. Back home, the trees are still gold and crimson and the air is spiced with apples and hay. Here, it's nothing but smoke and the fresh, crisp scent of fresh snow.

I check my watch, grinding my teeth as I wait for this man to just give in like the rest.

"What happens now, if I agree?"

"You and your family will pack immediately and board the next train to Eastonia, and from there, you'll be escorted by me into a disclosed location, a safe house, within a community of… others like you."

"And my king?"

"He'll be under the impression you're taking a long sabbatical for a family emergency on your mate's side, seeing as she's from Eastonia. It was easy enough to arrange."

"So he's unaware–"

"He's aware to an extent," I lie, "but on paper, you're taking leave of your post for an extended period of time. Other than that, you disappear. You and your family will be safe and cared for, and the only stipulations are that you don't leave the community, and you don't ask questions."

He eyes me wearily before nodding. Again, I find myself curious about what's inside the file. Everyone I've moved receives one shortly before I arrive, which I find odd, seeing that I've never given the Architect an exact schedule or idea of where I'll be, and when.

"How much time do we have to pack?"

"Twenty minutes."

"That's not enough–"

"Take what's irreplaceable, and the rest will be supplied to you. Twenty minutes." I set a timer on my watch while he stalks out of the room to speak to his bewildered, nervous mate. In eighteen minutes, I have a family of five in the SUV I rented at the border, driving through the middle of night to the train station.

It's been months of this. The last time I was back at the safe house outside of Twin Rivers was shortly after the coronation, when I returned to gather what I'd need to travel around for a while. I've been all over the place since then, and now, sitting on a train the morning after delivering the last mark and his family to their home for the foreseeable future, I wonder where, exactly, I should go next.

The Viper has given a mark or two over the past five months. Both deaths, of course, which ended up being two of the three Beta's I safely moved into hiding. It's been busy, to say that least, and that's a fucking blessing.

Any time I sit down and have a moment of peace, I think of her.

The train pulls into a small station deep in the Roguelands. Morning sunlight stretches over the golden landscape, a soft breeze plucking dried leaves from the trees. I hike my backpack over one shoulder and pull my ball cap down to cast my face in shadow before moving off the platform, walking into a sleepy, but mid-sized, town split between two Alphas. I check into a motel on the outskirts of town, showering off three days of travel. I change into jeans and a sweatshirt then take a short walk to a run-down dive bar with a brunch service.

It's not even 10:00 A.M. when the bartender slides a frosted glass full to the brim with a dark, rich ale in my direction. I press a few dollars onto the counter before walking to a booth in the back corner of the bar and sit down, sighing, before drinking half of the beer in one go, barely tasting it.

A TV over the bar is playing the news. I watch in silence as images of the Roguelands bleed into Moonrise, where Maeve appears, waving to spectators as she steps off a private train car surrounded by her guards.

"Queen Maeve has just returned from her tour of Tarsian," the anchor announces as the footage cuts to video of Maeve meeting with the Alphas and Betas of Tarsian. The voice of the anchor fades, and all I can see is her. Her, moving through a crowd of excited onlookers. Her, dressed finely in suits or gowns. Her, looking... worn. Tired, maybe even a little sick. The dark circles under her eyes are mostly masked by the golden glow of her skin that seems to shine brighter than usual, like she's actively using her powers in some way during this tour.

Keeping a shield around herself, perhaps. In fact, footage from a ball held in her honor shows her surrounded by high ranking men, all of which can't come within three feet of her. Shields, for sure.

"Smart girl," I smile into my beer before finishing it off.

The door to the bar opens, sending a bell chime pinging from wall to wall. A shadow passes over me before a man slides into the booth, his hands covered in black gloves and face shielded by a familiar mask.

A black ball cap covers his hair, but he's still dressed impeccably. A tailored suit jacket covers a black button down shirt as I scan him before raising my gaze to his masked face.

"You have an uncanny ability to sense my next moves," I tell him shortly then rise to get another beer. "Do you want one?"

"It's not even 11:00 A.M."

"Suit yourself."

He's still at the booth when I return, his face tilted toward the TV still covering Maeve's long, tortuous tour of her new kingdom.

"Queen Maeve will remain in Moonrise for the next six weeks before attending a summit with the Kingdoms of Crescent falls, Celestoria, and Lunaria to discuss the latter kingdoms joining the Allied Kingdoms..."

I eye the Architect as he watches the screen, toying with my fresh beer, which I've suddenly lost a taste for. "What do you want now?"

He pulls an envelope out of his jacket and sets it on the table.

"I'm done, man. I've been out in the field for five months–"

"This is the last one."

I shake my head, leaning back against the cushioned booth. "Why are you doing this? Moving so many people... The King of Crescent Falls will catch on, especially with one of his commanders now missing–"

"Leave him to me," he says, pressing his finger on the envelope and sliding it closer to me. "This is the last job I have for you, at least for now."

I take the envelope, but he remains in the booth. I grind my teeth as I open it. There's no cash in this one. A check for an outrageous sum of money linked to a private bank account slides free, followed by a note on graph paper. The money is enough to pay my debt, and Patton's, ten times over.

But the name on the note tells me all I need to know about this job.

"You can't be serious," I murmur, shaking my head.

"She dies."

"You're joking."

"I'm not."

I lean forward, glancing around to make sure we're not within earshot of anyone else. The Architect's scent hits me–it's icy and sharp, like fresh snow. Like a bitter cold winter's day–clean, and fresh, with a hint of a dark, musky cologne. "You realize she's heavily guarded twenty-four hours a day. There is no way I'll be able to get close to getting her alone."

"You have very little time on this one. Three months at the most."

"I can't do it."

"You can, and you will."

"I can't," I argue, chuckling. "You realize she's my boss, right? She's the one pulling the strings day to day for the Spider himself. You take her out, and you'll have him to answer to. I'll have to answer to him–"

"And that is exactly the point," he says, leaning forward over the table. "The Viper is going to be sending you new marks very soon. Waiting to pay off your debts has been in your favor, Soren, you were smart not to go to her immediately. She's starting to panic, and the Spider is breathing down her neck."

"How do you know all of this?"

He leans back and goes silent for a moment. "It doesn't matter how I know. Every mark she gives you over the next month needs to die. Do you understand? I won't be intervening because I need you in her good graces. Do not pay off your debts until after the third mark is complete."

"No," I bite out. "No, I planned on paying my debt off now–within the week. I'm done. I'm done with her, and with you." I slide the envelope back to him. This is the most we've spoken to each other in years, since he first approached me with a proposition to aid him in... whatever scheme he had going.

I turn back to the TV as Maeve appears again, this time in a series of paparazzi photos taken in Moonrise. She doesn't look well. Her eyes are dead and hollow as she walks along the upper balcony beside Jane, the two of them looking down at the tablet while Maeve directs a horde of maids to do... something.

"You asked me where my loyalties lie," the Architect says. "I hadn't realized how loyal you were to the very queen you've been working against for years."

"Nothing I've done was done in spite of her," I reply under my breath.

"But everything you do now is for her benefit? I didn't take you as a man who bows to authority–"

"I'm an enterprising man," I correct. "I bend the knee when it benefits me. And this no longer benefits me."

"But it would benefit her," he says, tilting his head toward the TV where a celebrity gossip show is now talking about Maeve. The hosts discuss an array of options–single Alphas and other high-ranking young men–for Maeve. I feel a pang of... rage. I curl my hand around the beer while the hosts laugh, matching Maeve with some prince in the distant kingdom of Lunaria, saying how they'll meet formally at the summit...

The pint glass splinters under the pressure of my grip.

The Architect chuckles darkly, shaking his head as he watches the same program play across the TV set. "I always find it interesting that people assume the queen needs, let alone wants, a man. Whoever it is will never rule beside her. He'll be a background actor."

"Is there something wrong with that?" I ask hotly, and he turns back to me.

"You're awfully committed to Her Highness."

"She's our queen. Of course she has my support."

He watches me for several long, drawn out seconds–long enough to make me wonder if I've gone too far and given myself away.

"Then you will support her in this. Getting rid of the Viper puts the onus of her operations on the Spider, and we need to draw him away from his web."

"There is no *we* in this," I argue. "We are not partners. I don't know your name or your face. Find someone else."

"There's no one else I trust."

"That sounds like a personal problem."

The Architect exhales deeply, leaning back against the cushions. He tilts his head toward the TV, saying under his breath, "Have you noticed that your escapades have been silenced? There's no more mention of the assassin on the news and hasn't been for months, even though you've been killing again."

My jaw tenses as I watch his masked face.

"All anyone wants to know is what Queen Maeve is up to, why she hides herself behind her powers, keeping her shields high, and who she'll end up with. Everyone seems to believe the summit is where she'll meet the man destined to stand in the background while she rules. I know many, many Alphas are desperate to get close to her in any way they can to give themselves a shot at being king–"

"They wouldn't be king."

"Ah, but that's what you're not understanding. Not everyone appreciates the queen like you do, Soren. Not everyone believes she's capable of this, of doing this on her own. Even Queen Ella had a man by her side–"

"Queen Maeve would kill a man before she let anyone take her throne from her."

"That's what she'd like everyone to believe," he says under his breath like an afterthought, and I hate that I agree. "She's always been that way." He rises as a prickle of unease shoots up my spine.

"Do you know her personally?"

"Do you?" he asks.

He pauses a beat before turning, walking back out into the fall sunshine, leaving the envelope on the table.

FOUND OUT

MAEVE

IT'S SNOWING IN CRESCENT FALLS. I WATCH THE LANDSCAPE RUSH BY AS I ride in the back of a blacked out SUV, resting my hands on the swell of my growing belly.

I'm nearly eight months pregnant now. The reality of my situation hasn't set in yet. I think back on that day when I'd sat on the bathroom floor with Jane, spilling my heart out, often. Everything since that moment has been a blur.

Within days of confirming the pregnancy, I started my grand tour of Eastonia. First, I traveled through Moonrise and the towns and villages surrounding the main city, formally introducing myself as their queen. Then, I spent a few weeks in Veiled Valley with my family while navigating my royal duties and guarding my secret. I didn't tell my mom I was pregnant. She still doesn't know. I don't know how to say it.

I left Veiled Valley and traveled through the Roguelands, with many dozens of stops, meeting face to face with every Alpha, Beta, and Luna. I sat in on pack meetings, listening to the trials and tribulations of the people I'm meant to rule and guard. From there, I went to the Deadlands, where I spent over a month and a half traveling, speaking publicly, and attending their fall festival before taking a boat to Emberfyll where I spent a few weeks with Brie and Logan and toured their strange island home. But even then, I couldn't tell anyone. I kept my growing belly hidden using my powers, putting a shield around myself that made it impossible for anyone to pick up my scent and see the changes happening–like how tight my clothes began to fit, how much more rounded I was becoming.

I didn't tell Brie. I couldn't do it. Telling her would have meant opening the floodgates and saying the name I've spent the last eight months trying to forget.

My tour of Tarsian was the distraction I needed to get through the worst of it. When I left Emberfyll, I spent over a month back in Moonrise where I quickly started to spiral. Nothing worked. Nothing made me feel better. My heart felt like it had been cleaved into pieces, and there was nothing I could do to put it back together again.

With my tour of Tarsian, the largest kingdom by far, approaching, I kept myself busy preparing for what that would entail. Tarsian is a mess as it stands, even now, after my tour. It's far too big, even with three Alpha Kings ruling at one point. But, its mass and the sheer amount of Alphas and high-ranking officials I had to meet with kept me busy and distracted for over a month, and by the time I returned to Moonrise again for a break, six months had passed since I last saw Soren.

You'd think I'd be over it by now, right?

While in Moonrise again, wasting time until this current journey for the summit in Crescent Falls, I… took a trip on my own.

It had been a rushed decision. My pregnancy hormones are to blame, I assume. I snapped my fingers and jumped, using my magic to travel for the first time in months instead of joining the procession of warriors and guards in cars and trains, and I jumped to the cabin in the dead center of the Roguelands.

It was quiet. The small, two-story cabin blended with the dark trees under a canopy of deep gold and muted crimson. Leaves were falling in the lightest breeze, crumpling to the ground as the wind carried a stiff chill, and the dark clouds overhead promised the first snowfall of the season.

When I'd been there last, it had been early summer. Everything had been the brightest green and just... lovely. Gorgeous. But that day, it was a shell of what it used to be. I crossed what could be construed as the front lawn, noticing the empty, leaf covered chicken coop on my way to the house. The windows were boarded tight, and the front porch hadn't been swept in ages.

No one was there. I figured it would be that way. Even if I had come back, and Soren had been there, I didn't have anything I could have said to him. I'm still not sure what I'd say if we were ever face to face again.

But I'm pregnant.

The fact that he doesn't know, and I have no way to tell him, has been killing me.

So that day, after sitting on the porch for an hour, I wrote him a note. It wasn't anything long or wordy. Just a few words, words I hoped he'd one day read and know that I was still thinking about him.

"I miss you."

I didn't sign it.

I simply... jumped back to Moonrise and went about my life and my royal duties for a month hiding an advancing pregnancy, and now I'm in another car, driving to another place, my last stop on this grand, seemingly never ending tour.

I feel a pinch of exhaustion in my powers when the massive gates of the castle in Crescent Falls open, and the driver, one of my warriors, silently takes me down the long drive lined with snow covered trees. Everything is white and silver in the moonlight as the car kicks up snow. I lean my head against the window with a sigh. Tomorrow is the summit where I'll meet the heads of both Celestoria and Lunaria, Crescent Falls neighbors to the north, and the northernmost kingdoms of our great continent.

And, yes, I'm aware of what the media is spinning about me meeting Alpha King Julius's son, Prince Eric of Lunaria.

The castle comes into view after a winding turn, and before I can blink, the car rolls to a stop in the rear of the castle. My guards in the trio of cars behind us quickly fan out, and I exit the car, not bothering to wait for one of the guards to open my door.

Sarah rushes out of the exterior door leading off the garage, her violet eyes shining in the moonlight. She wraps me in a tight embrace while my magical shields simmer, making it look, and feel like I'm the same as I've always been... not growing more and more round and swollen by the day.

I can thank my ability to shape-shift for this trick, even if my powers are easily drained these days. I'm itching to drop the shields and go to bed, but Sarah takes my face between her hands, beaming up at me. "You're late! You missed dinner!"

"We got held up on the highway," I say with a sigh. "I'm sorry."

"Don't be. We're just happy you made it. The last storm was terrible. I feel like the winters are getting worse year after year." She guides me into the house while the guards deal with my luggage. The castle expands around me in a mix of dark wood and cream-colored walls. Great Grandma Isla's design touch hasn't been changed since her death two decades ago. Floral wallpaper greets me as we walk down a long, narrow hallway and pass the informal, family style kitchen and cross into the grand foyer where she turns me toward the formal sitting room with yellow wallpaper and a roaring fire in the white marble hearth.

Sydney smiles as I walk into the room with Sarah at my side. Liam, their second oldest son, is resting by the fire with a book in his lap but looks up at me and grins politely. He's the spitting image of his mother with icy blonde hair and a softly handsome face. His violet eyes are muted, however, compared to Blake's and Sarah's. He has the eye color, but none of the powers that come with them.

Their twin daughters both attend Wellington University and aren't here, and neither is Noah, who's also away at the University of Tarsian in Serpentia, which reopened ten or so years ago, after the war.

But it's the woman leaping from her perch on a nearby couch that steals my attention. My breath leaves my lungs in a huff as Brie's body collides with mine.

"What are you doing here?" I gasp as shock ripples through my system, making my powers tremble. I rein them back in so I don't blow my cover, but they nearly slipped through my fingers this time.

"It was supposed to be a surprise, but you're hours late!" Brie replies excitedly, holding me at arm's length. I haven't seen her in months, not since I visited Emberfyll. She searches my eyes before releasing me but grips my hand tight.

"Ready for tomorrow?" Sydney asks before sipping from a glass of what I believe is scotch, knowing him.

"I believe so. Is there anything I should know about the Alpha Kings and their Betas before the summit?"

He shakes his head. "Nothing we haven't already discussed."

"You look exhausted, Maeve. You should go to bed. We can all have breakfast together in the morning before the summit starts, okay?" Sarah bustles me out of the sitting room with Brie hot on my heels, and within minutes, I'm ushered into a guest room on the third floor of the castle, surrounded by my luggage. A maid already laid out the outfit I designated for tomorrow.

Brie is staying in the room next door. She's not here with Kieran and Logan, but she briefly explained why before telling me she was going to take a shower. The whole family is meeting in Maatua next week for Winter Solstice, and Logan and Kieran are traveling there with Aviva and Ryan, giving Brie what sounds like a much needed break.

Unpacked, I run myself a bath as the castle goes quiet, and the moon rises high overhead. I shed my robe, sighing as I drop my shields and let my shapeshifting magic finally rest after a full day of travel, and sink in the tub. My fingers splay over the tight rise of my belly where the baby rests.

I'm having a girl.

I wonder if she'll have his eyes or mine.

I close my eyes against a torrent of tears. This grief comes in waves–some soft, others violent and crashing, leaving me curled in a ball in the middle of my bed.

This can't be right. I already know this feeling isn't rational. He's the only man I've ever kissed, ever lain with, ever let myself touch… and somehow that bound him to me for life.

He probably hasn't thought about me since we parted ways, has he?

Feeling ridiculous, like usual, I step out of the tub and dry off, the robe barely covering my stomach as I brush out my hair. My mind drifts back to Soren, pushing past the barriers I've been building to keep his memory at bay, when the sound of the door opening in the bedroom alerts me to someone's presence.

Brie calls out my name, but I don't have time to lock the bathroom door nor shield myself with my powers before the door opens and she steps inside. "Do you have toothpaste I can borrow? I must have left mine at the hotel I–"

My heart skids to a stop as Brie's eyes leave my face and drift down to the very noticeable swell of my stomach. Her lips part in a sharp gasp just as my chest caves in.

SPILLING IT ALL

MAEVE

"MAEVE–"

"I can explain–"

"You're pregnant?" Brie's voice cracks, her dark brown eyes wide with shock and then a sudden, choking grief. "*What?* How? When?"

I raise my hands in surrender, trembling, wondering how to even begin, but Brie steps toward me, her brows furrowed in confusion. "Maeve, you're massive!"

"Uh, thanks," I snarl, but tears begin to prickle along my eyelashes.

"You're–you have to be nearing the end of the pregnancy, aren't you? Why haven't you told anyone? I didn't know. Mom doesn't know–"

"I wanted it that way."

"You didn't tell the family? You've been pregnant this whole time, on the tour." Her eyes widen as she thinks out loud. "You were pregnant during the coronation, weren't you?"

"I didn't know yet, not at that point, but a few days later–"

"You found out when the family was gathered, and you didn't say anything?" Tears stain her cheeks like ribbons of silver. "You didn't tell *me*?"

"What the fuck was I supposed to say?" I bite out, the room around me blurring as tears fill my eyes.

She shakes her head, her lips pulled tightly together. "I don't believe you. How could you–"

"It's my baby, and it was my decision to keep this a secret for her safety–"

"You're having a girl?" Her anger shatters for a moment, and it's enough to absolutely wreck me.

I desperately try to rein myself in, but my entire body is shaking at this point. I nod in confirmation, sniffling, teetering on the edge of losing control entirely.

"I figured it would be best to just introduce her to the family when she arrives. I didn't want the public to know I was pregnant. It was none of their business."

"Goddess, Maeve–"

"I've been fine. We're both healthy. I have a midwife–"

"You've been going through this on your own–"

"I am fine," I press, talking over her.

"What about her father? Who is he?"

I close my eyes against the anguish twisting to life, rendering my lungs useless.

"Where is he? Have any of us met him?"

"No," I whisper, curling my arms around my middle, squeezing tight in an attempt to shield myself from the feelings trying to claw free.

"Is he–he's helping you, right?"

I open my eyes to meet her astonished gaze. Tears slide free, drenching my cheeks, and her expression fumbles into outright confusion.

She's never seen me like this–this... emotional. This broken. No one has.

"I had a plan," I say without meaning to speak. "I'd have the baby, and... everything we know about the Firestone queens points to their use of breeders. I'd say her father was chosen for specific traits and strengths, that I chose him as a breeder, and…" I suck in a breath. "Everyone would understand. That's what I told myself. I'm cold and blunt by nature. They wouldn't question my decision because–because I'm *me*. I don't feel things like affection and love–"

"Maeve–"

"It was going to be just business," I say pointedly while tears continue to flood down my face, slipping down my neck and into my robe. "I had it all planned out."

Brie exhales sharply, her breath rattling.

"And I was going to just forget about him eventually. I tell myself that every day, that I'll forget. That eventually I won't remember his name–"

"Oh, gods, Maeve," Brie says under her breath as I begin to shatter into pieces in front of her, the space of a bath mat between us.

"*But I can't*," I grind out through tears, the words laced with pain. "I hate this. I feel like I'm stuck underwater, and I can't breathe. I force myself to eat. I haven't had an appetite in months. I can't function, Brie. I feel like I'm–I'm living outside of my own body, and who I was before is just gone. I can't find her." I brace a hand on the counter to stop myself from falling to my knees. My sister is silent, watching me dissolve into sobs. "I barely knew him, you know? People hook up all the time, and it means nothing, and I figured… I figured what I felt in those first days would pass. The confusion. That tightness in my chest whenever I thought of him–"

"Maeve–"

"I don't understand why this is happening to me," I gut out, meeting her eyes. "I don't get it."

She opens her mouth, but nothing comes out. Her lips shut tight as her gaze falls to her toes, her hair still wet from her shower and curling around her shoulders as she shakes her head. "What happened, Maeve? Where did you meet him?"

"He broke into the castle and stole all of my jewelry."

"What?"

I laugh through the tears at the absurdity of it.

"You're joking–"

"He stole my jewelry, and I beat the shit out of him for it, but he escaped, and I… followed him, and then went on the adventure of my life for the next week or so and…" I look down at my hands, imagining Soren's body pressed to mine in that abandoned building. I imagine him pressing my wrists above my head, his fingers woven with mine. "He broke my moonstone necklace. It's why I stopped wearing it. I… it was a few weeks before the Rite. I didn't have power left after chasing him down, and he… he got me home safely."

Brie looks lost, but… It doesn't matter. There's nothing I can say about what happened to me that wouldn't blow his cover. I promised to take his identity to the grave, going as far as to erase any news about the assassin from the media. Three more Alphas were found murdered over the past few weeks, and I knew it was him. I sent the Ghosts on a wild goose chase in the wrong direction on purpose. I've been protecting him.

Even against… my own sister.

"You have to tell me everything–"

"There's not much to say."

"Maeve, are you serious? You–you love him–"

"I–" I cut myself off, shocked that that's what she's most worried about, not the fact that I just told her the unorthodox way we met and how I was technically missing for week without anyone knowing.

"Where is he now?"

"I don't know–"

"Does he… know?"

I shake my head, tears flying free. "No."

"Why not–"

"Because we can't be together, Brie. For fuck's sake, I know you can't understand, and there's so little I can say, but we… we both knew that there wasn't a future for us. I'm the Queen of Eastonia, and he's… he's not… he can't."

Brie steps closer but doesn't reach for me. Her hand hovers near my shoulder before her fingers form a fist and drop back to her side. I turn to face the counter. I'm not shocked by my reflection in the mirror. I look like I've been dragged through hell because I have, for months.

"I can help you find him–"

"No."

"Maeve, be serious–"

"I'm deathly serious, Brie. He doesn't know, and I think it should stay that way. He'll feel like he owes me something–"

"He's the father of your child–"

"And that's it. He can't possibly match the way I feel. I'm obsessed, and it's unhealthy–"

"You're heartbroken. It's obvious. You were so–so disconnected from everyone when the family was in Moonrise for the coronation, and now I understand why. You should have told me what happened."

"I can't tell you anything–"

"Why not? I'm your sister!"

"Because his life is at stake."

That confusion flashes behind her eyes again, but I wave her away.

"Maeve, I don't like this–"

"It's not your responsibility–"

"What is he like?"

My heart quakes. Her words are so soft, so gentle, barely a whisper in the steamy, post-bath air. "He's… annoying," I whisper, chuckling around a weak sob. "He's temperamental and brutal. He doesn't have a filter for his words. He flipped me off once, but I deserved it." I close my eyes. "He doesn't ever think about himself. Everything he does is for someone else. He's loyal to a fault, honestly, but he doesn't realize it. He thinks he's a bad man, someone people need to stay away from, but he's really just… terribly, unequivocally, devoted to those he loves."

I reach up to wipe my tears. My cheeks are soaked, and my skin is heated, but… a burden lifts from my chest with each word I say. I haven't spoken about him out loud in so long. It feels good.

"He's tall," I continue, sniffling. "Taller than me. My head reaches the crook of his shoulder, and that's a feat in itself. He's handsome.

He's young, twenty-six when we met, and… he's had a hard life. Still does."

"And what was he like with *you*?"

My knees start to give out as exhaustion washes through me, dragging me into its current. I grip the counter and slide to my knees then rest against the cabinets. Brie follows me to the floor, her back against the glass door of the shower.

"He hated me at first, I think. I hated him. At least, I thought I did. He was, and still is, the only man outside of the family who has ever looked me in the eyes. He wasn't afraid of me. If anything, he egged me on. He broke my necklace and wasn't sorry about it, wasn't afraid of the promise of what I could do to him when my powers returned. In fact, I think he wanted to see it. And… when it was clear that I didn't have a way to get back home on my own, he took me in. At first, he was standoffish, but there were a few… situations where… where he was possessive of me. Protective." I close my eyes against the detailed memory of killing Duke and the event leading up to, and following, that night. "But he was also… funny, and sarcastic. He'd tease me constantly, and I feel for it all the time. He loved getting under my skin, and I loved that he could."

I lick my lips, finding them impossibly dry.

"I saw a different side of him the night we…" I taper off, my cheeks glowing red. "Afterward, I made him tell me everything– everything that made him the way he is, and I learned… too much, I think. If he were really as bad as he thinks he is, as bad as he wants me to believe, I could have pushed past these feelings, but… he's just trapped in a cage, and he can't get out. He knows it. I know it." Fresh tears spring free. "And he wouldn't drag me down with him even though I begged him to come with me. He wouldn't. We went to bed that last night, and… for a moment I had everything. I was warm, safe, and loved. And then we woke up, and I think we both knew it was over."

"And I… I grew up knowing I'd never find a mate. It's not in my blood. I let myself grow cold and emotionless, thinking I'd never be able to feel that strongly for someone else, but then I saw you and

Logan together, and I... I was jealous," I admit, meeting her eyes. "Seeing him love you. Seeing him love the child you gave him.... I want that. But... I left my heart in the Roguelands, and I don't know how to find it again. I think it's gone forever."

"Then let me help you find him–"

"We can't." I sniffle, sitting up and shaking my head. I know Brie wants every detail, but there's so little I can say.

"Is he... in danger?"

"Yes."

"Our family–"

"He'd be in danger around our family, too. More so, I believe, if..." I shake my head again. She can't know. I swore to myself I'd take his identity to the grave. His past, his future, and his name.

Brie scooches closer to me, reaching a tentative hand toward me. Her touch is warm and soft, a comfort I hadn't realized I needed.

"You're using your magic to shield the pregnancy, aren't you?"

I nod, and she smiles sadly.

"I won't tell anyone, Maeve, but Mom is going to be heartbroken."

"I know. I just can't."

"I get it. It's going to be okay. You should have told me. You should... find a way to tell him." When I start to protest, she shakes her head, continuing, "I just mean that he should know. He should know you feel this strongly about him."

"It's crazy, isn't it–"

"Not at all."

IS IT TRUE?

MAEVE

THREE KINGS SIT BEFORE ME AT A LARGE CIRCULAR TABLE IN A SIMPLE, but bright, room within the temple in Crescent Falls. Sweat prickles along my brow line, but my magic keeps my nerves under wraps as King Lucius of Lunaria smiles at me, pleased, I think, with how the summit went.

King Evan of Celestoria, however, keeps his expression cool and collected, while Sydney sits somewhat smugly nearby, glancing at his watch. We've been here for hours, covering everything from trade to the relationships between the territories under our separate control. With so much migration and tourism between our four kingdoms these days, not to mention a massive boom in population that followed the War of Tarsian twenty years ago, the agenda was long and tightly managed, but long nonetheless.

I'm tired, hungry, and ready to leave.

I smooth the fabric of my neat, perfectly tailored black and gold suit jacket. My hair is tightly woven into a bun at the nape of my neck, and Brie did my makeup this morning, which is simple, but perfect. No frills. No show of my magic. No crimson. I am here as the Queen of Eastonia, plain and simple.

King Lucius continues to grin at me until I can't take it anymore.

"I believe Celestoria and Lunaria will benefit greatly from joining the Allied Kingdoms," I say to the group. It's the reason I'm here. So far, the Allied Kingdoms have only encompassed Eastonia and Crescent Falls, but they want in.

Sydney, to his credit, was leaving it up to me. I wanted a summit with them first. I was mostly curious about the shrewd king of Celestoria who has been a hard man to pin down when it comes to trade negotiations.

I continue, "I'm willing to sign whatever treaties come my way."

"And would those include Eastonia's promise to come to our aid in times of crisis?" King Evan asks dryly.

"Of course. My army is your army when duty calls."

King Lucius continues to grin. I glance at him then quickly look away. "Well, then. I believe we've discussed everything I came here for. Sydney, do you have anything to add in conclusion?"

He shakes his head, but King Lucius says, "Will you be joining us tonight at the castle for the ball held in the queen's honor?"

He's talking about Sarah, of course. It's her birthday party–at least, the birthday she and Sydney decided upon since neither know her actual date of birth.

"I will not," I reply, giving him a polite smile. "I'm traveling with my sister to the port. My next stop on this tour is Maatua." It's a half lie. I'm not going for work. The family is gathering in Maatua for the Solstice, and since Brie traveling via my powers would be risking her life, I agreed to sail with her to the island instead. It gives us two days together, alone, to try to sort out my life.

King Lucius's smile fades, and Sydney's small, knowing smirk makes me bite down on a smile of my own.

I rise, and so do the kings, who bow to me, and I bow them, and *blah, blah, blah*. This side of being queen is dreadfully boring. I like the other stuff–talking to commanders and warriors. Having to be mean and firm when it comes to Alphas who dare to not acknowledge my leadership. I like those things.

Talking about trade? Kill me.

Blake would be much better at this. He should be here for me, actually, but is still dragging his Goddess-damned feet about leaving his title behind and joining my court, the bastard.

In the car, just me and Sydney, on the drive home, he says with a smirk, "King Lucius is desperate to introduce you to his oldest son."

"Prince Eric?" I laugh, my powers flickering as they continue to shield the pregnancy he doesn't know about. "According to the news, we're already very much in love."

"Have you given any thought to the prospect of marriage?"

"You sound like Grandpa Ryatt right now," I accuse bluntly, shooting him a glare. "And no, of course not. I have no interest in that."

"You might change your mind. I've heard Eric is very handsome."

"Introduce him to Briar and Celeste, then. Have them fight over him."

He groans, but I laugh, and it's a sound I haven't heard in a long time.

It's a quick turnaround once we reach the castle. My bags are already packed, and Brie's waiting patiently in the foyer, dressed comfortably, and itching to get on the yacht waiting for us at the port. I change and say quick goodbyes, and within minutes, my guards are driving our procession to the port of Crescent Falls.

Brie, sitting beside me in the back seat, rolls up the partition so we're not overheard, then turns to me. "How'd it go?"

"Exactly like I thought. It was boring and could have been an email."

She smirks, rolling her eyes. "You have to get used to these things. It's all I do these days."

"You're far better at delegating than I'll ever be, and plus, you have an Alpha King by your side. You can split up the work. I can't."

She searches my eyes, her smile fading. "You could find–"

"No," I bite out, shaking my head.

"You know, you never told me his name."

I chew my lower lip, casting her a weary glance. I haven't said his name out loud in months. Sometimes when I lie in bed at night, I dig up the courage to whisper it into my pillow but always chicken out before it leaves my lips. I desperately want to call him into existence, but he's... gone.

I need to accept that eventually.

But today, I decide to be brave.

"His name is Soren."

Brie smiles softly, nodding. "That's a nice name."

"I thought so, too."

"Theoretically–" she begins after a beat.

"No."

"If," she cuts in as the highway bleeds back into a coastal city now that we've left the sprawling metropolis of Crescent City and spent the last half hour driving through woodlands, "if you did find him again, he could be in your life, Maeve. He wouldn't be the king, so to speak, unless you gave him that title–"

"He wouldn't accept it–"

"But if you offered, and he did accept, then he'd rule beside you. You wouldn't be bearing this burden on your own–"

"You don't know him–"

"But you do! I–I've always wondered what kind of man you'd fall for one day and what you described is exactly what I thought he'd be."

I narrow my eyes to cat-like slits. "I described him as annoying and hot-headed–"

"Exactly. He doesn't balance you out. You've never needed that. You've needed someone to fight with, Maeve. Someone who riles you up and matches your energy–"

"Well, that sounds like a recipe for disaster–"

"Look at Aviva and Ryan and tell me that kind of dynamic doesn't work." She arches a brow in challenge. I chew my lower lip, shrugging, then face the window. "See. Not everyone is like Mom and Dad. They needed that balance. Logan and I needed that balance. You... you would've eaten alive someone who bowed to your every whim."

I snort a laugh, throwing her a look over my shoulder, but she frowns at me.

"You look exhausted, Maeve."

"It's my powers. Keeping my shields up all day is one thing, but shapeshifting really drains me."

"Well, the second we get on the yacht, you should drop them. I already spoke to the captain, and he's a discreet man. It's a small crew, too. I've already paid everyone a handsome bonus for keeping their mouths shut. Don't worry."

I throw her another weary glance. "I suppose…"

"Your guards will be on another ship, anyway. I think one or two will be aboard at the most, and they can be dealt with."

"You've really put a lot of thought into this."

"You look like hell frozen over and reheated," she says with a yawn. "And I'm mostly trying to keep myself busy so I don't wring your neck for not telling me."

I smile against the window as the car comes to a stop. The yacht is beautiful, of course, and belongs to Grandpa Ryatt and Grandma Ella. We board but sit in the bay for quite some time as a light storm passes over, causing a bit of a traffic jam. Day fades into a startlingly vibrant sunset as we bob in the water, sitting on the main deck drinking tea and ignoring the bite in the air.

I dropped my shields ages ago, just like Brie said I should. I feel large and wobbly as I curl into a blanket, but it's not big enough to cover my neck and shoulders. A few other boats linger nearby. Brie watches them, narrowing her eyes, then looks back down at her book.

"I'm going to get another blanket," I grumble, shimmying to my feet. "I don't fit in this one."

"Let's just go downstairs and get ready for bed. It's freezing."

I nod my agreement and set the blanket down in a heap on the slightly frosted lounge chair I'd been resting on, but a flashing light briefly catches my attention on the water below. I squint down as a boat soars past the yacht and out of sight.

"I think we're finally leaving the bay now," Brie says with a sigh. "Thank the Goddess. I told Mom we'd be there in two days, tops."

And two days pass. It was the break we both needed for sure. Brie did nothing but read and show me the thousand pictures of Kieran on her phone. I did nothing but sleep and eat to my heart's desire, finally regaining an appetite. I credit Brie for that.

I didn't open up about Soren again, however, and she didn't push me. But just… talking about him? It helped.

Morning sunlight drifts over the main deck as the yacht pulls into the private dock owned by my family. I squint into the sun, my shields up and my shapeshifting powers hard at work. I convinced Brie to keep my secret until I'm ready, even if it means spending the four or five days in the company of my entire family, and even if she doesn't like how I'm going about this.

I'm just… not ready. I'm not sure I'll ever be ready to explain that I fell desperately in love and my entire life got turned on its head, and now I have a little souvenir to show for it.

"Oh! That's Mom!" Brie says excitedly as the yacht bobs to a stop. She bounces on her toes and waves at the dark-haired beauty hurrying down the length of the dock, followed closely by Misty, her golden hair streaking out behind her. "Why are they running? Why is Misty pulling on Mom's arm like that?"

My guards grab our suitcases, stepping past us toward the ramp now lowering against the dock. Misty yanks Mom to a halt and says something to her that I can't hear, but the worried look on Mom's face and the nerves pinching Misty's eyebrows together makes my stomach hollow out.

"Something's wrong," I murmur, grabbing Brie's arm. We race down the ramp as Dad comes into view, followed by Grandpa Ryatt, the two men looking stern and cold as they walk side by side.

Something isn't right. A prickle of unease shoots up my spine when Mom yanks out of Misty's grasp and whirls to us, her eyes wide in shock, maybe even… disappointment.

"Maeve–"

"Hey," I smile, glancing at the four people now closing in on me and Brie. "What's wrong? Did something–"

Misty steps in front of Mom looking grave. Brie pales as she looks between us then over her shoulder at Dad and Grandpa.

Mom opens her mouth but chokes on what I think is a sob, but Misty says, "Kenna, everything is fine."

"Maeve, is it true?"

"Is what true?" I ask, my cheeks beginning to prickle. "If this is about the Prince Eric of Lunaria again, I swear to the Goddess–"

Misty holds up her phone so I can see the screen. Brie leans in, gripping my arm as my world shatters at my feet.

A picture of us on the main deck several days ago stares back at me. It's hazy but clear enough to see... to see me, and my advanced pregnancy, in full color.

It's all over the news.

It has been for days.

"We tried calling you!" Mom says in a near shout, her eyes frantic as she looks between me and Brie.

"We didn't have service," Brie says, but her eyes water as she looks at our mom then our dad then me.

But I'm looking at Grandpa Ryatt. His silver gaze bores into mine.

I straighten my spine, squaring my shoulders, and that's all he needs to know the truth. He turns on his heel and walks away, leaving me in the center of my mother's downward spiral.

"Drop your shields, Maeve," Dad says on a breath.

SO MUCH FOR VACATION

Maeve

Waves beat against the pristine white sand of the private beach a short walk from the fabulous vacation house Maddy and Isaac now call home full time.

I cross my arms over my chest, resting them against my belly as a warm breeze ripples through my flowy sundress and sigh.

Well. I guess I deserved the shocked looks and whispers when I'd reached the house, stormed inside, changed, and let the family dissolve into chaos before racing toward the beach to gather my thoughts. It's barely midmorning when I splash through the surf, watching the glittering, crystal clear water rush around my increasingly swollen ankles. The sun warms my skin, making it prickle with the promise of a tan, or sunburn, depending on how long I plan to spend hiding.

"Maeve."

I hesitate before turning toward my dad's voice. He's walking beside Mom, who looks like she spent the last two days crying her eyes out, which makes me feel worse than being stabbed repeatedly in the heart.

I hug my stomach and slowly turn to face them, walking out of the gentle surf, careful not to slice my bare feet on any of the large seashells scattered across the shore. Dad's dark green eyes hold mine as he closes the distance between us, Mom only a few steps behind him, struggling to keep up with his long stride.

I wish I'd known them when they were young–before I came into the picture. To be totally honest, I often wonder how two people with such differing personalities ever found love and common ground. Mom is so gentle and soft. She's prone to anxiety and deep, unwavering emotions, but she's also the most loyal, loving person I know.

Dad is… quiet and stern. He thinks through every word he says. He's calculated and hard as nails. But I've seen them in quiet, stolen moments. I've watched him smooth his thumb over her hand while they sat together in the evenings while Mom told him about her day, about us, while we played loudly and made an insane amount of noise and mess in the room around them. I've seen him calm her with nothing but a touch to her arm, a hand on her lower back, a whispered word not meant for anyone else to hear.

He's a strong man but not a proud one. He's humble. Honest.

The idea that I've disappointed him is gut wrenching.

"Dad, I–"

He takes a step into me and pulls me into an embrace that totally catches me off guard. I stand perfectly still for a moment, my heart hammering, before sinking into his arms and burying my face in his shirt.

Mom sniffles beside him, gently patting my back like I'm five again, and I've just gotten railed on by Aris for stealing his toys, like he's called me a monster, which I likely deserved.

Dad pulls away, holding me at arm's length to look me up and down, then sighs, trying to hide the grimace.

"I know you're disappointed–" I begin, but he shakes his head, unable to find the words he wants, and needs, to say to me.

Mom, however, has had two days to decide what to say and immediately jumps in with both feet. "Why didn't you tell us?"

"It's complicated," I rush out. "I–I understand my duties, Mom. I know you understand them, too, both of you."

"You're so young," Dad says in a voice like gravel.

I purse my lips to stop a rattling breath from leaving my lungs. "I'm a Firestone. The only one of my kind. You both knew—you had to know, based on what Aviva and Misty have told the family—that my purpose is to have daughters, right? I'm having a girl, Mom." I turn to her, teary eyed. "I'm due in about a month, give or take."

Mom looks down at her sandals and closes her eyes.

My heart sinks to my bare toes. "I–I didn't tell anyone because—because I didn't know how to." It's true, at least. "I didn't want the public to know. I had the tour, and I wanted both of us to be safe. I didn't want to deal with the paparazzi swarming us and the public questioning my every move and who the father is."

"And who is the father?" Dad asks sternly.

This is where I lie, I guess. This is where I spin a web of deception I'll be trapped in my entire life. "You–you don't know him. But he's–he's exactly what I wanted in–in a breeder–"

Dad turns around, unable to look at me. Mom, however, is staring up at me wide eyed. "Why?

"Why, what? Why would I use a breeder?" I understand how bad this is. I'm lying to my parents, but I have to. Soren's life is at stake otherwise. Dad would know who he is. I know that much. He'd remember someone like Soren. He's impossibly hard to forget. "I'm the queen, Mom. I… I have other things to worry about right now other than finding a husband. But I needed an heir first and foremost. You have to understand. The public is already torn about my ability to rule, my ability to give them stability, and now I have. I am having an heir for Eastonia, the next Firestone queen. She has powers like me. She'll be a full-blooded Firestone. In a month, I will have completed my destiny."

"What about *you*? Is this really what you want? Raising a child on your own?" she asks.

"I won't be alone. I have–I have Jane. I have you," I say, but my words wobble over the last part. "If you'll forgive me for keeping it a secret."

"Of course you're forgiven," Mom says tearfully. "But I–you shouldn't have gone through this entire pregnancy on your own."

"Brie said the same thing," I murmur, sniffling despite my eyes remaining dry. I'm not sure I have any tears left at this point. "I'm fine. I'm healthy. She's healthy. I'm well taken care of by a midwife you trained, Mom."

"And when, exactly, are you due?" Dad asks, but his voice is soft. I can tell he's going through it, carefully keeping his back to us so I can't see the emotions flaring behind his eyes. Grief, I'm sure. Disappointment, maybe a pinch of anger.

"Three weeks, but my midwife thinks the baby is going to take her sweet time. I'm not showing any signs of labor whatsoever, so... a month, perhaps." I turn to Mom as guilt rages through my body. "Will you be there when she's born?"

"Yes," Mom says with a tearful nod. "Of course, I will." She squeezes my hand, her tearful smile lighting up her face again.

"Is... Grandpa mad?"

"Ryatt would like to speak to you, but I don't think it's wise," Dad says, turning to face us.

I furrow my brows.

Mom purses her lips, shaking her head. "Ev, come on. Everyone else is excited. My mom said–"

"Ryatt's right," he tells her, bringing up whatever tense conversation I'd blown past when we'd first arrived at the house. "Maeve isn't safe unless she's back in Moonrise. She can't stay for the Solstice."

I blink, looking between my parents. "What?"

"Grandpa made a good point," Mom says somberly, wincing as she looks at Dad. "While you and Brie were traveling, the news spun the paparazzi pictures out of control. It's a mess, darling. Isaac and Maddy have been fielding off reporters for days, here, in Maatua. Someone got a hold of the manifest about where the yacht was going. The whole continent knows you're here."

"That doesn't matter–"

"It does," Dad says under his breath. "For your safety, you need to return to Moonrise immediately and remain there until the baby is born. Blake is going to stay with you."

"What does Blake have to do with this?" I snarl, letting go of Mom's hand. "If he's in on this plot to ruin Solstice it's because he doesn't want to come here and spend time with the family!"

"He's been in Moonrise dealing with the fallout. You need to return and prepare a statement about the photo and the pregnancy. You need to announce it."

"I don't have to do anything. I am the queen. It's up to me," I cut in bluntly, my voice sharpened to a fine edge. "Do you both really agree with this? Making me go back? I just got here!"

"We're going to go with you and spend Solstice at the castle," Mom says. "Brie, Logan, and Kieran, too–"

"No," I say, shaking my head. "Everyone has been looking forward to this for months. Maddy planned everything out–"

"You are in danger," Dad says harshly. "Now more than even."

I shake my head. "Is that what Grandpa told you to convince you of this? He's mad at me, guys. That's all. This isn't about my safety. I can write and release a statement from here."

Mom and Dad exchange looks that tell me my fate has already been decided.

I might be Queen of Eastonia… but Grandpa Ryatt's word is law.

I whirl from the waves, stalking away from them.

"Maeve, wait!"

I stop, my powers simmering as rage whispers through my body, untangling a knot in my brain. I lose focus as I whirl back to my parents, who look stricken and guilty even though I'm the one lying and scheming.

To hell with it all.

I'm tired of this. This secret.

"Tell him," I growl, balling my hands into fists. "That this wasn't some plot of my own design. Tell him I fell in *love*."

Mom gasps, grabbing Dad's fingers.

"Tell him," I continue, "that her father isn't a breeder. That I didn't pick him out of a lineup. I didn't choose him for traits I wanted in my bloodline. No, I wanted *him*, and I can't have him because he's enslaved to the Roguelands just like Grandpa was. And he won't let me help him out of it." Tears of rage and grief burn down my cheeks. I'm so sick of crying. I'll never cry again after this. I swear on the Goddess Herself. "Tell him that I loved a man and had to let him go because of the talons wrapped around his heart that forbid him from loving me back! Tell him I've spent the last nine months in a hell Grandpa Ryatt designed–a hell where I am queen and the burden of my birth has separated me from the only man I'll ever love! Tell Grandpa Ryatt that, and then tell him to never look me in the eyes again!"

I'm gone in a flash, the beach replaced by empty nothingness that I reach for, thankful for the silence for a few precious, quiet moments. The stillness is ripped away as quickly as it came, depositing me in an office I haven't stepped foot inside in several months.

I slowly turn to the neat desk of dark wood, where Blake blinks at me, tilting his head ever so slightly as he looks me up and down and sighs.

"Well," he begins, leaning back in his chair, "you've really done it this time, Maeve."

"I'm going to prepare a public statement about the baby and read it tomorrow morning. I want all eyes on me when that happens."

"Noted."

"From there, nothing. No interviews, no meetings, not until this spring."

"Am I suddenly being demoted to your assistant?"

I wave him off, shaking my head as my mind tries to grasp what just happened, what I've done to my family. My heart lurches when I think of Grandpa Ryatt. Mom will repeat what I said word for word, knowing her.

I take several seconds to compose myself before asking, "What would you like for Solstice dinner, since we're both now the outcasts of the family?"

"It's not like that for you. Ryatt will calm down. I've heard Ella has already given him a mouthful about his opinion on the matter. He only wants you safe."

"He's just proved he's never trusted me and doesn't trust I can lead this kingdom."

"That's not what this is–"

"Then what is it, Blake?" I sneer.

Blake doesn't reply.

I turn out of his office, saying in passing. "I'll see you in the morning. We have work to do."

FINAL PAYMENT

Soren

Snow falls in heaps that stick to hanging neon signs coated in ice. Street lights flicker as I move through the shadows, keeping my head down and my eyes covered by a thin strip of black fabric. A group of drunk patrons stumble out of a bar in front of me, tumbling into the ice covered street, carrying music and the scent of beer in their wake, but no one looks in my direction.

It's easy to go unseen in a city this size.

In the distance, between the gaps between old apartment buildings and shops, shadows rise over the icy river. There used to be a city there. Now it's a wasteland, nothing but ash.

Twin Rivers has a sordid history. I hate coming here. It's noisy and dirty but constantly bustling. It reminds me of some of the bigger cities in Crescent Falls that fell out of the influence of the royal family. Crime runs rampant here, practically unchecked. I know this city is on Maeve's radar. It's the largest city in the Roguelands, with twelve packs claiming territory in the city boundary alone, and over a dozen more spread out in the nearby neighborhoods on the outskirts of the city.

This used to be my home. I came here as a kid, lived in a shitty one-bedroom apartment with a brother I didn't know existed until I ended up on his doorstep.

I'm never coming back when this is said and done.

The file I left tucked between my bed frame and the mattress at my safe house a hundred miles south of here flares in my mind. I can't act on the Architect's desires today. I'm not here to kill the woman responsible for ruining my life and Patton's life, but I am here to try to tie off loose ends before I start making plans.

I pass a tea shop and pause as the scent of chamomile drifts through the air. I brace a hand on the cold stone wall of the building, closing my eyes for a moment.

It's been months. Eight months to the day, to be exact, since I jumped on that train and kissed Maeve for the last time. Her memory burns through my body like wildfire, uncontrolled and scorching through every wall I've built around her memory.

I've stopped watching the news. I don't have a phone with access to social media, so I've been able to stay out of the loop. I thought not seeing her and not hearing her name would help, but I find constant reminders of her everywhere I go like my body seeks them out without my permission. The smell of chamomile tea. A woman passing me in the street with perfume scented like magnolia blossoms. A couple lovingly bickering a few rows ahead of me on the train while the man brushes his fingers through her hair, etc.

I can't sit by a fire without imagining the fireworks she sent over Moonrise all those months ago.

I assume this is just what I'll feel like for the rest of my life–empty.

So be it.

Wherever she is, she's safe.

That's all I have to keep me going.

I cross a street, weaving between a group of wolves out on a midnight stroll. Solstice lights still decorate the windows of shops shuttered for the night, a month and a half after the holiday. Patton cooked a feast for Solstice and brought out his best plates and glasses.

I barely tasted it.

A building of stone comes into view at the very end of the street where the lights have long burned out, casting an entire block in cold shadows. A single corner store is open and two people linger near its lit entrance. I pass through their cloud of cigarette smoke and into the darkness, my boots crunching through the snowy street no one bothered to clear and reach the five-story, otherwise abandoned, building casting its shadow on nearby apartment buildings and boarded up storefronts.

I cross into the center of the street when the main doors open, and a tall man steps outside, holding the door open like he's expecting me.

"Well, well," he drawls, his face covered in scars, "long time no see, Soren."

"Shut the fuck up," I grumble, brushing past him into the darkened foyer of what used to be a hotel. Music drifts through vents along the baseboards as I pass through a shadowed archway and take a set of stairs into more darkness. The music grows louder, vibrating through the floorboards. Two more men appear–bouncers tasked with guarding the gates to this tunnel to hell.

Neither stop me. They know who I am, and their shared expression of surprise warns me that they're actively sounding the alarm about my arrival.

I'll be in and out of here in twenty minutes. That's as long as I'm willing to stand in her presence and do what needs to be done.

A nightclub expands around me. Strobing lights dance across walls of red velvet. Dancers twist on a low stage wearing nothing but string, but my eyes are on the black double doors on the far end of the bar where people swarm the counter for refills.

I feel the curious glances of onlookers as I wade through the crowd. A young woman presses her hand to my chest, drunkenly asking if I want to dance. I shove her away, and her yelp fades into the music.

I burst through the doors, and the music falls into a sucking kind of silence that makes my skin tingle with unease. She knows I'm here based on the four burly men standing outside her office door, their arms crossed and eyes honed on my every move.

I pass them, open the door wide, and step inside the Viper's den.

Andrea lifts her head from her phone screen with a bright red, seductive smile, her chin-length black hair rippling with the movement. "*Soren.* I've been wondering when you'd come back here. You and I have unfinished business."

She's beautiful. Graceful and thin, she leans back in her chair and swivels from side to side, her long, pointed fingernails painted a blood red as she toys with the pendent of a snake she wears on a long, pure silver chain.

But her skin isn't marred by scars. It's flawless, as pale as snow. Her sharp, unnerving green eyes follow my progress to the center of her office where I sink into a chair in front of her desk and pull a large bank bag out of the inner pocket of my jacket, tossing it on her desk.

"That's everything. Enough to cover Tom's debt, my debt, and Patton's."

She licks her lips, tilting her head ever so slightly to drink me in. I resist the urge to bristle as her fingers drift down the seam of her impossibly low cut blouse. "That's all you came here for? I don't even get a hello? How are you? How have you been?"

"I don't give a shit how you've been."

Her smile is bright and deadly. She chuckles low, her voice a deep, sultry hum that licks up my spine and explodes through my mind like a death knell. "I've missed you, Soren. You've always been my favorite."

I rise, motioning to the bank bag. "There's enough to cover everything and then some. Consider it interest–"

"Your debt to me has tripled."

I blink then slowly meet her eyes. "What?"

She leans forward, tapping her nails on her desk. "You owe three times what you did a year ago, Soren. That's an impressive sum. An impossible sum, actually."

"We're done, Andrea. I'm not longer under your control–"

"Because you broke free of your band?" Her answering laugh reverberates through the room. "Soren, my love, no amount of money will help you out of the mess you've made, and over what? Rumor has it you fell in love with some pretty little witch, and now you're throwing it all away." She rises and sways around her desk. Her tight, black dress shows off what could be considered curves if she wasn't so desperately thin. She's tall. Taller than Maeve. Taller than any woman I've ever met.

She perches in front of me, leaning her hip against her desk, and reaches out to draw a line along my jaw.

"You'll never leave me, Soren. You belong to me."

I lean out of her touch, and she snickers, reaching to the side for a pack of thin cigarettes. "Got a light?"

"Fuck you."

"I'd love that. It'd be like old times."

My answering growl only makes her smile widen. She puffs her cigarette, sighing around the pull of smoke before releasing it. "You thought I wouldn't find out about Duke, huh? He was one of my best runners. His debt to me had grown substantially, you know, after all that gambling he was doing up north. I had to bail him out more than once."

"I'm not taking on his debt. Find someone else."

"But you killed him, right? Or was that someone else?" Her eyes flare as her smile fades into a knowing smile.

"We're done here. Duke's debt isn't my responsibility."

"Do you realize the mess you made killing the Hounds?" she snarls, teeth bared and pointed. "I had to answer to Hannibal for that, Soren. You'd be dead by now had it not been for my intervention. I had to convince Hannibal of your worth–"

"Fuck Hannibal," I say calmly, leaning in to brush the words against her temple, "and fuck you. I'm done. We're even."

"I know you have more money than this," she hisses, grinning around the words. "Do you think we don't know that you've been busy again, Soren? Or should I call you the Blade? Hannibal is impressed by you. He always has been. But your abilities as an assassin aren't enough to keep active and alive in his eyes. I had to grovel for your life–"

"We're done," I repeat sharply. "If more money is what you want, take it–" I reach into my jacket, but she grabs my wrist, and her men move into the room.

She steps into me, tucking her hair behind a pointed ear, and says, "Hannibal has a job for you. One more mark, Soren, and it's over, and his grand plan can finally come to fruition."

"No–"

"Do you think I didn't know about *her?*" she whispers against my cheek, brushing the words to my ear. "Your precious little *princess?*"

Dread hollows out my stomach as I feel the presence of her guards behind me, boxing me in. Andrea takes another drag of her cigarette, her mouth tilting over mine, and exhales. "You're mine, Soren. I don't like to share."

Her guards shove me down into the seat. I try to kick out, my wolf powers prickling to the surface of my skin, but it's too late. They hold me down, one of them yanking my arm free and slamming it on her desk. She chuckles, walking to the side of her desk as she puffs her cigarette one more time before pressing the cherry to my skin.

I grunt in pain, my eyes watering, but I hold her gaze through it.

Until she absolutely shatters my world and says, "Queen Maeve is *pregnant* and due any day now, from what I've been told. Hannibal wants that dealt with."

I can't breathe. My chest convulses as her men bear down on my back, forcing me to stay seated. *No. No, no, no!*

Andrea drags the tip of her nail over the old scar left from the original band. My skin flays open at her touch as her powers drag into existence like a heated blade, leaving molten silver in its wake.

"He wants that baby dead. Immediately. Make it messy, Soren. Paint the castle with its blood."

I grit my teeth, biting back a scream of pain I can't contain as she creates a new band. Blood rushes down my wrist, pooling on her desk.

"He wants the queen alive for now. He has business with her," she continues as the band expands and her powers fade. "But... do it in front of her. Make her watch."

The edges of the silver band meet in a perfect, seamless circle around my forearm.

The second her men ease up, I move, stumbling out of her office at what feels like the speed of light. I can't breathe. It's not even from the pain.

She's pregnant?

The second I pass the corner store I dip into an alley and spill the contents of my stomach, blood gushing from the band and turning the snow at my feet a deep, dark crimson.

I scream into the night before tearing myself from the city, jumping on the last train and slumping to the ground as it speeds away from Twin Rivers.

It's morning when I stumble up the steps to the safe house, covered in blood, my mind in shambles and heart tearing out of my chest.

This can't happen to her. To *them*. How could I have been so stupid to leave her?

Patton's sitting at the kitchen table pouring a cup of coffee when I explode into the room, crashing through a side table and knocking over two chairs before rushing him, grabbing him by the shoulders.

"Goddess, Soren, what the fuck?" he shouts, his eyes wide with panic, but I'm beyond rationality. He notices the band and pants, "No, Soren–Fuck! What–"

"She's my mate," I shout, then slump to the ground, dragging him with me by his shirt. "She's my fucking mate–"

"Soren–"

"Maeve is *my mate!*"

ON HER OWN SCHEDULE

Maeve

I've heard some of my family say, albeit under their breath, that the old Maeve is back. The temperamental one. The rash and hard-headed on. The one with little patience and a tongue sharp enough to cut glass.

Sometimes I wonder if that's all people think I am.

Maybe it's for the best, I guess. Maybe I now understand why Blake hides his true self behind his powers. I… I had someone to be soft with once. It feels like a lifetime ago.

"You're not even close," Ginny, my midwife, says with a sigh. "Have you taken the herbs?"

"Religiously," I grumble, and Jane, at my side, nods as Ginny smooths the fabric of a bright yellow nightgown–the only thing that fits me at all these days, back over the enormous rise of my belly.

"There are other things we can do, but she's quite cozy in there as it stands," Ginny says with a frustrated sigh. "You're only a day past your due date, and I don't give much stock to those anyway, but the clock is ticking now. You should walk as much as you can. Take the stairs often."

"I'm sure one of the guards is strong enough to pick me up and shake me around like a rag doll to get her out."

Jane bites back a small laugh. Ginny frowns at me, but I shrug. She removes her gloves and tosses them in a waste basket then joins Jane in the arduous task of helping me upright and off the exam table. I grimace against the pressure between my legs. Every movement of my body is difficult these days. I'm constantly winded and feel like I'm too full to eat even though I can barely stomach a bite of food these days.

"Otherwise, you're in good shape, and she's perfectly healthy."

"Great," I whisper, nodding, but flinch when my sweet angel of a daughter drives her foot into my ribs and kicks me several times. "What else can I do to get her out?"

"Well, there is one thing," Ginny says with a shrug but her cheeks go slightly pink. "Some… relations may help start labor."

I arch a brow, loving the way her cheeks begin to fade into a deep crimson. "Relations?"

"Sex," she says pointedly.

"Well," I sigh, "I guess she'll be staying put for a while longer."

"Just keep track of any contractions that are painful or an increase in the practice contractions I told you about."

"I will," I nod, allowing Jane to help me into the satin robe that matches my gown. I retwist my hair into a claw clip before slipping my feet into the fluffy slippers I've taken to wearing most days, seeing as everything else hurts.

I'm starting to wonder if Brie had it easy having Kieran so early but banish that thought as quickly as it comes.

Arm in arm with Jane, she weaves us through the clinic and through a servants hallway leading into the castle proper.

"Should I call your mom and have her come?"

"Not yet. I have more days to suffer, I think."

"Your grandmother called this morning for you. She sent a

package and a bouquet of flowers to try to cheer you up. It's in your office."

"I'll call her later, after I've settled in for the night. I have to talk to Blake first, before he leaves for... wherever he's going. I can't remember."

My brain feels trapped in a perpetual fog these days. I can't think of anything but the baby. I've rearranged my closet at least a dozen times over the past week without any idea as to why. Anything to keep my mind off him, I suppose, as the day our daughter is born nears.

I don't even have a name picked out. I have no idea what to call her. What if she hates her name?

"Maeve?"

"Yeah?" I say, blinking down at Jane.

"I asked if you wanted to retire to your suite after meeting with Blake. I can have a bath ready for you."

"I won't be able to get in and out of the tub without assistance at this point, and I don't want to further scandalize the maids," I huff. "Don't worry about me. I plan on going to bed directly after I meet with Blake, so just... well, I'll see you tomorrow morning, then." We come to stop on the fifth floor where Blake keeps his suite and office. He's been hanging around often these days, especially after the Solstice debacle wedged a knife between me and my grandfather.

Brie visited after Solstice with my parents, Logan, and Kieran. Now, everyone is back in their own little worlds patiently awaiting the newest arrival to the family while I keep everyone at a safe distance.

It's just easier to be cold, I guess. Just like they think I am.

I watch Jane walk away until she disappears around a corner, then I slip into Blake's office without knocking.

He looks up from the briefcase he's hurriedly packing, rolling his eyes. "Do you ever knock?"

"Is there someone hiding under your desk half clothed that I should know about?"

He shoots me a glare. "For your information, I'm late for a meeting with the Mystics that's bound to go all night." He checks his watch then glances at the first inklings of sunset beginning to paint the mountains a deep fuchsia. "Doing your job, technically."

"They could come here and stand around my bed," I say with a shrug, leaning my weight against one of his massive black armchairs that cost a ridiculous sum to purchase and ship to Moonrise from Tarsian.

"I'll be back later tonight. You can't hold off the meeting with the Alpha of Ransom Creek any longer, Maeve, I have him on my schedule for the morning."

"He's the most inconsiderate bastard I've ever met. Make him wait."

Blake smiles, which is entirely uncharacteristic of him, and throws me off guard. He shuts his briefcase with a snap and leaves without another word.

Honestly, I think I was right about how Eastonia was the best place for him. He's... brighter now. Less intolerable. He smiles sometimes, even.

He'll never admit I was right.

I sigh, looking around the office that he says is strictly off limits. I'm shocked he didn't drag me out of here on his way out the door, but he's distracted, it seems. More so by the day.

I round his desk and sit down, testing the limits of his fancy office chair. It's better than mine, that bastard. I reach for the phone to call down to Jane to ask if she can send an army of maids up here to switch the chairs before he comes back, but something catches my eye.

Blake has been splitting his time between his duties here and in Crescent Falls, which includes his work as an architect at his father's old engineering firm. He's brilliant, honestly. I look at blueprints scattered over his otherwise neat table, every line perfectly straight and hand drawn, but it's the stack of graph paper that makes my chest tighten.

My mind whirls, trying to unlock some long forgotten memory I can't place. I smooth my hand over the first page, over incredibly neat handwriting that tickles something deep in my mind. It's perfect, unnervingly so, like it was printed from a computer instead of scribbled by his hand.

"What a weirdo," I mumble then rise with effort, dragging the chair behind me into the hallway.

There's no one around, of course. I wheel the chair to the elevator and press a button on the intercom directly beside the controls, saying into it, "This is Queen Maeve. I'm stealing Blake's office chair and putting it on the elevator. Can someone fetch it, put it in my office, and swap my chair for his?"

A soft laugh echoes through the static before someone, possibly one of the male servants who do the heavy lifting around this massive palace, replies, "Sure thing, Your Majesty."

Smiling to myself, I hike to the sixth floor but stop in the center of the stairwell.

I have a sudden flash of memory from when Soren lifted me into his arms the night I killed Duke. I pressed my cheek to his chest and breathed in his scent while he cradled me in his arms. I turn around, looking down the stairs, backtracking a few steps. I swear I caught his scent–that crisp, forest scent after a heavy rain.

The baby rolls and kicks.

I shake my head, closing my eyes for a moment as my belly tightens into a painless contraction, then continue on my way.

This happens from time to time. I think I see him in a crowd. I think I hear his voice. But then I wake up, and my bed is cold, and his scent isn't there. It's not even on his jacket that still hangs in my closet, which now smells like me and the salt of my tears instead.

The one thing that hasn't faded yet is my grief. To be honest, it's been easy to bury, but when I'm alone and it's quiet, I think of him against my will, making up little daydreams about what could have been, about what could be if he ever came back.

I dream about him being here to meet his daughter when she

comes into the world. I imagine her looking like him, having the same expressions he does, even though I know seeing that in her will be my undoing.

I've just been… coasting.

I'll coast forever. I'll survive, but I've come to the conclusion I won't fully live.

So be it.

I walk the long hallway to the main entrance of my suite, huffing and puffing after climbing the stairs, which made the baby more active than usual. I reach the door and find it unlocked, shaking my head over being so careless, but my attention span is probably three seconds at the most these days.

I shut the door behind me, leaning my weight against it for a moment while I try to catch my breath. The strain in my lower back is getting to the point I can barely handle walking from my office on the second floor to the royal suite on the sixth, but it's good for me to keep moving during these final days of the pregnancy, or so my midwife says, even though all I want–all I can think about–is lying down.

The baby shoves her foot into my ribs again. I wince, chuckling as I smooth a hand over the slope of my belly, the satin fabric of my tent of a nightgown already incredibly tight and snug on my skin.

But then I… look up from where my fingers rest, feeling a strange sensation sweep through my body, my senses, that tells me with certainty that I'm not alone.

"Jane?" I ask, my voice traveling down the length of the snug hallway, through the archways and open doors leading to the various rooms of my suite.

It's not Jane. It's not. I can–I know who it is–

My feet start moving before my mind, and heart, have a chance to catch up, to stop me from hurting my own Goddess damned feelings and getting my hopes up, again, for the thousandth time, but… I turn into the main room–that wide, open, beautifully decorated living area with cream colored couches and ceiling height windows overlooking the sparkling turquoise lake, high above the golden city.

The shadow leaning against the back of one of the couches slowly turns to look at me as the air leaves my lungs in a silent, but strangled, gasp.

"Soren?"

A MANGLED MESS

MAEVE

MY HANDS MOVE TO MY STOMACH ON INSTINCT, CRADLING THE HEAVY swell and the baby currently kicking the absolute life out of me. My lips part with another heavy breath, but words fail me as the phantom, the man who blesses my dreams, lifts his head and meets my eyes.

He looks... the same, but different. That wry, charming boyishness has bled into something hard and dark-hollow, just like I've felt for nine months. He's wearing that same dusty blue backward ball cap, but his hair is a little longer, curls poking out around his ears. His eyes are the same trio of colors but lined with dark circles-exhaustion, I realize, as I take another tentative step into the room, not daring to blink lest he disappear.

The column of his throat bobs as he holds my gaze, searching my eyes, my face, his eyes uncharacteristically wetting as he licks his lips and lets his gaze lower to my stomach.

I feel a sudden jolt of uncertainty, maybe even shame.

"Soren," I suck back the word as it splinters into a shallow, choking sob I can't contain.

He moves, taking four long, swift steps, his hand suddenly caressing my cheek, his thumb swiping tears from my skin, and I know then, without a shadow of a doubt, that this isn't a dream.

"Oh, my Goddess," I croak, and he carefully, gently, presses my cheek against his chest and curls around us–both of us. Me and *our* daughter.

His hand glides down my back, resting right over the sore, aching spot that's been bothering me for days, pressing in just a bit, like he can feel it, too. His other hand brushes down my arm before smoothing over my stomach. He presses a kiss into my hair before inhaling deeply, sighing, his body damn near trembling as we stand in the center of the room, late evening sunlight playing over our bodies.

The baby kicks against his hand. I feel his soft smile against my temple as more tears slide free from my lashes.

"She's yours," I whisper.

"I know," he says so softly I almost miss it. "Maeve, I–" He pulls away enough to look down at me, taking my face between his hands.

I look up at him, my hands holding his waist, and... and I know I should say something. That he should say something, anything, but... we can't. Nine months of what I can only describe as anguish flash before my eyes. Nine months questioning the power of what I felt for him, what it meant, if it was even rational or if I'd lost my mind entirely.

Soren just shakes his head, his mouth parting in a rushed inhalation of breath, then says, "Gods, I fucking missed you–" His mouth crashes into mine before he even finishes his sentence, pressing the words against my lips instead.

I sob against the kiss, the dam of emotion I've been building since the day we parted ways releasing in a torrent of feeling so strong I can't feel anything else. He breaks from the kiss to embrace me again, squeezing me but careful of the baby between us.

"What are you doing here?" I manage to ask, pressing my face against his chest, breathing in his scent of clean, forest air and everything male, musky, and sharp. Goddess, he smells amazing. The same way he used to, I'm sure, but I didn't realize how much I missed until I couldn't find that scent again anywhere, and I craved it.

He tilts my chin to him with his finger and kisses me again, deeply, his hand gliding down my back. He doesn't answer the question. Not right away. I'll ask again later. There's much I need to know, so much he needs to know, but that doesn't matter right this instant, does it?

Have I not wished for this? Begged for it?

But then I smell something new, something that brings back a rush of memory when I start sliding his leather jacket from his shoulders, and my hands stop, pressed to his chest. "Soren? Are you bleeding?"

My hands travel down the length of his arms as I take a step away, shoving myself out of the haze of reunification and into reality. He flinches sharply when my hand grazes over his right forearm. Dread fills my body as I look up into his eyes, seeing more pain than I've ever seen there.

"What happened?"

"Maeve, I need you to listen to me," he says gravely, taking me by the shoulders. "You need to go."

"What? What are you talking about–"

"Go to your parents and grandparents in Veiled Valley. You'll be safe there. You need to pack now, and I'll take you there myself. Please–"

"What the fuck is going on?"

He shakes his head but then goes suddenly pale, like the blood is draining from his cheeks in real time.

"Soren? Soren?!"

He starts to slump forward as the smell of blood swells. Blood seeps down his wrist, dripping onto the white carpet as I catch him to the best of my ability, kneeling against his weight as he starts to fall to the ground.

"JANE!" I scream, sending her name down the mind-link between us; a similar link, I suppose, between shifters as it is to witches. But in the event she's nearby already, I scream again, now on my knees with Soren's head in what's left of my lap.

He grimaces, his eyelashes fluttering.

"Don't move, okay?" I tell him nervously, sniffling as I try to pull his jacket free of his arms. I grunt with the effort, then stifle a gasp as his undershirt–long sleeved and deep gray–soaks with blood from his elbow to his wrist on his right arm. "Oh, Soren," I breathe, my heart rate skyrocketing. "What have you done?"

The door to my suite opens, and Jane's rapid footsteps carry through the hallway, echoing behind her. "Your Majesty–"

I turn to her, my eyes glassy. "I need–I need five healing drafts. *Please*. Hurry!"

Jane stares at me, looks down at the man in my arms, then back to me again. She swallows what questions she had on the tip of her tongue and nods, hurrying away without a single word.

I close my eyes for a moment, taking a deep, deep breath, and start tearing his shirt open at the shoulder. His skin, even on his upper arm, is mottled purple and an even angrier red as the fabric tears down, and down, until...

"No," I whisper, tears flooding down my cheeks as my chest convulses.

A bandage soaked red with blood covers his forearm... right over the scars left from the silver band. I beg myself not to react, swallowing past the lump in my throat, and shiver uncontrollably as I unwind the bandage.

I want to scream, but I can't. Nothing but a choked whimper leaves my lips, pursed tight, as the bandage falls away. His arm is completely mangled, skin flayed, burned in places, with glimpses of bone. A ring of new wounds around his forearm tells me all I need to know. The band was put back on... and he somehow got it off by himself without the use of magic.

"How bad is it?" Soren asks weakly.

"It's infected, you fucking idiot," I sniffle, struggling to maintain my composure.

That wry smile.... Goddess, even at his worst, that smile works its way through my body, untying the knots around my heart. "Who did this to you?"

"An ironsmith," he says, his eyes opening to slits as beads of perspiration appear on his hairline. "An expensive one."

"You paid someone to do this to you?"

"I had to."

"Why?"

"I had to come to you. When I found out, I had to come. I should have–I should have been here months ago. I shouldn't have let you go in the first place."

My chest squeezes around his words, making it impossible to take a breath.

Jane's footsteps sound through the hallway again as she huffs and puffs, desperately out of breath from sprinting what must have been the length of the castle and back. She's bright red when she skids to a stop beside me, kneeling with two handfuls of healing drafts clutched in each hand, her eyes wide and mouth gaping as she sees Soren's arm. "It's not going to be enough–"

"I know, I know," I cut in, waving her off. "It'll be enough to help, at least, until I... until I decide what to do." Who to call, more like it. I grind my teeth as we start popping corks. Soren tries to shy away, growling his protests after I dump the first draft into his mouth, and he promptly spits it out all over us. It's bitter, I get it, but he needs it.

"Stop–"

"Shut up and take your medicine," I bite out, clutching his cheek, pinching his mouth open until he stops fighting and allows us to help him.

Jane collects the empty vials, dumping them into a wastebasket in one of the side bathrooms, then hurries back to my side. "What do you need me to do?"

I wonder if she recognizes him. She has to, given that she tied Soren to a chair once, watched as I dumped icy water over his head and slapped him repeatedly. Now, his head is in my lap, his cheek pressed against my belly, where his daughter is repeatedly kicking him, unused to someone else touching her. I doubt he's aware enough to notice much of anything right now, let alone that, but he leans into the sensation as the drafts begin to wind through his body, his tense expression relaxing.

I wrack my brain for solutions, chewing my lip as I devise a solid plan of action, at least for the next few hours. "I can't lift him into bed, so I'm going to stay here with him for a moment, and when he gets some strength back, I'm going to–to put him up with me," I tell her.

She nods, dutifully knitting her fingers together over her apron.

"Soren is an honored guest of my court," I continue. "If anyone asks, he's my guest, but no one is allowed on this floor for the time being, especially here, in my suite."

"Patton," Soren breathes, wincing.

We look down at him. "Patton? What about him?" I ask hurriedly.

"He's here. In Moonrise."

"Where?" I give his cheek a few gentle pats to keep him awake and talking while the healing drafts begin to settle, some of the bruising on his arm already fading.

"One of the hotels near the train station. The big one… with the blue paint."

I turn back to Jane. "Have… Niall fetch him. He's tall, with dark hair and blue eyes. Have Niall tell him he's being summoned by the queen. He'll come. And Niall needs to be discreet about it. No signing in. No ID checks. Nothing like that."

"I'll make sure." Jane nods. Niall is one of my favorite guards at the castle–kind and always joking around but serious and deadly when he needs to be. I trust he won't ask questions.

"Other than that, can you find him some clothes? And have a tray of food brought up when he wakes? Something warm and hearty. Stew, steak, red meat or whatever the kitchen has that can be made and brought up as soon as possible."

"Whisky," Soren says through gritted teeth, the color in his face returning.

"Don't get ahead of yourself," I reply sharply, sucking in a breath. "Wine is better for this. Uhm, have Trinity in the kitchen fortify it with herbs and heat it just a bit. I'm thinking... cinnamon, nutmeg, and other warming spices. Heat it in iron."

"For the healing. For the blood," Jane nods, likely recalling the rigorous potions curriculum every witch in Moonrise had to pass during our school years, including me.

"Exactly."

Jane turns on her heel and leaves, shutting and locking the door behind her, and silence swells.

Soren takes a heavy breath, then another, struggling to keep his eyes open. I wince as I stretch out my cramping, aching legs, readjusting his head on my thighs, and wait.

His arm is far too mangled to be healed using drafts. It'll kill the infection, I hope, but otherwise... I need *Misty*. I might even need Cole, to be honest. I could, I guess, use the clinic downstairs, but the questions that would arise....

"You're huge," Soren says almost dreamily, riding the edge of what I assume will be a full body stupor in a matter of minutes.

I glare down at him. "Did you really just say that to me?"

"How much longer?" he asks, his eyes finally closing.

I chew my lip to stop it from trembling as I absently run my fingers through his hair. "Until you heal? I don't know. Several hours, but it won't be complete–"

"Until *she* comes?" He turns his face against my stomach, his words slurred as potion induced sleep washes through him, his body relaxing more than I think it ever has in his life.

"Any day now," I whisper, fighting tears again, forcing myself not to think about what happens now.

YOUR HOME NOW

THE NEXT PERSON WHO ENTERS THE SUITE IS FAMILIAR, AND IT'S A relief. Patton, only half an hour after Jane left to start spreading the word to those we trust, arrives in a hurry, his face washed in concern, then frustration, when he races down the hallway with Niall hot on his heels.

Niall, tall and muscular, with dark hair and brown eyes, his skin a rich golden brown against the deep crimson of his guard uniform, skids to a stop when he sees me on the floor in nothing but a night-gown and robe with a stranger's head in my lap—a stranger who broke into the castle, no doubt, sliding past my guards, and my shields, for Goddess's sake.

"Maeve," Patton rushes out, trapped between what he feels is duty to me as a friend, as Soren's friend, and being in the presence of a royal. A queen. He gives me a weak, awkward bow before giving Niall an unsure glance and moving closer to us.

Niall, unaware of the situation and what he was walking into, grabs Patton's arm, but I shake my head, holding out a hand.

"Niall, please help me put this man in bed. You and Patton can lift him. I… I can't." I motion to my stomach, giving my guard a flat smile, but my tone leaves no room nor invitation for argument.

Soren is out cold, which I expected. His arm is no longer bleeding heavily, but I'm worried that'll change when the herbs start wearing off. The food and new clothing hasn't been delivered yet, but I'm under the impression Jane is waiting until the coast is clear, giving Niall time to fetch and deliver Patton. She might be meek and shy, but she's smart. She knows how precarious this situation is, and judging by the look on Patton's face as he gazes down at me and Soren, it's worse than I think.

Soren isn't just hurt. Something else is wrong–very wrong. Wrong enough for him to break whatever unspoken vow we made in that run-down cottage when we tore ourselves apart and parted ways. Something that brought him here, mangled, bleeding, and desperate.

I keep my lips clamped shut as I watch the men pick Soren up. I wordlessly rise and direct Niall to put him in my bed, ignoring the look of shock and curiosity flashing behind his eyes when he and Patton deposit Soren there. I hang back, my arms resting on my stomach, but then follow Niall into the hallway, stopping him with a touch to his forearm.

He nearly shies away in shock from me touching him but recovers himself as I say, "Keep quiet about this."

"Yes, Your Highness."

"I mean it. I trust you, Niall. These men are my guests. Jane is already tending to his injuries, and I am safe." I step closer to him, keeping my gaze locked on his, dominating him despite our small difference in height. "I want extra guards on patrol–at least double the normal amount. The main gates are closed to the public until further notice, and any deliveries made to the clinic and the staff entrances will be limited and heavily overseen going forward."

"Yes, my Queen."

I step into him, closing the distance between us to the point I can almost feel him on the cusp of shying away, but I squeeze his arm, keeping him locked in place. "You're a fantastic guard. You're respected and admired by your colleagues, and I see that. I want you leading them. You do this for me, keep this quiet, and keep the castle locked down, and I'll make you head of security. You have my word."

His jaw goes momentarily slack before he takes a sharp breath and nods, eyes wide.

"Go," I say under my breath, releasing him, and he swiftly disappears, the main door to my suite snapping closed. I race to the door, locking it tight, before whirling and rushing back to my bedroom where Patton is pacing at Soren's bedside looking immensely stressed.

Soren groans weakly before slumping again.

"What happened?" I ask, but Patton rounds the bed, his blue eyes shining in the fading light of sunset. In two quick steps, we collide in an embrace.

I didn't realize how much I needed this. Tears sting my eyes, but I blink them away, squeezing him back. My hand drifts down his arm until I reach the silver band he still wears, and shy away, stepping away from him. Why hasn't he been freed yet? That was the whole point, wasn't it? The whole reason Soren remained trapped in the Viper's clutches? To save Patton and pay their debts?

"Are you all right?" he asks, genuinely concerned.

"What do you think?" I squeak, unused to the amount of... feeling choking my body. "Of course I'm not okay. Soren just walked back into my life and is–is so hurt. What happened? Why did he do this to himself?"

Patton chews his lower lip before replying, "I warned him. He was adamant he had the band removed."

"But I removed his band months ago!"

"He went to the Viper to pay the debts–our debts. She... she wouldn't let him go."

My stomach hollows out. "But he could have paid the debt this past summer? I don't understand–"

"He's been lying low. He had to–"

"He hasn't, though." I step toward him, balling my hands into fists at my side. "I know everything, Patton. I know he's working for someone he calls the Architect. I know three more Alphas disappeared, and two more died since this summer, among a slew of others either dead or in hiding. You have no idea what I've had to do here, as queen, to keep Soren safe–"

"The Viper wants you–she wants the *baby*. She told him the baby was his next mark. He didn't know you were pregnant before that, Maeve." Patton closes his eyes, a shiver running through his body as he begins to recount what happened. "She put him in a band again. He was held down, from what I believe, and she forced the matter. He came straight to me in a panic, saying–" He cuts himself off abruptly, shaking his head. "Saying he needed to go to Moonrise. We came straight here. I don't know how he got into the castle–"

"I do," I murmur, closing my eyes against a burst of frustration. "He told me I needed to go to Veiled Valley to be with my family."

"And you should–"

"We're safest here. Both of you are safe here. I can't promise I can keep you safe if we involve my grandfather, though. You both need to understand that." I open my eyes and hold his gaze. "He's like me. Suspicious and cold. It'll take time to talk him out of killing you both. He'll act on impulse first."

Patton swallows hard, nodding. Someone with his level of knowledge about my family would know that there are two men in my family that shouldn't ever be fucked with. The rest... well, they would at least hear them out.

But Grandpa Ryatt and Ryan wouldn't waste that kind of time, especially the former.

"You're going to stay here, in the castle," I tell him. "There's a suite next door. It's Jane's, my assistant. She's trustworthy and knows Soren, knows he's the father of my baby. She's already aware of the situation."

"I can stay in the hotel."

"No, you're a guest. A friend," I cut in.

His mouth twitches into what I could describe as a smile if he'd let it happen, but he takes a breath, nodding.

I step closer to him, though, motioning for his arm. "You're not going back to that life, Patton. When I said I knew everything, I meant… everything. Everything you've been forced to do, as well."

His cheeks heat, and he drops his gaze to the floor.

"You're going to stay here, with us. You can live here, work here if you want. I miss your baking."

He chews his lip in an effort to not look excited. "I have my chickens to think about."

"They can come, too," I offer with a small smile while my chest tightens. "This is over, okay? I'll deal with the Viper. The two of you have been through enough."

"Soren won't stay."

I ignore the pang of disappointment radiating through my chest. "It's not up to him anymore. I'm not letting him go this time."

Patton finally smiles, but it's brief.

I gently take his arm, my powers already simmering, waiting to strike. "This isn't going to hurt that bad. I promise. I'm stronger than I was when I did this for Soren."

"I don't care," he says, meeting my eyes. "Just do it."

I grip his arm but keep my eyes locked on his as I send a painless rush of my magic over his skin. I hadn't noticed it the first time, but the band isn't just silver. When I'd taken it off Soren, we'd been in the middle of a terribly violent fight, and I'd thrust every bit of my power into his, breaking past what I think is some kind of shield–*magic*. It has to be. The silver shimmers as I tighten my grip. Patton winces, exhaling in a growl of pain but holds himself steady. My powers tear through whatever binds the silver in place, shredding the metal until it pops free of his arm and falls to the ground with a clank.

Patton stumbles a step back, smoothing his hand over his gnarled skin.

I step into my bathroom, gathering a towel and a few healing drafts from the cabinet. They're not as strong as what I gave Soren, but the unhealed burn on Patton's arm will take to this easily.

"Take both of these, and go rest in the suite next door for a few hours. No one will bother you. I'll have food and drink sent up, and I'll check on you after a while, but don't leave the suite without me, okay?" I press the healing drafts into his hand then bend, my belly straining, to pluck the silver band off the floor with the towel, wrapping it tight.

"Is Soren going to be okay?"

"Honestly, I don't know," I reply, stepping out of the bedroom with him and shutting the door behind me. I walk the length of the hallway toward the sitting room and toss the towel in the fireplace, sending a blast of fire from my fingertips to ignite the fabric. "His arm is… I can't fix him, Patton. Whatever the ironsmith did to get it off, it's… I can't take him to the clinic or bring nurses here to mend it, given the circumstances, and even if I could, I don't think they'd have the ability to fix the damage."

"He's going to lose the arm. I told him that. Even the ironsmith told him that, but he wouldn't listen."

"Maybe not. I'm working on something, but I just haven't decided yet. But I swear to you, and to him, that I'm not going to let him lose his arm, or his hand, or his fingers. I'll fix this."

I walk Patton across the length of my suite to a connecting door that leads into the adjoining, much smaller, suite. "This entire floor was for my grandparents' private use," I tell him, leading him into one of my favorite spaces in the entire castle. "I just finished renovating, but this suite used to be my grandmother's. They shared a bedroom, of course, but she liked her space, and he wanted her to have a studio that faces south because it has the best light." The smaller suite opens up with a simple, airy living space and three adjoining rooms. Grandma Ella's old studio is lit from within by the last light of the sunset as Patton looks around in awe.

"The bedroom is to the left. It's a brand new bed. You'll be the first to break it in. Jane still likes to sleep in her old room downstairs in the maids' quarters, but she does keep some of her things up here."

"I'm not in the way?"

"No, I'm happy you're here." I squeeze his arm before leaving, walking steadily back to my suite, closing the connecting door but keeping it unlocked.

Silence swells, and it's welcome. I move into the bedroom where Soren is lying on his side, his mangled arm open to the air.

I gather some from a kit in my bathroom and sit beside him, careful not to wake him as I wind them bandages over his skin.

But he stirs, twitching, his eyes opening to slits as he takes in his new surroundings… then turns to me.

I don't say a word as I slide into bed beside him, exhausted, my back and lower belly aching from the strain of my advanced, nearly overdue, pregnancy.

He turns to curl his body around mine, tucking his arm under my neck so I lay my cheek against his bicep, his hurt arm draped over what's left of my waist, which isn't much these days.

I watch the sun slip below the mountains and the sky turn a deep, starry purple, then close my eyes to try to catch a few hours of sleep before I make a decision that will change everything.

But only if he stays.

WHO THE F I AM

Maeve

I wake to total darkness, shooting upright as my heart thunders in my chest. I rarely dream, but I felt… uneasy, to say the least, about something that now I can't fully remember. I reach up to rub my eyes, exhaling, then inhaling deeply before going completely rigid as the events of the last several hours come back to me in a rush.

I fly out of bed–at least, I roll–stumbling into a pair of slippers while cradling the swell of my belly and groping in the dark for my robe. There's a slight chill in the late winter air as I rush out of the bedroom, sliding around the sharp corner into the living room where a single lamp is on, illuminating the two figures sitting around the fireplace, which has burned down to embers.

Soren lifts his head to look at me, his eyes dark and details blurred by the shadows. Patton rises, the frantic look in his eyes softening as he swallows hard, his Adam's apple bobbing. I obviously just interrupted a tense conversation judging by the look on both of their faces.

I press my hand to my chest, panting, my other hand braced

against the wall as I struggle to catch my breath. I bend ever so slightly in a weak attempt to fill my lungs–which the baby has been using as punching bags–and nearly miss the silent exchange between Soren and Patton.

Patton gives Soren the sharpest, dirtiest look I've ever seen before striding past me in the direction of the door that adjoins the two suites, saying in passing, "I'm sorry if we woke you."

"You didn't," I pant, but he's already fading into the shadows. I close my eyes, inhaling deeply as my belly tightens into one of those practice contractions my midwife keeps hounding me about, and when I exhale, Soren's by my side, taking me by the elbow in an attempt to steady me.

I can feel the tension pouring from him as I struggle to straighten, weakly waving him away.

"You need to go back to bed," he says, his voice a low, deep whisper in the silence. "It's late."

I squint through the darkness, catching the faint glow of the silver light drifting through the windows. It's snowing again, falling in dizzy sheets that catch the light of the outdoor lights as it falls to the ground in thick clumps.

"Maeve," Soren says under his breath.

"I'm fine," I rush out, straightening, still bracing my hand on the wall. "What are you doing out here?" I reach for his arm, but he moves away, gripping my elbow as he guides us back around the corner toward my bedroom. "Soren–"

"You shouldn't be up like this," he says gruffly, and I rip my elbow out of his grasp.

"I'm pregnant, Soren. Not injured." I whirl into my bedroom and turn on the lamp on my bedside table, squeezing my eyes shut against the sharp glow before whirling back to where he's standing in the doorway. He looks beyond exhausted. A tight, blood stained bandage covers his arm. I was right about the bleeding starting up again. I knew it would. With a heavily annoyed sigh, I stride past him into the ensuite bathroom and start rifling through the cabinets, grumbling,

"Patton told me everything, Soren. You can drop the hero act. I'm not going to Veiled Valley."

Soren doesn't move from the doorway as I clutch another vial of healing potion and move back into the light, coming to a stop a few feet away from where he's standing. "The Viper put another band on you when she told you to come here and kill our baby, didn't she?"

Soren sees red. I can taste the tension, the fury, pouring off him as I roll the vial between my fingers, keeping my gaze locked on his.

When he fails to respond, I add, "I'm safest here. You're safest here–"

"I can't stay–"

"You are. You're staying."

"Maeve–"

"I'm not letting you go. I can't." I grip the vial hard enough to warm the glass. His expression shatters for several seconds before he regains his composure, his eyes going characteristic hard and sharp.

"You know who I work for. You know who *she* works for–"

"I don't give a shit," I snarl, my eyes flooding with tears I can't blink back. "Do you know what I've had to do over the past nine months? What strings I've had to pull to keep you a secret while you gallivanted around the Allied Kingdoms killing more and more people for the Architect? I don't know what you're trying to accomplish, but I made it possible for you to do it, Soren. I sent my own father's forces on fake missions to keep them off your trail because they got fucking *close*, okay? I've been lying to *my family* for you. I've been lying to Eastonia for *you*, and you're going to stand here and tell me you can't stay and let me help you out of this?!"

"This is why," he says through gritted teeth, taking two rushed steps toward me, more blood soaking the bandage. "*This* is why, Maeve. What kind of future did you think we had? I'm a fucking murderer. I've spent the last ten years of my life working against the very kingdom you now rule–"

"I don't care–"

"I do," he rasps, but his eyes betray his tone. That steely darkness retreats, giving a glimpse of what he really feels but can't voice. Pain. A desperate, twisting kind of agony I've never seen before.

"Did you come back for me?" I ask through my tears. "Or just to warn me that the Viper put a mark on my–*our*–unborn daughter's head and try to force me to leave–"

"I came when I knew–"

"Did you come for me?" I shout, pushing past a sob. "Are you here–are you here for me?"

He searches my eyes, his chest rising and falling with each shallow inhale. "Look at what I did to you, Maeve, and tell me I have the right to even grovel at your feet and ask for forgiveness," he says in a near whisper, shaking his head.

My hands instinctively cradle my stomach. He takes another step in my direction.

"I got you pregnant," he continues darkly.

I tilt my chin in what I hope is a look of defiance. "Well, it's not like we took the necessary precautions."

"Don't fuck with me right now."

"Don't come into my house trying to boss me around, you fucking bastard, and expect me to bend the knee and do what you want! I am the Queen of Eastonia, Soren. I'm not going to run and hide because some crazy bitch wants to kill my baby!"

"You're on Hannibal's radar, Maeve!" he shouts, his eyes darkening as he lets his real feelings flare. "He knows. He knows about *us*. The Viper knows about *us*. She knows the baby is *mine* and knew I'd come straight here. We're not safe here–any of us." He motions to my stomach, reaching for me, but hesitates, curling his fingers into a fist.

"Have you forgotten who the fuck I am?" I snarl, letting my powers flow. My eyes burn crimson, my fingertips crackling with embers, my magic scenting the air with iron and flames.

Soren watches me closely but holds my gaze, unwavering, even as my magic begins to fill the room.

A fiery electric current scurries around us, but he's totally unfazed. In fact, his eyes narrow, his expression tightening into annoyance. "*Stop.*"

There he is.

My powers abruptly shut off, and the electricity in the room snaps. He flinches, rubbing his neck, while continuing to glare like my magic snapped him like little rubber bands all over his body, and honestly, I hope it did. "I'm not afraid of the Viper or Hannibal. I want them to come. I want them to try their best. I hope they fucking do. It will save me an immense amount of time tracking them down to punish them for what they did to you!"

He steps into me, taking me by the shoulders. "You're not fighting this battle for me."

I shove him back. "I never asked your opinion. You came here just to warn me they're coming for me and our baby, right? Now you're going to leave again–"

"I'm escorting you to Veiled Valley–"

"I don't need you to escort me anywhere," I snarl, those tears of pure frustration prickling into existence again. "I can take myself there with a snap of my fingers. I'd be there in seconds."

"Then do it," he growls, gripping my arms. "Go–"

I shove him back, but he doesn't budge. I shove him again, my mouth pulled tight in a pained grimace as nine months of pure, unfiltered emotion breaks through the dam I built, spilling in a tidal wave that's nearly strong enough to bring me to my knees. I grip his shirt as a sob tangles in my throat and makes my next words sound like gravel when I ask, one final time, "Did you come back for me? Was there any part of you that–that–came back because you–you just wanted to be here, with me?" My voice is small, almost weak. I can't even look him in the eyes right now. I hate this–begging like this. Feeling broken and small as his body closes in on mine.

I don't pull away when his arms wrap around me, tugging me close. His scent blurs my senses, turning my fury and turmoil into liquid heat I'm forced to ignore, trying to keep my head clear and safe from what my body desperately wants, trying to keep my focus off the fact my feelings for him never faded, but maybe for him, they did.

"I've never done this before," he admits in the softest tone he's ever used with me. "I've never had something that–that didn't make any sense, that fucking sucked to lose. I don't know where to go from here, Maeve."

"It doesn't matter–"

"But it does. You're the queen. Not just any queen, either. A Firestone queen."

I curl my arms around his waist and press my cheek to the crook of his shoulder, closing my eyes.

"I'm… uneducated. My parents were rogues who never amounted to anything and are likely dead. I spent my life trying to survive. I had no goals, no real home. I have enough blood on my hands to fill a small city, and I can't… I can't ever take back what I've done."

"You were forced–"

"There were things I did willingly," he cuts in, his hand smoothing down my back. "You know that."

I keep my eyes closed, barely able to breathe as I wait for him to shove us apart again.

But he grips me tighter, closer, his other hand unraveling from around my body to press against the side of my stomach. The baby rolls, kicking him, and I feel the softest, saddest smile against my temple when he says, "I did *this* to you, and you've been going through this alone for months."

"I had no way to tell you."

"It doesn't matter. I put you on that train knowing I was making a mistake, but I couldn't see a way out of it. The only thing that mattered to me then, and now, was your safety and reputation. I wanted to say fuck it all and take you away, settling us somewhere in the Highlands where no one would be able to find us. I let myself imagine what that would have been like–a home together. A place where you weren't the queen and I wasn't something out of your family's nightmares."

I pull away, looking up at him. "That's what you're worried about? My reputation?"

He searches my eyes as I pull away even further, taking several steps away from him.

"You're worried about what people will think if they find out about us?" I press, trying not to laugh. "Soren-"

"I'm fucking terrified of anything bad happening to you, Maeve," he growls, his eyes going dark as iron again. "I can't handle the thought. It's been eating me alive-"

"I'm fine. I'll always be fine. I'm a Firestone witch, for fuck's sake! I'm more powerful-"

"You're my mate!" he shouts, his patience snapping and shattering around the room, which goes perfectly, completely still-so silent I can hear the snow falling beyond the windows.

A SLIGHT MISUNDERSTANDING

MAEVE

"WHAT DID YOU SAY?" MY MOUTH GOES PAINFULLY DRY. I TRY TO swallow but fail, humming a choked sob as I search his eyes for understanding.

The four feet of distance between feels like an ocean when he balls his hands into fists at his sides, widening his stance like he's preparing for battle, and maybe he is. I can feel my own power prickling over my skin as it stands.

"You're my mate, Maeve."

I imagine this is what it feels like to be stabbed in the heart. I clutch the corner poster of my bed for support as I sink onto the mattress, overcome by... a sudden, overwhelming understanding that makes the last nine months make absolute sense.

This whole time.

All of these feelings–this insane, otherworldly heartbreak...

"How long?" I ask, unable to look him in the eyes. "How long have you known?"

"Since the morning after you danced on that table at the hotel in the Highlands," he admits, his voice level and deep, like he's holding back whatever he's feeling. "I nearly–"

"You almost marked me," I say under my breath, finishing his thought. I remember that morning clearly, like I'm back in that room right now, watching him fighting for his life while he yelled at me to go shower, to wash off that *scent*. "You–you kept your distance from me the entire walk back into the Roguelands."

"I wasn't sure what was happening until we–until I realized we'd been spotted and followed." He moves through the dark, his body casting mine in shadow as he sinks onto the edge of the mattress beside me with a soft groan.

I look at him then, taking in the expression sharpening in the planes of his face. I always forget how young he is. He'd be… twenty-seven now, I suppose. I don't even know his birthday, but he's lived what seems like a dozen lives compared to my single one.

Those lives show when he scrubs a hand over his face and turns ever so slightly to look at me.

"I want to know everything," I tell him, and he nods.

"I know."

"You–you knew this whole time, and you didn't–"

"You can't feel it like I can, Maeve."

"What makes you think this has been easier on me?" I whisper, unable to raise my voice like I want to. How often have I lain in this very bed, alone, talking myself out of scaling the castle walls to scream my despair from the rooftops, praying he could hear me? Find me? Save me from this torment? How often have I wanted to claw out my own heart and inspect it for Soren's brand, like he laid claim to it, forcing me to forever carry the weight of my feelings when he was so, so out of reach?

I feel it, too, I realize, and it's… shocking. I rub my upper chest on impulse, trying to feel the strings binding us, but it's… faint. A taste of what it could be if I had more shifter blood, I suppose.

It's still completely overwhelming.

I steal a glance at him, and I see the pain he's been wearing since he came here, waiting for me, likely stealing his way into the castle to get to me, and realize it has nothing to do with his arm.

He was coming back for the mate he forced himself to leave behind.

"I realized we were being followed," he begins, "shortly after we dropped back into the Roguelands. I took us down that old road knowing it was going to be difficult for them to maneuver into that ghost town in their wolf forms. The whole time I was thinking that I… that I couldn't keep you safe, that I'd die there, protecting you, if it meant you'd be able to get home. That's when I really knew that you were my mate. I was going to die to ensure you got home, when just a few days before I… I was begging the Goddess to take you away somehow."

I choke back a laugh, but Soren isn't laughing. He's entirely serious as he glares at my obvious attempt to rein myself in and then rolls his eyes to the windows with a sigh.

"I'm sorry," I whisper, wiping a rogue tear from my cheek. "Go on."

"This isn't funny to me."

"I know. I also know that you really hated me for a while."

"I never hated you." He breathes, glancing in my direction. "I hate that I–" He cuts himself off abruptly and takes several heartbeats worth of a pause before continuing, "I hated that I wanted you, Maeve. From the moment you absolutely beat my ass in my old apartment, I wanted you. I was curious about you from the beginning."

I'm not sure what to say, so I say nothing, folding my hands over my belly instead. He shifts his weight, his thigh brushing mine as we stare out the windows at the falling snow for several long, silent seconds.

"You shifted for the first time in years that day, in the village."

"Yeah," he answers with a nod.

"Is that when it snapped into place?"

"No. Well, I guess, yeah. It did." He chews his lower lip, closing his eyes as if summoning the fine details of the memory. "In the hotel, that morning, when you slid out of bed, and I could smell you over the blood… that nearly did me in, as you remember. I was out of my mind. Then, in the village, when I shifted and saw you getting dragged away, I honestly blacked out. There was nothing in my head but ripping the Hound off you, off *my* mate. So, I did, and I took you inside."

"And I kissed you." I look at him, my heart beginning to beat out of rhythm.

"And you kissed me, and my mind went blank save for me… claiming you." He runs his hand over his face like the memory is suddenly too much to bear. "I was so hard on you–"

"I liked it–"

"It doesn't matter, Maeve, and that's what I'm trying to say right now. I didn't have control over my wolf at all that night. I wanted you, badly. Fucking desperately, and that had nothing to do with being able to shift again, but you were my mate, and that part of me was desperate to keep you. But I still put you on that train and sent you home. I had to. I saw no other way to keep you other than sending you back because I'm not–I'm not the kind of guy you need. I'm not someone who can stand by your side while you rule. Stuffing me in a tailored suit wouldn't have changed who I am and what I've done. Your family would have found out who I really was eventually. Your public would be curious, and it would have been just a matter of time until the truth came out, and where would that leave you? Dealing with very public fallout, Maeve."

"It wasn't just your decision to make for the both of us."

"I did what I had to do. I made sure you made it back to Moonrise safely. I kept tabs on you. I made sure you weren't followed during your grand tour, or whatever the hell the media called it, and kept the Viper busy while you were out in her domain. I gave us a clean break so you could fucking live your life as queen–"

"You sent tea to the castle."

Soren closes his eyes with a sigh.

"The night of my coronation and the Rite… you sent tea to the castle. You had it delivered to Jane. You said–you–" My eyes fill with tears.

"You never needed that necklace," he finishes, his voice a soft whisper. "I remember."

"This whole time you've been... you've just been making sure I was safe? But you knew I was. I have guards, Soren. I have my powers–"

"I couldn't fucking sleep, Maeve. For months. I just... I wanted to feel close to you somehow." He picks at his shirt, his hand directly over his heart as he watches the snow falling in dizzying silver sheets beyond the frosted glass.

Soren and I are alike in so many ways. This is terribly hard for him... talking about how he feels. Putting those feelings into words... I know because the past months have been impossible for me to describe.

I buried it, just like he buried our bond. It ate me alive, just like it's eating him alive now.

"Why did you come back?" I ask, knowing the conversation could go two ways. He'll pull a stunt, rejecting me, telling me it's what's best for us, or... I wince, looking down at my hands.

"Enough time passed that I felt it was safe for me to go to Twin Rivers to pay the debts we owed. Patton didn't want me to. He stayed behind, but I wanted out, officially. Your tour of Eastonia and the summit in Crescent Falls kept the Viper busy. She couldn't move contraband like she normally does, and I figured she wouldn't fuss when I gave her what I owed her, but... it didn't go as planned."

He pauses, and I wait for him to resume.

"She... told me I had another mark, that she couldn't let me go yet, and when I refused, I was held down, and she made another band. I found out... I found out about the baby then. The news had gone public. I went back to the safe house and..."

"Nearly cut off your arm?"

He rolls his lower lip between his teeth, casting me a narrow-eyed glance. "She made this band tighter than the last."

"Would you have... would you have come back regardless if I was pregnant or not?"

He looks toward the window, his eyes shadowed by the lamplight.

Beyond the frosted glass, the first inklings of morning light are starting to fade into view.

"I don't know how to do this, Maeve," he replies under his breath. "I don't know how to be with someone. I don't want to hurt you." His eyes meet mine. "I don't know how to be a mate, or a father, fuck, I…"

I reach for him, placing my hand on his thigh. His fingers absently find mine. "Would you have come back for me?" I ask again, my heart on the verge of shattering. Shattering for him–and for us. Shattering for the little boy who used to get in fights, who had a future given to him then ripped out from underneath him, and the man he was forced to become.

"I've been coming back here from the beginning," he says with great effort. "Going to the tea shop, sitting on a roof wondering what you were up to."

My lower lip quivers.

"I came back," he says, turning to me, "and broke into the castle–easily, I should add–because I couldn't fucking take it anymore, and I wasn't going to leave you alone with our baby. And now you have to go–"

"Listen," I interrupt, clutching his face. "I can deal with the Viper, all right? I'm not going to go hide in Veiled Valley. But the second you set foot in Veiled Valley dragging me back there, my dad is going to kill you while my grandfather watches. We're safest here."

"You're not understanding–"

"I don't need you to protect me. I should be protecting you–"

"That is not how this is going to work."

"Because you're a man? Because you've spent your life fighting to keep it? I can't–what you've been through, Soren, is terrible. It's horrific. I think about it all the time, and I don't–I can't let you go back to it. I won't."

He smooths a hand over my cheek.

"You're not afraid of me and what I can do, but you should be," I say in a near whisper. "You don't understand what I'm actually capable of. My powers aren't even fully mature yet and won't be until she's born. I could wipe out the entire kingdom with a snap of my fingers if I willed it. I am not afraid of Hannibal or the Viper. I'm afraid of losing you..." I meet his eyes.

He just... stares at me, searching my eyes for understanding, like he can't place the feelings ricocheting through his chest. For the thousandth time, I remember this man, this good, honest, devoted man grew up thinking he was a plague to society. That everything he needed came with the price of violence, paid in blood. A man who was beaten and abused as a child. A man whose worth was decided by how hard he could fight and how much pain he could tolerate before bending, and he never bent.

"*I love you,*" I whisper.

Soren blinks, pulling away from me just a touch, and looks momentarily confused. His mouth moves, but no sound comes out as he runs his fingers through his hair then scrubs his hand over his face, his freshly shaven jaw, like he did his best to look... nice for me. "No one has ever said that to me before."

"I know," I bite out, fighting against another torrent of tears.

Silence fills the space between us. I let it, letting the truth of my feelings sink in, telling myself I won't be heartsick if he can't say them back because the fact that he's here is enough.

Soren reaches for me but flinches, drawing in a sharp breath as blood seeps into the bandage. I rise, wiping my eyes, and hurry to where I left the healing draft on my dresser, but he shakes his head. "I'm not taking any more of that."

"It'll stop the bleeding!"

"It'll put me to sleep," he argues. "We have things we need to talk about first, Maeve."

"Let me see it, then, and I'll decide what we do."

I sit beside him again, taking his arm. The wound is just... massive. Massive and all wrong. It won't heal, even with the healing potions still lacing his blood. I could... cauterize it with my magic, I suppose, but there has to be an easier way...

And there is an easier way, it just means bringing my family into this.

A sharp knock echoes in the recesses of the suite. I turn toward the sound, furrowing my brows as footfalls stretch through the darkness.

Soren rises, on edge, hackles raised, but I beat him to the door and step into the hallway just as Blake speeds into view, looking relieved to see me awake.

"We have a situation," he says as he stalks toward the doorway to my bedroom. "You need to move, now, to a safer location."

"What's going on?"

Soren, only a few paces behind me, and out of view of the hallway, stiffens. I glance at him, noticing the odd look crossing behind his eyes when Blake replies, "There's a possible intruder in the castle. I was just informed there's a broken window in the gallery."

I throw a look at Soren, but his eyes are narrowed to slits when Blake turns into the room, reaching for me.

"Guards are going to clear your rooms–" Blake freezes, his eyes sweeping toward Soren.

"There's a slight miscommunication," I begin. "I have guests–"

"What the fuck are *you* doing here?" Blake snarls.

"*You?*" Soren says in disbelief, chuckling.

Blake makes the grave mistake of grabbing my arm... in front of my *mate*.

YOU ALL ALONG

Maeve

When I was young, Aviva told me a story about her early days in the Silverhide pack and the first time she ever saw Ryan in his beast form. I didn't understand why back then, but she explained that newly mated couples occasionally go through a bit of a rough patch in the first days of their relationship. The men, she explained, were generally uncontrollable and often territorial of their new mates, going as far as to attack other males for even looking in their direction.

Touching another man's mate, however? *Especially* his heavily pregnant mate?

That's a death sentence.

"Soren!" I rush out, but it's too late.

Soren and Blake collide, Blake's iron grip on my upper arm snapping away in an instant, leaving me teetering off balance in the dark hallway. The sound of the men colliding with the wall and my new plaster cracking and falling to the floor brings me back to startling focus, and I quickly flip a light switch, flooding the corridor outside of my room with glaring light. "You fucking assholes! STOP IT!" I scream over the sound of Blake's fist meeting Soren's jaw and vice versa.

"SOREN!" I screech, waddling down the hallway after them, but both men are practically foaming at the mouth. Blake's eyes begin to glow, and I panic, raising my hands and sending a blast of heat in a warning to calm the fuck down, but they ignore me.

"You–fucking–bastard!" Soren snarls, rolling on top of Blake and pressing his forearm across Blake's throat. "This whole fucking time–"

"Shut the fuck up," Blake croaks, teeth bared, "Don't say another fucking word–" He shoves Soren hard enough to send him careening to the side, and then Blake is on top of Soren, but this time has his hands wrapped tight around Soren's throat.

I rip a lamp out of the wall, the cord trailing behind me, and run as fast as I can, wielding the lamp like a sword and aiming directly at Blake's fat head.

Patton sprints into view, sliding then stumbling past the mouth of the hallway before backtracking.

"Stop them!" I shout over the snarled, mumbled shouting match taking place between Soren and Blake, and Patton nods, wild eyed, and takes two hurried steps in their direction…. But Blake raises his hand toward Patton, and Patton goes still, his eyes open but unseeing, his jaw slack.

"No!" I cry out. "Blake, stop!"

Blake slam's Soren's head into the floorboards while fresh blood seeps through the bandage on his arm, sinking into the pristine, white carpet runner.

I act on impulse and swing the lamp. The lampshade smashes against the side of Blake's head, the lightbulb shattering on impact, knocking Blake off balance.

"ENOUGH!" I shout, but Soren rolls with Blake, immediately gaining upper ground.

Blake, distracted, releases Patton from his power grip. Patton faints, knocking his head against the corner of the hallway, and lies prone and useless on the ground only three feet from where Soren and Blake are continuing to beat the shit out of each other like rabid animals.

When Blake grabs Soren by the face, and his eyes glow a fierce, otherworldly violet, I act.

My powers flare. An eruption of light explodes through the hallway, shattering every sconce and bulb, showering us in glass. The fading light is replaced by brilliant streams of crimson magic that pour from my outstretched fingers and turn into strips of silver flames, and Blake's back is their target.

But he rolls, dragging an increasingly spent Soren with him, straight into my line of fire. I can't rein in my powers fast enough. Soren's grunt of pain tears through my mind, stopping my heart mid-beat. My powers shudder out, and then I'm moving as fast as my swollen feet can carry me. I grab Blake by the throat, digging my nails into his skin until I draw blood and shove him off Soren, whose arm is now raw and blistered to a fine crisp.

Soren goes ghostly pale, panting, but tries to rise, his hand outstretched in my direction. Blake tries to rise as well, desperately out of breath, but I send my fist against his cheek, and blood sprays from his lips, staining my plaster walls.

Blake stumbles away as Soren falls back to the ground.

"No, no, no," I cry, falling to my knees and dragging him toward me by his shirt. "I didn't mean to–"

"Get away from him Maeve," Blake snarls, his hand pressing down on my shoulder.

I drive my elbow into his upper thigh. "Don't touch me!"

"He's a murderer," Blake spits, his face shadowed by anger. It's the first time I think I've seen him show emotion, and it's jarring, but Soren groans, cursing sharply under his breath.

"Touch her again, and it'll be the last thing you do," he warns, and Blake gives him a quizzical look before taking a single step away from us.

"What is this?" my cousin asks in a sneer, looking between me and

Soren while I fuss over his mangled arm. "You know each other? How?"

Soren's smile is murderous. He sits up with great effort, panting, spitting blood onto the floorboards. I murmur for him to lay down, but he waves me away, saying, "Maeve, this is your cousin Blake, right?"

I don't like the tone he's using. There's something sinister there, something secret and dark lacing between each syllable.

"Yes," I murmur, glancing at Blake. "Why?"

"She doesn't know, does she?" Soren croaks, his teeth stained with blood from several splits along his lower lip.

Blake stiffens, nostrils flaring. "Shut up–"

"What's going on?" I ask over Patton's groan as he comes back to reality, rolling over onto his side a few feet away.

"I've always wondered what you looked like behind that mask," Soren says, and Blake's expression darkens to the point I think he's about to use his powers. I shimmy in front of Soren, blocking his body with mine while Blake looks down at us in mingled confusion and fury.

"Don't say another word," Blake hisses, but Soren's cutting laugh snakes through the tight hallway, pinging from wall to wall.

"What game are you playing? You... you sick freak, doing all of this behind her back–"

"What are you talking about?" I snap. Unease weaves up my spine, knitting between vertebrae. "Soren–"

"I knew something was off," Soren continues, shifting to his knees then methodically rising as the tension in the snug space reaches a peak, "when you found me in that village in the Roguelands and gave me my last mark."

"What?" I rush out, turning my head to look at Blake. My stomach curls into a knot as the memory of being in Blake's office yesterday hurdles back to the forefront of my mind. The graph paper. The handwriting. I couldn't place the memory at first but now... "Blake, what have you done?"

"Get out," Blake snarls at Soren, but Soren laughs again, taunting him.

"No... I think I'll stay... for a while, actually, and if you ever touch my *mate* again, you'll lose your arm."

"*Mate?*" Blake's eyes widen as he glances between me and Soren. "No. No, that's not possible–"

"You did all of this without her knowledge, didn't you? What's your endgame?" Soren asks, but that taunting tone is still in his voice, woven through every word, like he's... challenging Blake, but I don't understand why.

Blake snarls as he lunges for Soren, but I send a jolt of my power right into his chest. He flies back against the wall with a sharp grunt.

"Enough," I grind out, ignoring the sharp, twisting pain in my lower belly. "That's enough. One of you fuckers needs to start talking, now. What is this about? How do you know each other?"

Soren presses his back to the wall, gritting his teeth as his arm continues to sizzle, his skin a bright, angry red bordering on white. "Tell her, or I will."

"Tell me what?"

Blake's panting against the opposite wall, glaring viciously at Soren while Patton continues to moan, holding his head like he has a blinding headache.

"Tell her," Soren shouts, baring his teeth.

Blake shakes his head. "I–"

"He's the Architect," Soren says pointedly, looking down at me.

My stomach hollows out as I slowly look at Blake, waiting for him to argue, to say it's not true, but the look he's giving me...

"You," I whisper as shock burrows through my system. "You've been..." I can't finish. My brain won't function beyond trying to process this shocking, maddening truth. I turn back to Soren, closing my eyes as another jolt of rippling pain echoes through my lower back and belly before it tightens. I hiss out a breath, and Soren's hand presses into my lower back.

"You need to go lie down."

"No. No, I want to know that truth. How long have you been working with each other?"

"Not now," Soren replies, shaking his head as he tries to move toward the door. "I'll deal with this later."

"You're hurt. I hurt you–"

"I'm fine," he lies, and throws a cold look over his shoulder at Blake before guiding me into the room and helping me into bed, and I let him, my body numb from shock, unable to process any thoughts.

Early morning sunlight begins to fan through the curtains, casting ribbons of shadow over Blake as he steps into the room, hanging back in the doorway. I can feel him watching Soren's every move as he tucks me into bed despite my protests otherwise. I'm not sure I can protest. A sharp, deep pain radiates through my back, sending a warning siren bouncing through my skull. I grab Soren's hand when he starts to pull away, looking at the wound I created over his already terribly healing arm.

It's worse than I thought. Much worse.

"This is bad," I whisper, meeting his eyes through tears. "I'm so sorry–"

"You didn't mean to do it," he says levelly like he can't feel the pain, but I know it's there. He's pale, his eyes slightly glazed. "I'll be fine."

"You won't. Soren, you're going to lose this arm–"

"Is she really your mate, or have you imprinted on her?" Blake barks from the doorway.

"Get the fuck out of my room," I snarl, but Soren shushes me, tucking me back into the cushions almost aggressively.

"You're the father of that baby, aren't you? You fucking bastard–"

"You and I have unfinished business," Soren growls, looking at Blake, probably the scariest man in existence, at least in our generation, in the eyes. "But right now, I'm going to take care of her. You owe us both an explanation now, Blake. Especially her." His voice cracks painfully as he trembles, going even paler than before. He slowly sits on the edge of the bed, taking a deep breath like he's on the verge of passing out.

I make a decision even though I'm not sure it's the right choice.

My family was so… so untrusting and worried when they found out I was pregnant. I haven't spoken to my grandfather since then, and it's been a month, at least.

I shove Blake's deception to the side for now, and say, "Get Misty and bring her here, now," I tell him, holding his gaze.

He begins to shake his head, replying, "We need to talk about this. He's not–"

"He is my mate, Blake. Go get Misty before I kill you where you stand. I'm not bluffing."

Blake hesitates before gritting his teeth and disappearing in a whirl of black and violet mist, his magic sending a shockwave through the room that disturbs the curtains and makes the framed art rattle on the walls.

Soren rises and walks into the hallway where Patton is still on the ground.

"Are you okay?" he asks, his voice laced with pain.

"What happened?" Patton grumbles, panting.

"Well, if you can speak, you're fine, I guess."

"Soren," I say, sitting up. "There's an intercom near the front door of the suite. Press one, and it'll call Jane directly. Have her come up to help with Patton–"

Another burst of magic fills the room, cutting off my words, and Blake reappears, gripping Misty by the arm. She huffs out a breath of surprise and annoyance, dressed in pajama pants and a bathrobe. It's the middle of the night in Crescent Falls. He likely pulled her out of bed.

"What the hell is the meaning of this?" she snaps, ripping her arm free of Blake's grasp. "What are you–" She pauses when Soren steps into the room, her eyes locked on his arm. "Oh, *fuck me*. What happened?"

"Misty, I need your help," I say, her eyes slowly meeting mine. "But you need to keep this between us."

BALL OF SILVER

MAEVE

MISTY DOESN'T ASK QUESTIONS, AND I'M THANKFUL FOR IT. BLAKE watches with a scowl as Soren sits on the edge of the bed and extends his arm to Misty, who inspects it then looks at me.

"It was an accident," I tell her, swallowing past the guilt, and honestly, shame of hurting Soren like this. "I meant to do that to Blake."

Misty glances at Blake with a frown. "What the hell has gotten into you two?"

Blake widens his stance, crossing his arms over his chest and looking down at his shoes instead of answering her question.

"Later," I breathe. "Can his arm be healed fully?"

Misty nods, but her eyes betray the motion. She inspects his wounds with a sigh then motions for him to lie down. Soren looks at me with a skeptical expression shimmering behind his eyes but does what she asks, and in a matter of seconds, Misty's light begins to dance around the room.

Soren takes several shallow breaths as she grips his hand, sending her magic of light and healing deep into his veins. I watch, tilting my head as I follow the magic up his arm and into his shoulder then his chest. He's lying next to me while I sit in the bed, my arm wrapped around his shoulder and my hand resting protectively on his chest. I can feel her powers, taste them. Misty is very powerful. She inherited her powers from Isla, my great-grandmother, her grandmother, and it's… beautiful.

I look down at my hand before curling it into fist over his shirt.

My powers are of… death. Death by fire. Death by shadow and starlight. I can't heal the sick and wounded. I can't bring people back from the dead. I can't paint a picture of the past using fractals of mist or peer into the tangled threads of our futures.

I can destroy. That's all.

Soren's sharp exhale steals my attention back to the present. He slumps in the bed, trembling, his face going a ghostly pale. Even Blake takes a step closer to the bed, his eyes going wide and stance uneasy as he says, "What's wrong with him?"

"I can't–something's blocking my magic," Misty says with effort as she pushes the full brunt of her healing powers into Soren, gripping his hand so tightly her knuckles turn white. "It's not just a burn, is it?"

"No," I tell her, biting through the words. "He was bound in silver and had an ironsmith cut through it. I treated him with healing drafts, but it was only enough to kill what I thought was an infection–"

"It's not an infection," Misty cuts in. "There's something stuck… here." She presses against the tight muscle of his triceps, gritting her teeth as her eyes flicker with light. "Shit. My powers can't even touch it–"

"There's something in his arm?" Blake asks, now looking suspicious as hell. I watch my cousin move toward the bed, and my hackles raise.

"Don't touch him, Blake," I warn, my tone dropping several octaves. Even Misty looks up at me, glancing between us.

Blake looks me up and down before asking Misty, "What can we do?"

She releases Soren's hand, her powers shuttering out in a flash. "I need Cole for this. I can feel it. I know where it is, but I can't heal him. Whatever's in his arm is making it impossible."

"It's silver," I breathe, shaking my head. "It has to be."

"Cole can cut it out," Misty says, "Unless you can get him down to the clinic–"

"No," Blake and I say in unison, and Misty narrows her eyes at us.

"No," I repeat, shaking my head, and Blake disappears in another burst of violet mist and starlight.

Unstable footsteps echo in the hallway before Patton appears in the doorway looking unsteady, still gripping his head. He blinks several times to clear his vision before looking at me under his lashes, then turns to Misty, a total stranger, then Soren.

"What happened?"

"Come sit down for a minute, Patton," I urge, silently praying Blake didn't totally scramble his brain.

But Patton comes to completely, his head snapping back in Misty's direction. He gapes, then snaps his lips shut. I smile to myself as I slide out of bed and guide Patton into a chair at the very moment Blake reappears with an incredibly angry Cole, also pulled from bed, but gripping a large, metal medical kit in his hand.

Patton nearly faints.

"I'll introduce you to everyone in a minute, okay?" I promise him, and he nods, glancing between Misty and Cole like this is the moment of his life, a dream come true.

"Would either of you care to explain why you ripped my mate from our bed?" Cole snarls, dropping his kit on the ground at his feet. "It's the middle of the night in Shadowcrest–"

"Cole, I need you," Misty says calmly, a soft, almost secret smile touching her lips, and Cole turns to her, seeing Soren for the first time.

Everything from that moment happens quickly. Blake and Cole move Soren into the living room as the last inklings of the sunrise break through the curtains, illuminating the damage done in the hallway. Plaster and glass coat the ground, and the walls are scorched, and while I watch Cole kneel on the ground, directing Patton to roll

Soren onto his side, Misty comes to stand beside me, leaning in to ask, "Who is he?"

"He's mine," is all I can muster.

Misty, one of the more... level headed members of the family, just nods.

"He's the dad, then?"

"Yeah."

"What exactly happened in the hallway? I remember how much you fretted over this plaster when it was installed."

I cross my arms over my chest, wincing as the baby rolls, her little feet fluttering under my ribcage. "Ask Blake," I say with effort while Cole dons gloves and unpacks several scalpels.

I force myself to watch. Misty joins Cole and Patton, the latter pale but doing his best to support his friend. Soren weakly refuses when Misty offers to put him to sleep using her powers, and allows Cole to slice into the meat of his upper arm.

Blake hovers behind me in the shadows for several minutes, watching in solemn solidarity as Soren finally succumbs to the pain and passes out.

"Do you realize what you did to him?" I whisper into the fading darkness as sunlight drifts toward my toes. "What you made him *be* for years?"

"Do you feel it like he does?" he asks after several seconds of a sucking kind of silence broken by Cole's soft grunts as he flays my mate open in search of whatever Misty felt, whatever her powers couldn't pass. "He could just be saying he's your mate–"

"I do," I reply. "Maybe not like a shifter would, but... I understand why I couldn't forget him now. He's... branded on my heart, has been from the beginning, I think. I... jumped to him," I say, looking over my shoulder at my cousin. "My powers were so weak, but I had just enough to get home, and instead I woke up in a forest, and he was there, just a few yards away. When I told my powers to take me home, they took me to him. I should have known then."

Blake doesn't say anything. His eyes remain locked on Soren, those wells of violet dancing with flecks of starlight, like the entire universe lies just behind his gaze.

"Did you know about us?" I ask.

"No. I never bothered to look into his future because I wasn't going to keep him alive when I was done with him."

I stiffen at the knowledge. "Why did you do it? Why him?"

"Because he could handle it," he says, finally meeting my eyes.

He's not wrong. Soren is the strongest person I know. Nothing seems to faze him. Nothing but me, I realize with heartbreaking clarity.

"But why, Blake? Why kill Alphas—"

"Most are in hiding."

"He told me. He told me all about the Architect. Does our family know? Are they in on it?"

"No."

"What is the reason?"

He licks his lips as he deliberates his next words. I'll take them as a half-truth. He won't tell me the entire reason why. Maybe me and Blake aren't that different after all. "I realized early on that I was the only one who could ever come close to finding the Spider. He's like us, Maeve. Powerful. Unexplainably so. It was easy enough going off the information our parents have gathered on his people—his den leaders, including the Viper. I knew there was someone special in their midst, someone the Viper trusted more than others, and... I was able to find Soren. He was easily swayed, already disenfranchised and wanting out from under her thumb. He needed money to get out of her debt, and I have plenty of it, so when I asked for his help, he accepted."

"You turned him into a killer."

"He was already a killer. I turned him into a hero, Maeve. The people he killed at my command were working directly, or indirectly, with the Viper. The people we moved into hiding were at serious risk of death along with their families."

"Our family will find out what you've done—"

"They will," he says, unblinking. "But not until after the Viper has been taken down. She's his neck mark. His last mark."

I turn to him, shaking my head. "Do it yourself. He's not going back–"

"Don't touch it!" Misty screeches, and we both whirl to the bloody scene in front of us. Blake brushes past me, his body suddenly lighting from within as his powers surge, drawn to whatever just fell from Soren's arm onto the floor. Blake grabs a circular ball of silver with his bare hands then suspends it with a burst of his magic, pressing it tightly into a shield of what I only describe as starlight.

He quickly banishes himself from the suite, moving at the speed of light. I watch him go, then turn to Cole and Misty, torn between Soren and following my cousin to what I believe is his office, his lair in my palace.

"Heal him," I croak, my voice cracking, and Misty replaces Cole's spot next to Soren, letting her powers rain down on him to their full extent.

Cole pulls me aside, walking me into the corner of the living room, and says, "I'm not going to ask what happened here, but do your parents know what's going on?"

I shake my head, and he curses under his breath, looking back at his wife.

"Whatever was in his arm is unlike anything I've ever seen. This needs to be discussed–"

"Blake is going to figure it out, and we'll go from there."

Cole searches my eyes then sighs, "Maeve, I've done this before. Kept secrets, tried to be the hero and refused help at all angles. You know how that ended."

My chest convulses. "I understand, but for now, my priority is him. His health. Is he going to heal? Can his arm be saved?"

"It's saved." He turns away, running his fingers through his dark blond hair as Misty rises, asking Patton if he's all right, but he's still completely starstruck.

Soren is moved back to my bedroom. He's tucked in bed but begins to stir while I ask Cole and Misty to stay and to keep things quiet for a while, at least until Blake and I have more answers. Misty accepts this even if Cole looks like he's about to find the nearest phone and snitch on me to my parents.

I'll deal with everyone else later.

They leave, and silence fills the room for several minutes while Patton and I watch Misty's magic fade from Soren's skin.

"Maeve?"

"I'm right here," I say to Soren as he opens his eyes with a start, sitting straight up in bed. Patton rises from a chair near the window as Soren drags his arm from under the covers, inspecting the... totally healed, flawless, scarless skin.

His eyes meet mine then Patton's.

"Later," I whisper, grabbing his hand.

Jane's gasp, then hurried footsteps, echo through the destroyed hallway into my bedroom.

"Oh, shit," I murmur under my breath, coming to the realization that no one got in contact with her about what happened during the night.

She rushes into the room, her eyes meeting mine and relaxing when she sees me in one piece, but then goes completely, utterly still.

Soren straightens, his eyes on Patton.

Patton stares at Jane, who slowly turns her head in his direction.

A mate bond snaps into place in my bedroom between the kindest man I've ever known, and his feminine counterpart, the best, sweetest woman I've ever met.

"Finally," Soren says under his breath, and I smile, squeezing his hand.

CONFRONTING THE ARCHITECT

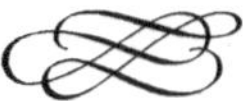

Soren

Maeve's room is painted in sunlight that reflects off the pale pink wallpaper inlaid with what I believe are real rose petals. This room smells like her—warm and rich with that underlying, unmistakable magnolia blossom scent that makes my mouth water despite my best efforts to remain neutral and calm throughout this entire ordeal.

If anyone had asked me what I was actually planning on doing when I reached Moonrise two days ago, I wouldn't have had an answer. I broke into the castle—shattered a fucking window knowing how easily I could have been overtaken by guards—but at that point, nothing mattered. I had to get to her, but when I did, and I saw her... fuck.

Everything has changed.

I watch Patton cross the room, taking several cautious steps toward Jane, who's clutching a spiral bound planner like her life depends on it. Jane's light brown hair is neatly pulled away from her softly beautiful face as she looks up at him, her cheeks burning a deep crimson.

"Jane, would you give Patton a tour of the castle, please? Take your time with it," Maeve says from the foot of the bed.

The maid blinks, startled back into reality, and nods. But Patton glances at me, raising a brow. I shrug, unsure how the bastard got so lucky, and watch as my closest friend follows his fated mate out of the bedroom and closes the door behind them with the softest click.

Maeve and I look at each other.

"Is that what it felt like?" she asks, clutching the fourposter and leaning her weight against it.

"What do you mean?" I slide my legs out of bed and make a fist with my freshly healed hand. I haven't seen my skin unmarred by scars in a very long time—since I was a teenager, actually.

"When you felt the mate bond snap into place?" Her cheeks are dusted pink, but her eyes are heavy with fatigue as she stands only a few feet away, a vision in butter yellow as she rests her arm over the swell of her stomach.

Seeing her like this is… hard to describe. She's stunning. A work of art. Something created by a master hand, but also… I did this to her. I'm normally so careful. I'm not a fucking saint, and I can readily admit it, but with her, it was different. I wanted this deep down, I think. I wanted her. I wanted a piece of us in the world as a reminder of what happened and what we could have been.

I did this to her, and she's been alone, hiding it, for months. I feel awful about it.

"Does your family know?" I ask, already forgetting what she asked before. Oh, right, the mate bond. I stand, smoothing the fabric of a shirt that doesn't belong to me over my stomach before turning to her, taking her in, watching her thick, dark hair falling in soft, bouncy waves over her shoulders and back. "It feels like a snap in your chest," I explain, "like someone's plucking the strings of a violin. It doesn't hurt."

I walk to the windows and look out over a view of the lake and the city beyond. The lake is frozen, glowing in the sunlight. Spring is only a few weeks away, I hope.

"My family knows," she says under her breath. "They were made aware recently, and it didn't go well."

"Are you… feeling well, though?"

It shouldn't be this hard to speak to her, but it is. It hurts. Nine months have passed since we sat on that train platform and let fate snatch us apart. It feels like an entire lifetime. And then, in the days that I've been here, too much has happened. This… wasn't the plan. I didn't think past the need to get her to safety. I didn't think about what it would feel like to see her again after so long. I didn't think about what would happen *after*.

"I am," she replies softly, likely sensing something's off. A glimmer of skepticism flashes behind her eyes before they turn sharp again. "You're not leaving me again, Soren. I'm not talking about it again."

"I know."

She takes an audible breath then winces, and I notice the fabric of her dress loosening as her belly tightens, and she bends ever so slightly over the rush of pain I feel in my own chest. Pressure. An enormous amount of pressure. Even her scent changes, turning from that sharp floral to something much sharper that sends warning bells skittering through my skull.

I've never liked seeing her in pain. My spine locks as my mind spins over what needs to be done. I don't know what our future looks like. I don't know if we'll have a moment of peace or even an easy life together. I don't know how to be with her or to be what she needs me to be because I truthfully don't know what that is. I've never been in a… relationship. It was never an option. It was never something I desired until the thought of being separated from Maeve made me feel like I'd be better off dead.

I don't know how to be with her while she rules as Queen of Eastonia, but there are things I can handle… like all of *this*. Her bastard cousin. Hannibal and Andrea. Her family.

I can take that off her plate.

"Please lie down."

"There's too much to talk about," she says through gritted teeth. "You, Blake–"

"You don't have to worry about that. I'll handle that."

"Blake is the Architect? How—why would he do this? He was undermining me. Lying to my face!"

"I realize that, Maeve, and I'm going to handle it. You need to rest."

"I don't want to–"

"I need you to."

"Misty pulled something out of your arm. What was it?"

"Maeve, it doesn't matter now. Not right now. Will you let me take over for a moment so you can just… lie here in peace? Please."

She sniffles but slowly straightens as the pain subsides. With a curt nod, she resigns herself to her mattress and curls around the baby resting in her belly while I close the heavy curtains against the spray of sunlight.

"Where can I find Blake?"

"His office is on the fifth floor," she says with a tight yawn, her eyes already fluttering as the room descends into darkness. She hasn't eaten since I arrived, either, and I make a mental note to find a way to have food sent up for her.

Maeve falls asleep before I've even walked out of the bedroom. My pants are bloodstained and coated in dust, but the empty hallways of the sixth floor greet me as a total contrast to my current disheveled-ness. Everything is spotless and shiny. Every mirror I pass is free of prints and streaks of dust. I take a familiar stairwell to the fifth floor, which is also empty of maids. I trek to the eastern wing, following Blake's icy scent, like a snowstorm on the coldest day of the deepest point of winter.

I don't bother knocking when I enter his office. Cole, Misty's mate, is bracing his hands on the surface of Blake's desk. He's a tall, stern man in his mid to late forties or so, and he looks over his shoulder at me, pale gray eyes narrowing before he sees that I'm not here as a threat.

I suppose running into a royal in-law is better than, well, practically any of the other men in this family.

Blake watches my progress toward his desk, however, but I stop short of it, crossing my arms over my chest. I'm under the impression he doesn't want me saying a word to Cole about why we tussled in Maeve's suite, and I'm not in the mood to discuss it, either. Not with a crowd.

Then I see the silver ball on Blake's desk. "Oh, that," I murmur.

Cole straightens, and Blake narrows his eyes to slits.

"It's a tracking device," I tell them with a shrug. "In case the bands come loose. We all have them. I'd totally forgotten about mine."

"How long was this in your arm?" Cole asks. "Years, I assume? You had massive amounts of scar tissue around it–"

"I was sixteen, I think."

Cole blinks then glances at Blake like he has all the answers to several silent questions, and Blake clears his throat, saying, "Cole, your discretion is appreciated–"

"You're going to Ryatt with this," Cole cuts in, shaking his head.

"In due time," Blake bites out.

"Actually, I'd like to speak to Alpha King Ryatt and Commander Evander as soon as possible. This morning. Now." I widen my stance. Both men glance at me like I'm the unwanted guest in whatever conversation they were having, which is probably true. I'm beyond giving a shit.

"Why?" Blake growls.

He thinks I'm going to snitch, doesn't he? What a pussy.

I turn to Cole, saying, "Maeve was in some pain. I understand you're a physician. I didn't like the look of her and came down here to find you. Would you mind checking on her? I think she'd like her mom here."

He's a smart enough man to read between the lines and sense the lie, but I know my way around healers and physicians. I've seen both– dozens over the years–and know for a fact that their first priority is always their patients. Plus, Maeve is his family.

Cole grinds his teeth before asking, "What do you mean?"

"I think the baby is coming, possibly within the next two days or so. I can sense it. Her scent is different. I caught the change while upstairs with her just now." My eyes slide to Blake, who's watching with a predator's intent, waiting to make a move. I ignore him and look back at Cole. "She's tired. I just want to make sure she's as comfortable as possible."

Cole runs his tongue along his lower lip. "I'll be back shortly in the event I need to stitch the two of you idiots up after this," he says with a soft growl, then leaves, the door closing on a phantom wind.

Blake rises, but I slump into a very fancy armchair, twisting back and forth to get comfortable. His glare deepens. "Do you mind? You're filthy, and that's Tarsian leather."

I make a point of kicking my dirty boots together on his pristine, black and silver rug before sitting still and resting my arms on the armrests, arching a brow. "Tell me everything, you fucking bastard."

"There's nothing to say–"

"I beg to differ."

Blake sinks into his desk chair, grimacing as he adjusts the chair, which doesn't match his office whatsoever. He picks up the ball of silver and twists it between his fingers before pinching it, and it warps, falling in on itself. His eyes burn violet as his powers turn the ball to a pile of ash, which he dusts off the surface of his shiny black desk, and looks at me. "You shouldn't have been able to shift with that in your shoulder. It was a backup plan to keep your abilities at bay, wasn't it?"

"Probably."

"You're so nonchalant about this–"

"The Viper gave me a final mark before I came here," I tell him, cutting him off. "Which was to kill my own child. That's why I'm here. To protect Maeve. To get her to safety, but she won't leave."

"Where exactly did you think you could take her where she'd be safer than here?"

"I broke into the castle so easily it would have been hilarious if I wasn't so fucking enraged at how much of a cake-walk it was," I growl. "Her security is lacking. She isn't safe, and she's nearing labor. She can't stay here. I want her in Veiled Valley with her family."

"She's burnt a bridge or two because of the child you left her with."

"I had no idea she was pregnant until the Viper had her men hold me down while she gave me a new band."

"And if you'd known earlier, you would have come back? I find that hard to believe."

"I don't care what you think, Blake. Maeve is mine. I will decide what's best for both of them."

He arches his brows, laughing dryly, "She's yours? You think the Queen of Eastonia belongs—"

"She is my mate, and what you've done to her—to us? You owe her the truth. I asked you once who you worked for, and you told me you worked for *your* best interests. What interest is that?"

"How dare you come in here—"

I rise and stare him down. He doesn't flinch, but the look behind his eyes—the expression he's trying to hide? He's not used to this. Someone looking at him—an all-powerful being—like he's just another man. Like he's not a threat. Yeah, that throws him off, for sure.

"The Viper said Hannibal is going to make a move. I don't know what that means. I don't know what he plans to do, but whatever you've been up to—whatever you've been using me to accomplish—its pushing him to the edge—"

"Good."

"No," I snarl, "Not good. Not when my mate and our daughter are the next intended targets for his *grand plan*. I have a feeling you know what that is, don't you?"

"I don't." He rises from his chair. "And you're not welcome here, Soren. You're leaving. I'll force you out myself."

"And Maeve will never forgive you."

"You act like you can waltz in and out of her life as you please." He growls, rising slowly, bracing his hands on the desk. "She is the queen!"

"I'm well aware."

"And what are you, Soren? Filth. Murderous scum with no place to call your own? No family, no connections—"

"I separated myself from my mate." My voice takes on a brutal edge, sharper than the finest knife. "I spent the last nine months in a personal hell thinking it was the only way to keep her safe, the only way to keep her out of this while you've been playing with my life and hers. This whole time you've been *here*, with *her*, using me as a puppet and keeping her in the dark. I'm not going anywhere. I will *fucking* kill you before I leave her again. That's a promise. You've put her in danger, Blake."

"It's Prince Blake to you–"

"Fuck off," I chuckle darkly, rolling my eyes to the vaulted ceiling. Everything about this room is cold and modern–like him. Lacking all color, all creativity. A cold, dark box. A cage. "You know," I smile, sucking my teeth, "if I didn't know any better, I'd think your best interests align with Hannibal–"

"You don't know what you're talking about."

"Then fucking enlighten me before I do something Maeve will never forgive me for." My wolf claws to the surface, begging for release.

Blake stares at me. I stare back, refusing to so much as blink. Whatever kind of being he is... he's unnerving. Those purple eyes make my skin crawl, but I hold steady.

The door to the office opens, and Cole steps inside, sighing against the tension. "Maeve is asking for you," he says, and Blake steps around his desk.

"He's talking to *me*," I smile and turn to leave.

ONE THING LEFT TO TRY

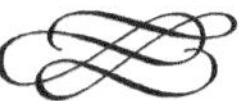

MAEVE

I BLINK INTO THE SHADOWS OF MY ROOM. THE CURTAINS ARE STILL drawn, but strips of deep, golden sunlight creep between the seams of the fabric, alerting me to the time. It's nearly sunset. I slept most of the day, save for Cole occasionally checking on me, but now my stomach is tight with hunger, and my body feels… strange.

I smooth my hand over my belly, but the baby is sleeping, curled in a snug ball right against my ribs, her favorite place to kick.

The door creaks open. I pop my head from beneath the blankets as a tall, dark shadow steps inside the room, carrying the scent of food with him. "Are you awake?" Soren's voice is… soft. Casual, showing no signs of pain or stress.

I lift onto an elbow as he steps into the room and walks to the windows, opening one of the curtains enough to softly illuminate the space, and turns to me, his eyes scanning mine.

"What've you been doing all day?" I ask, my tone lifted in suspicion. "It's nearly nightfall."

"I've kept myself busy." He rocks on his heels, now dressed in fresh clothes–black slacks that fit him like a glove and a plain white T-shirt that shows off his muscled frame. I feel an ache bloom to life that I've been ignoring for months now, burying that deeply rooted want along with everything else I felt for him.

"Doing what, exactly?"

"Well, telling my entire life story to your… whatever Misty is to you. A cousin?"

"I have a large family. I've always considered her more of an aunt."

He shrugs, closing the door behind him. "She likes to talk."

"That checks." There's something in the air–something electric that crackles and snaps as he scans the room like he's making sure we're alone.

"Patton and Jane are nowhere to be found, as it stands. I hope you didn't have a full schedule for her today."

"Obviously whatever plans I had for the day are totally off the table now."

"Are you hungry?" he asks, moving toward the bed.

I sit up all the way, inhaling sharply as my body protests the idea of leaving the cocoon of warmth I've been rotting in all day. "Are you suddenly going to be nice to me going forward?"

Soren arches a brow as he comes to a stop, his hands resting at his sides. "I feel like I've been about as nice as you deserve," he replies, his voice low and teasing.

Something settles deep in my chest. A flicker of familiarity I hadn't been able to find since he catapulted back into my life spreads like wildfire, igniting that flame once again.

He notices the change and tilts his head, looking me up and down with an appraising gaze as time slows to a crawl, and the outside world no longer matters.

I wonder if he cares that I can't feel the mate bond like he can. It bothers me more than him, I think.

"There's something we need to discuss," he says, his eyes on mine as he loosens the fabric of his shirt from his belt.

"What?" I smirk. "My cousin's deception? Your mangled arm? Our friends being mates? How I'm going to tell my family about us?"

"None of that." He takes a tentative step in my direction before halting, his fingers resting on his belt clasp. "I took care of that. It's none of your concern."

"I am the queen and this is my house–"

"*That* is what we need to discuss." He pulls his belt free in a smooth, intoxicating motion that sends a burst of warmth licking down my spine. "You keep telling me I'm not leaving. What is that going to look like, Maeve? Am I your prisoner?"

"Yes," I smile.

His jaw tenses as he braces his hands on either side of me on the bed, leaning down so we're nose to nose. "If I stay," he whispers, brushing the words over my temple, "I won't be able to stay out of your way. Your subjects will know you have a man playing house with you. They'll be curious."

"Let them be–"

"A certain prince might take this as an affront."

I blink, glaring at him as he pulls away ever so slightly. "Prince, who?" He arches a brow, and I cut a laugh, "You mean Prince Eric of Lunaria, don't you? You know I've never met him face to face."

He narrows his eyes, and I laugh even harder, teasing him. "You're jealous, aren't you? That's the real reason you came back, isn't it?"

"I don't get jealous. I wouldn't have let that relationship get that far, anyway."

"Oh, you're so scary and tough–"

His mouth meets mine, but he pulls away as quickly as the kiss began. "I don't want to share you."

"You wouldn't."

"I also wouldn't stand beside you to rule. I'd be in the background. I'd be with her." His hand comes to rest on my stomach. "No one would have to know who I am or even my name. It would be the easiest and safest thing to do."

I want to say I'm not concerned about my reputation and his social status. I want to ignore how odd it is that we're even mates given that he doesn't have a drop of royal blood. I want to banish the questions that've been burning in the back of my mind about how my

Firestone ancestors established their dynasties—whether love was ever involved.

But I can't ignore the man bracing himself against the bed, his mouth chasing mine as I say, "Can you be happy living in my shadow?"

"I'm honestly looking forward to the break," he says with a shocking amount of relief, a sigh leaving his lips before he takes mine in a hungry kiss that ignites more of the desire I've been tamping down.

"Then you'll stay?"

"I'll stay."

"If my family doesn't agree—"

"I told I'd handle it, and I will. It's nothing you have to worry about." He takes my hand. "Come, I'm going to run you a bath. Your back is bothering you."

"How do you know?"

"I'm your mate," he says. "I can feel it. Not like you can, but it's… it's bothering me that you're in pain."

"I'm overdue."

"What do you mean?"

"She was supposed to be here by now."

He chews his lip as he looks down at me. "What can be done?"

"Nothing I haven't tried already… except…"

He arches a brow. "Except what?"

I guide his hand back to me, placing it on my side. "Come to bed for a minute."

His eyes darken at my tone—the soft plea laced between the words.

I wait for him to tell me no, that he's worried about me and the baby. I wait for his rejection, but he kisses me instead, tender at first, before the kiss takes on a life of its own. Memories of our kiss in the abandoned building rush through the walls I built around them, tearing down the shields I built to keep my heart from falling into unmendable pieces. I wrap my arms around his shoulders and pull him into the bed, and he rolls with me so I'm straddling him, his hand large and firm as it presses down my back, finding all the places that ache.

His other hand reaches between us to undo the button and zipper of his pants. I lift on my knees to give him room to shimmy out of his slacks and boxers, but when he reaches along the skirt of my night-gown, I pause, going suddenly rigid, my heart in my throat. My hand falls on his and presses down to prevent him from lifting the night-gown any further as uncertainty burrows through my body, making my skin heat with a rush of… embarrassment.

"I want to keep my nightgown on."

"Why? Because you're worried about how I'll react when I see you naked?"

I find it hard to swallow as I look down at him, scanning the hungry, heated look he's giving me.

"Y-yes."

"I've been dying to see you in just your skin. Let me."

"I'm–I'm different than I was the last time."

"You've never been more beautiful than you are right now," he whispers, his voice so incredibly heated it could scorch the room. His hand moves up my thigh beneath the fabric, testing, trying to creep past the boundary created by my… worry that he'll leave again. That I'll get hurt again. That something awful will happen to him, to us, and we have no future beyond this….

"Look at me," he whispers, grasping the back of my neck. "I'm here with you."

"I feel like so much has changed."

"It has," he replies steadily, softly, his eyes fading from that sharp black to his usual trio of colors. "You asked me to come with you once. I should have. I should have at least tried, and for that, I'm sorry. I never want you to forgive me for it. I don't deserve it. But, I can promise I'll spend the rest of my life making it up to you. I'm going to stay, Maeve. I don't know what that's going to look like. I don't know what the Goddess has in store for us, but I'll be here. I'll be here with you both."

"You don't even believe in the Goddess," I whisper, my voice edging on teasing, and he gives me that cocky smile that makes my blood simmer.

"She might have had a hand in this. I suppose I should give credit where credit is due."

"You're an asshole," I laugh, but the ice between us thaws, marking the return of something that feels… normal and good.

"Maybe. I doubt I'll change much, Maeve. So this is entirely up to you."

"I want you to stay."

"Then I will, but on one condition."

"You've already given me conditions–"

"No more shifting into your cat form."

"Why not?"

"Because I'm terribly allergic."

I bite back the smile tugging at my mouth, but he drags his thumb over my lower lip, forcing that smile to life. He gently guides me down to him, his mouth pressed to mine as the heat between us turns from a flickering ember to the beginnings of a flame, but then a tickle radiates through my brain a second before Blake's aggravating, annoying voice bursts through my ears, *'My suite, now. We need to talk. Bring your insufferable boyfriend with you.'*

"Fuck off," I growl, and Soren releases me, giving me a deeply quizzical look. "Not you," I assure him, bracing my hands on his chest as I straighten my back. "Sorry. Blake just summoned me. He wants to talk to both of us."

"Make him wait," Soren suggests, but I shake my head, sliding off him. "Is there anything I should know? Any secrets you need to tell me before we face him?"

"You know everything, at least from my perspective," he replies, following me out of bed. I watch him dress before padding to my vanity and pulling on a floor length robe, tying it over the swell of my belly, and quickly twisting my hair into a bun.

"Do you trust him?" Soren asks as he walks to my side.

I look up at him, noticing the lines around his eyes. He looks at our reflection in the mirror.

"That's the question I've been asking myself since we were kids," I admit, turning toward him, my hand pressed against the hard muscles of his abdomen. "I don't know yet, Soren. I want to believe Blake is good, but I don't think he is. Something happened to him. It changed him."

"Let's go see what he wants."

SORTING OUT SOREN

Soren

BLAKE'S SUITE, ESSENTIALLY A PRIVATE APARTMENT WITHIN THE CASTLE, is on the far eastern side of the palace. His view is of the more rural, affluent neighborhoods of Moonrise and the thick forest beyond—quieter and more secluded compared to Maeve's suite overlooking the lake and city center.

I take in the gray walls and modern furniture before turning to the man sipping a glass of scotch as the sun fades from view, the sunset broken by dark clouds promising another snowstorm, but it's warmer today. Humid. I can almost taste the rain on the horizon.

It's nearly spring.

I hope it's a good summer.

Maeve stares Blake down from the far side of the room, her eyes briefly flicking to mine before she clears her throat, "Well? What do you have to say for yourself?" She taps her foot impatiently, but Blake just looks her up and down before turning to me.

"Patton didn't have a tracker in his upper arm like you did. Misty checked. He's clean, otherwise." I grit my teeth, unsure what to say to that, but Blake swishes his drink and drains it, setting the crystal glass on a black glass side table between two dark gray leather couches. He looks at Maeve then, his expression tightening as he continues, "I looked into Soren's timeline–"

"*Blake*," Maeve snarls, taking several waddling steps in his direction as molten rage plays behind her eyes.

I step into the space between them, prepared to separate them, but Blake says, "He is, in fact, your mate. I just wanted to confirm he wasn't a lying, cheating bastard going after your wealth and power." His eyes flicker to mine before locking back on Maeve's face, which is murderous. "You're *fated*, which I found hard to believe, so I… dug a little deeper–"

"*How dare you!*" she snarls.

"What the fuck are you talking about?" I cut in, grabbing Maeve by the arm as she tries to rush past me toward her cousin. I pull her back, stepping between her and Blake once more. "What do you mean by *my timeline?*"

"Your future," Blake says matter-of-factly.

I open my mouth to laugh, or say something, anything, I suppose, but nothing comes out.

"You had no right to do that," Maeve says, trembling with rage.

"I had to. There were things that weren't adding up–"

"Future?" I say so quietly I'm not sure I said it out loud, but Blake looks right at me with those deep, starlit wells of violet lighting from within. What a freak. He is, I notice for the hundredth time, a very powerful man. A scary one. The only man, other than Alpha King Ryatt, I surmise, that I would… tread carefully around… if I were smarter.

"You can see my future?"

"A bit," he replies with a shrug of one shoulder. "Your timeline is murky because Maeve has a fucking chokehold on you. She's been shielding you with her powers for months–"

I turn to Maeve, and she purses her lips, glaring at Blake. "I haven't been."

"It's the mate bond between you. I can't see your timeline, Maeve, because you and I are from different power groups, as far as I know. We are not compatible. We have magic on the opposite end of the spectrum, so while I was trying to figure out–"

"You will stay out of his head from now on!" I've never heard Maeve use this tone before, even with me. She's... absolutely livid– trembling with righteous fury.

But I'm curious. "What did you see, exactly? How many kids I'll have? Whether Maeve kills me in my sleep one day? The day I die?"

Maeve growls low in her throat, but Blake... smirks. It's a secret kind of smile that briefly flashes behind his eyes as he meets my gaze. "No. I had to look deeper than that. Your timeline is static. You've only had one, and all points led to her. It would've happened regardless of if you'd met here, in Moonrise, or during her grand tour after she was crowned. You were meant to fall in step with Maeve. You were meant to be the father of her daughters. Your blood is... royal, somehow. You have an ancestor from the time of the Old Kings, possibly *an* Old King, prior to Kane. Slave blood, on your mother's side."

Maeve goes completely still and quiet, but my heart begins to race. "You can see all of this?" I ask, dumbfounded.

"It's not... seeing, necessarily," he replies, pacing away from us to pour himself another drink–a heavy pour this time. He moves a second glass toward the edge of the bar cart but pauses, continuing, "Our world is woven in a tapestry that has no beginning and no end. Everyone born carries a piece of thread. Some are short. Some are long. Some fray and bend, weaving where they don't belong. Other's tangle. You've been perfectly woven with Maeve's thread for years, and I'm not the only one who's seen that."

Maeve makes a small noise in her throat while pressing her hand to her lower back. I absently guide her to one of the couches, forcing her down, and she obeys like her legs were already on the verge of giving out.

"Who?" I ask. "Who else has the ability to see these things?"

"It used to be just me," he says, pouring a glass of scotch for me, I hope. He turns with both glasses in hand and extends one in my direction, which I take without hesitation. "The Mystics see these things, but… it's like looking at our world upside down and underwater, through a thick layer of fog. They can pull prophecies from their visions and from the stars, but they can't read the stars like I can. They can't look into the heavens, passing the sacred veil of the living and the dead, like I can. They can't decipher the fabric of our world, and others, like I can. But he… he can. And he found you, and her, years ago."

"You're talking about Hannibal." The words leave my lips in a resigned exhale.

Maeve pales, her eyes going wide as our words sink in.

"Unfortunately, yes."

"So he's a Mystic?" Maeve says from the couch.

"No," Blake and I say in tandem then look at each other. Blake continues, "No, he is not. He's something else. Something… not from *here*."

I look at Maeve then back at Blake. "The Viper as well."

"Then you're aware of their differences to us? Not like us shifters, or witches, and Mystics, and… what my family is."

An echo of pain laces through my bond with Maeve. She's having another contraction, a strong one. Even Blake looks at her as she suffers in silence on the couch just a few feet away. But she asks, "How long have you known this, Blake? Did you know Soren was my mate years ago?"

"No," he says quickly, shaking his head. "I never looked into his timeline because… because I didn't care. I was going to kill him, you know, when I was done with him."

"Of course you were," I grumble into my drink before draining half of it.

"But after… this mess," he continues, motioning to us, "I had to. I had to confirm, and when I did, I felt someone else with me. Like someone had been there before, picking through the same frays of thread. It isn't something Hannibal can do naturally. I felt another force there. Magic. Perhaps a spell. Then, Cole pulled that silver ball out of Soren's arm, and when I destroyed it, I felt that same magic. Soren is the only one who had that in his body."

Blake moves to the window where wet snow is starting to fall, on the verge of turning to rain. "Years ago, when Hannibal's operation caught the attention of our fathers and grandfathers, they couldn't track him. It was obvious he was some kind of magical being. At first, my grandfather Isaac and Ryatt deduced we were dealing with another witch, like Gabriel of Draven Coven, someone with Old King blood or a stolen relic they were using to summon ancient magic. But I got involved, and the more we were able to find and interrogate his people, the more I realized Hannibal was two steps ahead of us, like he knew what we were looking for and when we'd find it. I had to stay a step ahead of my family from that point on. The people we'd find were lower soldiers employed by his den leaders. They were... weak. None of them wore bands." He glances at me before turning back to the window.

"Four years ago, the Viper fell onto my radar, and so did Soren. Hannibal was protecting them both using whatever powers he had, but he didn't anticipate *me*."

I can feel Maeve watching me, but my eyes are locked on the back of Blake's head.

"The Viper was different. I couldn't find her thread in the tapestry, nor Hannibal's. The other den leaders were easy to find there because they belonged here; they don't. They're from somewhere else."

"I don't understand what you're saying," Maeve says, shaking her head. "They're not... part of our world?"

"No, and they're here to disrupt it." Blake turns to us, his eyes downcast on his drink. "The murders began, and I realized no one else in the family was going to be able to get to Hannibal, or even his... stronger den leaders, like the Viper. She was, and still is, a huge obstacle in our way when it comes to tracking Hannibal down. So, without the family's knowledge, I used my powers to start tracking her people and putting our own people, any high-ranking wolves at risk, into hiding. It worked, with Soren's help. She kept her men in bands, and each was chosen for specific skills. Her men were the strongest, the ones Hannibal selected by hand, it seemed. Soren was one of them, but Hannibal's interest in Soren began after the two of you met for the first time, when your threads began to intertwine."

"The tea shop," Maeve says under breath.

I close my eyes, finding it hard to fill my lungs.

"He knew Soren was bound to Maeve as mates. That made Soren invaluable."

"Did you know?" I ask Blake. "When you found me and offered me a way out?"

"No. But I knew you were something neither the Viper or Hannibal wanted to lose, which made our scheme doable. When I inspected that ball from your arm, I realized it was more than a tracking device. It wasn't meant to track your movements but your progress. It was meant to ignite and lead him back to you once the mate bond clicked into place. I believe he meant it as more of a timer, giving him the green light to begin whatever plot he's working on. But even I don't know what that is."

"But they know I'm here now," I say, taking a much needed breath. "The Viper knew I'd come straight here, I know that much. She knew I wouldn't kill my own child."

"Yes, they're aware you're here."

I turn to Maeve. "This is why you need to be in Veiled Valley–"

"No," Blake cuts in, shaking his head. "That's what they want to happen. They want Moonrise to be vulnerable. If Maeve leaves, Moonrise will be ripe for the taking. If they're planning an attack on Moonrise, they don't want Maeve here for it. She is at her most powerful right now, pregnant, and once the baby is born, her powers will fully mature. That's why they gave you that mark. It's why I sent you to kill her, knowing full well you couldn't, but I needed you in her way. I knew something was happening. My powers... pushed me in this direction, but I didn't know it would lead you back to Maeve. I didn't know you were mates like my gifts were trying to show me, and for that, I'm sorry. But whatever Hannibal and the Viper are, they aren't a match for her, and they know it. They see this as a window of opportunity. They knew you'd come here trying to save her, hide her, because you are devoted, Soren. They know your loyalty is no longer, and has never been, with them. Hannibal needs Moonrise for something, and he's waiting for you to leave with her to take it." Blake moves in my direction, looking down at Maeve, who looks tired and wary.

I run my tongue over my bottom teeth, sucking in a breath, "We need your family involved now."

"Yes," Blake agrees, even if Maeve pales. "We do. Which is why you and I are going on a little trip. Hang on tight."

"What?" I ask, but Blake grabs my arm, and the world erupts, fracturing, then shattering like glass all around me.

Maeve's shout of protest echoes through my mind before everything goes black. My eardrums swell, on the verge of bursting. Pain explodes through my body as I'm pulled apart, but just as quickly as it began, the pain ceases, and the floor beneath my feet turns from soft, pristine gray carpet to hard, ancient stone.

I blink, then double over, bracing my hands on my knees, my glass of scotch shattered at my feet.

"Not bad for your first time," Blake says under his breath as I slowly straighten, an unfamiliar room spinning around me—all dark stone and tall stained glass windows letting in soft starlight. "Ready to meet the parents?"

"You fucking dick," I pant, hanging my head. "Where are we?"

"Welcome to Veiled Valley, Soren."

MEET THE PARENTS

Soren

A GRAND STONE STAIRCASE FUNNELS TO THE HIGHEST REACHES OF THE cathedral-style foyer where the stained glass windows stretch to the highest rafters. This place is ancient. From the dawn of fucking time, I think. Shadows hug narrow passages leading off the foyer, but Blake knows exactly where to go, I guess, because he grabs my arms and tugs me to the left. I balk, ripping my arm out of his grasp.

"Don't touch me again," I huff, smoothing the fabric of the rather fancy button down shirt I've been wearing most of the day. Jane brought me clothes and quickly disappeared again shortly after I left Blake's office this morning to check on Maeve. Patton, too, has been missing all day, but judging by Jane's slightly disheveled appearance, she'd been enjoying Patton's skill set for hours at that point, I wasn't going to interrupt them with questions... yet.

Now, I might not have the opportunity to see my closest, and admittedly only, friend find true happiness in the form of a mate because this is where I'll die, my blood painting the hallways, and my body in shambles at the feet of my mate's father.

"Tidy up," Blake hisses under his breath, glancing through one of the shadowed archways before turning to me and motioning to my halfway unbuttoned shirt and ruffled hair.

"I'm fine as is. It's not like I'm going to walk away from this looking any better than I do now. What's your game here, Blake? Throw me into the fucking fire while my mate goes into labor hundreds of miles away?"

"To be honest, I'm shocked you're even upright," he whisper-hisses as a rush of air funnels through every hallway then bursts around us, rattling the smoky quartz chandelier high above our heads. "Jumping normally makes the less powerful members of my family quite ill."

A chill snakes up my spine when the draft–at least, that's what I thought it was–curls around my feet and scurries up my body like a thousand mice. I want to jump out of my skin at the sensation, and I practically do, leaping out of the cool embrace and taking several steps away from Blake. "What the fuck was that?"

"Just the house. It likes you, apparently." He rolls his eyes and motions to the hallway to the left.

"The what?"

"The house. It's some entity that lives here. Don't worry about it. If it meant you harm, you'd know."

I gape after him as he starts moving to the shadows then warily look around. "You mean like a ghost?"

"Get over here," he snarls from the archway.

I do. I don't stick around in the grand foyer, but as Blake leads me down a narrow corridor, the sconces on the walls light on their own accord, swirling with magic that shines a deep, rich amber. My stomach tightens as a feeling of dread whispers through my body. I can feel someone–something–following me. *Right behind me.* Yet, when I look over my shoulder, there's no one there.

Whatever it is, it's just curious.

I hope.

Blake turns a sharp corner and ascends a set of stone stairs. I follow, sticking close, and within moments, the stairwell opens to another hallway, this one wider and warmer, its walls and furnishings more modern compared to the lower sanctum of the castle.

Blake turns into a room where the door is already wide open, and I step inside behind him without hesitation.

I know this place. I've looked upon this castle many times over the years. It's stunning. A work of art, although a quarter of the size of the golden palace in Moonrise. I know who lives here and who I'm about to face.

I also know Maeve… lied to her family for a long time about the baby, and they don't know my name to this day.

That's about to change.

"Blake," a lovely, middle-aged woman with the same thick, dark brown hair as my mate says in surprise from a couch in the center of the room. She rises excitedly, her silver eyes wide with delight, but then they turn to me, and her mouth ticks into a shy, surprised smile. "Oh. Hello. You brought a… a friend?"

It strikes me at the moment, judging by the look on her face, that she's not used to seeing Blake in the company of others, let alone a *friend*.

I bite back a smirk that Blake catches with a side-eyed glance in my direction, but I know he's about to get me back for it a hundred times over.

The screech of a chair steals my attention to the far corner of the room where a man is standing, green eyes locked on mine. My entire body reacts to a familiar face staring me down with such intensity I feel it in my bones.

The Royal Commander, the head of the Ghost army, looks me up and down with an expression so sharp it could cut glass, but his mate, Kenna, Maeve's mother, is oblivious.

"What are you doing here?" she asks Blake, gliding toward where we're standing near the entrance of the room, which is a cozy, dimly lit sitting room with couches, bookshelves, a desk and a large fireplace.

"*Where have you been?*" Commander Evander snarls from his position in the corner, which startles his mate so badly she jumps, rushing out a breath, her hand flying over her heart.

"Evander!" she scoffs, but he's moving in my direction, and I brace myself for impact.

"*You–*" he says, pointing a finger at me. "Where have you been?"

Blake glances at me before taking a step back into the shadow of the archway. I'm honestly at a loss as to what to do or say. I met this man once a decade ago. I was a kid. There's no way he recognizes me.

I take a step back and bow deeply to both of them. "Alpha Kenna, Commander Evander, my name is–"

"*Soren Sinclair,*" the commander cuts sharply.

I wince. It's been… years since I heard my last name–my father's last name–spoken out loud. I'd nearly forgotten it for good reason.

But Kenna steps in front of him, her eyes wide and worried as she looks from me to Blake, "What's wrong? Is it Maeve? Is the baby coming? Is that why you're here? And who are you? Evander, how do you know him?"

"No," Blake tries to cut in, but I shake my head.

"Yes," I breathe, a sudden sense of purpose taking over, forcing me to ignore the way the commander is boring holes with his gaze through my profile as I turn to Maeve's mother. My voice softens, giving a hint of my real emotions–fear, uncertainty, my utter lack of skill and knowledge when it comes to this type of thing–when I say, "She's hurting quite a bit. She won't admit it, but I think she knows it's time. I felt the shift earlier this morning. The baby is coming soon."

Kenna and Evander stare at me in sucking silence, like a vacuum of sound has just descended on the room.

I just gave myself away as her mate, didn't I? Only I would feel that shift, that change in her body, the soul interlocked with mine.

Blake lets out his breath with a sigh, and on that final second of exhalation, the tension snaps.

"Oh, my Goddess," Kenna breathes, her eyes going wide. "Are you– are you *him?*"

Him. Of course. She wouldn't have spoken my name. Her excuse was likely to keep me safe, wasn't it? Forcing herself into silence and burying my memory. I feel worse than ever when I nod, which is all I can muster, and I'm prepared and also not surprised when Evander grabs me by the back of the neck and drags me out of the room into the hallway against his mate's sharp, echoing protests.

Blake follows, finally looking somewhat alarmed when Evander backs me against a wall, his hand curled around my throat. "Evander, this is not the time," he tries to say, but Evander tightens his grip, his eyes searching mine.

That's how he recognizes me, isn't it? My strange combination of contrasting colors.

"Where did you go when you left training camp?"

"The Roguelands," I croak, holding his gaze despite the bruises he's leaving on my skin. "I didn't..." I suck in a breath, barely enough, and continue, "It wasn't my decision."

"Your shithead brother had something to do with it, I assume?"

"He's dead. It doesn't matter."

"Evander, let him go!" Alpha Kenna shrieks from the archway. I feel another presence nearby. Something dark, cold, and watching the scene play from the shadows. I assume it's the ghost Blake mentioned, but I'm proved wrong, my blood running cold, when the Alpha squeaks, "Dad, stop him!"

Dad. Fuck my life. One glance to the right confirms my worst nightmares. The Shadow King of the Roguelands steps into view, his silver eyes scanning his fretful daughter before narrowing on me and Evander.

He looks like Maeve. Their chiseled, sharp features are the same. The same mouth and teeth. The same nose. She's his feminine image.

I close my eyes against the black spots starting to sprout to life along the edges of my vision.

"Evander, that's enough," Ryatt says darkly, but Evander doesn't let go.

"It's fine. I deserve it," I manage to gasp, not bothering to fight.

He knocks me against the wall, still gripping me by the throat. "Where have you been? You were our best—our finest trainee—"

"I got wrapped up with Hannibal," I say, and the hallway goes silent.

Blake lets out his breath as Evander lets go and steps away. Maeve's parents and her grandfather look at me as I take several shallow, choking breaths, my eyes watering, then settle myself enough to breathe normally.

"Hannibal?" Ryatt's voice is smooth and monotone. I don't dare look him in the eyes.

"One of his den leaders, the Viper, was my boss." I glance at Blake, wondering how much of the truth he's going to tell them, but he remains silent, letting me drown without even thinking to throw me a life vest.

To my surprise, Evander says to Ryatt, "We were aware of what happened to him up until seven years ago or so. We knew he was working with someone linked to that network, but we lost track of him after that." Evander turns back into the sitting room.

He knew where I was?

He cared enough to… keep tabs on me?

I blink, looking at Blake, but he's just as confused. He turns after Evander, following him out of sight, but Ryatt and Kenna remain nearby.

I look at Kenna, shaking my head. "Look, there's not a lot of time to explain, but you have to come to Moonrise. You, and… and you," I look at Ryatt then quickly look away. "We have a situation."

"The baby?"

"The baby's fine," I grind out, finding it hard to speak in general. This is a first for me; meeting a woman's parents. No relationship has ever gotten even remotely this far. I wouldn't have let it. "But–Maeve *is* in danger, and we need everyone there. Everyone with powers–"

"How–how did you even meet my daughter?" Kenna asks, reaching for me. She's not what I expected. She's soft, somewhat frantic in nature.

But Ryatt is exactly what I knew he'd be.

"How do you know Blake?" he asks sternly.

"I–fuck, I don't know how to even begin to answer that–"

"Soren, that's enough," Blake says from the archway then turns to Ryatt, Evander within sight in the room behind them. "Soren and I have been working together for the past five years, moving Hannibal's marks into hiding and killing anyone working with him against the Allied Kingdoms."

Kenna gasps, whirling, but Ryatt just… stares at him.

"Soren is what the media calls the Blade. He was the Spider's assassin, but I turned him to our side. We have Hannibal exactly where we need him now. It's time to act."

"What have you done, Blake?" Ryatt asks coolly, and even Blake pales at the ice in his tone.

"What only I can do," he replies sharply. "We don't have time to discuss this further, not here. Where is Ella? Is she still in Maatua visiting my grandparents?"

"Yes," Kenna says, swallowing hard.

"Send word that she needs to come to Moonrise."

"Brie," I say, and all eyes turn on me. "Maeve will want Brie there, too."

Kenna's eyes soften as she nods, but her gaze searches mine, her lower lip trembling. "You're right. She will."

Ryatt, dripping with murderous rage, takes two steps toward Blake, laying his hand on his forearm, and they disappear in a gust of black shadows, leaving me with just her parents.

Evander remains in the sitting room, his back to us as he looks out a window at the star filled sky. I wonder what he's thinking. I wonder what I'd be thinking if the father of my future daughter's baby was someone, *something*, like me.

"Is she all right?" Kenna asks quietly.

"No," I tell her because it's the cold, hard truth. "I should have been here ages ago. I didn't know."

"She said as much." Her eyes slip to the ground for a moment then meet mine again. "Your neck is bruised. I can fix it."

"Don't bother. It's less than I deserved."

Evander turns ever so slightly and looks at me, his face cast in shadow. I can't decipher his expression. It's dark and lined with what

I can only describe as… guilt. Not for nearly strangling me, though. For something else.

"Are you her mate?" Kenna asks after a moment, her words soft and nervous.

I nod. "Yeah, I am. At least, I feel it. It's different for her, I think."

Kenna rushes out a breath and smiles, sniffling slightly. "Yeah, she's… she's… oh," she breathes, teary eyed, turning to Evander. "She must be so happy and relieved–"

But Evander looks grave, his eyes holding on his mate as a silent conversation passes between them. Kenna's face falls, and as she starts to look back in my direction, I look at Evander and say, "I love her, if that's any consolation. I've loved her from the moment we met, and had I known what she was going through alone, it wouldn't have gone on this long. This is something I'll carry for the rest of my life. It shouldn't have been this way for her, and for that, I'm sorry."

Evander doesn't say a word, but he nods, just once.

A gust of black shimmer coats the hallway before Blake, looking slightly pale, and Ryatt, looking furious, reappear. Ryatt grabs my arm, saying to Kenna, "Go to Emberfyll immediately and get Brie and Kieran. Logan stays behind to be ready with the Ghosts stationed there."

"Ready for what?" Kenna cries out, but Ryatt sends me into a free fall of noise and darkness once again.

MARCHING ORDERS

MAEVE

GRAY MORNING SUNLIGHT SPREADS ACROSS THE CARPET AS I PACE THE corridor outside of the library where a screaming match is taking place between Blake and Ryatt. Soren and my dad's voices occasionally lift over the snarls and growls but otherwise blend with the chaos.

They came back last night, and it's been a mess, to say the least. I came out of Blake's private suite to the sound of my mother's frantic voice echoing through the halls where we collided in an embrace, and the first thing I asked was if Soren was still alive.

And, he is. Thank the Goddess, and it sounds like he's holding his own.

I should be in the room. I know that, but this pain... I can't work past it anymore. My entire body is in turmoil as the contractions I've been having off and on over the past two days grow closer and closer together but then slip away entirely, leaving me breathless and frustrated.

Now, I'm stressed out, and all I want is a moment alone with

Soren to make sure he's okay and no one in my family maimed him beyond repair.

Cole slips out of the library, his face drawn in shadow, and sees me standing in wait nearby. He closes the door against the voices inside and sighs, running his fingers through his dark blond hair as he walks in my direction. "Maeve, you should be upstairs–"

"I have nothing to do," I rush out, balling my hands into fists. "Mom left hours ago to go get Brie. She won't be back for a while, probably not until tomorrow or the next day, given that jumping with Brie and Kieran means having to stop in the Deadlands for them to rest and to dose more herbs." I swallow back my nerves and scrub my hand over my face, my fingers trembling. I feel swollen and heavy. Jane came in to brush my hair away from my face and braided it tightly down my back. I'm wearing another nightgown that brushes my knees and a robe that sweeps across the floor, and I'm barefoot because my slippers don't even fit anymore. Cole's gaze takes me in, chews me up, and spits me out.

"Don't look at me like that," I whisper, shaking my head. "I know what I look like–"

"You look incredibly uncomfortable. You should go rest," he says bluntly, taking a heavy breath. "Has your water broken yet?"

"Look, I get that you've delivered half of the babies in this family, but I am fine, okay? I'm just huge, uncomfortable, and really going through it right now, all right?"

"All right," he echoes, raising his hands in surrender. "I'm going to be with Misty making arraignments for our kids when they get here, if you need me."

Soren's voice tears through the barrier of the heavy, ancient wooden door into the library, and my body moves on impulse, shoving past Cole and into the sanctum where my male family members have been fighting over the best course of action like they have any say in what we're doing.

What I'm doing.

"You don't know the Roguelands like I do," Soren bellows, pointing an accusatory finger at Blake, who's standing with his arms crossed over his chest a safe distance away from everyone else. Soren doesn't even glance in my direction when I lean my weight against the library door to close it, the click of the latch echoing seven stories high to the domed ceiling. "You go there with an army, and the only thing you can expect is to piss off every Alpha who claims territory there and send the people you're seeking deeper into hiding! That forest will eat you alive, Blake. I swear to the Goddess, going in with an army is going to get everyone killed and put us ten steps behind Hannibal and the Viper."

Blake rolls his eyes, but my grandpa, who I haven't seen in over a month, braces his hands on one of the many tables scattered across the lowest level of the massive library. "He's right, Blake. The Roguelands is a different animal entirely."

Soren blinks then looks secretly smug at the fact that my grandpa agreed with him, but Blake is furious.

"Are you seriously considering–"

"I am seriously considering bringing your father and grandfather here to deal with you," Grandpa snaps back, eyeing Blake with so much vitriol I can taste it. "You've made a huge mess that I have to clean up. Do you realize that? Your cousin has been slaving away running this kingdom and brought you here to help, and you did *this*? Undermined her authority? Undermined your father's authority in your own kingdom?"

Blake looks at me, narrowing his eyes.

Grandpa Ryatt, who hasn't noticed my presence, continues, but softer, "You can't continue like this, Blake. Your powers are too immense, and you're too young to be using them this way. You have no real world experience–"

"I will determine when and how to use my gifts–"

Another shouting match rattles the hundreds of thousands of books all around us, but I catch my father's gaze, and he shakes his head at me, then tilts his head toward me, mouthing, *"Just go."*

I shake my head. "Will all of you shut the fuck up?"

Blake glowers, but Grandpa Ryatt slowly turns his head to face me.

"I think you all may have forgotten who is now in charge here," I spit, my hands on my hips. "I've had enough of your screaming tantrums this morning. I have a vicious headache. I'm a thousand pounds and fucking tired. I'm sick and tired of the noise. *Enough*. I will determine what happens next. Blake," I turn to my cousin. "You will bring every single person, including their families, that you hid away back to Moonrise. They will be housed here for the near future until we can find a way to bring them back to their packs without a media shitstorm to clean up afterward."

"That's impossible," Blake says coolly. "And I'm not doing it until the Hannibal issue is solved–"

"You are not being honest with us," Grandpa Ryatt snaps, teeth bared. "What have you seen?"

"It doesn't matter what he's seen," I interject, pacing toward the group. "If Hannibal is planning something, we need to be prepared for war. War on Moonrise. Potentially war on Eastonia." I look at my grandfather, waiting for him to brush me off, but he just stares at me, waiting for me to continue, so I do. "I'm shutting down the borders immediately. Sydney will deploy his army to the border between here and Crescent Falls to ensure whatever happens in Eastonia doesn't spill into his kingdom. Travel between the kingdoms of Eastonia will be severely limited until the threat has passed, and I want every single Alpha in Tarsian, the Deadlands, and the Roguelands prepared to deploy their personal warriors to my cause in the event Hannibal has an army." I glance at Blake as I move back across the room. "Moonrise will be under full shields from this moment forward."

"You cannot use your shields to that extent hours before having a baby," Dad says, his voice uncharacteristically tangled by grief.

It takes me aback, but only for a moment, because I look at Soren next, and that cocky fucking smile is stretching across his lips as he watches me... take control. He arches a brow, giving me a little nod in a silent command to keep going.

"I serve Eastonia above all else," I gut out, and my powers stretch, simmering as I ignite the shields around Moonrise. Invisible to the naked eye, but I feel the pull of the magic as it leaves my body and fashions a dome around the sacred city and its more rural towns. "It's already done."

"Maeve," Dad warns, but I shake my head.

"Veiled Valley is already secure, and it will stay that way, but I need the entire force of the Ghosts prepared to move out at any given second," I tell my dad. "And–"

"There will be war," Blake says, and the room goes still. I slowly turn to look at him, my spine lengthening vertebrae by vertebrae when I notice the shattered expression flashing behind his eyes. "A war that will… test our limits. I can't see an outcome for either side."

"What have you seen?" Grandpa repeats under his breath like he didn't mean to say it out loud.

"When?" I ask Blake, turning to face him fully. "Where?"

"Soon, but we have… months, if not a year or two, to prepare. Something happens in the meantime, but I can't see it clearly." His eyes shine like starlight as his powers shimmer behind them. "They'll come from the coast of Tarsian and the Deadlands."

"They?"

Blake shakes his head. "They'll invade."

"Who?" Grandpa growls.

I glance at Soren, who's rapt, watching Blake with a hawk's eye as my cousin raises his hands to his face, pressing his temples like it hurts, badly.

"Hannibal's… people… I can't–I can't see that far. Something's in my way."

"Enough," I tell him as his magic begins to fill the space between us, riling my own. I turn to face my mate. "It won't get that far. We will stop Hannibal here. There will be no war. Not while I'm queen." A rope of pain curls around my lower stomach. I clutch the top of a chair, sighing through the tightening sensation threatening to pull me to my knees, and say, "For now, everyone in the family gathers in either Moonrise, Veiled Valley, or the capital in Crescent Falls. Blake, alert your parents–" I grit my teeth as the pain reaches a peak, and then Soren is beside me, leaning down to whisper in my ear.

"I can't stand here and watch you do this. Come with me, please."

I nod as tears of pain well in my eyes. The men behind me are silent. I've given my orders. They know what to do and how to do it.

Within minutes, thanks to the elevator, I'm back in my suite watching Soren run me a bath. He looks just as worn and exhausted as I feel. I want to ask how it went when he met my parent., It was against his will, but it still happened. I gather Mom was excited for us. Dad will barely look in my direction.

But instead, too stressed and unfocused to fight it, I lean my cheek to his chest as he gently pulls the robe from my body, his hands warm and solid on the bare skin of my arms as the silken fabric falls in a puddle on the floor beneath us. He unties the laces of the nightgown, loosening it enough to pull it over my shoulders. His hands brush down my naked body, calming, reassuring, and I don't blush or shy away from him seeing me this time.

His mouth brushes against my temple as we stand there in the bathroom, alone, at peace, while the world begins to burn all around us.

The bath works wonders for my aching, too heavy, body. Soren doesn't leave his perch against the counter and is there to help me out and to wrap me in a towel that barely covers me. I grip his arm as he leads me into the bedroom, now sparkling with midday light, but rain pelts the windows, signaling an early start to spring.

But when he helps me into bed, I stop him with a hand on his chest.

"I missed you," I whisper, the only words I can think to say.

He nods, swallowing back a reply, but then… kisses me. It's tender and light, and after a moment he pulls away, resting his forehead against mine.

I rise on my toes and kiss him back, letting the kiss take on a life of its own. I feel him coming to life around me, his touch harder, more demanding, and I melt into him, forgetting the strain in my body and the unraveling world outside the confines of my room–our room now.

Because this is our home.

And he's mine.

And nothing is going to change that. I won't let it.

Soren stops the kiss to look at me with a silent question drifting behind his eyes.

"I want you," I whisper, nodding, smoothing my hands down his chest. "Right now. *Please.*"

He nods, breathless, and backs me against the bed.

THE MATE BOND SNAPS

MAEVE

I EXPECTED THIS TO FEEL AWKWARD. SO MUCH TIME HAS PASSED. WE had each other for a single night, and then months went by. Should I have forgotten what his hands feel like? Should my body be tense and unyielding when he climbs next to me, carefully bracing himself with a hand to the mattress as he leans over to kiss my lips, my jaw, and down the slope of my neck while his free hand glides over my hip to my thigh?

Instead, I melt into his touch. I drown in him. Every ache and pain fades and is instantly replaced by a dizzying sense of belonging and being beloved. It's natural. It's like touching and being touched by him is something I was built for, like he was made for me and I him. Yet, I'm not as agile as I was once. Moving around–being thrown this way and that way is obviously off the table, but Soren... knows what to do.

"Oh!" I cry out, gripping the sheets when his mouth dips between my thighs, his arms snaking around my legs and pulling me down the mattress. My eyes flutter closed as his tongue parts my folds, and he growls against the tender, aching flesh, sending a vibration of pleasure skittering down my spine that settles where he's now licking and sucking me into a heated frenzy.

I haven't been touched like this since him. Since that morning before the train. I continue gripping the sheets as he tugs me further down the bed until he's kneeling on the ground at the foot of the bed with my thighs resting on his shoulders, my ankles locked and toes curling when he slides his fingers inside of me to further push me toward the edge.

"You were," he rasps against my clit, smiling as I moan against the sensation of his voice and fingers pleasuring me in tandem, "amazing down there, Queen Maeve."

"In the library?" I pant, already too overcome to stop myself from falling over the edge of reason, the edge of no return.

"I love it when you're mean." He grins, and then his tongue drags through my folds again, rendering me useless.

"You're acting like our world isn't crashing down around us right now," I whisper then whimper a moan.

"I'm kneeling for my mate," he breathes, pressing a rough kiss to my inner thigh. "The rest can fucking wait."

All I see is stars as he showers me with me praise and fucks me with his tongue and fingers until I'm begging for him to let me come, but every time I get close, he slows his movements, savoring the way I'm begging and pleading his name.

"I want you inside of me," I beg, clawing his shoulders as I try to sit up. "Please, Soren, I'm dying for it."

He rises and takes off his shirt, then his pants, holding my gaze as he skillfully drags his belt free of the loops. But I can tell he's hesitating, likely going over the logistics in his mind as he scans my naked body. He reaches for me, kneading one of my breasts—so much larger than they were when we were together the last time—and trembles with a sigh. "Fuck, Maeve. I'm not going to last long when you're like this," he says hungrily, his pupils blown wide like he's on the verge of shifting. "Seeing you like this... I want to keep you like this forever."

"Keep me pregnant forever? Absolutely not!" I scoff, glaring, but he shushes me, leaning down to kiss me and stealing the words from my tongue.

"Turn around," he says sternly against my lips.

My heart is in my throat and beating out of rhythm as I slide off the foot of the bed and turn, closing my eyes against the sensation of his arms wrapping around me and his mouth pressing into the crook of my neck. He leans us forward so I'm bent over the edge of the bed, my hands braced on the mattress, his mouth leaving searing kisses along my shoulder blade.

His cock teases my entrance before he slowly guides himself inside of me, hissing out a breath as my inner walls grip him tight. "Fuck," he growls, kissing my shoulder. "I missed this."

I rise on my toes, breathing through the stretch as he fills me up, holding himself there for a moment like he needs a second to regain his composure.

He finds my breasts as he begins to thrust, taking his time as he pulls out and presses in again until we both begin to groan, and the pressure builds.

"*Yes,*" I gasp as tension coils in my lower stomach. "*Goddess, yes.*"

"Are you going to come for me, Princess?"

I arch my back as he grips my ass, thrusting into me harder than before. My inner walls spasm and clutch his cock so hard he bites down on my shoulder but not hard enough to break the skin. It still fills me with so much heat I nearly scream his name, and his teeth graze my skin as he loses himself in my body…. It's enough. It rocks me to my center, and I fall over the edge into blinding, white-hot pleasure.

He grips my throat as I ride out the orgasm, his other hand braced on the mattress at my side, but then he tilts my head to the side and…

I suck in a breath, biting back a scream as he sinks his teeth into the crook of my neck, marking me.

The smell of blood briefly reaches me. He bites down harder, groaning as he rocks into me. Another orgasm sweeps through me, taking me by surprise, and then he's coming unglued.

Soren grunts, his teeth still clamped to my neck, and spills inside of me.

Gasping, he pulls away, his forehead pressed to the ridge of my shoulder while I struggle to catch my breath. A bead of blood drips down my neck and trickles between my breasts, but I don't feel pain.

I feel… everything else. Everything warm and rich.

The mate bond echoes through me at first, like a warm summer breeze. It's… beautiful. But still just out of reach.

I turn around to face him, caressing his cheek, and press a soft kiss to his mouth before moving to kiss his jaw, then down his neck…

He clasps the back of my head, pressing my face against his neck, "Bite me. Mark me, Maeve."

"Is that possible? I'm a witch–"

"I don't give a fuck. I'm yours. I want to carry your scar."

Something unexpected ripples through my body. The faint mate bond I feel burrows deep, igniting my powers, which shimmer through my skin. I lick his neck, and he groans, tangling his fingers in my hair, his cock growing hard again as my teeth graze his skin.

I bite down on his neck, hard, hard enough to break the skin.

But I'm not a shifter.

I'm something else.

I'm the only one of my kind…

But I have him.

My powers burst, sending a flash of heat where we're joined. Soren grips me harder, hissing in pain, and I pull away, tasting his blood on my tongue.

Muted crimson light sparkles from the mark I left on his neck. It sinks into his skin, leaving a smooth, silver scar in its wake–fully healed.

But my magic travels through his body, giving him a faint golden glow.

I look up into his eyes. He looks down at me, panting, as the magic fades, and the mate bond between us snaps together–and I feel it.

I feel the full force of it.

It's enough to make me cry.

"You felt like this for nine months?" I whisper, completely and utterly overwhelmed.

"I love you, Maeve," he whispers, leaning his forehead against mine and taking my hand, smoothing a kiss across my knuckles.

SOREN

SHE'S SLEEPING AS I GRIP THE TOP OF THE DOORFRAME, LEANING forward to stretch the aching muscles in my back and shoulders. I feel like I lived ten lifetimes in the past... forty-eight hours or so. My brain can't grasp everything that happened, but honestly, I really don't give a shit about Blake being a weird fucking mutant dickhead, or "Grandpa Ryatt" stalking around like a shadow, or Hannibal, or the Viper.

Everyone can go to hell because we have... twelve hours, I'd guess, until this baby is born.

I watch Maeve twitch in her sleep, sighing around another tightening that grasps her entire body, but nothing strong enough to make any real progress. It's frustrating seeing her like this. I want to help her somehow, but... I suppose just being here is enough. There's not much we can do for her now, according to her mom and Misty.

I close the door and step into the quiet, still destroyed hallway, and run my fingers through my disheveled hair with a heavy sigh.

I let my body decide where I'm going next, which ends up being a cozy but wide study or parlor located on the fifth floor. I'm not the only one seeking refuge here because I find the one man I really didn't want to be alone with sitting in an armchair near the fireplace, swirling a glass of whiskey as he squints down at the phone in his hand.

Ryatt follows my steps toward the bottle of whiskey he left open on a built-in bar along the far wall. I fetch a glass from a shelf above my head and pour myself a heavy dram, exhaling deeply through the obvious tension filling the room.

I turn, nodding at him in greeting, then move to a dainty antique chair in the far corner of the room, and sit.

Minutes tick by in silence. I'd surmise he thinks I think I own this place now, moving around from room to room as I wish. I drain my whiskey. He drains his. He grumbles at his phone. I check my watch, timing another rush of pain through the mate bond.

I'm pouring myself a second glass of whiskey when the Shadow King, an absolute legend in the Roguelands where I'd spent the majority of my life, says, "We're not all bad. You're meeting us at a… complicated time."

I glance at him over my shoulder to confirm he's speaking to me and not taking a phone call, and when his eyes meet mine, I feel… I feel like Patton would likely feel coming face to face with this man. Starstruck.

"This entire situation is my fault," I tell him, turning back to the bar to take a sip of my drink so he can't see how badly my hand is trembling. "I got Maeve into this."

"It's not your fault, necessarily. There's been some… rifts in the family for a while. And, she would have gotten herself into it eventually. You were her target for so long." He exhales as I turn to face him. "That's all she cared about, all she talked about for years when she was shadowing Ella. I'm going to find and kill the assassin. I'm going to bring him to justice. I'm going to rid the world of him and the Spider. Little did she know those feelings were… the mate bond trying to guide her home."

"I can't stand here and pretend to be a good guy," I reply hoarsely. "I'm not going to grovel for acceptance, if that's what everyone is expecting from me. I did what I had to do to survive and keep someone I loved safe. I would do it all again. Every kill, every lie. I don't regret any of it."

"I know. I understand completely." His soft, almost secretive smile is something I realize I might not get the opportunity to see often, if not ever again. "The Roguelands are… uncontrollable. That's the reason why it's still a hotbed for illegal activity. It'll never change. It'll never be tamed. Only someone who has lived there, who has bled there, knows that." His gaze holds mine for several seconds before he looks down at his drink.

I chew the inside of my cheek while wondering if I should start asking him questions about his time as the King of the Rogues. Everyone knows the history, of course. The Roguelands was... nothing back then. A deep, dark forest. Dark enough to hide in. Dark enough to disappear in. He gathered an army there out of misfits, bandits, and slaves. He ruled as king when there wasn't anyone to rule. He overthrew an evil regime with forces whose training was nothing more than a life of survival in the same forest I've called home for so long.

He understands. He's still the king there, in some shape or form... at least, until Maeve came into power.

I think we both know her authority doesn't mean shit in the Roguelands.

A gnawing, clawing sensation drifts through my body. It's something I've been ignoring for weeks, maybe months... years, I suppose.

The Viper's end, and the liberation of men like me, men unable to get out from beneath her, will be at my hand, but I can't do it from here, can I?

"I'll stay here with her," he says as if reading my mind, bringing his drink to his lips. "She'll be safe. Ella just arrived, and Kenna will be back soon–with Brie. She's surrounded by family again. She's not alone, Soren. *She's safe.*"

A tingle of understanding prickles over my skin as the... the truth of the matter that I've been burying starts clawing to the surface like he *knows*. Like he can see right through me, see through the mask of bullshit I've been wearing since I arrived here.

Since I came face to face with Blake, the only man I think can help me end this for good.

"She's going to be okay, and you're going to come back to her, but you need to do what needs to be done. You have to go back."

I grind my teeth, nodding, and bring my drink to my lips. "I'm taking that freak with the weird eyes with me. He owes me."

Ryatt smirks, leaning back in his chair, and nods.

EXITS AND ENTRANCES

MISTY LINGERS NEARBY AS GINNY, MY MIDWIFE, RISES FROM BETWEEN my legs, her face cast in the shadow of the sunset sending golden and crimson streaks of light through the curtains. The snow is melting. Ice thaws on the windows. I relax my legs with a grimace, Misty coming to my side to help me back into a seated position.

"So?" Misty asks as Ginny disposes of her gloves. "Is this happening?"

"Slowly, but yes. She's quickening now. Her contractions will grow stronger from her, but they're still far enough apart that I believe we have some time. A day or so."

"A day?" I whine.

Ginny and Misty give me mirrored looks of sympathy, but it's obvious there's nothing more that can be done.

"Well, that means you have a full day to finally decide what her name is going to be," Misty quips, shrugging a shoulder. "I'm leaning toward *Misty*, but I'm sure your Mom and Sarah would beg to differ."

I playfully narrow my eyes. "If she ever makes her arrival, I'll give her a name. Until then, I'm going to continue wallowing." I roll over, grunting with the effort, and hug one of the six pillows currently stacked around the bed while Ginny murmurs to Misty about whether I'm planning to have the baby here, in my room, or at the clinic.

I watch the sunset fade, picking at the tassels on the pillow, wondering what the men are up to. I woke up to Soren puttering around the room, taking bites of a sandwich and looking incredibly bored. I'm not sure he knows what to do with his time here, which makes me wonder what I'm going to do when it comes to him having a life here, with me, with our baby.

I can't see Soren finding any kind of solace in a soft life where he can watch TV to his heart's content and take up a hobby, like... underwater basket weaving, or something.

But I can see him... going to work at the same training facility where he was given a shot at a real future all those years ago. He's incredibly gifted as a warrior.

The idea of him trying to wrangle a group of teenagers in the fourteen to sixteen class makes me chuckle, however, into my pillow. He doesn't have the patience for that, but they'd love him. They'd worship the ground he walked on and run home to their parents with a colorful new vocabulary I wouldn't stop hearing about for years to come.

But... he wouldn't have a title. He'd be a background character.

Would he be okay with that?

He's never given me the idea that power is something he wants, but... he's an Alpha. It's in his blood. He's a born leader.

Keeping him locked up in a gilded cage is the same as trapping him in a silver band, isn't it?

I curl around the jolt of guilt now ripping through my body.

"You okay? Hungry? Thirsty? Want to go on a walk?" Misty peppers me with questions.

I shake my head, rolling over onto my other side in an attempt to get out of bed completely. "I should go check on Soren, actually. I worry about him being alone with Grandpa and my dad for this long."

"As far as I know he's holding his own," she murmurs, clutching my arm to steady me as I lift my legs off the mattress with a grunt. "Your dad's being weird, though. I've never seen him like this."

"He feels guilty, I think." I sigh.

"About what? I didn't realize you were fighting with him, too. Everyone was under the impression you left before Solstice because of Ryatt–"

"Well, that last part is true, I guess. I wouldn't call it a fight but…" He overstepped my boundaries by forcing me back to Moonrise during Solstice, but now… now I realize he was right. Soren coming back confirmed it. I was in danger. The baby was in danger. I close my eyes, waddling toward my dresser where I left my robe wadded on its surface, and shake it out, saying, "Dad knew Soren, I guess. Soren was a trainee in the Ghosts, and he… he didn't come back from leave. I don't know the details of what it looked like for Dad and his captains but… I think something else happened, something Soren doesn't know about."

"Your mom told me your dad had Soren pegged as a future captain before he even came into wolf powers."

"I wouldn't be surprised," I whisper, more to myself than to her. Misty takes her leave, and I dress as best I can. Fatigue clutches my body. I move at a snail's pace into the tidy living area of my suite, but I find Jane there carrying a tea tray.

"Oh, I was hoping to surprise you," she says with a soft smile. There's a new light behind her eyes, and her cheeks are… softly pink. She looks warm all over.

I smile to myself as she sets the tray down and turns to me, tucking her hands behind her back. "How're you doing, mistress? I feel like I haven't seen you in days."

"You've been busy," I tell her, and it's not just because of Patton and their mate bond. While I've been dealing with my family and the first signs of labor, Jane has been doing everything else. Clearing my schedule, handling questions from the press about why the family is gathering here, etc. "And I'm all right. Just tired. I was about to go find Soren–"

The door to my suite opens, sending an echo through the network of hallways and archways leading to the living room. Soren's footsteps are undeniably set in determination as he rounds a corner, but when he sees me and Jane standing in the center of the living, he pauses in an archway, and his eyes...

"What happened?" I rush out.

Jane steps beside me and turns to face him, still gripping the tea tray. It's the chamomile blend from the tea shop. Soren and I notice the scent at the same time, and his dark, steely expression deepens.

Blake fades out of the shadows, and Jane looks at him, her nostrils flaring as Blake leans to murmur into Soren's ear, "Patton is in the Roguelands gathering your contacts. He'll be meeting us in Twin Rivers within the next hour–"

"What?" I gasp, looking between my cousin and mate.

Blake licks his lips. Soren steps forward, resigned, and holds out his hands in surrender.

But I already know what he's about to say and do.

"No," I whisper, looking from him to Blake and back again. "No, Soren–"

"Listen," he says quietly, edging toward me cautiously like I'm about to burst into flame before his eyes. "Maeve, this ends with me. I have a chance, okay, to kill the Viper. She's the one in the way of your family finding Hannibal and putting an end to his–"

"It's not your responsibility–"

"It is."

"But I can do it. I can do this for you–"

"No," he breathes, holding my gaze as he shakes his head. He gently takes my arm and guides me back into our room, closing the door behind him, and pulls me against his chest.

I'm too tired to fight. My body is honed on the changes actively taking place inside of me. My powers are... loosening, changing in a way I can't explain, like they're making room for something greater– the full strength of my powers as they mature.

"I spent the last ten years of my life fighting to take it back," he whispers into my hair. "I killed people. I hurt people. I stole and fought to keep my head on my shoulders." He pulls away enough to look down at me. "I laid in the Vipers bed and let her fuck me, Maeve, to protect Patton. Now I have to protect you and her." He places a hand on my stomach, where the baby is silent, still, lying in wait for her grand entrance to the world. "And I will."

I shake my head, but in my heart, I know this is done. He's been in and out of our room all day, and most of the day yesterday, as well. He's been plotting and scheming, making sure every detail is in place for me.

"I am here," he says in a whisper, "to take a burden off your shoulders. This won't be the first time I step up and tell you to step aside for me. You're my queen, but you're also my mate. Let me protect you–"

"I have powers, Soren."

"Save them for her. Save your strength for her."

Tears sting my eyes, but don't fall as I… give in. Give up. As I go against every fiber in my being screaming to chain this beautiful, infuriating man to my bed and rush off to do this myself.

But I can't. I don't know where the Viper is. I don't know her people. I'm not familiar with her games.

Soren is. He knows her on a level that makes me sick to my stomach.

"Come back to me," I whisper into his shirt, closing my eyes against a surge of grief that burrows through my chest.

"I swear on the Goddess that I will come home," he replies sternly, like he's branding the words into existence. "We have it all planned out, Maeve. Your father has Ghosts undercover in Twin Rivers already. I've given him the Viper's location, and they're clearing the way for us."

"Us?"

"Blake and me. Blake took Patton to the Roguelands today, jumping him from place to place to alert the people we trust, people who want out just as much as we do. Blake shattered their bands."

I swallow past the lump in my throat. "I don't know if I fully trust Blake. I feel like he's hiding something."

"He might be, but he's clear on what he wants. He wants her dead as much as I do. He needs her out of the way to take down Hannibal. Once the Viper is gone, and the baby is here, you can handle Blake however you want, but I need him right now."

"And what do I do?" I whisper.

"Stay here with your family. This won't take long, Maeve. Hours, at the most. We're leaving at nightfall."

"Promise me something," I say, holding him at arm's length. "Promise you'll be here when she's born."

He smooths my hair out of my face.

"Promise me," I repeat, gripping his arms. "I want you here. I want you to see her."

"I will be here," he says, his eyes locked on mine. "I swear. I will be here when she's born. I will come back to you, even if it means I have to walk through hell to get here. I will come home."

He brushes his thumb over the healing mark he left on my neck, his eyes dropping to my lips, but he kisses the corner of my mouth instead.

Time moves in a blur for the next two hours. I sit in the living room with Jane, who's ghostly pale and uncertain. Patton didn't even get to say goodbye to her before Blake whisked him away, but I know Patton wouldn't have left her behind if he didn't believe we all had a shot of a life without the worry of the Viper or Hannibal chasing them down, hurting them, hurting us.

I watch my father fit Soren with new Ghost armor—something top of the line. Dad doesn't say much, but seeing them together... seeing my family accepting him while knowing the truth... it's overwhelming, to say the least.

I was wrong about them. About everyone. I drove a wedge between my family members thinking they'd never understand, and maybe they never will, but Soren is now the bridge between us.

Goddess, please let him come home.

I refuse to say goodbye. Soren, too, simply turns to Blake, both now wearing plain clothes with their Ghost gloves tucked in their jackets, and they disappear. Jane leaves to cry herself to sleep, I suppose. I sit on the couch, watching the stars prickle into view, and see twin shadows in the archway.

Grandma Ella comes to sit beside me. Grandpa Ryatt stays put, his eyes on his watch.

An hour passes, then another, and the world keeps spinning.

"Your mom is going to be here in the morning. She just confirmed they're leaving the Deadlands at daybreak. Kieran can jump without the herbs, I guess, but Brie is still terribly ill," Grandma says, smoothing my hair away from my face as she draws a bath for me. I stand in the bathroom as the water surges out of the tap, fragrant steam billowing toward the tiled ceiling.

"Grandpa should have gone with them," I tell her, hugging myself as another contraction soars through me. I wince, but Grandma Ella bites her lip.

"He wants to be here, with you."

"I didn't understand why–I thought he was sending me away from Maatua because he didn't trust me."

"He built the world you inherited, honey. Knowing what you're going through now is killing him. It makes him feel like he didn't accomplish enough."

"That's not true," I whisper, shaking my head, but just as the contraction fades, another begins, worse than before.

I double over, gripping the counter, and groan through the tight, deep pain threatening to snap my spine.

"Oh, dear," Grandma huffs. "Okay, this one was bad."

"I–" I can't talk through it. The pain steals my breath away.

"Maeve, just breathe–"

Water spills between my legs, tinged with blood.

I meet Grandma's eyes.

"I can't—not until he comes back–Oh, Goddess–"

"Don't panic, Maeve," she whispers, but her skin pales as I double over again, clutching my stomach. "Ryatt? RYATT!"

TAKING DOWN THE VIPER

Soren

Twin Rivers is cast in darkness and flickering neon lights as I trudge beside Blake, our heads bent against a spray of slush. The streets are clear of ice but soaking wet, and my boots leave deep imprints in the rotten snow as I cross a street, Blake staying in step with me. My eyes are covered by my usual mask–a simple strip of dark fabric. My ball cap casts the rest of my face in shadow as we cut through an alley between two lively bars. We have to side-step between the crowd to gain access to the next street.

Blake begins to don his gloves, but I stop him, shaking my head. "She needs to see you as you are. That's part of the plan, remember?"

He grits his teeth and slides the gloves back in his pocket.

"Having second thoughts?"

"No," he rasps. It's impossible to tell what he's really thinking. His face is set in a mask of indifference as the city bleeds around us. Twin Rivers is a hotbed for nightlife. Bars and clubs rage even in the darkest hours of morning. A group of young women croon at us, but

Blake keeps his head down, strategically adjusting his hood to cast his face, especially his eyes, in shadow, and we keep walking.

"How much further?" he asks as the city light begins to fade behind us, the streets ahead dark and run down.

"Two blocks."

His eyes light from within for several seconds before fading. "Evander's Ghosts are nearby. They've cleared a path. We won't be bothered at the entrance."

"Andrea's going to be aware something's going on," I tell him, and he tilts his head in consideration.

"We want her desperate, don't we? Also, I didn't realize you were on a first name basis."

"I know her far more intimately than I want to."

Blake stops walking in the middle of the street and turns to me. I shove my hands in my pockets, gritting my teeth as I face him. "What do you mean by that? Do you have a history with her? A romantic one?"

"Why does it matter when she'll be taking her last breath within the hour?"

"Because you're linked to Maeve now." He steps into me, squaring his shoulders. "I know you don't fully trust me, but everything I do, and everything I've done, has been to protect those I love, which includes her–"

"If you're asking if I used to date the fucking Viper and may have lingering feelings for that bitch," I hiss, "the answer is no. It wasn't like that. Not at all."

He searches my eyes for understanding, and I let him see it.

Blake steps away, clearing his throat, and begins walking again even though he has no idea where he's going.

"This way, idiot," I grumble under my breath, turning to the left to stalk down a poorly lit road with shuddered apartment buildings towering over us on either side.

A shadow moves across the street dressed in a rather fancy puffer jacket from a high-end sporting goods store right across the street from the castle. Patton glances around before hurrying to my side, whispering, "We're clear. She's alone."

"Have you been inside yet? Nice fucking jacket, by the way."

"No I haven't been inside," he growls, but then his cheeks glow pink as our trio passes under a flickering streetlight. "You like it? Jane said her favorite color is navy blue. I got the matching hat."

Even soulless, emotionally inept Blake snorts a laugh.

But that laugh cuts short as we near the building towering over the street. No one greets us at the door. Music still wafts from below, but it's a quiet night in the exclusive underground dance club. Blake glances at the dancers sitting on the stage, barely dressed and kicking their legs as they scroll their phones instead of twirling on the poles. The bar is completely empty, no one manning it, and no guards stand outside the double doors to hell itself.

"I don't like this," I say, unable to stop walking to turn to the men beside me. "What exactly were the Ghosts told to do?"

"Keep watch on this building and side street. I know a small diversion was created to make it possible for you to bring us in, but that was supposed to be it," Blake says, each word sharp and dripping with apprehension. "Something's up."

"I know." I think of Maeve. I think of the moment she brings our daughter into the world. I promised her I'd be back for that, and I will be. Even if I have to crawl my way back to Moonrise, I'll be there.

I open the double doors and feel a momentary burst of relief to see two guards standing outside Andrea's office. One of them looks at me but then looks down at his hands, and the nerves return. Odd. I don't recognize these men, and I know everyone.

Into Patton's head, I say through the mind-link now active between us, *"What about our guys? Where are they?"*

"Beckett, Louis, Sean, and Maverick are lying in wait just outside the city if we need help getting out," he says as we move closer to Andrea's office door. "The rest are three blocks away, lying low at a bar under the guise of attending a concert. They'll be here in twenty minutes."

"Good," I say out loud then turn for the door and shove it open without knocking.

Andrea is sitting at her desk. She smiles at me as I walk in, but I see through it. Her eyes dart to Blake and her brows raise. "Well, well, well. I did not expect this tonight."

I motion for Patton to remain by the door, which I left open. But Blake steps in front of me and sits in one of the twin armchairs in front of her desk, looking directly into her eyes.

He drinks her in, taking in every detail like he's memorizing her. His gaze narrows as she tucks her chin-length black hair behind her pointed ears and smiles at him kindly, looking as stunning and evil as ever.

"Prince Blake. *What an honor.*"

"I understand you have some type of agreement with Soren regarding my cousin, the Queen of Eastonia?"

I cross my arms over my chest as unease ghosts through me. I have to remind myself this is the plan. Blake knows what he's doing. Nothing he's about to say, or offer, is how he really feels, but he's really fucking good at this. Too good.

"The child was born last night," he lies. "A full-blooded Firestone female, the heir to Eastonia after Maeve."

Andrea tilts her head, shrugging. "And is the child dead, like I asked my dear friend Soren to arrange?" Her eyes flicker to mine with a flash of annoyance.

"No. I have something better in mind," Blake says. "I can get you Maeve. I can hand her over on a silver platter, and you can feast on her bones."

"I don't need the queen. No one can get close to her. Even my best. My sweet Soren has failed, hasn't he? That's why you're here, isn't it? He called in the cavalry?" Her smile is sickly sweet.

But Blake is playing ball. "The queen asked me to be her second a few months ago. I haven't given her an answer yet, but I've been taking a share of some of her duties over the past months for obvious reasons. I am her closest advisor. She does anything I say without question."

It takes all of my strength not to laugh.

Andrea tilts her head and looks interested, for once. "But if you're here, in my den, you must want something she can't offer you."

"Precisely."

"And what is it that you want, Seer?"

"I want it all," he says smoothly, his mouth stretching into a sick smile I'd believe wholeheartedly to be true had we not just discussed what he was going to say to her. His eyes glow softly in the dim light, not enough for her notice yet, but while he's keeping her talking, he's slowly sending his powers into her mind, clawing past what I assume are mental shields.

That's the whole plan. Break into the bitch's head, find out all of the secrets she keeps, get a location on Hannibal, and then boil her gray matter, or whatever the fuck Blake is capable of doing.

"What are you suggesting, princeling?"

"I want in on whatever your boss is planning. I want Eastonia. I want Crescent Falls. I want the kingdoms beyond. I can make a deal with him."

"And what of your ever powerful family?" She laughs, but she's enraptured, slowly leaning over the desk as his eyes glow brighter with each passing second.

I let my hands fall to my side, brushing over the twin blades tucked against my thighs, out of sight.

"My family is a waste of power. I'll take what I can from them, drain them, and dispose of them. They trust me without fault. I've been using that to my advantage for a while, but Maeve is the one standing in my way, and right now, she's vulnerable." He rises, bracing his hands on the desk, and leans toward her. His eyes glow like fire-lit amethyst as he concludes, "It was a long, hard labor. They barely survived. She's weak now. I can make this happen. I can pluck them from this world and give Hannibal the green light to *invade*."

I realize the mistake the moment Andrea's expression flattens. Blake's eyes grow bright, but she... holds strong. I can see the tension in his knuckles. He's gripping the desk like his life depends on it and starting to tremble as he sends his powers into her, but she… she's not like us.

He told me that once.

I realize with a start that she knew we were going to be here somehow. She was waiting for this. No, she never sent me to Moonrise to kill my child. Blake mentioned Hannibal has similar powers to him somehow. Hannibal knew. Hannibal was, and will always be, two steps ahead.

"Fuck," I say under my breath.

She chuckles, which turns to a shrill laugh that pings from wall to wall. Blake stands, panting, and takes a stumbling step backward, and I… I act.

Two steps is all it takes to leap onto her desk, brandish my blades, and pin her to the wall with my daggers crossed against her throat.

She giggles, running her tongue along her lower lip like a snake. "I missed playing with you, Soren."

"Shut the fuck up. This is what's going to happen. You're going to die here. I'm going to chop off your head and drag your lifeless body into the street. My men are actively canvassing Twin Rivers for any of your people and disposing of them in a public way. You're done, Andrea. This is over."

"Oh, Soren, you are *so* late to the party."

A ripple of unease shoots up my spine. Blake teeters, catching himself on the edge of the desk, and lunges for us. I slice into Andrea's neck and beads of blood appear along the blade's surface, but it's not enough to even hurt the bitch, not yet. Blake slams his palm against her forehead and screams as his powers surge, her eyes turning a bright violet as her scream fills the room.

But then Patton yelps, gasping, and hits the ground behind us in silence. The sound is the catalyst for the end of life as I know it, but I realize that a moment too late.

A blast of energy explodes through the room. Andrea's shrill scream of pain when one of my blades cuts deep into her throat and the reek of her blood follows, coating the room with the scent of iron, but my vision cuts out. I feel my body hit the wall next to her, then turn as slow, steady footsteps echo through the sizzling chaos.

"Well done, Andrea," Hannibal says, his voice as smooth and deep as an aged scotch.

"Kill them," The Viper gasps around a mouthful of blood.

I open my eyes, but I can see anything. Something's wrapped around my head, my eyes, blocking everything but light. I can't move. I'm… being squeezed…

"Not yet. I want to play with this one first."

Blake grunts in pain, and then everything goes black as the world around us falls away.

This was not part of the plan.

But I'm an enterprising man with a mate resurrected from the seventh level of hell, and she'll come for me, one way or the other.

She'll finally get what she wants.

I submit, smiling, to the darkness that swallows us whole.

SHE WON'T BE STOPPED

I CAN'T BREATHE THROUGH THE PAIN ANYMORE. IT GRIPS ME, TEARING through my back, splitting my spine.

I grip Misty's arms as I howl, tears streaming down my face. Misty's trembling, holding me upright, her healing powers hard at work mending the bruises and scratches I've left on her skin.

It's been four hours of this. Six hours ago, Soren, Blake, and Patton left.

Soren told me he'd be back within an hour. Maybe two, at the most.

I've been counting the seconds.

"Maeve, you should try to lie down," Misty says gently, coaxing me toward the bed, but I furiously shake my head and writhe through another contraction that begins to build at the base of my spine.

"No, no, no, no," I mumble then gasp as the pain curls around me in an iron embrace.

"Ginny, how much longer?" Grandma Ella says sternly from my

other side as I stand between the two women, my legs shaking, but I'm unable to find the strength to move.

I feel Ginny's hand glide between my legs. The pain is unbearable. I lean my forehead on Misty's shoulder and cry out against the feeling begging me to push, to let her into the world, but *I can't.*

"Maeve, you need to push now–" Ginny begins to say with a hint of panic in her voice.

"NO," I shout into Misty's shoulder. "No! He promised–he promised he'd be here. He swore!"

"You cannot hold her in," Grandma says firmly, her hand pressed against my lower back to try to alleviate the pain, but it does nothing to soothe me.

"S-something's wrong," I bite out. "He–he should have been back by now. Where is he? Something happened!" I feel it in my gut. It's a raw, aching sensation that tells me nothing is okay, and everything went wrong. Dread curls through me, yanking at the strings binding me to Soren, calling out to him, begging for him to find me again.

"Maeve," Misty growls, losing her patience, "you have to do this. She is coming *now*. She's ready."

"I'm not ready," I groan. "Please–" The worst pain yet rips through me, rendering my voice useless. I cry out Soren's name as an empty feeling spreads across my chest and settles like an icy, uneven weight. My powers surge, my skin prickles, and then I know, without a shadow of a doubt, something went terribly wrong. "No," I rush out, letting go of Misty's arms. "No–no–"

"Maeve? Maeve, listen to me–" Misty tugs me close, shushing me as I begin to unravel.

The door to my bedroom flies open, revealing Grandpa Ryatt and my father. Two women rush past, however, beelining for me. Mom immediately grabs Ginny for a synopsis of the last four hours of a very painful, very fast and intense labor while Brie replaces Misty, her dark amber eyes holding mine.

"Oh, Maeve," she breathes. "You're going to be okay. I'm here now. We're going to do this together–"

"Where is Soren!" I scream.

"Ella," Grandpa Ryatt says, but his voice is drowned out by a burst of magic that fills the room, followed by a gurgling sob and two more familiar voices.

"*Goddess above*, everyone out!" Grandma shouts, her sea-green eyes blown wide with frustration, but I turn my head to see Sydney with an arm around Sarah's waist, her face shattered and smothered in tears. Her eyes are glowing, however, with her magic. She looks lost as she trembles, unseeing.

She's scrying.

"*No*," I choke, gripping Brie, who just arrived from the Deadlands and is weak from the herbs in her system, but she stands tall and immovable. "No–"

"Where is Blake?" Sydney asks with heartbreaking quiet. "Ryatt? Where is he? We felt–we felt something. I can't explain it–"

"I can't–I can't find him," Sarah sobs. "He's gone. *I can't see him*–"

Dad steps forward, his eyes dead and hollow as he urges Sydney and Sarah out of the room, but I shout, "What happened?! Dad!"

"EVERYONE OUT!" Grandma roars, her Firestone magic flaring behind her eyes, so similar to mine.

I shove away Brie, limping and cradling my aching stomach as I round the bed to stare at the family members gathered in the door-way. "Where the fuck–" I demand, shaking as another contraction burns to life along my spine, "is my *mate?*"

Mom and Brie reach my side, but I rip out of their grasps, my eyes on Dad, who pales. Sweat drips down my temples and along my jaw as I wait for what feels like a century for him to say to the room at large, "We have reports coming out of Twin Rivers. The Ghosts went to meet Soren, Blake, and Patton at the... abandoned hotel where the Viper keeps her den."

My mouth runs dry. I barely feel the contraction this time. My powers simmer, ready to explode if someone would just light the match. He continues, "They went into the building and couldn't find the men. But there was obviously a battle. They confirmed it was the Viper's den–"

"Where are they?" I whisper as my heart shatters. "She has them–"

"We're actively tracing any leads as to their location," Dad says gravely.

I clutch my dresser to keep myself upright. Mom's hands steady my waist as I lean, crying out through the deep ache spreading through my lower belly. Blood drips between my legs, but the only thing I feel is… rage. Fury I can't contain.

Grandma Ella sees it before anyone else does. Tall and graceful, she turns to the crowd of unwanted guests in my bedroom, and snarls, "Go away. Do not come back in here unless you have found him—found *them*. Do not set foot in this room until this baby has been born!" She turns to Sarah and her cruel, icy expression fades in an instant. "We will find Blake. I promise. Sydney," she says, her voice shaking just a touch. "Put Sarah to bed and go fetch Maddy and Isaac from Maatua, all right? Go now—"

My scream of pain blurs her words. Tears fog my vision, and then hands are backing me toward the bed. Brie's touch is the only one I truly feel. Her voice is soft and calming as she shushes me, running her fingers through my hair. Mom and Ginny take up my vision. I blink the tears away, and in the edges of my line of sight, Misty talks in low tones to a stressed looking Grandma whose fingers are pressed over her lips as she nods, then shakes her head.

"She's fine standing. We can deliver the baby in this position," Mom says to Ginny.

"I'm worried about the shoulders," Ginny replies with effort. "The baby has been in this position for an hour now, at least." She lowers her voice while my gaze and focus remains locked on my grandma, wishing I could read her mind. She's torn between this room and following after the rest of the family, isn't she?

"Maeve is refusing to push. Her body is doing it anyway," Ginny continues in a whisper that I ignore.

"Where is he? He promised!" I scream as contractions bleed through me, bending bone and muscle. "SOREN!"

"Maeve, please," Brie whispers, coming from behind to stand in front of me. "Look at me."

"I won't do it. I want him here. He should be here." My voice cracks over the words. The fury wanes, replaced by a searing desperation almost strong enough to bring me to my knees. "I *just* got him back, Brie."

"She needs you right now. She's ready to meet us. You have to let her come."

"I won't–" I suck in a breath, biting back a scream as my body pushes against my will. I don't even register Ginny kneeling behind me, her hand between my legs.

"She's crowning. Good job, Maeve. *Keep going*."

"I won't," I repeat, looking Brie in the eyes. "Don't make me."

"You have to," Brie whispers, her eyes full of tears. "Let her come."

"He promised me–"

"He will come back to you." Brie grips my sides, leaning her forehead against mine. "Let her come."

I shake my head but scream as white-hot pain erupts through me.

"Her head is out. Keep going, Maeve! Kenna, I need you," Ginny says frantically, and my mom kneels.

Misty begins to hover. I can taste her magic in the air as she waits, holding her breath in the event we need her healing gifts.

But as I scream through the feeling of Ginny turning my daughter's shoulders into position, my eyes are on my grandmother.

Her eyes are exactly like mine. Bright and the purest sea-green. We're the only people in our family, maybe the world, with that specific shade of blue–polished sea glass, they call it. She tilts her chin, looking down her nose at me as I pant, choke, and scream my daughter into existence.

She almost died having my mother. Ryatt held her as she bled out, and my mom came months too early and was born quiet. But we're Firestone. This is what we're meant for. Our ancestors came from a matriarchal society where motherhood was considered the greatest, most powerful source of magic of all.

She gave her life to bring my mom into the world, not knowing if she'd ever see her child's face, or her mate, again. She risked it all then became the most powerful woman Eastonia had seen in three thousand years.

All because of love.

She went through that to see her own daughter have three children.

She went through that for me to be standing here in this room, in this palace, ruling over the kingdom she united with her mate by her side.

All for me.

All for... this baby. My daughter. My heir.

Soren's daughter.

"One more push, Maeve, come on!" Ginny says with effort.

Brie clutches me, whispering praise, her mouth pressed to my cheek as I sob through the agony, but then...

"You swore," I send down the bond as... a sweeping, ethereal sensation shimmers through my body like a wave of light.

I gasp as the pain dies in an instant. I sway, my eyes fluttering as I lose my grip on reality, and the room blurs.

Ginny's voice is lifted in triumph over the hushed prayers of thanks and squeals of excitement all around me, but I feel... weightless.

The soft cry of an infant reaches me. Hands touch me, guide me onto my back. The sunrise filters through the windows in soft shades of butter yellow and the softest baby pink.

And she's placed in my arms.

A thousand voices ring out in my mind—voices raised in thanks and praise. Voices of the Firestone mothers who came before me, all of them, a chorus singing for me, welcoming me into my full... *power.*

It surges in my veins, thrumming and twisting, knitting everything broken and weakened by the birth. My powers soar to their full maturity in an instant, rendering me... whole. Untouched.

I blink and turn to the women gathered on the side of the bed, chattering and crying together, but my eyes slide to Misty, who's staring at me in awe, her powers shuddering out in a puff of mist that snakes between her fingers.

She takes a step away from the bed to stand beside my grandma while Brie, Ginny, and my mother fawn over me, oblivious to the change my body just went through.

Only when my powers fade into an echo of feeling do I look down at my child. Our child.

She's... beautiful. A soft, healthy pink and... rather big, I believe, for a newborn. Ginny gently dries her off while she rests in my arms, her perfect lower lip trembling as she opens eyes the color of onyx.

"Sweet girl," I whisper, realizing I'm quite out of breath and utterly overwhelmed.

Mom reaches out to touch her, smoothing her hand over the baby's head where soft golden curls spring free.

"She's blonde," Brie giggles through a torrent of happy tears. "I didn't expect that."

"She's perfect, Maeve," Mom gushes, her face wet from crying as she presses a kiss to my forehead. "You did so well."

The baby opens her eyes to slits and looks right at me. I look back at her, and a rush of emotion sweeps me off my feet and carries me away on a current I can't fight.

She looks like him.

She looks like Soren.

"Take her," I say, my voice like gravel as despair clouds my mind, tearing my heart right out of my chest. "Someone–someone take her!"

Brie grabs the baby the moment I sit up and swing my legs out of bed. Everyone except my grandma rushes me, their voices overlapping as they try to convince me to lie down, but I'm fine. Healed completely. Like I didn't just give birth. Like I haven't been in back-breaking pain for... weeks now.

Fury replaces every emotion as I turn to my sister, now clutching her newborn niece in her trembling arms.

The door opens behind me, and Grandpa Ryatt steps inside, likely called here by Grandma through the mind-link because she knows exactly what's about to happen, doesn't she?

I ignore him for a moment and bend, pressing a kiss to my daughter's forehead, and say a soft, silent prayer to the Goddess to thank

Her for giving me a family that will care for this child if I don't come back.

Because I will burn our world to ash if there's even a scratch on Soren's skin.

That's a fucking promise.

"Name her before we go," Grandpa says gravely.

I slowly straighten, ignoring the gasps of protest, and turn to him. His powers flare behind his eyes, and he nods, tilting his head toward the baby.

"Name her. Give her a name, at least, in the event we don't return."

"Dad?" Mom's gutted tone rips through me like a heated blade.

Tears sting my eyes, but I refuse to let them fall. I won't live in a world where my daughter doesn't know her father. Once, I'd accepted that fate, and it tore me apart.

Never again.

I look at Brie as my powers embrace me, turning my sweaty, bloody clothes to armor of silver and crimson made of fire that cools to something as hard as diamond but weightless. Ginny faints. Misty lowers her head, closing her eyes as if praying. Mom looks murderous with rage.

But Brie gives me the softest, most knowing smile, and says, "I'll take care of her until you come back."

I look at my daughter, my heart ripping to pieces, and I say her name. A name she gave me the moment she was born, and my powers came into their maturity. A name her ancestors painted in the stars for us.

Fallon.

"I'll be right back," I whisper, and the room ignites with my magic, turning the pockets of sunshine to starlight, but I'm not alone in the ether that follows.

MIND SCRAMBLE

Soren

Water dribbles down heavy mildew stained stone as I blink into the glare of flickering fluorescent lights. Patton pants beside me, grunting in pain as my mind catches up to my body.

My wrists are bound with iron shackles and strung up over my head with a chain connected to the ceiling. My back is to the wall, however, and I'm... seated, my legs stretched out in front of me, my thigh brushing Patton's.

I close my eyes against a searing pain along the left side of my head. I taste blood when I lick my lips and realize I must have been struck on the side of the face with something heavy and blunt.

"Pat? You good?"

"I dunno," he murmurs. "I can't feel my legs."

I open my eyes, straining my neck to look at him and notice the blood seeping through his thick, goose down jacket now flayed open down the center. He got stabbed. That's obvious, but I think we've been out for a while judging by the total numbness in my arms, so the fact he's awake and talking is a good sign.

A rattling echoes toward us down a long, narrow hallway. A door only twelve feet from where we're bound is resting ajar, and a shadow moves into view.

My hackles raise as an unfamiliar man steps into view, leaning down over Blake, who's strapped to a chair, blood pouring from his eyes, nose, and ears.

I might have seen Hannibal once, at least I thought I did. Andrea always had powerful, rich men around, especially when Patton was her whore, but I would have never forgotten this man.

He has to be over seven feet tall–tall, and… thin. His dark, golden blond hair shakes as he turns ever so slightly to the side where sharply pointed ears poke through the silken strands that fall over her shoulders like golden satin. He's… a fucking attractive man. Beautiful, like a woman. It's odd, really, looking at him, trying to place him, trying to fit this creature to his name. He's… younger than me. He has to be. His skin is flawless, showing not a single sign of age.

"You're as strong as I thought you'd be," he croons to Blake who's trembling so hard his iron shackles rattle incessantly as Hannibal places his fingers against his forehead. Light shimmers over Blake's skin, and he screams–an agonizing scream that settles in my bones and twists my stomach into a tight knot. "Let me know, Mystic. Drop your shields and show me your secrets."

Blake spits blood, his eyes a milky violet lacking their normal luster, like he's being drained minute by minute.

"What are you hiding?" Hannibal continues, smoothing his hand over Blake's forward when the light retreats.

Blake lurches like he's just come out of Hannibal's magical grip and slumps forward, struggling for breath. Tears mingle with blood on his cheeks. So much blood.

Hannibal's torturing and killing him right in front of me.

I don't like Blake. I fucking hate the guy, but he doesn't deserve to die like this.

Metal sings as Hannibal turns back to Blake wielding a knife this time and traces it over his forearm. "You're an odd man, Blake. I haven't seen one of your kind so strong in… thousands of years, admittedly. The gods would be so jealous of what you can do and see." He slices through Blake's shirt, smiling to himself. He draws the tip of the blade over Blake's forearm until he draws blood, smiling as he says, "I didn't think you'd bleed red. Oh, it's a shame, really. To think that I have to wait another generation or two for someone from your line to come into their full powers. You're still mixed with beast blood. Unclean, we call it back home."

Blake holds his gaze, unblinking, unafraid.

Hannibal inspects the bloody knife as he brings it to the light then tips it toward Blake's forehead. "I suppose studying your brain would show me everything I need to know."

Blake grunts, his chains rattling, and closes his eyes as Hannibal slices over his forehead, and I…. Not like this. Blake, the biggest fucking prick I've ever met, isn't going out like this.

"Fuck off, you fucking monster," I snarl, my voice echoing down the hallway where Hannibal pauses and turns to look at me over his shoulder.

His surprise is quickly vanquished and turns to a sick kind of smile, and his eyes are… nearly white. White and silver, a strange, unearthly combination. I bristle as he straightens, turning toward me, his lanky, too tall to be real body stepping through the doorway.

He tucks the knife in his belt as his smile fades, his eyes narrowing on mine.

Patton hangs his head with an exhausted groan.

"Hello," Hannibal says with the softest, most curious of smiles. "You're Soren, aren't you? I've heard so much about you."

"I bet you have," I remark, rolling my neck.

He turns his head to look back at Blake but then settles his gaze on me again. He looks me up and down appraisingly, then sighs heavily. "I would have had you culled years ago had Andrea not begged me to keep you alive. Apparently, you're rather exceptional in bed." He hums a laugh, glances at Patton, and leaves, saying as he passes the door into Blake's torture chamber, "I'll be back soon. Think about making this easier on both of us in the meantime."

His footsteps recede down the hallway until silence hugs the space, and the echo of a heavy, likely guarded, door rushes toward me, confirming, I hope, that we're alone.

I shift to my knees to give my arms some slack, but suddenly the iron shackles give way, falling to pieces. My numb arms fall to my side out of my control. Patton's, too, slump, and he rocks forward, wincing as the same tingles rip through his muscles as our blood supply returns.

"Soren," Blake grinds out, his voice choked with pain. "Come here. Hurry."

I rise with effort, scanning the broken pieces of iron as I rub my arms to wake them up. "Did you do that? With your powers?"

"Yeah–"

"Break yourself out, then, come on," I urge, glancing around the stone room where he's bound to the chair. He shakes his head, his face and neck covered in blood.

I lose my patience and start yanking on his iron shackles until the metal warms and bends.

"Blake, you have to help me out here–"

His powers surge but only faintly. Metal clicks, and I pull the shackles open, but the second he's freed, he grabs my shirt and pulls me close, our noses touching.

"Blake, come on, we don't have time for this–"

"Take Patton and go," he says, his tone dark and pleading. "Get out of here. There's a door at the end of the hallway. It's unguarded. She has men guarding the exterior, but you can get out. Go to the shore and wait. They're coming–"

"Come on," I bite out, grabbing his arms to pull him out of the chair, but he twists the fabric of my shirt, refusing to move. "We're not doing this dramatic, leave me behind, save yourself, shit."

"You have to leave me here to die."

"Fuck that. *Get up.*"

"You must–you don't understand–you can't–"

"I don't give a fuck, Blake. Maeve will kill me if I don't bring you home. You're going home. We're going to get out of here and you can use your powers to spirit us back to–"

"Go to Crescent Falls," he rasps, the light draining from his eyes in real time, "and find Marianna. She lives—she lives in the Wildstone Pack territory, near Shadowcrest."

"Blake, you're getting out of here—"

"You have to find her and t-take her where—where you hid your marks." The panic in his voice gives me pause. He's shattering right in front of me as blood gushes from his ears like Hannibal scrambled his brain. Maybe he did, in fact, break Blake beyond repair, because this emotionless bastard has tears in his eyes as he says, "I tried. I tried to s-save her. I did everything I could. Every mark I gave you—"

"Blake, enough, we need to go. You need to get up!"

His grip tightens on my shirt, but his hands shake.

"Our d-daughter—" he cries out. "You have to take them. You have to hide them, Soren, please!"

"Daughter?" My mind reels without a place to land. I lean away from him, but he pulls me back in, gritting his teeth.

"Skye," he breathes. " She's—she's six. Marianna will understand—understand why she's going away. She knew—she knew from the beginning that something like this might happen. She'll know what to do. We had a plan. Please—they both have to go. You have to hide them—"

"From what?!" I shout, grabbing his shirt and tugging him upright. "You've lost your mind, Blake. You don't really have a daughter. Hannibal fucked with you—"

"You have to save them," he whispers, and his expression is so raw, so broken, so absolutely, utterly unhinged. "*I tried.* I've been trying for years to save Marianna, but she—her timeline—I can't—I can't fix it." He starts to pass out, gasping for breath, and I've had enough.

"We're not dying here Blake. Look at me!" I slap him soundly, trying to bring him back to reality. "You've been tortured, okay? Your brain is coming out of your ears. I have to get you out, but you have to help me, okay? Patton got stabbed. I don't know how bad, but I can't carry you both. You need to walk—"

"Take them where you—"

"No, you're going to shut the fuck up now," I growl then yank him out of the chair. We stumble backward, but I steady myself against the wall as Blake slumps in my arms, unable to hold himself upright. "Blake, come on, man, you gotta work with me here. We're getting out, okay? I'm not dying here. I'm not letting you die here."

Blake has a kid? *What the fuck?* Obviously no one knows about this. Maeve would have mentioned it. No one in the family said a Goddess-damned word about it.

"Fuck," I curse, dragging him through the doorway where Patton is feeling along the wall, trying to remain upright. "Pat, you gotta help me. We have to go."

Patton grabs one of Blake's arms, draping it over his shoulder. Together, we drag the bastard down the hallway until we reach the door, which is, in fact, unguarded, but only from the inside.

Andrea whirls toward us the second the door opens, her face twisted in murderous rage. A room comes into view, half of it exposed to the elements, where a bleak, gray landscape spreads out in the distance and wind whips a thin layer of snow into a frenzy.

Beyond that, nothing but miles, and miles, of an angry sea take up the rest of my vision.

Where the hell are we?

My eyes lock with Andrea's, ignoring the two burly men–Hounds–rushing toward us to her aid.

"I'm really going to enjoy this," I tell her, smiling wickedly.

Her eyes flare a bright green with her magic. Her fingertips turn silver as her lips part in a snarl, but then the floor beneath us trembles.

Stone falls from the roof and shatters on what remains of the brick floor.

Andrea's murderous rage flickers to confusion as she glances behind her. "What–"

A shockwave of energy rips through the building, sending more stone caving in. I rip Patton and Blake to the side as rocks the size of small SUVs fall, landing on the Hounds with a wet crunch. Andrea screams, but it's too late. I fall to the ground, covering Patton and Blake with my body as bright, searing, silver fire erupts all around us.

BANSHEE BATTLE

MAEVE

MONTHS AGO, WHEN THE TREES WERE GREEN AND SUMMER BLOOMED all around me, I used my powers to try to spirit home from the Roguelands. My powers did, in fact, take me home, but... not to the home I expected.

I should have realized it then.

Now, the landscape coming into focus is desolate and barren—an icy hell of wind beaten grass and rough seas... but he's here. My powers brought me here, back to him, back home.

Firestone witches can have mates, and I've found mine, but my powers recognized him before I did.

I like to think the Goddess had a hand in our first two meetings—that She drew him to that tea shop on the same night as me, seeking quiet companionship. That she urged me in his direction after Brie and Logan's elopement just so we'd cross paths ago, planting the seed of our bond in both of our chests.

Now, my powers have called me home again, but I have no idea

427

where I am. A cold, angry sea laps against a beach of sharp, dark stone. Cliffs overlook the roiling black water, and fog hugs the shoreline as I land, my powers roaring around me in a haze of crimson starlight. Through the magic shielding me, a wind-blown field of gray, dead grass lightly dusted with snow spreads as far as the eye can see around the building in the distance–a small manor, I guess.... No–a lighthouse.

My chest tightens as my powers settle, and I step out of the magical shield.

The lighthouse is long out of use. Dark stone is covered in a thick layer of salt, ice, and centuries of grime. The house beside it has long fallen in on itself, leaving a shell of what it once was–four stories of stone now scattered across the barren island.

There are lighthouses dotted across Eastonia, but I've never seen nor heard of this once. My powers surge, giving me an idea of how far I am from Moonrise right now, but the mark Soren left on my neck tingles to life, and I know, without a shadow of a doubt, that he's here.

I look over my shoulder for the force that followed me into the ether, but Grandpa Ryatt is nowhere to be seen.

The gem-like armor covering my body glistens in the gray, foggy daylight as I turn back to the building, my magic sizzling in warning as several shadows break from the fog and rush in my direction.

Wolves and armed men charge at full speed, weapons raised and sharp teeth glistening in the bleak daylight. Beyond them, people stream out of the house shouting and cursing commands.

Why would they even bother? Don't they know who I am?

I raise a single finger and send my powers soaring in a spray of curling crimson starlight, wiping out at least a dozen men in the space of a heartbeat. Their bodies vanish in thin air, falling to the ground in fractals–burnt to a crisp–nothing but glowing embers.

The men in the rear of the charge skid to a stop and immediately turn back, running toward the lighthouse, but I'm beyond showing mercy. I'm not thinking straight. Every step I take over the crunchy, frozen grass is a step away from my newborn daughter and a step toward the man I know is being held here against his will. If he's so much as bruised... gods, I'll kill every last one of them.

My hair billows out behind me as I raise both hands and send a spray of pure, white-hot silver fire toward the lighthouse, scorching the men trying to escape. My power booms like thunder, sending a shockwave across what I believe is a very small, insignificant island off the far northern coast of Tarsian, perhaps, over the impassable mountains that mark the eastern edge of our great continent. It doesn't fucking matter because I'm going to send this entire island toppling into the ocean if I don't... rein... myself... in....

I scream, the full force of my fury sending a tidal wave of flames across the barren field with me in its center. My power radiates from me like live flames–in the pit of hell itself–and I let it. I let it flow through me at its full strength, and I don't feel an ounce of ice. No, I'm hot. Burning from the inside out as my next scream paints the ground black with embers, and the sky goes dark from the smoke left in my magic's wake.

"WHERE IS HE?!" I screech, sending another blast of magic toward the lighthouse, which scorches, my flames shattering the windows and sending old stone toppling to the ground.

The air around me goes thin and silent as I let my powers simmer before retreating. The smoke clears, driven by the wind coming off the water, but even the waves crashing into the jagged cliffs seem to draw away from my fury, the water going suddenly calm.

There are no bodies left to step over. My boots crunch across blackened, burnt grass as I move toward the lighthouse and the manor beside it. They're caved in even more now, with large chunks of stone piled neared what could have been an entrance at some point but is now a gaping hole exposing the inside of the house to the elements.

And then I see him.

"MAEVE, MOVE!" Soren shouts, dragging a totally limp Blake onto the scarred grass as he exits the building. Patton's at his other side barely able to hold himself upright and grips Soren's shoulder for support…. But it's the woman climbing out of the rubble that catches my attention–my magic's attention. Pale skin and short black hair. Big, wide, green eyes. A sick, twisting smile of surprise as she spots me and sucks in a breath.

Her banshee scream knocks me off balance. It rattles through me, vibrating like I'm being hammered against my temples. I cover my ears as my powers hiss and curl away from the sound.

Soren's scream of pain echoes, and his mark on my neck scorches, hot enough to blister. He buckles, falling to the ground in agony on top of Blake. Soren covers his ears like her scream is slicing into brain, slicing him from the inside out. Patton passes out after a long, guttural howl, but Blake remains motionless–lifeless.

My stomach curls as dread fills my system, temporarily distracting my powers.

The Viper frees herself from the rubble and rushes in my direction, her left leg obviously weak and dragging behind her when she raises her hands. Her fingers glow silver from her powers surging between her fingers, knitting into something solid–twin blades that grow and stretch with each wobbly step she takes toward Soren.

I drop my hands from my ears and match her scream, but louder, sending the full force of my powers careening toward her in a shower of crimson light that makes the ground shake and rolls. My flames erupt next, turning from streaks of silver fire into the form of… a wolf. A great, sleek, wolf made of flame and starlight. It leaps over Soren and soars through the air, jaw slack, its coat flaming and teeth gleaming as it collides with the Viper.

But she slices through my flames like butter, her swords of silver cutting the wolf down in an instant.

The pain reverberates back to me. My arms quake, but I hold steady, swaying just a touch. She raises her swords over Soren, and I… I…

A burst of shadow covers the island in darkness before an explosion of power explodes, knocking me and the Viper to the ground. Grandpa Ryatt appears in silence, his face set in determination as he wields the Shadowsword, it's hilt inlaid with gems glowing bright, and swings, metal singing as it splits the air around us into pieces.

The Viper flies backward, caught in the current of his immense powers of darkness and shadow.

Grandpa Ryatt slowly turns his head, his eyes holding on mine. "Now."

"MAEVE!" Soren shouts, struggling upright as he drags Blake's useless body with him, "DO IT! KILL HER!"

I hesitate, my powers flickering as the high of righteous fury that's been carrying me for the last... ten minutes... fades as quickly as it came. I look from Grandpa to Soren, then to the woman struggling to get back to her feet, her body bloodied and in shambles but her strength returning in real time. She shouldn't be alive. There's no way she could still be alive.

"MAEVE!" Soren screams, his eyes meeting mine in the smoky haze, but his voice cracks. I can see the confusion, exhaustion, and surrender in his eyes.

The Viper begins her banshee scream a second time, but I silence it, raising my hands, and give her everything I have. My powers flow through me in silence. It's painless. Slow. Like time is standing still. Maybe time is standing still as my powers fill the air–heavy and all-consuming.

I'm... trained. I trained for this. I spent a decade testing and honing these powers but never–never at this strength. I painted the sky red for Moonrise. I pulled power from the eclipsed moon and the shadowed stars that night, bringing back the light, but... this feeling is different. This power takes up space. It fills me, twists me, and brings me to my knees as I keep one hand raised to the heavens and one toward Soren, where I try to shield him from what's going to come next.

He calls out my name before falling back to his knees, his eyes holding mine to the last possible second. He has to know. He has to know one flick of my fingers will bring this island into the sea. He has to know I could send a wall of flames toward the heavens that will consume everything, and everyone, left standing. He has to know I could—I could open a portal and suck the Viper into it, couldn't I?

Can't I do that?

Soren blinks, his eyes uncharacteristically wet, and he... smiles. He laughs, yelling my name, egging me on.

He's not afraid of me. Even now.

The bond yanks me back to reality. I scream as my powers surge, draining, and then snap in a burst of heat so extreme it turns the lighthouse and the manor to nothing but ash in a single second. The Viper just... dissolves, disappearing into a puff of ash as her banshee screams cut out for good.

But my powers don't just flicker out. A shockwave bounces back to me, knocking me off my feet. Grandpa grabs my arm, and we roll to a stop. Silence creeps in again while my body starts to go numb.

Wind rushes over us, whipping my hair into a frenzy. Grandpa's screaming at me as he clutches my face between his hands, but I can't hear him. I taste... blood. My vision darkens at the edges and his image fades.

A faint tug in my chest brings him back into focus for a few seconds, but it's not enough. Soren's yanking on the bond, trying to tug me back to life. I feel him there, pulling the strings, refusing to let me fade into the darkness.

Grandpa's eyes search mine. His mouth moves, his brow pinched in desperation. He says my name—screams it—and shakes me by the shoulders. A shadow passes over him, and suddenly, Soren is here, pulling me upright, pinching my cheeks as he shouts in my face. His voice is loud, vibrating through my body, and his eyes are... angry. Absolutely fucking livid.

"Do not give up!" he screams, clutching me to his chest and pressing my face against his neck. "Maeve, for the love of the Goddess, if you die here I'm going to find a way to resurrect you so I can kill you myself!"

I blink, blearily looking over his shoulder at the scorched remains of the island. A man is standing in the center of the devastation I caused, his body covered by a cloak billowing around his too tall build. His strange, almost white eyes lock on mine, and his mouth is curved into the softest, most wicked of smiles. But he's... hazy. The way he moves is... dreamlike.

Hannibal. It has to be.

He turns his head to look at... Blake.

My dying heart thumps, lurching, as he raises a hand, snaking, violet light curling between his fingers and creating a swirling... vortex... a portal... right over where Soren left Blake lying face down in the ash.

"No," I croak, gasping for breath. "NO!!!"

I shove Soren back as the last of my powers rage to awareness, and I send them flying, slicing through the distance between us, and cut through Hannibal's magic before it snatches Blake. Hannibal slowly looks at me with that same smile that makes my stomach twist with disgust.

His voice booms through my head, loud and clear, *"We'll meet again, Firestone. It has only just begun."*

His form falls away, drifting like flakes of ash on the brisk wind.

Grandpa watches the ash float away, his eyes dark and expression searing, then rises, sliding the sword into the hilt along his back in one swift, smooth motion, then moves to tend to Blake and Soren.

Soren lowers me against the ground, rising over me, casting me in his shadow.

"Look at me," he says hoarsely. His face is covered in bruises, and his eyes are rimmed red.

"You look like shit," I croak, and he blows out his breath, chuckling darkly.

"You don't look much better."

My eyes flood with tears—happy ones. The Viper is gone. Hannibal... left. To where, I don't know, but Soren is free.

"Did you have blond hair as a kid?" I ask as he smooths his hand over my cheek.

He searches my gaze for understanding and finds it with startling consequences. He takes a shallow breath, hanging his head for a moment before meeting my eyes again. "She's here?" he whispers, his eyes wide and damp.

I nod as energy rushes around us. Sydney, my father, and a legion of Ghosts arrive to clean up the mess and guide us home.

To our daughter.

FALLON

Soren

It's dark in Moonrise when we return to the palace–to Maeve's entire family in wait. Blake is whisked away by his parents and a trio of healers. Jane, blubbering, reunites with Patton and the two disappear to the clinic to have his wounds tended.

Sydney brought us back within minutes of Maeve using her magic to scorch the island into a blackened heap of rubble, and we're back, but... everything feels different.

Ryatt stayed behind with the Ghosts and Evander, but I feel his presence everywhere I step. Maeve clutches my hand tight, her fingers like ice, and we rush through the castle toward her suite. Our suite, I suppose.

Toward the daughter I promised I'd be here to witness coming into the world.

Maeve's armor clicks as she moves like the wind, ignoring the shouts coming from the end of the hallway where we landed only moments ago. Warriors and healers rush after us but neither of us turn around. My heart is in my throat as we climb the final staircase to the sixth floor.

Kenna steps out of the grand double doors marking the entrance to the royal suite. Her thick, dark hair is pulled back from her face, and her silver eyes shine with relief when she sees us and opens the door wide, stepping out of the way while Maeve drags me beside her.

My legs feel like lead. My lungs refuse to cooperate as we cross down a hallway and into the open, fire-lit living room where the curtains are drawn against another dreary, late winter day.

Brie rises from an armchair, her glossy, light brown hair falling down her shoulders and back. She turns with a blanket-wrapped bundle in her arms. Kieran, the little boy I'd seen throwing a knock-out, drag-out tantrum on the balcony all those months ago, clutches his mother's robe, hiding behind her.

Maeve lurches forward. Brie places the baby in her arms and scoops Kieran up, resting him on her hip. And I stand perfectly still several feet away, unable to move.

The sun is only just starting to rise over the mountains when Brie brushes past me, reaching out to squeeze my arm. "It's nice to meet you," she whispers with the softest of smiles. I follow her as she heads toward the hallway where she stops to speak quietly to Kenna.

But I see Kieran in full then. Dark, coiling curls bounce around his… pointed ears. My stomach hollows out. I meet Kenna's gaze, and she knows exactly what I'm thinking right now based on the withdrawn look on her face.

A question was just answered for the family, wasn't it?

Brie leaves, her footsteps soft and echoing before I hear the door close, but Kenna remains as a quiet presence when I turn to look at my mate and take in what she had to do for me.

Maeve's fingers are nearly blue as she tucks our daughter into her arms, shushing the baby as she rocks side to side, like she's always had a baby there to comfort. Golden blonde hair peaks from the blanket in gentle curls as fine and thin as silk threads. I close my eyes while my chest caves in with guilt.

"I promised I'd be here."

"She couldn't wait," Maeve says in a sing-song voice, such a sharp contrast to how she normally sounds. She turns to me and lowers the velvet soft, yellow blanket away from the baby's face, and I… see her.

She's… indescribable.

"Do you want to hold her?" Maeve looks up into my eyes, but I'm looking down at the child we made, a vivid reminder of our love. Our journey. Of every sin and injustice I had to commit to get here.

I don't deserve this, and I know that.

"I've never–I've never held a baby," I murmur, the words wobbling off my tongue.

Kenna appears at our side with her hand resting on my forearm. "You won't break her. They're surprisingly sturdy little creatures." Her smile lights the room but does nothing to calm the storm brewing in my heart.

"I'm filthy," I argue, but Kenna forces me into a chair, and Maeve holds my gaze as she places our girl in my arms. She's… so small, but heavy, I guess. Heavier than I thought she'd feel. She has a perfectly round face with chubby cheeks, and her tiny mouth forms a perfect O as she jerks, surprised, then settles. I don't so much as blink, let alone breathe.

"Go change. I left some herbs in your room that help speed up your recovery. You depleted your powers again, didn't you?" Kenna's voice sounds far away as I gaze down at the baby in my arms. "Don't worry. I'll stay with them."

The world around me fades, replaced by a memory that took place several months ago during the single night Maeve and I had to truly be together.

She'd fallen asleep in my arms to the sound of rain pounding the rusted metal roof. Darkness cloaked the room, shadows creeping between crates and dust covered furniture, and we'd lain on the floor covered by nothing but our skin and a filthy blanket. I traced every inch of her that night. I pressed my lips to her skin and memorized her scent. I laced my fingers through her thick hair and worshipped her like the goddess she is, laying myself at her altar like a sacrifice, begging her to take my life, to let my blood be what stains her hands in exchange for never living another day without her, but she wouldn't do it.

I knew she was my mate then and couldn't bring myself to reject her. I wanted that… piece of us. Something that bound me to her for eternity, even if it was selfish. Even if I had to lie about how I felt and how it felt to watch the train speed into the distance without me on it beside her.

A cup of tea is placed on the coffee table in front of me. Kenna sits across from me, weaving her fingers together, leaning toward us, smiling at the baby.

"We all agree that she looks like you," she says softly. "The blonde hair really surprised us."

I close my eyes, my jaw clicking as it flexes. "You shouldn't even be letting me hold her right now."

Kenna's kind expression fades to something sharp and lightly frustrated. "Soren–"

I shake my head. "Take her, please. I need to–"

"To what? Leave my daughter?"

"No–"

"Soren, you don't know us well enough yet to understand that… none of this comes as a surprise. You and Maeve. Your history–"

"I should be in prison," I say through my teeth, arching a brow. "Not cuddling the Royal Princess of Eastonia."

"She's yours," she whispers, her eyes a deep, glowing silver. "Nothing is going to change that. And you don't belong in prison. You deserve every award for what you went through, for what you had to do to survive. Your circumstances were a failure on our part."

I begin to shake my head again, but she interrupts by raising her hand to silence me.

"Evander remembers you. You were a boy when you came to the academy. The youngest and smallest in your class by three years. You trained with the fifteen-year-olds at only twelve, and your trainers kept you there because you had nowhere else to go."

"I had a brother–"

"Tom," she says, nodding. I'm surprised she knows, but she says,

"Admittedly, Misty used her powers to paint us a picture of your past when you came here. Tom was who got you wrapped up in this."

"He–he was a victim of circumstance. I could have gotten out. I had the skills I needed to get out and return to Moonrise–"

"You stayed for your friend."

I close my eyes, holding the baby a little tighter than I mean to, but she remains blissfully unaware of the fact her father is starting to spiral.

"You don't think you're good enough for her," Kenna says in a hushed whisper as Maeve, dressed in nothing but a bath towel, walks past us in silence, glancing at me and the baby with a tired smile before disappearing into the hallway. Kenna waits for her to move out of earshot before continuing. "Maeve wouldn't be here if my mate hadn't gotten over that himself. He's spent his whole life feeling the need to prove himself to not only me, but my parents, when in reality, I've been the one working to be worthy of him all these years. You protected her against all odds. You guided her home, knowing you were separating yourself from your mate–"

"I'm a murderer," I cut in, and she sighs.

"Blake," she says under her breath, "is at fault for that. It will be dealt with."

My lips part with the words, *Did you know about Skye?* but they fizzle out on the tip of my tongue.

"You love her," Kenna says. Maeve appears again, carrying a stack of clothing and disappearing into our room. "And Maeve is… an almost impossible person to love, and I mean that in the kindest way. She's… multifaceted. She's glorious, beautiful, and funny. She feels so deeply and is kind, and strong. Being loved by her is like… being in the center of an epic storm. It's electric. But she's also… anxious and unsure. She can be terrifying, and I know she scares herself. Her powers are… untouchable. Just… immense. But you knew that. You were never afraid of her. You never once made her dim her powers. You make her shine, Soren."

I swallow past the tight knot in my throat, unable to look her in the eyes.

"That's what the family sees, not the assassin you were forced to be. And now you're here, and she'll never let you go, and your daughter will be the same. They will shine because of you, and that's why you're here. No other man could stand where you've stood and survive. No other man will be able to stand in a family of Firestone witches and hold his own. But you will. You have been, since the beginning, haven't you?"

I absently smooth my hand through the baby's silken hair.

"What now?" I whisper, my jaw flexed. "What happens now? Hannibal is still out there. Maeve isn't–"

"She's safe, and you're free. The rest… we'll figure out in time, but for now, sleep. Eat something. Spend some time with your girls. Evander will find you when he returns."

Kenna rises as Maeve, now dressed in a bright pink pajama set, steps out of her room and stands expectantly in the doorway of our room.

But a shadow I didn't notice is lurking in the hallway. Queen Ella. I rise as she steps into view and stares at me with a smile I don't think I deserve, but she turns with Kenna and leaves the suite, her voice a whisper in the darkness as she says, "He reminds me a lot of your father when he was younger."

The door shuts tight, and silence funnels toward us.

Maeve walks toward me looking refreshed, a new golden glow to her skin. She smells like magnolia blossoms and amber. She moves to my side, her hand a light touch against my lower back.

"You stink," she whispers, running her knuckle over the baby's cheek.

"Me, or her?"

"You," she smiles, chuckling. "You smell like a bonfire."

"I have you to thank for that," I whisper into her hair before pressing a kiss to the top of her head, but I don't move away. I close my eyes, inhaling her scent, letting it wrap around me in a tight embrace.

"She has a name," Maeve says, leaning her head against my chest.

"Fallon, I know," I reply, my eyes still closed. "She told me."

"You can hear her, too?" She looks up at me, slightly taken aback.

"Not like… words. She's not even ten hours old. But… the name has been stuck in my head for a while now, and I didn't know why. But the second I saw her, I knew."

"It's great, honestly. We won't have to come up with a name for the next one if they're all like this—predestined."

I smile against her hair. "What do we do now, Maeve? Now that I'm… free?"

"Watch TV," she says, roping her arm around my lower back. "Drink tea. I don't know. What does a trophy mate do in his free time?"

My laugh wakes the baby, who looks up at us, her dark eyes not yet fading into what I know will be the same color as her mother's.

Polished sea-glass.

Fallon smiles before falling back asleep in my arms.

THE ROYAL PRINCESS

Soren

PATTON LIMPS DOWN THE WIDE, GOLDEN HALLWAY SOMEWHERE ON THE fourth floor. He's dressed in a brand-new tuxedo, something of Jane's doing, I'm sure, but it fits him like a glove. He checks his watch.

Voices drift through the air and the sun beams onto the pristine, crimson carpet. I catch my reflection in one of the many mirrors along the golden walls and stop to adjust my hair, sweeping the chestnut curls away from my forehead.

The black-on-black tuxedo I'm wearing was Evander's idea, even though I could be in sweatpants and a T-shirt right now. The electric hum of the crowd gathered around the palace walls reaches the upper levels of the grand house I now call home, but it's been like this since the earliest hours of the morning when Maeve sent warriors out into the street to proclaim the birth of the princess.

She was, technically, born three days ago, but we've had a lot to do since then. Mostly... rest. In fact, Maeve, Fallon, and I haven't done much but sleep, eat, and sleep some more since Maeve came to rescue me when Blake's grand plan went sideways.

But, I've had to face the men in her family a few times since then. I met Alpha King Ryan, who I adore, to be honest. He's... perfect. He was exactly the kind of buffer I needed when his twin brother, Sydney, began grilling me about what Blake had been up to for the better part of five years, with me as an accomplice.

Ryan seemed to be more entertained with my stories of the Roguelands than anything else, as were his daughters, Nora and the foreboding Lexa, who might be the only woman in the world other than my mate who could kick my ass and make it hurt.

The one man I really wanted to speak to was Blake, however, and he's been holed up with his parents for days.

"How do I look?" Patton asks under his breath before we reach the archway where a dozen voices mingle.

"Expensive," I say with a shrug.

"Good," he breathes, adjusting his lapel.

He steps into the room before me, smiling grandly at the faces that turn in his direction–the celebrities he idealized and now falls into the same social circles with, living in the same palace. Jane beams when she sees him, and I lose him in the crowd of family and friends gathered to listen to Maeve's address to her people to mark the birth of Fallon, our royal princess. My daughter.

Fallon, being the new baby of the family, is being passed between Ella, who wants me to call her Grandma, but I've refused so far, and... Maddy. Yeah, that's her name. She's Isaac's mate–the tall, silver-haired man standing in the corner talking in quiet tones to Ryatt, who *hasn't* asked me to call him Grandpa, thank the gods.

A brute force hits the back of my legs and topples away, a quick, shrill whine splitting the air before settling into a grumble of half-words and broken vowels. I turn ever so slightly as Kieran uses my legs to get back on his feet, rubbing the back of his head and scowling at his light-up sneakers.

"You good, man?" I ask, and he blinks up at me, his deep green eyes narrowing before he nods, trying to look tough, but he's on the verge of tears.

It takes all of the strength I have to ignore those all-to-familiar pointed ears I've yet to bring to anyone's attention. I scoop him up, settling him on my shoulders, where he tangles his hands in my freshly gelled hair and screeches with delight.

Brie looks up from her conversation with Misty and Cole and smiles, waving at her son, but the men in the room turn to watch us. I move toward my mate, who's standing just a few feet from the balcony and just out of the view of the sea of people below.

Instead of a sweeping, ethereal gown, she's wearing a sleek crimson suit jacket with matching trousers that pinch at her narrow waist. Her royal crown of jewels from every corner of her kingdom rests atop her head, sparkling in the sunlight as winter finally submits to spring.

Kieran pats the top of my head like a drum while I hold Maeve's gaze and turn him toward Brie, where I kneel, allowing her access to the wriggling little boy, who must be about three years old, Ella appears beside me.

She gently releases her hold on Fallon, who slumps sleepily in my arms, dressed in a cream colored dress of lace that makes her look like a frosted cupcake. "It's a ridiculous dress in my opinion," Ella teases, glancing at Maddy, who scoffs.

"I made it myself!"

My mouth tugs into a half smile. I turn back to Maeve, Fallon resting in my arms, and walk to her side.

She glances at her watch before meeting my eyes with a soft, almost nervous smile. I inspect her crown, saying, "Now, this one would've fetched me a damn good payday at the fence."

"I doubt you'd have been able to even carry it. It weighs a thousand pounds."

She reached up to adjust its weight with a wince.

Brie floats over and steals her attention for a moment, and I turn to scan the room. Everyone's dressed all neatly, but they're not pulling out all the stops like at her coronation. There's a tension I can't shake but I assume it's because these people welcomed me into the family with very little reservations. I scan the room, catching Blake's gaze, and hold.

He's standing near the far wall, alone, nursing a glass of scotch. His eyes are... withdrawn, lacking their usual light. I move through the crowd on impulse, but he shakes his head at me, and turns, leaving the room all together.

"Don't take it personally," Evander says, walking past me as he moves through the crowd. "He's going back to Crescent Falls for a while, I guess. I just spoke to his parents."

"Is he all right?"

"He's fine, I assume. He's always like this." Evander halts his progress to stand beside me for a moment, but Kenna sees him and waves him over. He sighs, checking his watch, and says, "You and I need to talk. You'll be in Veiled Valley next week for the start of our Mating Festival. We'll speak then."

"About what?" I ask, but he walks away, side-stepping between Misty and Cole.

I stay where I am, bouncing Fallon. She opens her eyes and looks around, squinting up at me. I wait for her fussing to begin, but the second I take a step back in Maeve's direction, Ryatt's voice reaches me in a low, near whisper.

"He wasn't born there, you know."

"Then I don't understand your line of thought, Ryatt," Isaac says in the same low murmur, a conversation obviously meant for just the two of them.

"I don't doubt it. You haven't spent time in the Roguelands—not like I have, or like he has."

"I thought Aris would inherit the Roguelands."

"No. That's not how it works. Aris will be Alpha of Veiled Valley. He's meant to stay there. That's his kingdom, his little pocket of territory, as it has been for thousands of years. The Roguelands didn't choose him as king."

Isaac's disbelieving chuckle reverberates through my bones. "You're saying the forest decides to whom it bows?"

"Yes," Ryatt says with marked certainty. "It chose me long ago. Me, a child of slaves. Me, a boy who led an army of bandits and rogues.

I've spent the last two decades looking for my successor. The Rogue-lands finally gave me one."

"You're going to make him Alpha King?"

Ryatt brings his drink to his lips and nods. "The Roguelands already did. It's decided. It was never my decision."

Isaac's brows raise, but then he slowly, slowly, looks at me from across the room. My heart drops into my stomach as Ryatt follows his gaze, the patriarchs of each line of the family looking at me while carving my future into existence.

I choose to ignore them. The roar of the crowd below reaches a peak. Maeve steps out onto the balcony. I quickly skirt through the room to stand just out of sight, ready to pass Fallon to her when she gives the order.

Maeve... doesn't say a word. She doesn't need to. The people below scream in excitement when she steps to the railing and waves down at them, beaming, scanning the crowd. She doesn't give them a magic show. She doesn't let that smile falter to look cold, fierce, and unforgiving like during her coronation. She just smiles—a real, genuine smile—letting her people see that she's like them. Young and excited. Young and unsure. Young and trying her hardest to be what they need.

And that's enough.

When she turns back to the doors, the crowd goes silent in antici-pation. I step forward, remaining just under the cover of the archway. We discussed this moment in length. She wanted me to be the one to hand Fallon to her so she could show her people their princess. I will stay out of sight, in shadow, with her family.

Because I'm not a king.

I'm just... her mate. That's enough for me.

Fallon frowns, her face scrunching as sunlight plays over her eyes, and Maeve reaches for her, but then her eyes meet mine.

"I love you," she says, and squeezes my wrist.

"I love you," I echo, smiling, but that smile fades to a shocked grimace when she tugs on my wrist, and I stumble into view of the crowd below–and the dozens of cameras perched on rooftops broadcasting the event all around our world.

Maeve steps back to the edge of the balcony. The crowd remains silent. Then, she turns, motioning for me to stand beside her.

And I... I do.

The reaction of the people below starts as a startled hum of confusion, then it ripples, the gasps turning to screams of glee from the street to the tallest rooftops.

"What do I do now?" I ask over the thundering voices all around us.

"Show them our baby." She smiles, her cheeks burning pink, and her eyes... they're beautiful. Bright and swirling with her powers.

I step into her and press a kiss to her lips. The crowd screams loud enough to rattle the windows on the highest level of the palace, and when I pull away, she's still smiling, but with tears in her eyes.

I turn from her and lift Fallon, showing the world our girl.

STARLIGHT FLICKERS OUTSIDE. I CLOSE THE CURTAINS, THE CITY BELOW still thrumming with life as a festival in Fallon's honor rages.

Fallon, however, is having a hard time settling. Her whimpering cry of protest when Maeve tries to unlatch her from her breast pings from wall to wall. I turn, thankful to be out of my tux and in a soft shirt and sweatpants instead of the form-hugging fine fabric.

Maeve looks more beautiful than I've ever seen her right now, her hair spilling over her shoulders. She frowns down at Fallon, who's now turning purple with rage. "She can't still be hungry," she says, exasperated. "She's been nursing for over an hour." She switches her to her other breast, not bothering to adjust the thin straps of her tank top, and meets my eyes. I edge toward the bed, giving me a sharp look. "Don't gawk at me, Soren."

"I can't help it." I slide into bed beside them, reaching for her, drawing my fingertips over her exposed breasts. "You're gorgeous."

"I'm covered in milk."

"I like milk. What man doesn't?"

"You're a sick freak, you know that?"

I lean over her, pressing a kiss to the top of her breast. I want her. Badly. Deep in my bones but... we now share a bed with a baby who wants her as well, and I have to wait my turn, I guess. For whatever reason, my mind storms back to Blake, which ruins the mood immediately, and I lean away, falling back against the pillows with a sigh.

"Maeve?"

"Yeah?"

"Has Blake ever mentioned someone named Marianna to you?"

"Oh, of course. She was his teenage sweetheart or something." She scans my face. "He refuses to talk about her, though. Where did you hear her name?"

Fallon unlatches, finally falling asleep with a deep, dramatic newborn sigh. I roll over onto my side, and Maeve lies down as well, Fallon sleeping like a starfish between us.

"Did he ever mention the name Skye?" I ask, my stomach twisting in a knot I haven't been able to untangle since the moment Blake said her name.

Maeve thinks about it, her lips pursed tight, then shakes her head. "No, he hasn't."

Fuck, she doesn't know. If she doesn't know, no one knows about Blake's... daughter.

I need to get him alone. I need to talk to him about this.

Because I can't keep a secret like this from my mate.

"Maeve, don't... freak out about this."

"About what?" She laughs then takes in the stern, unsettled expression painting shadows over my face. "What is it, Soren?"

"I think Blake has a kid."

THE END

BONUS: READY FOR HER

MARIANNA

"I DON'T UNDERSTAND." I SWALLOW HARD PAST THE LIE, FOLDING MY hands over my lap, meeting the headmaster's shrewd gaze. She's an otherwise lovely woman in her late fifties, I believe, with raven-black hair peppered with silver and bright brown eyes. Her pink lipstick crinkles when she gives me a sad, sympathetic smile I know all too well… because this has happened before. Twice. Three times now, if I count today.

The pewter stone walls of the exclusive, ridiculously expensive Children's Academy of Crescent City smothers me. She looks down at her desk for a moment, sighing.

"Ms. Abbot," she says, meeting my gaze again, her face washed in what I believe is empathy but could be something far less deep. "Skye doesn't belong here. She's too–too–" She waves her wrist in what I can only construed as dismissal.

"Too intense?"

She purses her thin lips. "I have other students to think about. We've given this a shot, haven't we? After her… premature *departure* from MoonWolf Preschool, I was reluctant to admit her here, and we've tried our best. You know we have—"

"She's six years old," I bite out, unable to hold back my emotions any longer.

It's always the same story, the same excuses. Skye is too much for her teachers. She's too intense, too... too big of a personality for such a small body. She doesn't pay attention. Her head is in the clouds—past that, these days. Her eyes are full of starlight and nothing else.

She can't make friends. She scares those few who get close to her and absolutely terrifies the rest with her *stories*....

"She's an incredibly gifted young girl," the headmaster says with the softest, but fakest, of smiles. "She's years ahead of her peers when it comes to her academics. I believe... *homeschooling* would be a better option for her. I mean that wholeheartedly."

"Homeschooling?" I mouth, my stomach going hollow, but I should be used to this feeling by now.

"I have some pamphlets I could share if you're interested. She could graduate from high school four or five years early and go on to do great things in college with peers who are... more mature and able to understand her—"

"There's nothing wrong with my daughter," I rush out, biting back tears I've cried a million times.

The headmaster gives me a look I know all too well. Skye's fate has already been decided. She is no longer welcome here.

End of story.

I gather my purse, stuffing the pamphlets I didn't have the strength or wherewithal to decline deep in the recesses of the bag where they'll find solace with some rogue sticks of gum and the rocks Skye likes to hide in there. I walk out of the school into the brisk spring air and breathe, filling my lungs till they're near bursting, and choke when I attempt to exhale.

My phone buzzes repeatedly, but I ignore it like usual. My mom, Leona, never texts me. She always calls. It's a new rule we have. It's how I know it's not her blowing up my heavily abused smartphone right now. No, the person who's sent me a hundred texts in the last hour is someone I hope I never see again.

Crescent City comes into view around me. The hustle and bustle of the city streets suck me in, drying my tears in an instant. I knew this was coming. I shouldn't have been surprised to see the email in my inbox from Skye's school. I should have known that day they called me to pick her up early and refused to elaborate as to why that something was wrong, and she was done, dropped from the exclusive program in an instant…

But it hadn't been an instant, had it?

I hug my purse to my chest and stand at the bus stop, fighting to breathe. Music fills my mind, unraveling the tangled network of thought and emotion fighting for dominance. I wish I could say this is the hardest it's ever been with her, but she's been like this since she started walking. Since she could look me in the eyes and show me what's really going on behind those beautiful, grayish-violet eyes of hers. Eyes that remind me so much of her father that it's nearly enough to bring me to my knees sometimes.

"Goddess dammit," I whisper over engine noise and chatter, leaning my weight against the plexiglass of the awning protecting the benches from the elements.

The bus arrives three minutes late. I board, swiping my metrocard and sitting toward the back, letting the rumbling vibration lull my senses into a stupor while the city bleeds past, the towering skyscrapers turning to silver blurs against the afternoon sunlight. It takes me all of twenty minutes to reach my stop, and I disembark without a word to anyone, walking down the street and into a wide, circular building–the royal performing arts center–as the first inklings of sunset turn the sky a deep orange.

Storm clouds funnel in the distance, casting shadows over the side streets. I rush through the lobby and through a doorway that closes me off from the world at large, and sucks me back into the one place where I can be me again.

"Anna," Jesse, fourth chair of the strings, says with a hushed sigh as I speed past him toward the locker where I left my violin two hours ago. "Michael's looking for you. Where have you been? You missed practice this afternoon."

"I had a meeting. He was aware of that," I grit out, fishing my phone out of my purse. "Did I miss something important? The music is already finalized for both acts—"

"There's a rumor going around that the prince is coming to the concert tonight," he says with effort, his cheeks going a ruddy pink, a sharp contrast to his nearly white-blond hair.

"The prince?" There's three. The chances it's him are… thirty-three percent, which means it's highly likely it'll be Prince Liam, a true lover of the arts, of his younger brother, Prince Noah.

Not Blake. Never Blake.

He nods, leaning his shoulder against the lockers. I slide my phone into view, but I don't even look down at the flashing screen. "For the last concert of the season, too. You'd think he'd have come to the opening show."

While Jesse inspects his nails and drawls on and on about the prince, whichever one, showing his face at tonight's finale, I reel, my fingers trembling as I quickly delete the seventy-six text messages clogging my notifications.

"Is Michael changing the music? Is that why he wanted to see me?" I ask, blindly dialing my first contact on speed dial—my mother—but I don't press call just yet.

"It kinda sounds like you have a solo tonight. The guest violinist can't make it."

"What?" My tone is lifted in actual surprise.

Jesse shrugs as he picks up his cello case. "That's just the word on the street. We got time. The concert doesn't start until—"

"Seven," I reply, checking the dainty wrist watch I've been wearing since I was seventeen. I haven't taken it off once. The white-gold band and matching face are a sharp contrast to my golden-bronze skin. "An hour and a half. I'll talk to Michael, okay? If I make any changes what-soever to the music, I'll call everyone together before we settle on stage. Can you let everyone know? Give me like, thirty minutes."

Jesse nods and gives me a bow that makes my spine tingle. It's a joke, of course. I'm not royalty. I'm just second chair of the strings behind Lorna Johnston, the real queen of the Crescent Falls Philharmonic Symphony, and I'm her assistant.

Well, not by definition. Her slave is a better word for it. I do all of the administrative stuff she hates because, as first chair, we're all terrified of her. I've never said no to the woman in my life, even if she's a cold, hard bitch who doesn't even know my name, and we've been working side by side for three years.

She's a legend. I'm just... me.

"Mom," I say into my phone, hurrying down a long, twisting hallway in the deepest depths of the arts center. "Everything okay? Did Skye eat her dinner without a fight?"

"She's fine, Marianna," Mom says with a short laugh. I can hear a kettle squealing in the background, and Mom's shuffling as she movies around our snug kitchen making her evening cup of tea. "How... how did it go?"

I lean against a wall, my eyes locked on the HVAC system weaving through the open ceiling above my head. "How do you think?"

"Everything is going to be fine. This was meant to happen, you know. The Goddess wouldn't have given you an opportunity like the one you're facing if you didn't have to close a door first."

"I wouldn't consider your granddaughter getting kicked out of a third school an opportunity–"

"Have you given *it* any thought?"

I smile weakly and wave at the bass players as they wheel their instrument cases past my perch. "Of course I have, but it would mean uprooting our lives, Mom."

She sighs heavily, "Anna, don't let this pass you by because you're worried about *him–*"

"I'm not," I rush out, gripping my violin case so tightly my knuckles turn white. "This isn't about him."

A tall, blond man walks into view, spots me, and exhales deeply as he rushes in my direction. Michael's eyes are pleading when he mouths something I don't catch, his hands extended in surrender.

"I have to go. I'll be home later tonight. Way late. I'm sure Michael will force my hand when it comes to the after party."

"Enjoy yourself, sweetie," Mom says in a light, sing-song voice before hanging up.

I've barely lowered the phone from my ear when Michael says in a whispered hiss, "We have a situation."

"What's going on?" I resist the urge to remind him that I'm *second* chair, so whatever drama is currently taking place should not be going from the conductor to *me*. It never works out that way though, does it?

Michael, a kind, slightly aloof, but incredibly talented, conductor glances warily around the now empty, but echoing, hallway and comes to a stop at my side. "Lorna isn't coming tonight. I need you in first chair."

I look up at him, squinting, like that'll help me hear better.

"She's not coming," he repeats, his cheeks growing pink. "She's in Celestoria, or something, with her new boyfriend–"

"The Alpha King," I correct, glaring at him. "Are you fucking serious, Michael? You're moving me into first chair an hour before the concert–"

"This concert is falling to pieces. We already lost the soloist performing tonight, so that's going to be you now–"

"I've never soloed as a guest–"

"You're going to solo as first chair. It'll be fine! You're far more talented than Lorna, anyway." He cuts himself off with a ferocious blush then amends under his breath, "Do not tell that witch I said that."

"I–I haven't practiced any of the music for Lorna's solos tonight, Michael."

"You can sight-read. It's fine."

"It's not–"

"Prince Blake is coming to the concert," he says over my rushed protest, and the floor cracks beneath me, threatening to pull me into the void. "With the Alpha King and Luna Queen."

I black out. At least, I wish I did. *Goddess, take me now.*

I gape, my mouth opening and closing like a fish.

Michael thunders forward, saying, "And Marianna, I'm aware of the offer you got from the Philharmonic in Moonrise." He leans in, resting a supportive hand on my shoulder. My just-above-the-shoulder-length, wavy dark brown hair brushes the top of his hand as he continues, "You should take it. This is the last concert of the season. Consider it a goodbye. You get your solo."

My eyes water against my will when he pulls away.

"Take the job," he says sternly, nodding. "You know I fought for you to get first chair when Lorna started… pulling away in favor of her boyfriend, but she's a celebrity and the board–"

"The Alpha King of Celestoria," I correct him under my breath even though he barrels over me again.

"You deserve first chair. You're the best violinist I've ever worked with. You're so talented, and it's been wasted here." His eyes drop from mine to the fading, yellow bruise under my left eye, and he sighs. "Plus, I think a change of scenery would be… good for you."

I jolt back into awareness and fix him with a cold, but professional, look, nodding. "I'm still considering it." I absently feel my pocket for the compact concealer that I've been carrying around so long it's left a permanent imprint in my favorite jeans.

He claps me on the shoulder and walks away, leaving me alone in the gaping, never ending tunnels running beneath the concert hall, where I'm sure guests are starting to arrive for early cocktails before the final show of the season begins.

I walk to a bathroom, setting my case down before catching my worn expression in the mirror. I dig the concealer out of my pocket and carefully pad it onto my cheekbone, covering the bruise that's taken weeks to heal.

A chill runs up my spine, and I turn ever so slightly to find a trio of women standing just a few feet away in what should have been an empty bathroom. Silver white robes brush the group as the center woman takes a step toward me, her face obscured by a mask of crystal, her hair covered by the hood of her robe.

I bite back a sob. "She's so young," I whisper, "I'm not ready to let her go yet."

The Mystic nods and says, "But she is ready for us."

And they're right.

I wonder if Blake knows.

He warned of this when she was born.

And we've done everything to give her a normal life thus far, haven't we? A life he's not in?

"Give me a few weeks, okay?" I beg, and the Mystics disappear, leaving me alone once again.

> *Thank you for reading! Book 15 is coming soon! Get ready for Blake's story!*

Chosen As the Breeder

Mated to Four Alphas

Threats Against the Breeder

At War for the Breeder

The Stolen Breeder

Four Alphas, Four Babies

Becoming the Luna Queen

Descendants of the Breeder

Desired by the Devil series

Whispers of the Devil

Banter of the Devil

Murmurs of the Devil

The Mafia Kings series

Indebted to the Mafia King

Loved by the Mafia King

Claimed by the Mafia King

Secrets of the Mafia King

Burned by the Mafia King

Kidnapped by the Mafia King

Dark Stalker Romance series

Tempted by Sin

Fated to Sin

Secret Billionaires series

Finding the Secret Billionaire by Olivia Bhelle Kildare

Falling for My Secret Billionaire by Bella Moondragon

Driven by the Secret Billionaire by ID Johnson

Wolf Shifter Alpha Kings series

Ravens and Ruins

Sundrops and Shadows

Snowflakes and Sabotage

The Vampire King's Feeder series

Claiming the Alpha's Daughter

Loving the Alpha's Daughter

Finding the Alpha's Daughter

Bewitching the Alpha's Son (coming Sept 2025)

Writing as B. Moon

The Boy Who Died

Sign up for Bella's newsletter here.

Or get a free novella from The Alpha King's Breeder series when you sign up here: The Beta and the Maid

Follow Bella on Facebook here.

Follow Bella on Bookbub here.